Cara Colter shares her home in beautiful British Columbia, Canada, with her husband of more than thirty years, an ancient crabby cat and several horses. She has three grown children and two grandsons.

Michele Renae is the pseudonym of award-winning author Michele Hauf. She has published over ninety novels in historical, paranormal and contemporary romance and fantasy, as well as writing action/adventure as Alex Archer. Instead of writing 'what she knows' she prefers to write 'what she would love to know and do'. And, yes, that includes being a jewel thief and/or a brain surgeon! You can email Michele at toastfaery@gmail.com, and find her on Instagram: @MicheleHauf and Pinterest: @toastfaery.

GU00372746

Also by Cara Colter

Snowed In with the Billionaire
Winning Over the Brooding Billionaire
Accidentally Engaged to the Billionaire

Blossom and Bliss Weddings miniseries

Second Chance Hawaiian Honeymoon
Hawaiian Nights with the Best Man

Also by Michele Renae

The CEO and the Single Dad
Parisian Escape with the Billionaire
Cinderella's Billion-Dollar Invitation
Consequence of Their Parisian Night
Two-Week Temptation in Paradise

Discover more at millsandboon.co.uk.

THE BILLIONAIRE'S FESTIVE REUNION

CARA COLTER

THEIR MIDNIGHT MISTLETOE KISS

MICHELE RENAE

MILLS & BOON

All rights reserved including the right of reproduction in whole or
in part in any form. This edition is published by arrangement with
Harlequin Enterprises ULC.

This is a work of fiction. Names, characters, places, locations
and incidents are purely fictional and bear no relationship
to any real life individuals, living or dead, or to any actual places,
business establishments, locations, events or incidents.
Any resemblance is entirely coincidental.

This book is sold subject to the condition that it shall not, by way of
trade or otherwise, be lent, resold, hired out or otherwise circulated
without the prior consent of the publisher in any form of binding
or cover other than that in which it is published and without a
similar condition including this condition being imposed on
the subsequent purchaser.

® and TM are trademarks owned and used by the trademark owner
and/or its licensee. Trademarks marked with ® are registered with the
United Kingdom Patent Office and/or the Office for Harmonisation in
the Internal Market and in other countries.

First published in Great Britain 2024
by Mills & Boon, an imprint of HarperCollins*Publishers* Ltd,
1 London Bridge Street, London, SE1 9GF

www.harpercollins.co.uk

HarperCollins*Publishers*, Macken House, 39/40 Mayor Street Upper,
Dublin 1, D01 C9W8, Ireland

The Billionaire's Festive Reunion © 2024 Cara Colter

Their Midnight Mistletoe Kiss © 2024 Michele Hauf

ISBN: 978-0-263-32140-1

10/24

This book contains FSC™ certified paper
and other controlled sources to ensure responsible forest management.

For more information visit www.harpercollins.co.uk/green.

Printed and Bound in the UK using 100% Renewable Electricity
at CPI Group (UK) Ltd, Croydon, CR0 4YY

THE BILLIONAIRE'S FESTIVE REUNION

CARA COLTER

MILLS & BOON

For the gifts of strength and hope
Kai ʻEhitu
Oh, yeah!

CHAPTER ONE

"Cassie," Brad Daniels said to his daughter, "it's the third day of November. You just got the Halloween things put away. It's a little early to be working on details for Christmas, isn't it?"

His daughter—he was the only one allowed to call Cassandra "Cassie"—gave him the raised-eyebrow look. It was so like her mother, Cynthia—in charge, would not suffer fools lightly, a need for perfection—that he felt a shiver go up and down his spine.

He used to call the pair of them his dream team.

"Dad! We're actually *behind* where we should be. The tree for the front lobby needs to be a blue spruce and it has to be twenty-eight feet tall."

"One foot for each year of your life?" he asked dryly. "By the time you're my age we'll have to raise the ceiling."

He was treated to *the* look again.

"The height of the tree has nothing to do with my age, as you well know."

He grinned at her, just to assure her that, yes, he did well know.

She sighed. "Do you think you just go to the Boy Scout Christmas tree lot and get one of those the day before you need it?"

His daughter was beautiful, as her mother had been. Willowy, fine-featured, blue-eyed. She had done something with her hair that turned the natural blonde to an unearthly shade of platinum that was extraordinarily striking, even as he wondered, *What is this generation's rush to gray? It would come soon enough.*

As gorgeous as she was, Brad found her intensity—a kind of earnestness—to be the most compelling thing about Cassie. He felt a rush of tenderness for her.

The last two years there had been only the most desultory efforts at making Christmas the spectacular event that was expected of the Cobalt Lake Resort, the ski and accommodation destination in Whistler their family owned.

Christmas had been one of the things they were best known for before the loss of Cynthia in a horrible accident had left Brad and Cassie reeling.

This year, from the almost feverish look of determination sparking in those blue eyes, it was clear that Cassie was planning to make up for it, with the best Christmas ever.

"You're right," he conceded. "Bring on Christmas. I'm sorry. I won't be much help. I don't have any idea where the Christmas stuff is."

"Oh, Dad, it's all in the main storage room, on shelves Mom labeled!" She looked at him indulgently. "Go back to running your empire, and I'll look after the resort. But remember, Christmas isn't a season, it's a feeling."

It was her favorite Christmas quote.

Brad groaned. "I have a *feeling* I'm going to be hearing that a lot over the next two months."

"It's not even two months."

"You're making my head hurt."

Cassie smiled at him then, and regarded him thoughtfully.

"Hey! Are you thinking I look old?"

"Not at all. You're only fifty-six. I was actually thinking how great gray hair looks on you."

His hair, salt-and-pepper when Cynthia died, had turned completely gray over the ensuing two years.

"Not every guy can say that," Cassie said affectionately, "but you look very distinguished, like Gregor Watson."

Watson, an actor, had just departed. He was one of many celebrities who had become a regular at Cobalt Lake, enjoying the upscale boutique nature of it, and that the resort was small enough they could go to great lengths to protect the privacy of their guests.

Security had had their work cut out for them this time, though. A couple of very determined members of the paparazzi had camped just outside the private property line, somehow having gotten wind of Watson's stay.

Security had nicknamed the most persistent of them "Gopher" because he kept popping out of various hiding places looking for the money shot.

He had not succeeded, however, in getting his prize—a photo of Watson, who had been named World's Sexiest Man about a million times.

"World's Sexiest Senior, here I come," Brad said dryly.

Cassie laughed.

As always, it was like the light had come on in his world. From the day Cassie had been born, it had been a source of amazement to him that two people as different as he and Cynthia could somehow create such a miracle.

It had been an accidental pregnancy. He remembered, clearly, on their twelfth anniversary, Cassie standing in front of them, hands on hips, doing the math.

"But I'm twelve! Did you get married because of *me*?"

"Oh, darling," Cynthia had said so smoothly. "We found out I was pregnant the very same day we had our engagement party. Which made it just about the best day of my whole life."

It was the tiniest of white lies, but what was important was that Cassie had been completely satisfied with the answer, and as far as Brad knew, it had never been mentioned again.

Brad sometimes wondered if that accidental pregnancy was

part of what had sent his wife's need to be in control into over-drive. And now, he found himself wondering something else.

He felt he and Cynthia had enjoyed a good relationship, based on mutual respect for each other and love for their daughter.

Cynthia had loved Cobalt Lake, and as his parents aged, she had basically taken over the daily operations of the resort. By the time his parents had passed, she had been shifting the place to fit her vision.

Brad had always pursued other business interests, thinking of Cobalt Lake, even though it was a substantial holding, as more of a family hobby than a viable business venture.

Cynthia had proven him wrong on that front. She had taken the property from what had essentially been—despite the de-lusions of grandeur of his mother, Deirdre Daniels—a quaint little mom-and-pop ski hill to one of the most sought-after vacation destinations in Canada.

And Cassie seemed intent on taking it to the next level.

Had Cynthia been as happy with the marriage as he had been?

He had thought so. And then, two weeks ago, in search of a paperclip, he had looked through the desk his wife had al-ways used. He had come across an envelope. It looked as if maybe it had been taped underneath the lip of the drawer, and the tape had dried over time, so that letter had whispered out of its hiding place, maybe even from him opening the drawer that had been closed for so long.

"You know, Dad," Cassie said carefully, drawing him back to the present, "maybe you're ready to meet some—"

"No," he said firmly, "I'm not."

The last thing he needed was his type A daughter thinking he needed to get back in the game. Much as he loved Cassie, Brad couldn't imagine anything worse than becoming one of her projects and having her devote her considerable energy to finding him a new partner.

He hoped his tone would be enough to make her back off, but, of course, that was not Cassie.

"Why not?" she pressed.

"I don't have the energy for it. If you think Christmas gives me a headache, you can't even imagine how I would feel sitting across a restaurant table with a perfect stranger, trying to think of things to say."

"It doesn't have to be like that. Traditional dating can be kind of lame. People need to think outside the box. Think how much you'd find out about someone if your first date was in a panic room!"

"I don't even know what that is." But he wasn't sure it could sound more awful than that.

"It's like a puzzle, only in real time. You get locked in this room, and you have clues and you find your way—"

He pressed his temples. "Here comes the headache."

She laughed. "Okay, okay, backing off. But if you did decide you were ready, you could tell me, and I could help you."

By locking him in a room with a stranger?

Really? At least the name was apt. Panic.

"I'm just letting you know," she said softly, "that I wouldn't be mad, or resentful that you weren't going to mourn Mom forever. I'd be behind you one hundred per cent if you decided it was time to move on. It has been two years."

He knew that Cassie's grief for her mother was still raw, and so, while misplaced, it was such a generous offer.

Under all that drive, there it was—a loveliness of spirit that she tried to hide from the world, as if it was a weakness.

"Thanks, sweetie. You'll be the first to know if I need a captain for Team Brad."

Not that it will ever happen.

"Go find your Christmas decorations," he told her gently.

She waved a hand at him, and left in her typical flurry of energy.

After she was gone, Brad got up from his desk and reached

for the jacket, which was hanging on the back of his office door. Time for a run. He'd always been a runner, and since Cynthia died, it brought him comfort he no longer got from the ski slopes. He called it his physical therapy.

It was cold and crisp today, the ice starting to form on the lake. He warmed up with a few stretches, but even when he started to run, his mind didn't clear.

He hated it that he had never questioned the strength of his and Cynthia's relationship while she'd been alive, or even after she died.

But that envelope, yellow with age, addressed in her firm hand...

Beloved

She had called him *dear* sometimes, and *darling* on occasion, but *beloved*? Never. So who was that letter for?

He had not opened it, or even decided if he would, but the questions it had stirred up were upsetting.

Was there someone she had loved before him? Had she married him only because of the pregnancy, because she thought she had to?

And an even worse thought: had the pregnancy been an accident at all? Or had his being a rising star in business—achieving billionaire status before he was thirty—been something that Cynthia, from a working-class background, wanted?

His mother had alluded to that possibility once or twice, until Brad had made it clear it would not be acceptable to him for his mother to air her habitual harsh judgments on the newest member of their family.

Cynthia had shown her mettle in very short order. She had left those humble beginnings behind her without a backward glance, sliding effortlessly into the world of prosperity that his business interests, more than the resort, at least at first, had provided.

She had been a perfect fit for that world, classy and refined. Okay, occasionally she'd overdone it, like using French words to sound chic. And when things reached her standard of perfection, she was fond of pronouncing them *marvelous*.

Still, any kind of accident, never mind pregnancy, was so out of her nature.

And yet, an accident had also killed her.

If she was happy, why had she loved those midnight skis by herself so much? Why had she taken a chance that night and gone into the avalanche zone?

Had she addressed a letter to *Beloved* before or after their marriage? Why had she kept it?

Should he open it, or respect the fact she had kept it secret? What if it blew apart everything he had believed about their marriage?

Brad shook off his thoughts, irritated with himself.

He had Cassie. And none of the rest of it mattered. At least not now.

It was colder out than he had thought it would be. His breath came out in icy puffs. He took the wide sidewalk that led him to the boardwalk that surrounded Cobalt Lake. He drank in the amazing view of Mount Sproatt. As always, the crisp air was a balm to his soul.

He caught sight of Gopher, hiding out in a group of trees just off the property line. He nodded to him, not letting on how annoying he found him, and thought to himself, *At least if he's here, unaware Gregor departed this morning, he's leaving someone else alone.*

He began to ramp up his speed, sprinting by one of the hot-chocolate-and-s'more stations provided by Cobalt Lake Resort. It was empty right now, but tonight the pathway would be lit up and people would be sipping hot drinks and taking—just as Cassie had planned—selfies against a magical backdrop that just happened to include the resort's logo.

It wasn't quite ski season, so there wouldn't be throngs yet. Christmas was the busiest time of year.

Brad noted the lake had formed quite a thick crust of ice around the edges. The water at the center was still open, though, and was the exact shade of dark blue that had earned the lake its name. If it stayed this cold, the lake would completely freeze over, and they'd be skating soon.

The ski portion of Cobalt Lake Resort was sandwiched between the two giants, Whistler Mountain and Blackcomb Peak, both of which he could see from here. Like their more well-known neighbors, Cobalt Lake was scheduled to open at the end of the month, snow conditions permitting.

They had a new ski pro, Rayce Ryan, arriving. He had been an Olympic gold contender before a skiing accident had shattered his leg.

Cynthia had always looked after hiring resort staff in the past, so this was Brad's first venture into it at Cobalt Lake. He hoped the new hire wouldn't come with the bitterness of dreams as shattered as his leg.

Skiing accidents had a way of changing how people felt. Brad lifted his eyes to the majesty of the mountains around him. All his life he had loved the mountains and the slopes so much. Cassie had been raised on skis.

Now, his daughter wouldn't ski at all.

And neither would he.

After Cynthia's death the resort had implemented a GPS tagging system for all their guests who ventured onto the slopes. It had already helped them find several skiers who had gone out of bounds and gotten lost.

But still, in the shadow of these mountains, Brad was aware how puny his defenses really were.

No matter what anyone thought, he was aware that the idea you could protect others was largely an illusion.

Again, he needed to shake off the shadows that threatened the beauty of the day. The sky was clear and blue, an osprey screeching and spreading its wings over the lake, the peaks of the mountains—Blackcomb, Whistler, Sproatt—shimmering with snow that had fallen at the higher altitude, but not down here.

Then, as if confirming Brad's thoughts about man's illusions about control, the perfection of the day was completely fractured. Suddenly, screams pierced the pristine mountain air.

CHAPTER TWO

THE SCREAMS HELD the pure and unmistakable—almost animalistic—sound of panic, the kind of terror of someone facing a threat to their very life.

It seemed to be coming from the area near the covered dock, which was located about halfway around the lake. Brad had already been running fast, but now he put on the jets, thankful that he was in great shape.

When he got to the dock, he pieced together what had happened in an instant. Out beyond the dock, on the ice toward that blue-black open water, a dog had broken through.

It looked as if a child—a girl, if the bright pink toque was any indication—was out there in the icy water with the dog.

The girl was screaming and scrabbling hard to get back on the ice, but every time she grabbed for it, the shelf broke away from her, like shattering glass. It didn't help her efforts that she wouldn't let go of the dog's collar.

A woman—the mother?—was racing back and forth on shore, dog leash in hand, screaming hysterically.

"Call 911," Brad called to her firmly She stopped, her mouth frozen open, and stared at him blankly, tears streaming down a face distorted by pure terror.

"Call 911," he ordered her. "Do it now."

He was thankful for the hours and hours of relentless training as a volunteer with the search-and-rescue team.

When he was satisfied the woman was following his order,

he looked around for something he could use as a reaching assist on the icy lake.

Search-and-rescue trained for this situation precisely, and so Brad found himself extraordinarily calm as he raced toward the flagpole at the end of the dock, pulled it from its holder and dropped down off the wooden platform onto the frozen surface of the lake, two feet below it.

He threw off his jacket. At first, where the ice was thick enough to support him, he ran flat out. But at the initial, barely discernable hint of the ice sagging under his weight, Brad dropped onto his belly. He tiger-crawled, using his elbows. He placed the pole well in front of him, horizontally, trying to distribute its weight across the ice as much as he could.

He inched closer and closer to the open water, to the flailing child and the frantic dog. The child was losing energy fast. The splashing was not so frenzied as it had been even moments ago, and the screaming had given way to a desperate gasping.

And still, she would not let go of the dog!

The ice creaked and groaned menacingly under Brad's weight.

And then, there was a giant crack.

It was sound like a gun going off and Brad braced himself to be plunged into the frigid water. He held his breath, but the ice, shockingly, held.

He inched forward again. Finally, he was nearly at the crumbling edge. Despite the fact that both the girl and the dog were tiny, Brad felt the surprise of how wrong he had been. This was no child in the water.

She was a mature woman, maybe his age, though the pink toque, with its huge pom-pom now completely bedraggled, looked like something a child might wear. Her soaked dark hair curled out from underneath it, and was plastered onto a face as white as the snow on the peaks that surrounded them. Her lips were already blue.

Her brown eyes, against all that white, looked huge, and filled with terror. The lashes were outlined in ice.

"You're going to be okay," he said firmly, deliberately keeping his voice calm and even. "Grab the pole."

He would not allow desperation to show in his voice, and he would not allow himself to get closer to the edge of the ice, even though he wanted to. There was no sense in all three of them ending up in the water. In fact, that was the possibility that Brad had to guard against most.

So, not daring to go any closer to that fragile edge where ice met water, he shifted the position of the pole, skidded it across the ice and felt an exquisite sense of relief that it was long enough. She could reach it.

Crazy to notice, right now, that she was cute, rather than beautiful. There was something elfin in her features, even as contorted as they were by fear and shock.

"Let go of the dog," he ordered her.

Even freezing, even in this perilous situation, he could see a certain raw determination residing side by side with her terror.

"I'll get you first," he promised, "then I'll get the dog."

Only with that promise did she loosen her hold on the dog's collar and make saving herself a priority.

She grabbed the pole with soaked woolen mittens. He could see her strength was nearly gone. That realization made his own power, adrenaline-fueled, ramp up a notch.

Inch by careful inch, Brad pulled her, but the ice just kept breaking as the weight of her body hit it. Still, he stuck to his plan. He kept backing up, kept keeping himself from the point where the ice would give way. He held his position and the ice didn't break underneath him, though it groaned threateningly.

Finally, they reached a place where the ice was strong enough for him to yank her onto the surface and out of the cold black water.

She lay there, exhausted, like a beached seal. He heard a little sob of relief escape her.

The dog had stayed close to her, and was paddling furiously in water and chunks of broken ice.

"Stay on your belly. Spread out your weight and crawl to me."

Finally, she was right in front of him, her face down, crying, her breath coming in great heaves.

"The dog," she gasped through chattering teeth.

He had a decision to make. Rescuing the dog did not feel as if it should be a priority. She was already very close to hypothermic, though her chattering teeth told him she wasn't quite there, astonishingly.

Brad decided to make one attempt. If that did not work, he had to make saving the human life his primary goal.

"Do not move," he ordered her, and made his painstaking way back to the edge of the crumbling ice.

Knowing he had given himself one chance at this, he focused intensely. He managed to get the pole, lengthwise, underneath the dog. It took every bit of his strength to use the pole as a fulcrum point to lift the dog out of the water. The ice held under the pressure. The dog, thankfully, was one of those ridiculously tiny things, maybe a Pomeranian.

Brad brought his full weight down on his end of the pole. It acted like a teeter-totter and flipped the dog into the air and onto the ice.

The canine looked like a drowned rat when it dropped in front of him. It deftly evaded his effort to grab it, and gave him a few half-hearted challenging barks, the ungrateful beast. It shook itself indignantly. And then, all four paws going in separate directions, the dog took off running, slipping and sliding toward the shore.

Brad crawled back to the woman. She had not moved, her coat rising and falling with her huge intakes of breath.

"Thank you," she said, her voice a hoarse whisper.

He was pretty sure she meant for the rescue of the dog, not her.

They weren't off the ice yet, but he didn't let her know they were still in danger.

"We're good," he said, deliberately using the same soothing tone he might have once used on Cassie for a scraped knee. "Just listen very carefully to what I tell you."

She nodded.

"We're going to go together. We're not going to stand up. Not yet."

"I don't think I can move," she whispered.

"That's okay. I can. That's what I'm here for."

And suddenly it felt as if that was about the truest thing he had ever said. That he'd been put in this place, at this time, to do this.

He slid his arm under her soaked jacket. It was candy-floss-pink, like the toque. He got a good grip on her. He was immediately aware that he was pumping heat, from exertion and adrenaline, but that she was dangerously cold.

He pushed, pulled and cajoled her, both of them crawling back across the ice, one painful inch at a time. It probably took minutes, but it felt like hours.

Finally, the surface beneath them felt thick enough to take a chance. He got to his feet and crouched. He got his arms under her knees and around her shoulders and scooped her up.

Her wetness soaked into his pants and shirt—it was about the coldest thing he had ever felt, like picking up a block of ice.

Despite the fact that she was soaked, and maybe because his adrenaline was running so high, she felt as light as a feather.

She was limp, and yet with her cradled body against him, it felt as if the bottom was falling out of his world.

Because he saw pure strength there.

There was the vaguest tickle along his spine, of knowing her.

Deeply.

Maybe that's just how adrenaline made a person feel after sharing this kind of dramatic life event with a stranger.

As if you knew every single thing about a person.

Their heart.

Their soul.

"Thank you," she said again, but this time her voice was stronger.

It was when he heard her voice, for this second time, not whispering, not a croak of desperation, that he knew.

"Faith," he said, not quite knowing if he was speaking her name, or if that's what she—and this incident—was restoring him to, in a world where he had walked without that particular quality for a long, long time.

CHAPTER THREE

"FAITH CAMERON?"

It had been so long since anyone had called her that, that Faith felt faintly puzzled. Or maybe it was shock.

Who was she, again?

"Saint-John," she said, correcting her rescuer.

Her voice felt like it was far, far away, detached from her, coming from outside of herself. She was so cold. She had never been this cold in her entire life. She wondered, foggily, if maybe it went deeper than being cold.

Maybe she was dead.

There had been a moment out there in that icy water when she had resigned herself to fate. *This is it.* She had fully expected to die out there, the price to be paid for that foolish decision to go after the dog.

Not that it had felt like a decision.

She'd felt compelled, and had been out on the ice in an instant. It was as if her brain had turned off, and instinct had kicked in.

Though she would have thought instinct might weigh a little more heavily on the self-preservation side. Faith mused that she could have spared a thought to her poor family. Hadn't they suffered enough?

She mulled over the possibility that she might be dead. She had read stories—scoffed at the time—of people who had died and been unaware of it.

Maybe all the rest of it—that man coming on his belly across the ice—had been a fabrication of hope.

And Faith, of all people, should know the dangers that lay in hoping.

So, possibly, she was dead. Somehow, it seemed totally unfair, that on death she would be greeted not by the husband she had spent thirty years with, Felix Saint-John, but by her first love.

But just as with hope, Faith Saint-John, should know life was unfair.

She squinted at her rescuer. Real? Or was her shocked mind fabricating? Or was he a greeter on the other side?

The other side had very sexy greeters if that was the case. Brad Daniels had changed, of course. Who didn't, thirty-plus years later?

His hair was completely gray, but the varying shades were exquisite, like storm clouds with the sun behind them. That same shade was in the faint stubble that speckled his flawlessly masculine cheeks and ever so slightly cleft chin. He had lines on his forehead, and crinkles around his eyes, but if anything, maturity had taken the raw handsomeness of his youth and refined it.

The lines around his eyes made him look as if he had laughed a lot. Once. Though laughter was the furthest thing from the intensity of his features at the moment.

His strength seemed unchanged, though. She remembered that about Brad Daniels. Strong, athletic, comfortable in his own body in a way so few people of that age were.

But those eyes! The same dark brown eyes that held a soul-deep calm that called to the very thing she thought she might have lost forever.

Some essential part of herself, gone.

Of course, she hadn't told her daughter that part. Only that she was returning to Whistler to fulfill the final wish of her father, Max—Maggie's grandfather—and have his ashes spread in his favorite place.

"Maybe you should wait until I can go with you," Maggie had said, but her daughter was a busy lawyer with two young children, which meant the right timing for her was a long way away. And Felix's illness had already delayed the granting of Max's request by far too long.

"Or maybe Sean could take some time off work."

Maggie was forever volunteering her good-natured fire-fighter husband for the Mom-needs-help projects, so much so that Faith referred to Sean as her saint-in-law rather than her son-in-law.

"How about Michael?" Maggie had suggested her brother.

For all her good intentions, there had been something mildly insulting about her daughter's insinuation that Faith wasn't up to making the journey on her own, so much so that Michael could be called home from his studies in Scotland.

Michael. Would he come home, if she asked? Of course. But would he come out of duty, or love?

Their poor family, so damaged.

No, asking Michael was complicated and out of the question.

"I'm going by myself," she had told her daughter firmly, shutting the door on further discussion even though she knew Maggie was only sensing what Faith was feeling. She was lost. Her name seemed to mock her, because that's what she had the least of after six years of giving everything she had to Felix. After six years of watching the man who had given her her whole life, and whom she had given her whole life to, morph into a stranger before her eyes.

And not a very nice stranger, at that.

"Unbelievable," Brad Daniels said gruffly, sternly, drawing Faith back, "that you would risk your life for your dog."

Faith frowned. If she was dead, that would mean Brad, greeting her at heaven's door, was dead, too. It seemed that the odds of her being welcomed to heaven by a lecture about dogs from an old boyfriend were ridiculously slim. On the other hand, what were the odds of being rescued from the cold jaws of death by her first love?

She managed to smile weakly. She couldn't take her eyes off his face. She wanted to touch it, to determine if he was real, but she couldn't move. Her hands were so cold that she doubted she would be able to feel his skin—what she thought would be the delightful texture of those rough whiskers—anyway.

"You know what's even more unbelievable?" she asked, finally managing to answer him. "It's not my dog."

Was he taking her clothes off? It seemed he was, dispensing with her sopping jacket, and then, quickly, the sodden blouse underneath.

She couldn't be dead! Would she care that he left her bra in place, left her some semblance of modesty, if she was dead?

In a flash, his own jacket was around her. That scent could be described as heavenly, so maybe... Then his hands were rubbing the outside of that jacket, firmly, relentlessly.

It was a good thing she couldn't feel anything, because she was pretty sure if she could, her every resolve would be weakening under his firm touch. At least his physical touch made her very aware that yes, she was definitely alive!

"The ambulance is coming," Brad said, cocking his head. "Almost here."

And sure enough, Faith could hear sirens getting louder and louder.

There was a woman hovering around Brad's shoulder, clutching the wet dog and sobbing. "Thank you. Thank you. I don't know how to thank you."

And then Brad was not at her side. Peripherally, Faith was aware of him putting his body squarely between her and someone else. A man, with a very bulky camera. Brad seemed highly annoyed. He blocked the man from taking a picture, and she could hear the sharpness of his tone, if not the actual words he was saying.

The ambulance was here. So much commotion! People asking her questions, more sirens in the distance, the dog giving sharp, bossy little barks. Then, she was being lifted onto a stretcher.

And Brad was beside her again, holding her hand, and the world felt quite, quite still.

"Why?" he asked her, with a kind of urgency, as if he might never see her again. "Why did you risk your life to save a stranger's dog?"

"Its name was Felix," she said, and then she was suddenly aware of the fresh pain she could have brought her family with that impulsive decision. She was crying, aware the tears felt unbearably hot on her cold face.

He let go of her hand and the first responders took his place.

"I'll come with you," Brad said as they moved the stretcher toward the waiting ambulance.

"No," she said firmly. So firmly it stopped him in his tracks. She tried for a softer tone. "It's okay. Really."

The stretcher was being loaded, the doors were shutting and the only warm part of her was where the tears had tracked down her cheeks. And the part she least wanted to be warm was the part around her heart, which she had resolved must be kept frozen.

So that it could never be hurt again.

That's why she had said no to Brad coming with her in the ambulance. She didn't want to see him again for the exact reason that she wanted to see him again.

Her heart was being pulled in two different directions: come back to life, and stay numb.

The next hour—or maybe more—went by in a blur as hospital staff worked on warming her up. Finally, they left her, wrapped in a cocoon of a heated blanket.

Beyond exhausted, she slept.

Faith woke up feeling the most beautiful sensation of warmth, but also a feeling of disorientation. That smell…

She opened her eyes, slowly. She saw a light blue privacy curtain and an IV pole, and heard the unmistakable sounds of a hospital—codes being called, shoes on squeaky floors, the hum of machinery. The smell was that mixture of disinfectant and despair that she had come to know too well.

She struggled to sit up. If there was one place she did not want to be…

There was a strong hand across her arm, staying her. She turned her head. Brad Daniels was sitting in a chair beside the hospital bed.

"Hey," he said.

It was really unfair that he had aged so well. He was one of those men who was getting better as he got older. It felt like such a terrible weakness that she was glad he was here, despite the fact she had asked him not to come.

"Hey," she said back, and sank against a cushion he put behind her back. The effort it had taken to sit up drained her, so she closed her eyes again, and just let an exquisite feeling of contentment float through her, replacing that moment of panic when she'd realized where she was.

"Feeling okay?" he asked.

"Yes, so good. Warm. You didn't have to come."

"Of course, I didn't *have* to. But I knew your clothes were wet."

She suddenly remembered him pulling her soaked clothes off her. It felt horribly embarrassing. She kept her eyes closed.

"I wasn't sure where you were staying so I didn't know where to go to retrieve some dry things for you to put on when they discharge you."

He laid a package on her lap, and she opened her eyes again, and looked at it, instead of him. Looking at him made her feel weak.

Swamped by memories.

Of a younger Brad, his lips on hers, awakening something in her that she had never known before.

Or since, if she was going to be completely honest about it.

She told herself, firmly, that what she'd had with Felix was so much better than fickle, youthful passion. It was steadiness, security.

"I've got your jacket and sweater, but I didn't bring them here. I think it's going to take about a year for that jacket to dry."

The package was wrapped in brown paper and tied with hemp twine, the way very exclusive shops would have done it. The paper had *Cobalt Lake Resort Boutique* subtly embossed on it, and a little green sticker that attested to its environmental friendliness.

She had barely cried since Felix had died, six months ago. Today, she was making up for it. Now, as she slid her finger under the twine, it felt as if she was, once again, choking back tears.

Faith drew out the items, one by one. Brad had obviously gone way beyond her basic needs. There was a beautiful new down jacket and a soft woolen toque in the same shade of sage green.

This was followed by a pair of navy blue yoga slacks, a plain T-shirt and a light zip-up hoodie that matched the slacks. Like the packaging, each item had a sticker on it attesting to how it was doing its part to save the world.

"Sorry about the leisure wear," he said. "They're kind of one-size-fits-all, so it felt like a good bet, since I don't know your sizes."

"No," she said, "it's perfect."

For someone who didn't know her sizes, the last items in the bag were underwear—a lacy white bra and matching panties. A quick glance at the label showed them to be sustainably produced, breathtakingly expensive and her size *exactly.*

She dared a glance at Brad and saw he was blushing, ever

so slightly. It was endearing. Was he remembering things best left in the past?

She quickly tucked those items under the brown paper and ran her fingers over that raised, tasteful embossing.

"So is the Cobalt Lake Resort still in your family, Brad?"

"Of course," he said, reminding her he was one of those enviable people who had always known what his future held.

"I don't remember there being a boutique."

"It was one of my wife's ideas."

It was one of the very questions she had wanted answered about him. Of course, he was married. No surprise there. The Daniels family was nothing if not traditional. In fact, it was *good* that he was married, a comfortable barrier for the niggling of attraction she felt for him, still, after all these years.

Or maybe it wasn't attraction at all. She was probably experiencing some kind of psychological phenomenon, some kind of bonding to the man who had, after all, just saved her life.

Faith slid a look at his ring finger to confirm. A band of gold rested there.

"Did your wife help you pick things for me?" That would put the *sexy* things in a different light.

He twisted the band.

"She died," he said. "Two years ago."

So much for the different light. He had chosen those things.

Still, Faith noticed Brad's tone was flat, as if he was deliberately trying to strip the emotion from it. But she saw an anguish, the kind that she was very familiar with, flash through the deep brown of his eyes.

Something in her went very still. What were the chances of this? Of the craziness of their reunion and then this interesting twist? That both of them had lost their life partners?

"I'm so sorry," she said quietly.

So many questions. How had his wife died? Did they have children? What directions had his career taken him in? Were his parents still alive?

Had he been happy with his choices? Or had his family's expectations—his domineering mother, to be precise—dictated them to him?

Suddenly, she felt as if she wanted to know everything about him. What had the last three decades held for him?

She could see the same curiosity in him as those dark eyes rested on her, inquisitive.

Her close call in the lake had made her feel weak. His thoughtfulness had made her feel weaker yet.

Faith was appalled to find she craved connection with Brad Daniels.

But life had taught her the inevitable link between connection and loss—even the companionship of a cat was destined to cause pain—and she could not leave her poor battered heart vulnerable to that.

She had vowed that her children, and her grandchildren, would be enough for her at this stage of her life, even as her daughter, Maggie, looked somewhat panicked at the idea of being her mother's raison d'être.

Mom. You've got to find yourself again.

Maggie wanted her to find herself, but ironically, didn't even want her to travel alone to the place she had spent some of her high-school years.

And maybe that concern was not completely unjustified. Look at the chance she had taken, racing out on that ice for a dog.

Faith felt a sudden jolt of panic. Maggie!

CHAPTER FOUR

"WHAT TIME IS IT?" Faith asked, after twisting her neck to look frantically for a clock in the hospital cubicle.

Brad slid back his cuff to reveal a gorgeous watch. While she and her husband—he'd been a university professor, until his retirement, and she had been a teacher—had always been comfortable, there had never been room for watches like that in their lives.

Brad's watch was probably worth more than the down payment on their beloved downtown Toronto bay-and-gable, pre-World-War-Two-constructed house had been!

"It's just after five."

"Oh! I was supposed to let my daughter know when I got here."

When Faith had arrived in Whistler her hotel room had not been ready so she had decided to delay calling Maggie until she could do so from the comfort of her room. Since she had not been able to check in, she had left her suitcase—with her dad's ashes inside it—in a secure storage room.

"Mom," Maggie had said, "I don't think you can just travel with, er, human remains. Or spread them wherever you want. I think you have to get permits."

Her daughter, the lawyer, would think of such things. But for once in her life, Faith was not going to do it right, or follow the rules. Her father would have approved. One of Max's favorite expressions had been "it's easier to beg forgiveness than ask permission."

So Faith had left the suitcase and then gone for that fateful walk around Cobalt Lake.

Another thought struck her, and her rising sense of panic increased.

"Where's my phone?" she asked. "My purse?"

Brad's brow furrowed, as he obviously was trying to remember the scene.

"I didn't have my purse when you pulled me out of the water?"

"Definitely not then."

"I hope I left it on the shore."

"I don't recall seeing a purse there. But I wasn't looking for one."

"What if my purse—and my phone—are at the bottom of Cobalt Lake?"

"You likely threw the purse down," he said, and there was something about him that was just so reassuring. "Do you remember where you entered the lake? Off the dock? Your purse might be there."

"I don't know where I went out onto the ice. Or if I threw or dropped the purse as I ran. It's all kind of a blur. All I remember, clearly, is that woman screaming for Felix."

"The dog."

"Yes."

"And something more?" he asked softly.

After a moment, she nodded.

"Who is Felix?" Brad asked, in a voice that felt as if it could call all her secrets from her.

She sighed.

"That was my husband's name. He died."

Brad drew in a sharp breath as he, too, recognized the coincidence in their shared tragedies.

Faith was aware she didn't need to offer anything else. But

the close call, the weariness, now the loss of her purse—one
blow after another—seemed to be lowering her barriers.

"Recently?" he asked quietly.

"Six months ago."

"I'm so sorry, Faith."

"Felix, my husband, had a horrible condition. A form of dementia most people had never heard of, until that action film
star got it. It was a behavioral variant. It affected his person-
ality, his judgment, his empathy."

She was slightly in awe of herself for managing to sound so
clinical about something that had been so utterly devastating.

"Oh, Faith." Brad did not appear to be falling for her matter-
of-fact tone. His deep voice was gravelly and showed genuine caring. His eyes on hers seemed to invite her to fall into
what they offered: the understanding of someone who had
also loved and lost.

She ordered herself not to say one more word. She ordered
herself to remember the danger of connections, particularly
to another human being.

Particularly given her shared history with Brad. But even
as she tried to warn herself of the dangers, she kept talking.
She glanced at the IV dripping into her arm. Was it possible
there was something in that?

"He left me a long time before he actually died. I couldn't
save him. No matter what I did, he just drifted further and
further away from me."

The clinical dispassion was leaving her voice. There was
a little wobble in it. This would be a really good time to stop
talking.

"I couldn't save him," she whispered, "but when I heard
that woman calling his name, it felt like maybe I could save
something."

Why was she saying this? It had to be the IV making her say
things she shouldn't. Feel things she shouldn't. For instance,
she shouldn't feel as if she *knew* Brad. As if she could trust

him with her grief and vulnerability, as she had trusted no one else, not even her daughter, or her son. You didn't know someone because they had been your *first.*

Well over thirty years ago.

There was probably nothing resembling truth in those first passionate encounters between Faith and Brad.

But even if she had not known him fully back then, she could not deny she the raw genuineness in him, coming out on that ice and rescuing her. Everything he was had been on full display, with no filters. Strong, brave, compassionate, wise, willing to put himself at risk for someone he had thought was a stranger.

It had also felt like raw truth in his eyes when he had told her about the death of his wife.

Still, obviously, she was in some kind of shock, or on drugs, which had made her blurt out personal details of her life like that.

And then, her defenses completely crumpled, and she was crying *again.*

Faith had an awful thought. What if she had come all this way, thinking fulfilling her father's final wish would help her find herself, and the hard truth was that the self she would find was weak and needy and given to sharing confidences with people she didn't know?

Well, that was not exactly true.

She *knew* Brad Daniels.

Or a version of him.

She didn't know him now. Ridiculous to feel as if she did, based on his heroics on the ice.

"Scoot over," he said, and she could no more disobey this command than the ones he had given her out there on Cobalt Lake.

He came up on the narrow bed beside her. Despite all her warnings to herself about the dangers of connecting, she did not tell him no, she did not push him away, she did not try to avoid contact with him.

She *liked* the feeling of his weight sinking down on the bed beside her. She *liked* his scent—subtle, masculine, mountainy—tickling around her nose.

He didn't draw back the thin blanket that covered her, and so his thigh was on one side of it, and hers on the other.

Still, the contact—the connection—was there. Subtle heat from his leg, her leg lying against the hard length of solid muscle.

And she liked that, too.

It had been so long since she had shared a moment like this with another human being. Except her grandchildren—Maggie's two daughters, Chloe and Tanya, four and six—who snuggled into her as she read them bedtime stories.

She had been away from home less than a full day, and suddenly she felt melancholy, homesick.

"I think there's something in the IV drip," she said with a loud sniff.

"There probably is," he agreed.

"I'm glad we got that sorted. That I'm being drugged. That I'm not like this. At all."

"Like what?" he asked huskily.

"You know. Needy. Weak. Talkative."

"I don't see you as any of those things," he assured her softly, then he drew her head to the exquisite broadness of his shoulder and let her cry as he murmured soothing words. It felt as if she had never known anyone in quite the same way she knew Brad Daniels.

"I'm really not—"

"Shh, give yourself a break. You've had a shock. You're probably mainlining muscle-relaxants."

She giggled at the suggestion, and relaxed into the comfort he was offering.

Finally, and with what seemed like just a touch of reluctance, Brad extricated himself from the bed and handed her some tissues.

She was glad it had been quite some time since she had put on makeup, because had it survived the lake it would not have survived this deluge of tears.

While she dabbed at her eyes and tried to stop the heaving of her chest, she watched as Brad took charge of everything. He was a man that had so obviously come fully into himself. He'd always been confident, but now maturity had added weight to that confidence. She could not help but admire how he handled himself as he made calls to the resort and sent staff out to look for her purse and her phone.

His manner was friendly, but also firm. There was an unmistakable power in him. There was an invisible line, even on the phone, that made him one-hundred-per cent the boss.

This is what she needed to remember, since it felt so good to just surrender to being the one taken care of—once she had been staff at his family resort.

And his mother had not had the people skills her son had. Deirdre Daniels—always Mrs. Daniels to the staff—had been rigid and condescending, possibly the worst boss Faith had ever had.

And that was before Mrs. Daniels had made it known, in no uncertain terms, that there was no room for a chalet girl— and probably particularly one with the last name Cameron— to have a place in her son's future.

But all that seemed a long time ago and far away as Faith let this next-generation Daniels take charge of her life.

When he was done making his calls, Brad handed her his phone. "Call your daughter," he said. "Let her know you're okay."

He kindly exited the room to give her some privacy.

His phone was still warm where it had been cupped in his hand. What an utterly ridiculous thing to find appealing.

She glared accusingly at the IV drip before punching in

Maggie's number. Of course, her daughter did not pick up, either because of the time difference—bath time for the babies, there was that sensation of homesickness again—or because it was coming up as an unknown number. Either way was a blessing, because Faith did not want to confess to her daughter that she had nearly brought more tragedy on the family, or tell her about the predicament she currently found herself in, or the circumstances that had led up to it.

It would just confirm all those doubts that had flashed through Maggie's eyes when Faith had announced her mission. She could practically hear the exasperated, worried, *Oh, Mom.*

"Hi, honey, safe in Whistler," Faith said with artificial cheer, leaving a voice-mail message. She glanced around the cubicle, glad it wasn't the video chat she would normally have used to connect with Maggie, Chloe and Tanya. The backdrop would have been a dead giveaway, that left to her own devices for the first time in years, Faith had managed to make a mess of it.

"Sorry to be letting you know so late. I seem to have misplaced my phone."

I knew she shouldn't go by herself, Maggie would say to Sean, when she heard that message. *How do you misplace your phone?*

"I bumped into a high-school friend who loaned me theirs," Faith continued. "I'll check in with you tomorrow."

She disconnected, thankful that her son, Michael, was away at university in Scotland and there was no need to keep him updated as to what was going on. She'd sent him a text about her upcoming travels, but she was not sure it had even registered with him.

Faith had the feeling that Michael had been grateful for the physical distance separating them when Felix was ill. The last time he had come home it had been a fiasco. It felt as if his sense of family had been deeply compromised by the trials of the last few years, and he had chosen a chilly withdrawal.

When she'd told him she was thinking about selling the house he'd grown up in, he hadn't responded at all, as if that part of life—and happier times—was far behind him.

And then there was Maggie, who cared too much.

How could she begin to repair so much damage to her family? Could she?

She sighed, and looked at Brad's phone, willing to take advantage of the diversion from the troubled state of her own thoughts. She was *not* the kind of person who would give in to the temptation to check out a few photos on the unlocked device.

Of course, she wasn't the kind of person who dashed out on the ice after a dog, either. Or unloaded emotional baggage in front of strangers.

Maybe she didn't know who she was at all anymore. Wasn't that at least part of the purpose of this mission that already seemed to be going so badly awry?

Of course, nobody would be more delighted by things going *awry* than her free-spirited dad.

Faith decided, even if she was choosing a new her, it wouldn't be someone who snooped on someone else's phone. She did like the wallpaper on Brad's lock screen, though. It showed a beautiful young woman with silvery hair, sitting in a mountain meadow and looking toward the camera with undisguised affection.

His daughter, she assumed, studying the similarities in the bone structure. The woman didn't exactly look happy—she had lost her mother, after all—but there was both strength and confidence in the set of her chin, and shoulders, in the directness of her gaze.

He had raised his children well.

She scoffed at herself for reaching that conclusion on the basis of one photo. She didn't even know if he had a daughter, or how many children there were.

It could even be a niece, though that wouldn't explain the

resemblance. Brad had been an only child, like Faith, so if it was a niece, it was on his wife's side.

When the door of her hospital room squeaked open, she hastily put the phone on the table tray in front of her as if she was a spy who had been caught looking at a file!

CHAPTER FIVE

IT WAS A doctor and a nurse, not Brad, who came into Faith's room. It was a sign of how much the world had changed since she was young—in good ways—that the doctor was a woman and the nurse was a man.

The nurse, who introduced himself as Adam, began to remove the IV.

"Is there something in that?" Faith asked him, as the doctor laid a very cold stethoscope on her chest.

"Yes, it's a heated intravenous solution of salt water. It helped warm your blood."

"And that's all?" Faith heard faint skepticism in her tone.

"That's it," Adam said with a smile. "If you're feeling not quite yourself—"

Whatever that was, she thought silently.

"—it's probably because your body sustained quite the shock. You're very lucky."

Lucky. Of course, she was. She had made a stupid, irresponsible decision and been saved from the consequences.

And yet, she was deeply suspicious of luck. Luck—chance, fate—had also selected her and Felix for a journey into heartbreak so breathtakingly painful nothing could have ever prepared her for it.

Still, with her rescue from the icy water of Cobalt Lake, her poor family had been saved from yet another blow, and for that she really did need to be grateful.

Even as she hoped they would never find out what she had done. The very thought of Maggie's tone, the look that would be on her face, made her cringe inwardly.

"Thank you for all your hard work," Faith said to the medical team. "I feel lovely now."

Except for the fact she had just discovered she had no excuse for confiding so deeply in Brad, for accepting the comfort of his body next to hers on the bed, his broad shoulder to rest her head on.

Faith was stunned by how much she missed those kinds of everyday intimacies. But those yearnings could make a person weak when they most needed to be strong.

"You'll need to take it easy for the next few days, but I think you're good to go," the doctor said.

But that was a dilemma. Go where? With no purse, no ID, no credit card, no phone? She wouldn't even have clothes if Brad had not supplied them.

The medical team left the room and Faith got out of bed, shocked by her lack of strength. Her legs felt as boneless as pudding.

She ducked into the tiny bathroom that adjoined the room with the clothes that Brad had given her. She pulled off the hospital gown—even that small effort sucked the strength from her—and sorted through the items.

She found herself blushing at his choice of undergarments. So feminine. Maybe even sexy. She had given up on sexy a long time ago, even before Felix got ill. Comfort had seemed way more important.

But even if it had been a long time since she'd worn anything but the most utilitarian underwear, she was too old to blush.

Still, she'd spent thirty years with the same man, so putting on undergarments purchased by her old high-school sweetheart felt oddly intimate, just like Brad beside her in that bed. But how had he gotten the sizes so right?

Her sense of embarrassment deepened as she recalled him yanking those sopping, cold clothes off her on the shore of the lake.

She hoped he was so busy in rescuer mode that he hadn't noticed that she wasn't eighteen anymore. Was rounder than the lithe teenager she had been.

But Brad wasn't the kind of guy who missed a thing.

Which included the scars of life, stretch marks and wrinkles, and things she had really thought she would never be brave enough to show another man in her life.

And yet, in this really lovely underwear, it seemed as if all her flaws were minimized. For the first time in a very long time, Faith felt exquisitely feminine. She realized why a woman might be tempted to spend so much money on lingerie.

She slipped on the yoga slacks and top. Both were products of a well-known designer—made from sustainable bamboo—and, as Brad had promised, one size fitted all, though maybe it was a bit on the snug side, hugging the curves of a body that had not been in a yoga class for at least twenty years.

Would yoga classes be part of her journey to find herself? Faith glanced in the terrible warped mirror above the sink.

The harsh hospital light wasn't helping, but she really did look awful. Her natural curls—dark brown threaded through with the odd strand of gray—were crushed to her head in some places and sticking straight up in others.

She pulled on the toque—the label said it was hand-knit by a local artisan—and that hid the worst of it. Her lips still looked faintly blue and she looked as pale as the death she had come close to experiencing.

She was annoyed at herself that she felt like she would have killed to get her hands on that little makeup kit tucked away in her suitcase.

Faith exited the bathroom. The small effort to get dressed had increased the sensation of heaviness in her limbs. She sank onto the edge of the bed, and ran her hand over the bamboo fabric of the slacks, trying to think what to do.

First and foremost, she had to break this sense of connection with Brad.

They were now, and always had been, from different worlds.

He was from a world of wealth and good taste. His mother had made it abundantly clear that a chalet girl—Mrs. Daniels's euphemism for a chambermaid—had better not have designs on her son.

Those had been her words, spat out, snooty and cuttingly judgmental. Her tone had been lady-of-the-manor to maid-who-emptied-the-pots.

Have designs.

Those words could not have come at a worst moment in Faith's life. Despite the bliss of loving Brad, real-life problems had been pressing up against her. Only a few days before, her dad had confessed he'd gambled away the money he had scrimped and saved for her college fund for as long as she could remember.

She had never seen Max cry before, but he had cried when he had told her, "I thought it was a sure thing. I thought I could at least double that money. That you could have gone off to UVic and lived like a princess instead of a pauper. It was a pony named Faithful Fate. I thought it was a sign…"

Could Mrs. Daniels have known about Max Cameron's terrible mistake? It seemed she did. Whistler remained very much a small town.

Because Mrs. Daniels had then held out the single carrot that Faith had been unable to resist. She had offered to pay all Faith's expenses—tuition, housing and a small allowance—for her entire four years at a prestigious university in Eastern Canada, a long, long way from where Brad would be going to school at the University of Victoria, on Vancouver Island.

Faith had been accepted at UVic, as well, but even with scholarships, after her dad's confession, she had been contemplating the financial aspects of pursuing a higher education with terror. She would be on her own. Though she had always excelled in academics—she loved to learn and knew early on that she wanted to be a teacher—she knew no matter how she stretched, or how many part-time jobs she managed to land, she wasn't going to be able to do it.

And, of course, by accepting Mrs. Daniels's offer, she hoped to somehow alleviate her father's shame and pain over his awful mistake, too.

To fix it.

Look, Dad, it all worked out.

Faith had insecurities—and plenty of them—before those words, and that offer, from Mrs. Daniels. By the time they'd arrived in Whistler, when she was in grade eleven, they had moved so many times.

Despite his horrible mistake gambling away her college money, Max had had only one addiction. It had been spectacular. It wasn't as if he didn't like booze and gambling, but those paled in comparison to his grand obsession.

Max Cameron had been a powder hound. It always seemed the place he thought he would be happiest was wherever he wasn't.

And so they had followed the promise of snow. Max had worked at Lake Louise, Sunshine Village, Aspen, Deer Valley, Jackson Hole and a multitude of others, loving how the one guaranteed perk of working at a ski resort was either free or discounted skiing.

He'd had great dreams for Faith, but she had never developed his love of the sport, possibly because it had cost her so much in terms of stability.

Instead, she had loved books and school. Max had eventually given up on a ski-racing career for her, referring to her affectionately as his little bookworm.

Books, though, didn't provide a complete barrier from the knowledge she had grown up with, of how resort towns worked. She was well aware that she and her father were on the bottom rung of a caste system, and that was before his many eccentric escapades were figured in.

Ski villages hosted very rich people who came for extended stays or owned the fanciest homes, and availed themselves to the posh resort lifestyles. They skied and hiked and went to spas, and sipped expensive wine in front of fires. If they had families, their children mostly went to private schools.

Then there were the business owners, like the Danielses in Whistler, who sold accommodations, or fine art, or exquisite furnishings, or designer clothes made out of bamboo. They were heavily community-minded, and that included support-ing the local schools.

At the bottom of the resort-town heap were the people, Max said, with a grin and a shrug of his shoulders. Like the Cam-erons, who actually kept everything running, the maids and the store clerks and the lifties and the mountain guides and the ski instructors.

These people couldn't actually afford to live in most of the famous ski resorts in North America, unless they were lucky enough to get staff housing. Otherwise, it was trailer parks and basements suites, or houses shared with other employ-ees. Faith had grown up experiencing all of those options at various times.

Max had been a seasonal worker, a chair-lift mechanic, and the absolute best at what he did. He had also been a true free spirit who had never conformed to what society expected from him.

He had been a single dad since Faith's mother had died when she was three. He had embraced that role with a star-tling joie de vivre.

She could remember him bursting in the door of her first-grade Christmas concert—where had that been, Big Sky in Montana?—looking panicked because he was late, his hands still black with grease and dressed in his work coveralls.

But the pride on his face, the love in that lopsided grin, had made her world. Though as she got older, it hadn't always felt like enough. Her dad's work could be as sporadic and unpredictable as he himself was. Especially in high school, when she had become aware money was tight and taken the job at Cobalt Lake to help out.

She'd been the new girl—again—and didn't have the right clothes or shoes, couldn't afford a good haircut and certainly didn't live at the right address. The money she'd earned helped pay the rent, it didn't buy baubles.

And so, when Brad Daniels—wealthy, athletic, popular, a member of the Whistler elite—had first shown interest in her, Faith Cameron, daughter of a lift mechanic and a lowly employee at his family's resort, she truly had felt like Cinderella, with a real live prince and a chance to dance at the ball.

She'd met him at school, not the resort. Having many experiences with moving, Faith had known the way to meet people was to join something, preferably not something that cost extra money. And so she had joined the school paper…and been mortified when her first assignment was to interview the athlete of the month, who had been Brad.

With his good looks and his athletic prowess, she had been expecting arrogance and superiority. Instead, she had found someone who seemed unaware of his social standing, or of hers. He was funny, humble and genuinely interested in people. He was one of the easiest people she had ever talked to. Sometimes it felt as if he was interviewing her, since he was so interested in all the different places she had lived.

Originally intimidated by him, she'd asked him for half an hour of his time. An hour later they had ended up going for sodas together at a local café.

He'd asked her, almost shyly, at the end of that time, if he could see her again.

She'd taken a deep breath, and admitted she worked as a

chalet girl at his family resort. She would never forget the slow, sweet smile that had come across his face.

"Oh, that's wonderful," he'd said. "It means I'll see even more of you."

As if her station in life, and his, meant absolutely nothing to him. And it never seemed as if it had.

Faith had allowed herself to get caught up in the fairy tale of first love and to believe good things could happen to a girl like her.

But then, as it turned out, even if Brad genuinely did not care about the differences in their circumstances, *somebody* had, and she cared very much.

Brad's mother.

She had flung those stinging, life-altering words at Faith. And then made her that offer.

That offer. She knew it was a deal with the devil.

Three days had passed without eating or sleeping. Crying until her eyes swelled nearly shut.

And then, Faith had done what she had to do. She accepted the terms—all of them—dictated by Mrs. Daniels.

Dealing with moving was nothing new to her. But dealing with heartbreak was. She missed Brad so much. She was dying to call him, to explain, to just hear his voice.

And Faith missed her dad, as well. He had been the constant in her life, and yet he seemed broken by the choice he had made, and the choices she had made as a result. Nothing she said or did when she called him seemed to make him feel better. Brad was out of her life and her father was drifting away from her.

She threw herself into her studies, blocking out heartache, trying to outrun that not-good-enough feeling. That, and the guilty awareness that she had somehow sold out. She had done what her father would never have approved of. Chosen security over happiness, the safe way over the unmapped route.

It had taken years to feel she belonged in her solidly middle-class life, especially with Max in the background, leaving Whistler at the same time she had, and going back to Banff. And then to Colorado. For a while, he'd been in Europe.

She'd had to send him airfare to come to her wedding, the first time he had met Felix. He'd taken her aside and suggested she "rethink" Felix, proclaiming him as dull as yesterday's porridge. Though he'd never been much of a drinker, he'd made an exception on that occasion. Max had gotten drunk and made a toast to a "boring and conventional life."

She'd been glad to put Max back on the plane, glad his presence in her boring, conventional life was sporadic. Because she loved *everything* about that life.

She had the life she had always hoped for—her own career as an elementary-school teacher, a husband who was stable and doting and, finally, motherhood.

Faith *loved* every single thing about family life and motherhood.

She loved it that she and Felix had aspired to the most ordinary of dreams. To have children, to buy their own house, to have a warm holiday in the middle of winter and to save their money so that Maggie and Michael could go to university, worry-free.

That life—those, oh, so ordinary goals—had slowly made Faith *finally* feel she was okay, that she was worthy of good things.

But then those good things had been snatched from her, in a dizzying flurry of tragedies. Her father had been diagnosed with liver disease—after ignoring the symptoms for years—and come home to her, only to die within weeks.

At about the same time, Felix's baffling changes in behavior had accelerated alarmingly.

And so, all those old insecurities seemed as if they had not been put to rest at all. They had just waited, patiently, for this past boyfriend to show up in her life and make her feel, at fifty-five, when she had really hoped to be beyond such things, insecure all over again.

It was not exactly, she thought wryly, what she had come back to Whistler for—to find herself in the grip of events that had happened well over three decades ago!

And she needed to remember the goal in her quest for discovery. Despite the insecurities of growing up in class-divided resort enclaves, when she was young, she had been so aware of her strength.

There had been a period when she had felt as if she could overcome any obstacle. During those romantic months of first love with Brad, at the end of their senior year, Faith had had a sense of being on fire with life, immersed in the moment, embracing the possibility that anything could happen.

So the ghosts of her former self had drawn her back here. That insecure girl wanted to find the roots of her self-doubts, exacerbated by Felix's illness; and that confident girl who thought she could do anything wanted to be coaxed back out.

Brad chose that moment to come back into the room. In light of the thoughts she had just had, Faith saw him through a new filter.

He carried himself with an enviable vigor for life. The air around him was practically shimmering with his amazing energy. He had an unshakable sense of himself, an innate self-confidence. It was in everything about him, in the way he dressed, in the way he carried himself, even in the polished cut of his silver hair.

The color of his hair was undeniably sexy on him. He looked like Gregor Watson. Only better, because he carried his looks without a hint of arrogance.

She did not want to be noticing anything *sexy* about Brad Daniels. But, given their recent close encounters—and his choice of underwear for her—how could she not?

"They tell me they're releasing you. Can I give you a lift?"

Of course, he could not give her a lift! She had to stop this right now! But what was she going to do? Walk back to her hotel? When her legs felt as if they were barely functioning? And then what?

"Yes, a lift would be nice. I'm not sure what I'll do about checking in. Without my wallet."

He tilted his head at her.

"I just arrived here in Whistler a few hours ago. The room wasn't quite ready for me so I left my luggage, but I'll have to see what the hotel has to say now that I'm without ID or a credit card."

He considered this.

"Maybe you should come back to Cobalt Lake with me until your things are found."

Such a bad idea.

Terrible.

Given the softness he was making her feel in places that had gone hard. That she had hoped were impenetrable for forever more.

That's exactly what she was afraid of.

That and the growing connection, if she allowed him to rescue her again.

"I keep a cottage at Cobalt exclusively for use of visiting executives. There's no one in it currently. You'd be welcome to it, until we sort out your difficulties."

It was a relief that he wasn't actually asking her to stay with him. That relief was somewhat nullified by his casual use of the word *we*.

It had been such a long time since she'd had a partner to help her with her decisions and difficulties. The kids had done their best, but it wasn't the same as this.

Someone to lean on.

"No," she said, with convincing firmness, "I've put you out quite enough. If you drop me at my hotel, I'll figure it out from there. I'm sure they've had guests lose things before."

CHAPTER SIX

BRAD WAS TRYING very hard not to stare at Faith. The outfit he'd hastily picked up for her from the boutique was made for someone with straighter lines than hers.

Her generous curves seemed beautifully womanly to him. Cynthia had been an athlete, all hard muscle and sinewy strength. She had never had a hair out of place, and her makeup had always been perfect, even when she stepped in, fresh off the slopes.

Faith, understandably, was having a bad-hair moment, that even the toque couldn't hide. Wayward curls were escaping out from under it, some sticking up, some flattened against her temples. Her face was makeup-free and her skin was so pale. It made her eyes look huge.

There was something distinctly waiflike about her. She was definitely vulnerable and he could not forgive himself if he just dropped her off at her hotel to cope when she was in a more fragile state than she seemed to realize.

There was something else about her, that he remembered from their shared past. In high school, that place that celebrated *sameness*, particularly in girls—same hair, same clothes, same fingernail polish—Faith had stood out.

She had not been the same.

The first time he'd ever even noticed her was when she'd interviewed him for the school paper.

Her wayward curls, that tentative smile, those huge earnest eyes, the *questions*. Nothing he'd been expecting.

If you could have a conversation with anyone, living or dead, who would you choose?

If you were stranded on a deserted island, who would you want to be stranded with?

At that point, he'd known Faith Cameron five minutes, and the answer to both questions had been *you*. Not that he had dared to admit that out loud. He had never been so completely captivated before.

And maybe, he realized, not since, either. Was there anything in the world that matched the thrill of first love?

There had been something about her…and still was. Something fresh and wholesome, wonderfully original and surprising. His mind settled on the word *real*.

He remembered, with startling clarity, the first time he had tasted her lips, how sweet and plump they had been, how she had been both innocent and eager. As he himself had been. They had discovered the brand-new world of passion together, with curiosity and boldness and reverence.

And joy.

Maybe especially joy.

He was appalled with himself when he realized he was comparing Faith to Cynthia. His guilt was instantaneous. Still, he needed to reassure Faith in no uncertain terms.

"It's not putting me out, Faith."

Brad contemplated the storm of feelings—oh, those most dangerous of things—that he was feeling. *Put out* was not one of them.

Aside from the guilt of catching himself comparing his wife to another woman, Faith's rescue had breathed to life a dying spark within him. The spark was that need a man had to be the warrior—to protect those around him.

Rationally, he knew he had nothing to do with Cynthia's decisions, the ones that had led to her accident and death, but a part of him felt, acutely, a sense of failure.

A powerlessness no man wanted to feel.

He had carried that sense of failure and powerlessness within him until that very moment he had succeeded in pulling Faith from the water.

Is that why he didn't want to let her go now? He wanted to relish this sense of having wrestled with fate, and won, this time?

He was being too complicated, he admonished himself sternly.

Faith Cameron—no, Saint-John now—had made it abundantly clear she didn't want any more help from him. Or at least, that's what her *words* said. But the *feeling*—there was that pesky thing again—that he was getting from her couldn't be more different than those words she had just spoken.

He wasn't sure what had possessed him to climb into that bed with her, and to take her in his arms, to comfort her, but he had, and it had changed everything.

Coupled with the rescue, he felt protective of her, something he had not felt for a long time, and something he needed to remind himself he had failed at—spectacularly—once before.

Still, it was pretty simple.

She was an old friend. She'd had a shock. She didn't have a wallet or a purse or a phone.

On top of all that, Gopher had been on the front steps of the hospital when Brad arrived.

"I got some great photos of you and that woman out on the lake," the paparazzo had said. "And the dog. The dog angle is the kind of thing that could make it go viral. It could be my break. Maybe even better than some shots of Gregor."

Without saying a word, Brad had pivoted and turned back to the parking lot.

"You could be a hero! I've got a really good writer interested in the story. She's here in Whistler, too, at the moment. But time is of the essence. Nobody will care about it a week from now."

Yay, Brad thought, still walking away.

"If I could just talk to you for a minute, it could make you famous."

Brad could not think of one thing he would like less than being famous. He always felt such pity for Gregor Watson, who could no longer do one normal thing without being hounded. But Gopher, a man who made his living preying on that whole cult of fame, would probably never understand that.

"And her. What's her name?" the annoying man had asked.

Brad had reached his vehicle with Gopher, undeterred, on his heels. He'd snarled at him, "Get lost, before I call the police."

He'd gotten back in his vehicle and made it look as if he was driving away, but in actual fact, he'd pulled into the lane at the side of the hospital.

A staff member on break had recognized him, and used his pass to open the locked side entrance.

"Good job out there on the lake, Mr. Daniels."

Oh, boy, it had never been one of his ambitions to be a hero in a small town.

Still, the notoriety cemented his desire to protect Faith. If ever a person needed a rescue, it was her, and if ever a person had needed to be a rescuer, it was him.

"Um…" he said to Faith now, after she had turned down his offer of accommodation "Do you want the good news or the bad news?"

They had often teased each other with that very phrase in those months they had been together as a couple in high school. He saw recognition dawn in her face, and a smile touched her lips.

It wasn't until she smiled that he realized how haunted she was, not just by the events of the day, but by what life had handed her with her husband's illness.

It wasn't until she smiled that he realized how much he wanted to make her smile again.

"The good news," she decided.

"Damn it," he said.

"What?"

"There isn't actually any good news."

And then she laughed, and it was exactly as he remembered her laughter being, a pure light in a world he hadn't even realized was dark.

"First of all, there's a reporter out on the front steps of the hospital who seems to think your rescue could be story of the year."

"A local reporter?" she asked.

"Unfortunately, no. He's been hanging around trying to catch Gregor Watson."

"The actor, Gregor Watson?"

"Yes, but he's not here anymore, a fact that hasn't caught up with Gopher."

"Gopher?"

"My security staff nicknamed the photographer. Gregor stays at Cobalt when he comes."

"Oh," she said, digesting that, looking at him as if there were facets to him that she had not considered.

"I don't want my children to *ever* find out what happened. Maggie, in particular, would put me on the doddering-old-fool watch list."

He smiled. "My daughter can also be pretty unforgiving of what she perceives as my senior-moment transgressions."

"I think I saw her picture on your lock screen when you loaned me your phone. She's extraordinary, Brad. Is she your only child?"

He felt that rush of pride that Cassandra always made him feel. "Yes, she is. She really is beautiful."

"Yes, I saw that. But there was something about the way she held herself that made me think she's very confident and strong, a credit to you."

He felt so pleased by those observations.

"She's a great young woman, even if she doesn't allow me to use the word *typing.*"

Faith chuckled. "I'm not allowed to correct spelling and punctuation in texts."

"I bet you're encouraged *not* to use them, right?"

"So right! And I was a teacher. It's like swallowing nails not to add a comma here and there. To plunk down a sentence with no capitals. To not scream in frustration at autocorrect."

"You became a teacher," he said, pleased. "That was your dream."

"Yes, it was. grade three and four. When they're still so lovely, and nearly fall over dead if they see you in the grocery store because they can't imagine Mrs. Saint-John actually eats."

It was his turn to laugh, but then he made himself get down to business.

"Aside from Gopher, the other bad news is that I know they can't allow you to check in at the hotel without a photo identification, and a credit card." He said this carefully, speaking from his long experience in the hospitality industry.

She contemplated that for a moment, then drew in a deep breath. "I should probably just go home. I can do what I came here to do another time."

It occurred to him, almost shockingly, that he did not know where *home* was for her.

"Do you think you could check flights to Toronto for me?"

He made no move toward his phone.

"I should just get you to take me back to Vancouver. To the airport." She blushed. "Or arrange for someone to do it. Sorry. It's a long trip. You're obviously a busy guy. Not a chauffeur. It's not like you're staff."

Why had she said it like that, with that funny little inflection in her voice on the word *staff*?

"Actually, if I could just borrow a bit of money from you,"

she said quickly, "I'll take the sea-to-sky shuttle to the airport. That's how I got here. It's a beautiful drive."

But that drive was two hours long, and it was evident to him that Faith was beyond tired, and practically swaying on her feet. She was in no condition to be making these kinds of decisions.

He decided not to tell her the resort had a helicopter at their disposal—another reason the celebrities loved visiting them—that could get her to Vancouver International in under half an hour.

But getting her to the airport was one thing, getting her on a plane was another thing altogether.

"Um… I hate to be the one to break this to you—" *not really* "—but if you don't have the right documents to check in to a hotel, you don't have the right documents to get on an airplane, either."

Brad watched as Faith figured out exactly how bad a pickle she was in.

"Oh, no," she whispered.

She didn't have to look quite that aghast that she was realizing she was highly dependent on him, at the moment.

"On the other hand, even if you could get on a plane, if you went home early, there would be lots of questions from Maggie, I'm sure."

She gave him a grateful look, for thinking of that angle, or remembering her daughter's name, he wasn't quite sure.

"How long were you planning on staying?"

She had to think about it for a minute.

"I'll be leaving Friday…if I can get things sorted out."

"Then let me look after you," he suggested, gruffly. "Whistler's still a good place, despite how much it has grown. I have every confidence your purse will be found or turned in, but until it is, just come to Cobalt."

Her shoulders heaved. "I guess I have no choice," she said with such genuine reluctance it stung him.

She reminded him, a little bit, of that ungrateful dog, barking at him after its rescue.

He frowned suddenly, remembering their senior year, and how they had discovered each other. He remembered the richness and excitement of first love. *That* feeling—made breathless by someone else's presence—that no matter where you went in life, no matter what other thrills you experienced, that one could never be replicated.

Firsts.

And then he remembered she had hurt him.

And that had been a first, too. His first broken heart. Brad reached back over the years, and the details were surprisingly sharp.

He'd been astonished to find a curt note from her, left at the front desk of the hotel, saying she was leaving Whistler to pursue her life and she wished him well with his.

He'd called her home phone—no cell phones back then—but no one had answered.

He'd driven by that trailer she and her dad, Max, lived in about a thousand times, but it had appeared to have been totally abandoned.

When he'd finally found the nerve to go the door, Max had been shirtless and swigging a beer. His eyes were red-rimmed and he'd looked at Brad with a sadness, as if someone had died.

"She's gone, buddy. Off to school."

"UVic?"

For a moment, had something like pity crossed that man's sorrowful features?

"No, she changed her mind."

Brad didn't want to beg, but he had. A phone number, an address, *anything.*

But her father had shut the door in his face.

Brad looked at Faith now, and saw in her expression exactly what he had always seen in her. Despite her reluctance to accept his help, there was an unguarded softness in her eyes and around the plumpness of the bottom lip she was chewing. She wasn't like that snappy little dog at all. He could see what she was: a person of innate integrity and kindness.

And yet, that note from decades ago had not been either.

The opposite, in fact.

A reminder that he had not *really* known Faith, any more than he suspected now, that he had ever really known his wife.

So, a warning.

To look after Faith, if she accepted his invitation, but to keep his distance, too. To protect himself from his inability to read the heart of the female species.

CHAPTER SEVEN

BRAD, WITH OLD-WORLD manners that did not surprise Faith, held open the door of his vehicle for her. They had exited the hospital through a side door, in case Gopher was still camped out at the front entrance.

She shuddered at the thought.

"What?" Brad asked her.

"Just thinking of my daughter finding out about my escapades because they've become front-page news," she told him.

"It's not 'front-page news' anymore," he informed her solemnly. "It's *going viral.*"

And then they were both laughing. It was the second time he had made her laugh. She thought she could probably count the number of times she had laughed in the last five years on one hand.

She noticed his vehicle was one of those very sophisticated, very large all-terrain sports vehicles. She had to step up to get into it.

She slid into the deep leather seat, and Brad shut her door with a click. He came around to the driver's side and started the vehicle with the push of a button. It hummed quietly to life and Faith was enveloped in a sense of luxury.

The scent was heavenly—part Brad, part new vehicle. The seats were heated, the interior was filled with the notes of a lovely acoustic guitar from a sound system so good the guitarist might have been in the back seat.

Like Brad's watch, the vehicle sharply highlighted the differences in their worlds. Faith drove a subcompact in Toronto. Felix had never been able to part with his old Volvo, which had been secondhand when he'd acquired it.

It was now nearly six o'clock, and the peaks surrounding the village had disappeared behind the shroud of absolute darkness that one only experienced in the mountains.

Brad pulled away from the hospital. "What hotel?"

She told him and then said, "The SUV is a bit of a surprise. If the boutique packaging is any indication, Cobalt Lake seems to have embraced all things eco-friendly."

He glanced over at her and grinned. "It seems like one of those gas-guzzling pigs, doesn't it?"

Had she sounded judgmental? She hadn't meant to. She'd just been trying to make conversation. "I'm sure it's necessary around the resort, and for unpredictable winter conditions."

"A bigger vehicle with four-wheel drive is necessary, but this is actually an experimental vehicle, a prototype that we'd like to produce if we can figure out how to get the costs down. It's an innovation based on hydrogen-fuel technologies."

"You own a vehicle company?" she said with surprise. "I thought you had inherited your family business, the Cobalt Lake Resort?"

"I did, but it never was at the forefront of my interests. I might have even let it go completely after my parents died."

"I'm sorry. I didn't know your parents were gone," Faith said, guiltily happy there would be no chance encounters with an aging Mrs. Daniels at the resort.

"My wife, Cynthia, loved it, and managed to drag Cobalt Lake Resort, kicking and screaming, into the twenty-first century. My daughter, Cassandra, does most of the day-to-day management of it now, so that I can focus on other things."

She heard the pride in his voice at the mention of his daughter's name. She had a sudden horrible memory of Felix brushing past Maggie, pretending she wasn't there, inexplicable hostility stamped in his features.

A reminder of how terribly wrong love could go.

She felt as if she had been punched and left breathless, as was so often the way when these memories surfaced. Thankfully, it was dark in the car, and Brad had that lovely gift for conversation.

"I'm a part owner of the hydrogen-fueled-vehicle company. I'm actually part owner in quite a few ventures. In university, I discovered I had a gift for sniffing out innovation, and figuring out which, of the millions of them, had potential."

This was said without even a hint of conceit, but with the enthusiasm of a man who truly loved his work.

"Right now, the most exciting project I'm involved in is developing an exoskeleton for human beings. It has amazing ramifications for the severely disabled."

Faith glanced over at him. In the light of the dashboard, she could see that he was, despite his losses, all of the things she was not. As in: fully engaged in life.

He pulled up in front of the hotel. "No, you stay there. I'll go get your things."

"I'm sure if they won't let me check in without ID, they're not going to hand over my luggage to a complete stranger."

He raised an amused eyebrow at her. "Stay here."

She watched him go, riveted by the presence he radiated. She saw him lift a hand to people he recognized, exchange quick greetings, once even stopping for a moment. There was a sense of him being where he belonged, and knowing it, in a way she found enviable.

Finally, Brad slipped through the doors of her hotel.

While he was gone, she put down her window and breathed in deeply. The mountain air had a texture to it—sweet, pure—that she had only ever experienced in these mountain villages.

Whistler Village had always been high-end, even in her growing-up years, but the atmosphere had morphed into something out of a fairy tale, an unlikely combination of cozy mountain meets cosmopolitan posh.

There was no snow and it wasn't anywhere near Christmas, and yet there was that holiday feeling with white lights threaded through the branches of every tree, and outlining every window, awning, railing and building.

The sounds of laughter, people chattering, cutlery rattling, glasses clinking, came in her open window and filled the crisp mountain air with happy sounds. Despite the chill of the evening, Whistler celebrated the outdoors in all seasons.

The patio areas of cafés, pubs and wine bars were open, the tables full, heat lamps glowing bright orange. People, colorfully dressed in parkas and toques and scarves, drifted in and out of shops, laden down with parcels. The was an air or excitement, prosperity and vitality.

A few minutes later, Brad emerged, carrying her suitcase by its handle. He was so strong it had not even occurred to him, apparently, to use the wheels to drag it along.

Again, she noticed him exchanging greetings.

He opened the back gate of the vehicle and tossed the suitcase in. He would live in that world of very expensive luggage. But if he had noticed hers was slightly travel-worn and certainly not a brand name, it didn't show in his face.

"I hope they at least put up a fight before they handed that over to you," she said.

"Yes, I did a tug-of-war with the desk clerk."

He laughed. His laughter was so wonderful. It shimmered with a promise of a life that held laughter again.

She wasn't sure if that was a good thing or a bad thing, but she found herself leaning toward a good thing.

"I'm pretty well-known around town," he said. "Not the one they're watching for to make off with luggage that doesn't belong to them. I seem to be especially well-known now. At least three people mentioned what happened at Cobalt Lake this afternoon. It's the talk of the town."

"Oh, no."

"Don't worry," he said, "I'll keep you out of the glare of the spotlight until this all blows over. In a week—or less, if we're lucky—they'll have moved on to something else. Last week the talk of the town was the stray-cat problem. The dog rescue is a little more riveting for now. But next week, who knows? 'Skunk family takes up residence under Banker's Bar? Bear misses memo on hibernation and is chasing tourists through Lost Lake Park…'"

He was making her laugh again. And then they were on the familiar rode to Brad's family resort.

If Faith thought Whistler had changed, nothing could have prepared her for Cobalt Lake.

Like Whistler, it was like something out of a fairy tale, every tree and every walkway lit up with millions of tiny white lights.

The lodge and grounds had been given a complete facelift.

No wonder Gregor Watson stayed here, and Brad appeared to be on a first-name basis with him!

"But where are the chalets?" she whispered, catching glimpses of gorgeous little cottages seeded among the stands of evergreen trees at the base of the ski hill.

"Oh, those old A-frames?"

Yes, the ones, she had cleaned to his mother's exacting standards.

"They hadn't been built properly, and were starting to have issues as they aged. Mold. Frozen pipes. Roof leaks. Decks that couldn't withstand the snow load. Cynthia replaced them with these cottages, one at a time, over the years. All the A-frames are gone now."

He skirted the main lodge, and took a side road that curved through a forest grove, lit with fairy lights. It looked amazing. Faith could just imagine how magical everything would look when it snowed.

Brad stopped in front of a delightful structure, set well

away from the other cottages. Faith went to open her door, but he lifted his hand, ever so subtly, and then came around and opened her door for her.

Again, such an old-world courtesy, and she *loved* it.

She stood looking at the cottage, trying not to let her mouth fall open. In what world was *this* a cottage?

It was a house, and a beautiful one at that. A tasteful sign showed it had been named Wolf's Song, and Faith remembered the name of the ski run directly behind it was Timber Wolf.

The Cobalt Lake Resort had always named their cabins, but they'd had cutesy names like All Decked Out, Misty Morning Magic, Mountain Standard Time and the Bear Cub Club. The new name signified a change in direction that was also more than evident in the new face of the resort.

A wide, curved stamped concrete walkway led the way, through manicured shrub beds that held plants chosen to keep color, even in the winter—emerald cedars, miniature mountain pine, dwarf burning bush.

The "cottage" had a craftsman-like style with an imposing stone-and-wood facade. Open trusses, huge and wooden, held up the roof over the covered entryway. Two flickering gas lanterns framed the large front door, which looked majestic and antique.

Brad carried her one shabby suitcase onto the porch and she followed him up the wide staircase. The spacious deck area had four deeply cushioned outdoor chairs on it, black-and-white-plaid blankets draped artfully over them.

Something brushed by her feet, and Faith gave a little squeal and stumbled back toward the staircase.

Brad dropped her suitcase and had her in a second.

"That darn cat," he said, annoyed.

Out of the corner of her eye, she saw a white form dashing away.

He didn't let her go, right away. She felt his nearness, breathed in his scent, and his strength.

"You're destined to rescue me today," she said. She intended it to sound light, but it didn't feel light. She was marveling at the sensation of having someone to lean on, of not having to rely on her own—admittedly quite wobbly—strength.

"My pleasure," he said, stepping away from her. "That cat! Such a nuisance. It's been hanging around here since the summer."

She suspected the cat was being used as a distraction, as if he, too, had felt a shiver of something white-hot with promise pass between them.

Brad punched in a code, and opened the door. He set down the suitcase inside. That poor suitcase had never looked more forlorn, and like it didn't belong.

"It's probably not the kind of luggage you're accustomed to," Faith ventured, as a way to tame down the white-hot-with-promise thoughts.

Brad looked down at the suitcase, genuinely baffled. "What?"

"Like not Louis Vuitton. Or even Samsonite, for that matter."

"Oh," he said, cocking his head and looking at her suitcase, then dismissing it with a shrug. "They all look the same to me. Cynthia picked all that stuff."

It occurred to Faith that maybe she was exaggerating the differences between them—focusing on the watch, the car, the luggage—as a form of self-protection.

But then Brad flicked on a light switch, and stood back to let her pass him. Faith stood in the foyer. No, she definitely was not exaggerating the differences in their worlds. The interior of the cottage was like something on the front cover of a lifestyle magazine.

CHAPTER EIGHT

"THIS IS INCREDIBLE," Faith breathed.

The decor was mountain-lodge, but in the most upscale way imaginable. It was a completely open plan, with expansive hardwood floors, huge windows, a floor-to-ceiling stacked stone fireplace. Logs crackled invitingly inside the firebox.

"You like it," Brad said, pleased.

And it seemed that was all that mattered to him, that she liked it. There seemed to be no ego—*look what I have*—in his statement at all.

"What's not to like?" she asked. "Did your wife do this, too?"

"She had a designer."

Faith had grown up in rented trailers and basement suites, with secondhand furniture and left-behind art hanging crookedly on walls.

She remembered her and Felix tackling projects in what they had thought would be their first house, with a kind of reckless enthusiasm. It had been modest, large enough, but in much need of repair. Its main selling point had been the location—walking distance to the historic St. George campus of the University of Toronto, where Felix worked, and the elementary school where she worked.

But it had also appealed because it had been on a block lined with mature trees that gave them shade in the summer, and that gave them birds to feed all winter. How Felix had adored coming up with increasingly complex plans to try and keep the squirrels from those feeders!

They had lovingly fixed the leaky basement and painted walls, and prepared nurseries, and bought throw cushions. They went through awful decorating stages, like sponge-painting walls and a Southwest theme and Scandinavian-style furniture.

When the time had come when they could have moved on, Faith, possibly because of her gypsy childhood, had been completely unable to let it go.

Their starter home became their forever home.

It had never—not once—looked like this, or even close to this.

But somehow, they had created a sense of home. And had so much fun doing it. She remembered the time they had painted the nursery in preparation for Michael moving out of the bassinette beside their bed. The color on the paint chip had been fine, but on the walls it looked hideous.

"My," Felix had said, mildly, "he's going to feel as if he's growing up inside an aquarium."

"Lucky boy," she'd said, deadpan.

And then, with paint in their hair and on the tips of their noses, they had started to laugh, and they had laughed until they were rolling on the floor.

Faith suddenly felt sorry for Brad. She bet he'd never had a moment like that in his entire life, poor guy.

She slipped off her shoes.

"You don't have to take off your shoes," he said.

"I can't imagine anything more un-Canadian than leaving your shoes on," she told him. Not to even mention the thought of scratching those beautiful floors could give her nightmares.

She let the great room draw her into it. "Who lit the fire?"

"Oh, I called ahead. One of the staff got it ready."

There it was again. *The staff.* Just in case she had any ideas about trying to forget the divide between their two worlds.

Their house had a fireplace. It had never drafted properly and every time they tried to light it, the whole house filled up with smoke and the fire detectors went off.

And for some reason, that was a good memory, too.

She realized, startled, that *good* memories had not been part of how she remembered Felix, so far.

She and Felix could not have afforded to stay in a place like this in a million years. What would it cost? A thousand dollars a night? Conservatively?

Even if they could have afforded it, she suspected they would have never done it, not even for a special treat. No, they would have opted to spend the money on a new furnace. Or bringing the kids home from university for Christmas, or building up their retirement savings accounts.

Yes, now that she thought about it, it was definitely building the retirement savings account that would have won out instead of a night in a fancy hotel. How important that had been to Felix... She shook off the feeling of sadness that was trying to edge in on her sense of genuine enjoyment of these posh surroundings, her surprise at finding herself here.

"Sit down," Brad invited Faith. "You look dead on your feet."

Not the impression one wanted to give, but she felt the same way she looked, and moved into the great room and sank into one of the deep inviting armchairs that faced the fireplace.

"I'll put this in the bedroom," he said and took her suitcase through a door off the main entrance. "I'm going to head over the lodge. I'll rustle up a cell phone for you, and bring something over to eat."

He was gone before she realized she had not said no.

In fact, she felt powerless to say no.

Faith settled more deeply into the comfort of the chair and enjoyed the flickering beauty of the fire, and the lovely light it cast over the stunning cottage interior.

She let her gaze roam around the room. Despite how undeniably grand it was, with its soaring ceilings, gorgeous light fixtures and priceless art, the room was somehow extremely cozy and welcoming. That's what designers did, she supposed.

She could see those professional touches in the upscale kitchen that was at the far end of the open space. It had a dizzying array of stainless-steel, high-end cabinets, stunning light fixtures. An entire bank of windows looked out toward the ski slopes, though the slopes were just a dark shadow at the moment.

Fresh flowers and a fruit basket were sitting in the center of an expanse of Italian marble that was the kitchen island.

Sadly, it felt like a kitchen not a single person had ever baked cookies in. She thought of Chloe and Tanya, standing on chairs beside her in her kitchen, as covered in cookie dough as she and Felix had once been covered in paint.

Still, as Faith looked back to the fire, she was aware of feeling slightly stunned to find herself ensconced in Wolf's Song.

Since Felix's diagnosis—no, way before that, because things had to become quite alarming before you even sought a diagnosis—she had felt as if she was being thrust deeper and deeper into a carnival funhouse.

Why were they even called that? Those places that kept your world feeling tilted and off balance. Those places of warped mirrors and hideous surprises and false exits. Those places where the panic rose in you as you became more and more lost in the mazes, and became more and more convinced you could never find a way out.

And yet here she was. She had popped out. Been released from the "fun" house nightmare.

She was sitting in this gorgeous cottage, in front of this soothing fire, only because her beloved husband, by now a stranger to her, had died.

How terrible, Faith thought, to feel relieved. To be so *glad* to be sitting here, instead of immersed in the day-to-day tragedies of living with someone who had been afflicted with bvFTD, or behavioral frontotemporal dementia.

She had been flattened by it. Numbed.

Was it the shock of hitting the frigid water that had jolted her out of the trance she had been in? She was aware that, starting this afternoon, for the first time, she had a real sense of leaving it behind her.

This is *exactly* what Maggie had wanted for her. Well, maybe without the dog, the icy lake and the near-death experience.

But this feeling of the flatness leaving her. Being in Brad's cottage felt just like being warmed up in the hospital.

That's what the memory of Felix and his obsession with the retirement savings account had tried—unsuccessfully, it would seem—to edge out.

A sense of the life force creeping back into her.

She felt alive.

And, okay, just a little bit frightened by the feelings Brad was drawing out of her. He had suffered a loss, too. Why did he still seem so vital? So engaged with life? It made her feel as if he had a secret that she needed to know.

She shouldn't really feel compelled to uncover any of Brad Daniels's secrets. In fact, it was dangerous. It felt as if, with the tiniest little shove, things between them might be right back where they had been when they were teenagers. Terrifying, indeed.

But why be afraid?

Hadn't life already done its very worst to her?

"Dad," Cassandra said over his phone, "what on earth is going on?"

Brad's phone was blowing up. It seemed every single person in Whistler wanted to know what had happened on Cobalt Lake this afternoon. He looked at it, alarmed, as the message counter kept ticking up. Fifty-six messages? Fifty-seven. Fifty-eight.

He'd put it on silent mode, but the phone was programmed to let Cassandra's calls come through. Even if he was screening everyone in the world—which it seemed he was at the moment—he always tried to be available to his daughter.

The signal was really bad—probably because Brad was in the wine cellar. The lodge had its own wine cellar, but this one, below their residence, had been Cynthia's private enclave.

He didn't even know when he'd last been down in this room, but like everything else Cynthia had done, it was beyond exquisite.

"Earth calling Dad," Cassandra said, and he realized he hadn't been listening to her.

"Sorry, Cassie, what? Bad signal."

"I asked you what is going on."

For a startled moment, Brad thought Cassandra must be referring to Faith being tucked away at Wolf's Song.

He realized, given their conversation this morning, he did not want Cassie to know anything about the woman in the cottage. Would his daughter take one look at her, and find Faith perfect for him?

He couldn't imagine anything more alarming that Cassandra deciding to play Cupid. For his own good!

Somehow, it seemed impossible that they had just had that conversation this morning. It felt to Brad as if a lifetime had gone by.

"My phone's going crazy," Cassie told him.

Join the club, he thought.

"So is the front desk. Everybody wants to know about the rescue on the lake."

"Oh?" he said innocently. "What rescue?"

"Dad! They're saying you saved a woman and a dog who had gone through the ice on Cobalt Lake."

"Oh. That. It was nothing, really. You know how people

love a great story. Remember when the gondola got stuck on Whistler and that ski-patrol woman went up on the ladder and got all those people off? Heroine for a week?"

"Dad! Don't downplay it. It sounds amazing," Cassie said. "And we still have lots of media people in town and hanging around the resort because of Gregor."

Cassie was usually working with security to protect their guests from the media, not approaching them.

"I could not have set up better publicity for the lodge if I tried," she breathed.

He went very still. "Catastrophe is not a publicity opportunity," he said sternly.

"But it wasn't a catastrophe. It was a disaster averted. From what I'm hearing, you prevented something terrible from happening."

"Leave it, Cassie."

He read her silence on the other end of the line as being slightly stunned.

"Dad?"

"Look, I've got a really bad signal. I've got to go."

With the tiniest niggle of guilt, Brad disconnected from Cassie and looked around the room that had been one of Cynthia's pride and joys.

Like the cottages, and the lodge, and even their private residence, this room had been done by a designer.

A very famous and expensive designer who had her own television show on the home-and-garden channel.

Cynthia had needed perfection.

He had felt indulgent of that need. She had come from a working-class background, and especially in the early days of their marriage, he thought she had felt she needed to prove herself to his parents, his mother in particular.

But had Cynthia lost something in that quest for perfection? Something of herself? Is that why he found Faith so compelling. *Real?*

He'd seen the expression on Faith's face when he'd said a designer did Wolf's Song. If he was not mistaken, it had been faintly sympathetic, as if he had missed something.

This room was beautiful by any standard, and yet now, as never before, he could feel it missing something, too.

Cynthia had loved collecting wine. Drinking it? Not so much. She wanted it "to age." Like everything else about her, the cellar was highly organized, with the rarest wines behind glass on the back wall, soft light sweeping down on the temperature-controlled display racks.

The cellar had been mostly for show. Occasionally, she'd hosted a wine afternoon for "the girls," but mostly, she had just collected.

Is that what he had been, too? For show? Where was her heart in this room? In those impeccably designed rooms? Where had her heart been in the marriage?

He hated these questions.

He wasn't indulging them anymore.

He went and inspected the wall that displayed her most valuable collectibles. Now, he saw there were probably five hundred bottles in this section.

If he drank a bottle every week, it would take him ten years to get through it.

Maybe he should break it out for Cassie's wedding—if his independent, fiery daughter ever found a man who was her equal.

Suddenly it felt ridiculous to "age" the wine, to save it for "special" occasions that never came.

They had *really* never come for his wife.

If there was a lesson to be had from Cynthia's premature death, maybe it was that. The time was now.

Still, he hesitated. Was it a special occasion? It felt like it was. But that was a feeling he needed to fight, not give in to.

But he was going back over there, anyway. Faith had to eat. They both did. Why not bring the wine? It had been a super-tough day. He didn't have to drink it with her—he could just present it to her, as a gift.

Feeling like a rebel—and slightly guilty, as well—Brad randomly selected a bottle from the most exclusive shelf and then made his way up to the restaurant kitchen to collect a dinner for two that Anita, the resort's long-time sous-chef, had put together for him.

He stopped at the front desk. "Hey, Kathy, any word about that purse?"

"No, sorry. Jim had a team out there looking, but they didn't find anything. He left a note here for you."

She passed it to him. Brad glanced at it, then shoved it in his pocket.

"He said your voice-mail box was full."

"Actually, while I'm here, I might as well grab a couple of cell phones."

"Of course." She went to a large cabinet where they kept an inventory of things guests might need, everything from toothbrushes to a selection of specialty pillows.

"There you go, Mr. Daniels. I heard what you did—"

He held up his hand. "That's why I need a new cell phone. Suddenly everybody in the whole village and beyond wants to talk to me."

"That explains the full voice mail. The world does love a hero, Mr. Daniels."

"Huh," he said. He opened one of the cell-phone boxes.

"This is the number," he told Kathy. "If the police call about that missing purse, you can give it to them. And to Jim, if he finds it. No one else. Am I clear?"

"But Cassandra, of course?"

He was shocked that he wanted to say no, but he didn't. He knew Cassie's phone number. If it came up on the caller ID of the new phone, he could decide then if he wanted to talk to her.

And then he stopped at his office and got rid of his own phone. The number of missed calls and texts was becoming ridiculous. Brad felt a startling sense of freedom as he slid it into his desk drawer. People needed to get lives.

As he walked away, he wondered when the last time was that he'd been without his phone.

It wasn't until he was on his way back over to Wolf's Song that he realized taking some back hallways out of the lodge had paid off. For the first time since she'd been born, he was happy *not* to see his daughter.

CHAPTER NINE

FAITH WAS SO glad she had not been able to find the energy to tell Brad no when he'd gone to get dinner for them.

Because the truth was, as the scents wafted off the containers he had brought back to Wolf's Song, she was suddenly famished.

She did wish, though, that she would have found the energy to go rummage around her suitcase, have a quick shower and throw on some attractive clothes, a bit of makeup.

Because it was the first time she'd seen him without a winter jacket on. He was in a plaid flannel shirt, the plaid in subtle shades of gray, almost identical to his hair. The shirt was open at the column of his throat. With it, he was wearing crisp, khaki mountain slacks, belted at his narrow waist.

Though he had obviously changed since the rescue, he didn't look as if he'd put much effort into it. Even when they were young, she never remembered him fussing over his appearance. And still, Brad Daniels looked front-cover-of-a-men's-outdoor-magazine-worthy.

She couldn't help but notice he'd left his shoes on, was a person who had seemingly never once in his life given a thought to a scratched floor, or puddles.

The *staff* looked after things like that. But she waved the thought away, like a pesky fly that was trying to spoil a perfect moment.

He knew his way around the cottage and refused her offer

for help, telling her just to sit at the built-in banquette in an alcove nestled in the windows of the kitchen. He opened the wine he had brought with the efficiency of one who had opened fine wines—as in corked, not screw-top—many times.

He poured a splash in two glasses and set them, and the bottle, on the table, then brought over plates and cutlery, and the boxed food, his movements efficient and comfortable.

She noted the tulip-shaped wineglasses had the unmistakable look of hand-blown crystal. The plates and cutlery had a similar aura—yes, he moved in a world where place settings gave off an aura—of being expensive and exclusive.

Finally, he sat down and lifted his glass to hers, and they clinked, the glasses giving off the crisp note that confirmed their high quality.

"What is this?" she asked, after her first sip of wine. It was a white, which was nice. Red always made her self-conscious about her teeth. Faith was certain she had never tasted a wine quite so layered in delightful, exotic flavors.

"Not sure." He studied the label and shrugged, much as he had when looking at her suitcase.

"Taste it," she suggested.

He took a sip. Unfortunately, it made her very aware of his lips. "Hey, that's pretty good," he decided.

That seemed like an understatement. "Have you ever tasted anything like that before?" she asked.

"Um… I don't know. I'm not much of a wine guy."

"Well, you don't have to be a wine person to know this is unbelievable. It's ambrosia."

Again, that easy shrug, dismissing the fineness of the wine in the same way he had barely noticed her suitcase. Brad served the food. It was a Parmesan-crusted chicken on fettucine noodles. The noodles had so obviously been made from scratch, not been dumped out of a box into boiling water.

It occurred to Faith that maybe, just maybe, the reason why

the wine and the food seemed so, so good was that it was all part of that intoxicating feeling she had of coming alive.

And part of that was from being with Brad Daniels. Okay, maybe quite a lot of it!

"So what brought you back to Whistler?" Brad asked. "After all these years? You said you had come here to do something."

The chicken was as exquisite as the wine. "My dad wanted his ashes spread here."

"Oh, Faith, I'm so sorry. I didn't know he'd died."

"How could you know? He didn't live here anymore. He hadn't for a long time. He left after I did. But this is the place he remembered with the most fondness. He worked at all of the top-twenty ski destinations in the world, at one point or another, but this is where he said his heart was. When he was sick, he asked me to bring him back here."

"The loss of your dad and your husband... You must be reeling." His voice was soft with compassion, and that same softness was in his eyes when he gazed at her.

It was hard not to fall into softness, like being invited to try a feather bed after years of sleeping on rocks.

"Dad predeceased Felix by about five years. That's why, when I realized I couldn't check into the hotel, I said I could just go home, and try again another time. I'd already put it off for so long, it felt like another few months couldn't possibly matter." She laughed, a little self-consciously. "My dad was a great believer in signs, and things don't exactly seem to be lining up in my favor."

Except, gazing at Brad over the lip of an exquisite wineglass, that didn't seem exactly true.

She had landed on her feet, sitting here with her teenage sweetheart, eating food and drinking wine that was top-notch, in a five-star environment.

"My dad was actually one of the first ones to notice things might be off with Felix. I had so much going on. Maggie, after finishing up her law degree, and in true Maggie fashion, deciding it would be nothing to get married, have a baby and start her career in a three-year period. Things got so chaotic that I kept putting it off."

Brad's gaze offered her what she had not offered herself. Forgiveness for the fact that life had gotten in the way of such a meaningful task.

"I think it's time, Faith. You're here. You'll regret it if you go back without doing what you came to do."

She nodded. "I think you're right. I'll figure it out."

"I can give you a hand."

"Oh," she said, "really, I've imposed enough."

"Did your dad want some place, specifically?"

"He loved the Feeney's Pass area. He mentioned the viewing point. I'll hike up there tomorrow. I won't need a wallet for that!"

"You're not going up there by yourself at this time of year."

She was taken aback by the firmness in his voice. It sounded like those orders he had snapped at her out on the ice. It reminded her a bit of her daughter, an implication she was some kind of incompetent moron who couldn't be trusted to do things by herself.

Not that her first day in Whistler had actually proved Maggie wrong. Or done anything to inspire Brad's confidence in her, either.

Still, she had to discourage him from thinking he could just order her around, despite the fact she had accepted his many kindnesses.

"I grew up hiking mountains all over North America," she said quietly. "I'm not worried about Feeney's Pass."

"Well, you should be." There was an edge to his voice. "There's fresh snow up there."

She felt a surge of annoyance, and realized how truly tired she was. Why else would she be so sorely tempted to tell him to mind his own business, when he'd been so good to her? Her irritability probably had more to do with the events of the day catching up with her than Brad. She checked herself.

Then—while busy biting her tongue nearly in half—she looked at him closely. What she saw on his face was distressing.

"Brad?"

"Cynthia died in an avalanche," he said, his voice husky.

"Brad! I'm so sorry." And so glad she had not reacted to her initial annoyance with him.

"She went skiing by herself. At night. She often did. I don't know why."

She heard so much doubt and pain in that confession. It occurred to her, that despite Brad Daniels appearing to have it all, she did not have a corner on suffering. Or insecurities.

"We've implemented a GPS-tracking-device system here because of it, but even so, I'm not comfortable with you going up there by yourself. I hope you'll allow me to go with you."

Suddenly she saw how important this was for him. She could not refuse him this, even as she saw their lives were tangling a little bit more deeply.

"My daughter thinks it's probably illegal," she said. "She thinks I probably need a permit to spread ashes. I don't intend to get one, just so you know."

"Ah," he said, and lifted his wineglass to her, "so we're to be partners in crime."

"No one would have approved more than my dad."

Brad grinned. She had always loved that grin, lopsided and boyish.

"Max was a legend as a lift mechanic, as you know," he said. "That's why I was a little surprised I hadn't heard of him dying. Ski communities are pretty tight."

It meant the world to Faith that Brad not only remembered her father's name, but had also said such a good thing about him.

"His last job was in Switzerland, until he got sick and came home. Well, not home for him. His home was always on the slopes. He had to come to Toronto, because that's where I was.

"He hated the city and then the hospice. I think he had always just thought when his time came, he would lie down on a mountain, and breathe in the fresh air, and that maybe an eagle would soar overhead. I think that's why he extracted the promise from me to let Whistler be his final resting place."

"I didn't know him well, but I always liked him, Faith—everybody did. He was so funny and outgoing."

"Outrageous," she said with a smile. "A true renegade."

"Here's to the renegades," Brad said, and lifted his glass to her father.

At Max's specific request, there had been no funeral. No words spoken. That casual toast by Brad felt so good, so right, so overdue.

They tapped glasses again, and took sips in memory of her father.

"I'm afraid I'm not much of a salute to his legacy," Faith said with a sigh.

"Don't say that. You are!"

She raised an eyebrow at him.

"Not a renegade, obviously," Brad said, "illegal scattering of ashes aside, but I was always so taken with the way you seemed able to be totally yourself, even given—"

He stopped, clearly uncomfortable. He didn't have to say it. *Even given* that she had been living in a trailer, *even given* that she did not have the good clothes, *even given* that she never had lunch money or even money to go for a Coke with the gang after school.

"I know my dad's legend was certainly not all about his mechanical skills," she said dryly.

Brad said, with unmistakable fondness, "Remember him at World Cup?"

"Oh, yeah," she said. Max had somehow gotten himself at

the start line, and launched himself down the course on his skis. The timer had gone off automatically as he passed it.

She'd been a spectator, and recognized her father's style and crouch immediately. She had never seen anyone, not even all those pro skiers, dance with powder the way he did. But that day, he had not been dancing. It had been a full-frontal attack.

She'd watched, with her heart in her throat, thinking he was going to be badly hurt. But, no, he had finished the course, straightened and waved his poles with a flourish at the roaring crowd.

"His time," Brad remembered fondly, "was the third best recorded that day. Legend."

"Unofficially. He got arrested for his mischief."

"Did he? I'm sorry, I didn't know that part."

"He said it was worth it," she recalled, with reluctant affection. "I was so mad at him at the time, though! And then it wasn't that long after, in the dead of night, that he scaled one of the lift towers."

"The talk of the town!" Brad said. "Forty feet in the air, and he managed to get himself off the tower and onto one of the chairs."

"He wasn't nearly as skillful at getting himself back off, and when they found him in the morning, he was nearly frozen."

"But the guy who found him said Max was quite merry, announced he had just been singing his death song to the dawn."

"In Celtic, apparently."

"Legend."

"It wasn't always easy being the legend's daughter," she said.

"I knew that, even then. And yet, you had some of that in you. The sense of humor, the sense of fun. I really did think you stood out from everyone else."

That had been so intoxicatingly evident at the time. And it was true, despite so many insecurities, that she had been fairly certain of who she was. Somewhere along the way, she had lost that certainty.

"It's because he loved me," she told Brad softly. "My dad had flaws, and many of them, but I always knew how much he loved me. I felt utterly cherished by him, and it did give me a sense of myself."

When had she begun rejecting that sense of herself given to her by her father? Perhaps with Mrs. Daniels's cruel assessment of her as not suitable for her son.

CHAPTER TEN

"BUT THEN, almost in reaction to Max's shenanigans, his free spirit, I became the opposite," Faith revealed, finding herself confiding in Brad. "Desperately seeking normal, liking rules and structure."

When she put it like that, it sounded as if she had become *uptight*, as conventional and boring as her father had once predicted she would be.

"And did you get that?" he asked softly, and there was no judgment in his voice.

"Oh, yes. Felix was one of my professors in university. He was quite a bit older than me. He acted as if he didn't know I existed, of course, which was so appropriate.

"That was one of the things I loved about him actually. He was always so concerned about what was appropriate. It was the opposite of what I had grown up with.

"But a year after I'd graduated and was in my first year of teaching, I ran into him in a coffee shop near my school. I found out later it wasn't an accident. He'd looked for me having let a suitable amount of time go by so that it was *appropriate*—and was kind of checking out the coffee shops in my neighborhood.

"He was most worried about our age difference. He was ten years older than me. But it never bothered me at all. A year later we were married." She sighed. "My father proclaimed him dull as porridge."

She shouldn't have said that! She looked at the wine the very same way she had looked at the IV drip earlier.

She glanced at Brad, a man who would never be called that by anyone! It made the words she had just said feel like a betrayal.

"But he wasn't," she said hastily. "I had the life I dreamed of."

There. That was a good note to end on. But somehow, she was still talking, and she was sure the wonderful wine was to blame.

"And then I didn't. And it's kind of left me wondering where all that adherence to the rules got me. My somewhat unpredictable upbringing made me think about every possibility for chaos and disruption, and head it off before it happened. So much energy spent doing that—and all that time the thing I'd least expected, the thing I could not prepare for, was probably already growing in Felix's brain."

"And that's probably why you dashed out on that lake," Brad said. "Leaving all those fears behind you."

"My dad would have approved of the doggy dash," she said. And it occurred to her that he would have. Not just of her giving in to an impulse, after a lifetime of controlling them, but of everything that had happened after.

Her unexpected reunion with Brad.

The loss of her purse, forcing her to adapt, to accept that the unpredictable was part of life, and that it could be a good part.

Look at where she was!

Something shivered along her spine, almost as if Max was sitting at the table with her, laughing. And then it felt as if she heard his voice.

Don't you love it when a plan comes together?

She really was way too tired. She really could not even have one more sip of that wine. She really could not spend one more moment with Brad. She shivered.

"You're still chilled," Brad said. "Let's move in front of the fire."

She shouldn't. She needed to beg off. To say she was tired, to wish him good-night, to go to bed.

But there was that question again.

All her life of doing everything she *should* do, and where had it gotten her? Since they were going to spend more time together, anyway, why not just surrender?

They moved to the couch in front of the fire, sitting together on it, nearly shoulder-to-shoulder. His scent was so completely and deliciously clean and male. Somehow, the wineglasses were full again, and he finally took off his shoes, hooking the back of them with his toes and letting them drop to the floor.

He put his feet up on the wooden live-edge coffee table that, from the size of it, must have been made from a thousand-year-old tree.

Faith laughed at his socks, which were bright red with little green monkey faces on them.

"What on earth?" she asked. "You're so cover-of-the-outdoor-gentlemen's-magazine, and then those?"

He wiggled his colorfully clad toes at her.

"Cassie got them for me last year for Christmas. It was her answer to 'what do you get the guy who has everything?' It's a membership to a sock club. They send me a couple of wild and crazy pairs of socks every single month. It seems to just tickle Cassie that I actually wear them, so I do."

Faith loved all the things that told her about Brad's relationship with his daughter. She was aware of feeling a drowsy sort of contentment. It was so much like it had been when they were young. It was easy to be together, the conversation flowing as naturally as a river.

She found herself telling him about the nursery painting disaster, and baking cookies with her grandchildren.

"You know," he said, "I've never baked a cookie."

"Come on."

"No, really, never."

For the second time, Faith felt something like pity for Brad Daniels, the man who seemed to have everything. He'd never painted a nursery the wrong color, never painted at all, in fact. And never baked cookies.

So she told him about some of that, about Maggie and Michael growing up, about the delight of grandchildren, about Maggie becoming a lawyer, and Michael following his heritage back to Scotland to get a doctorate in Scottish history.

"I've worried about how employable that degree will make him."

Brad laughed. "He'll probably end up a professor, like his dad."

She liked it that he seemed to listen so carefully, and that he spoke of Felix with the respect of someone who had not seen, firsthand, the horrible consequences of his illness, and how it had changed the relationships he'd had with everyone who knew him.

She encouraged him to share stories about his daughter, and Faith loved the tenderness and pride in his voice when he talked about her.

They laughed easily together, as they always had.

Somehow, silence descended, and into that silence an aching awareness of him rushed in. Faith glanced at the fullness of his lips.

Memories tickled along her spine.

Brad held her eyes, and then his gaze drifted to her own lips. He reached out with his thumb and scraped her cheek, and then the fullness of her lip. She should have pulled away from that thumb, but she didn't. She leaned into it.

Brad, to his credit, pulled away. He actually looked at his hand as if it was a soldier that had disobeyed a command.

"We're both tired," he said. "It's not the best time to make a decision."

Did that mean he did think the time was coming? To make

a decision? About touching each other's lips? And possibly more than that?

He was right.

It was not something to be decided lightly, not something to fall into because they were both beyond exhaustion, in the grip of the dramatic events of the day, and the surprising sweetness of their reunion.

Brad got up off the couch and stretched. It showed off the broadness of his chest, and a rippling of lovely muscles in his arms. His shirt lifted and showed the hard contours of his tummy.

It was breathtaking.

Faith reminded herself, sternly, that her tummy did not have hard contours. Thank goodness, they had backed off on what was developing between them before Brad had made that discovery!

"Oh," he said, "I brought you a phone." He picked it out of his pocket and laid it on the table.

"You just happen to have extra cell phones lying around?"

"It's probably the number-one thing our guests lose or break, particularly during ski season. Supplying loaner phones was one of Cassie's—Cassandra's—ideas, always offering that little extra service to the guests." He chuckled. "In the spring, though, it's a full-time job picking dead cell phones out of melting snow drifts."

"Thank you," she said, not opening the box just yet, and making note of one more example of her indebtedness to him.

She was shocked to see it was nearly midnight. Way too late to call Maggie. It would be 3:00 a.m. in Toronto. Really, was there anything worse than middle-of-the-night phone calls?

She felt a certain guilty relief about that.

"I had to grab a new phone, too," Brad said. "Mine is blowing up. Over the rescue thing."

"Oh, no!"

"I'm doing my best to keep the lid on that."

"Thank you."

"Why don't I come by around ten tomorrow morning, and we'll head up Feeney?"

He was taking charge of everything. She knew she should protest. But she wasn't going to.

"Thank you," she said again. "That sounds perfect."

He hesitated for just a moment. And then he bent, and dropped a quick kiss on her cheek. Completely platonic. Almost European.

"It's so good to see you," he said huskily.

Her silly heart, the one that was supposed to be frozen, had let the fire and his nearness warm it right up.

He slipped his shoes back on and was soon out the front door. She heard him locking it with the keypad. Another small gesture that, like the phone, and the meal, and everything he had done, made her feel intensely taken care of.

It just felt so good not to be the one in charge, to let go.

Faith went into the bedroom. Like the rest of Wolf's Song, the space was opulent, a luxurious symphony of soothing neutral shades and rich textures. The bed was a king. Who needed a bed so large?

She was suddenly so exhausted that it was a huge effort to get her nightgown out of the suitcase and wash her face.

The bathroom had a swimming-pool-size tub in it. There was a chandelier over the tub, hundreds of teardrop-shaped crystals suspended from it, winking with light. In the bathroom!

Finally, back in the bedroom, she pulled back those crisp sheets and climbed into that huge bed. There was a switch beside the bed to turn off the lights.

She was plunged into the kind of complete darkness that city dwellers tended to forget existed.

The expanse of the bed made her feel small.

And very, very lonely.

When she closed her eyes, instead of falling into deep and

exhausted sleep, the events on the lake replayed in her mind's eye. She had a terrible night's sleep, and despite that, Faith found herself awake early. She realized her internal clock was refusing to reset from eastern time.

It was nine o'clock in Toronto. She went out into the main area of the cottage and found where she had left the cell phone on the table. She looked out the windows. It wasn't raining, but it was a gray day in Whistler. The mountaintops were swathed in clouds.

She spent a few minutes figuring out the new phone, and then tapped in Maggie's number.

Unlike yesterday, her daughter picked up the unfamiliar number on the first ring.

"Hi, sweetie."

"Mom! I've been so worried."

Faith thought she'd seen that on a bumper sticker once: Live Long Enough That Your Children Worry About You.

"But I called you and told you I'd lost my phone."

"I tried your hotel, and they said you hadn't checked in!"

Faith had not considered that possibility.

"Can you imagine how that made me feel? So then I tried to call that number back, and I reached a message from a man named Daniel. I told him who I was and asked for a call back. I said it was urgent that I speak to you, but he never called me back. What kind of person is that?"

Faith remembered Brad saying he had put his phone away because of all the calls about the rescue.

"He just didn't have his phone with him."

Her daughter, from a generation that practically had their phones growing out of their hands, harrumphed with disbelief.

"And how would you know that?"

"We had dinner together."

"Daniel could have phoned me when you finished. I said it was urgent."

"His name isn't Daniel, it's Brad, and I'm sure he could

figure out a three-hour time difference might not make calling back the best idea."

"But how would he know there was a three-hour time difference?"

Faith could feel Maggie shifting into lawyer mode, and prepared herself for the cross.

"Shockingly, where I'm living now came up in our conversation."

"You never said your friend was a *man*."

"I didn't think it was pertinent."

"Mom, where are you? Are you really in Whistler?"

"What?"

"I'm scared," Maggie said. "I know there's something you're not telling me. I could hear it in your voice, in that message you left. You're vulnerable. And you're a woman of some means. Awful people troll the internet looking for people just like you."

Faith looked around at her beautiful surroundings, and almost laughed out loud. If only her daughter knew she was hanging out with a man who was the least likely to be an internet troll looking to prey on a weakened woman.

"You're right," she confessed, aware already she had no intention of confessing all of it. "I didn't tell you everything. I am in Whistler—of course, I am."

She almost said, "I would never lie to you," but realized an omission could be a lie and there was no way she was going to be telling her daughter about going out on the ice after that dog or anything that had happened after.

"I didn't just lose my phone," she continued carefully. "I lost my whole purse. So I didn't have any ID, which is a requirement for checking into a hotel. My friend, whom I've known since high school, and indeed is a man—*as is half the world's population*—put me up for the night."

"At his house?" Maggie breathed, aghast.

"No, sweetie. At the Cobalt Lake Resort. In a private cottage, like a VIP suite."

There was silence. Faith heard her daughter's fingers tapping away, and knew she was busy fact-checking. There was a reason she was such a good lawyer!

Finally, Maggie spoke.

"Mom," she said, "you know what comes up when I put in Cobalt Lake? Gregor Watson. Is he there right now?"

"Rumors abound," Faith said, tickled that her superpragmatic daughter was just a little bit starstruck.

"It's a gorgeous place. I'm on their website now."

"It's very beautiful," Faith agreed.

"Is it decorated for Christmas? Because it's absolutely spectacular at Christmas."

"Um…not yet." Last night that was one of the things Brad had told her his daughter was working on for the first time since her mother had died.

Her voice a whisper of pure discovery, Maggie said, "Brad Daniels is…"

Faith waited for Maggie to share what she'd found out. That Brad Daniels was the owner of that resort. That he owned quite a lot, actually. That he was most likely a billionaire.

But with all that information at her fingertips, that was not what Maggie said.

She said, "Mom. Brad Daniels is gorgeous."

CHAPTER ELEVEN

HER DAUGHTER'S ASSESSMENT of Brad was fresh in Faith's mind when he knocked lightly on the door and let himself into Wolf's Song.

He *was* absolutely and utterly gorgeous. He was obviously ready for an excursion in the great outdoors, in a down jacket and multipocketed canvas expedition pants. He had on light hikers, so she couldn't see what his sock selection for the day was.

Faith was glad she had freshly showered, done her hair, applied a bit of makeup. She'd chosen her outfit with care—a pair of slacks suitable for a hike, a beautiful white cashmere sweater that maybe was not exactly hiking material.

And she had not chosen the outfit just to send off her father, either.

"Hey," Brad said, "how did you sleep?"

She smiled inwardly. Brad was no more aware of the differences in her hair and makeup, the way she was dressed, than he had been of aware of the quality of the suitcase or that wine he had brought over.

And yet, when he took her in, that smile playing across the beautiful curve of his lips, she felt completely *seen*.

"Restless. I'd forgotten how quiet it is in the mountains. And how dark. You'd think those would lead to a better rest, but I think I missed the noise and light of the big city right outside my window. You?"

"Same. Restless. Had trouble letting go of the events of the day."

His arms were full and he went by her and set a bag and a drink tray with two steaming cups on the kitchen island. He opened the bag and pulled out a selection of croissants and bagels, and little pots of jam and cream cheese.

"That smells heavenly."

"Still take it black?" he asked her, passing her one of the cardboard cups.

Who remembered how you took your coffee after thirty some years?

"Yes. You're spoiling me."

He met her gaze. "You know what? You deserve some spoiling."

It should have made her feel as if she had confided too much in him, and had earned his pity, but that's not how she felt, and it was not pity she saw in his eyes.

It was such genuine caring it took her breath away. She went over and took the coffee he offered.

"Do you still take two creams and a sugar?" she asked him. Ridiculous to feel as if that was flirting.

But his grin told her he found it endearing that she remembered, too.

"You want the good news or the bad news?" he asked her.

"Good, of course."

"There isn't any."

She laughed and blew on her coffee.

"The staff searched around the lake extensively. No purse. I checked with the police first thing this morning, and no purse had been turned in there yet, either."

She considered the logistics of that. How was she going to begin the process of replacing at least enough things to get her home?

"Also, it's not a perfect day for going up Feeney. It's not

snowing or raining, but it could start. It's cold and damp out there. You're still okay to go?"

"Yes." Considering she had put off this task for so long, it now felt weirdly imperative that she do it.

"You can add to this morning's list of *not-so-good news* that my daughter is very annoyed with me."

"Hey!" he said. "Mine, too."

And they bumped their coffee cups, in silent congratulation for achieving the goal of having become an irritation to their children.

"It never occurred to me Maggie would call the hotel to try and track me down. I'm afraid the next time you check your messages on your other phone, you'll find a few from her."

"That's too bad that she worried."

"Takes after her mother more than she cares to admit."

Brad smiled at Faith, as if the worry gene was adorable. Then reached into a front shirt pocket and put a card down on the table.

"What is that?"

"It's a preloaded credit card."

"I can't take that!"

"What are you going to do then? Call me every time you want a cup of coffee?"

"That's a good point." His thoughtfulness was so compelling. "I'll pay you back as soon as I have access to funds, though."

He lifted a shoulder, clearly uncaring of whether or not she paid him back.

"I came on a quad," he said, referring to the four-wheeled all-terrain vehicles that were commonly used in the mountains before there was enough snow to bring out the snowmobiles.

"I wasn't sure if you'd prefer that to hiking, since the weather isn't that good?"

"Oh, I'd love that!"

"I'm glad you said that, because I wasn't sure about going as far as the viewing point on foot if it's going to snow."

"I haven't been on a quad since I left here."

"Really?"

"I'm afraid for the last thirty or so years experiencing the great outdoors meant taking a book and a picnic to St. James Park on a sunny afternoon."

Felix had been *not outdoorsy*, and not the least apologetic about that, either. Once, she had talked him into a camping trip with the kids. It had been a fiasco from beginning to end: mosquitos, poor-quality sleeping bags that had left them cold and the hotdogs burned to the point of being inedible over the campfire.

Startled, Faith realized that, little by little, she had surrendered her own interests to Felix.

But isn't that part of why she was here?

Not just to honor her father's last wish, but to discover some lost part of herself? The part of her father that was deeply ingrained inside her? Outdoors. Adventure. Challenges.

"Actually, I can't wait to get back on a quad," she said.

"We can get you your own, or you can ride with me."

"I don't know if after so long I'd be confident riding one solo, especially up the steep parts of that pass."

There was some truth to that, but even more truth to the irresistible nature of sharing the seat of a quad with him.

An hour later, Maggie would have been shocked to see her mother, in her puffy new parka, sitting astride a quad, her arms wrapped tightly around this fabulously good-looking man.

Faith had her nose buried in Brad's rather gorgeous shoulder as they traversed the rocky, steep trail.

A box of ashes, in a velvet drawstring sack, was on her lap, squished tightly between them, and that was all that prevented Faith from being pressed even more intimately into Brad Daniels.

She was glad for the warm coat Brad had provided her with

the day before, and for the fact he had given her gloves, as well. It really was a cold morning.

She was also very glad she had left the driving to him. Despite the thick, cold mist, every now and then she would catch a heart-stopping glance of the steep drop-offs beside the trail.

Soon, the warmth radiating off Brad and the pureness of her surroundings edged out the chill.

It was replaced with a sense of exhilaration, almost homecoming, as they headed into places so high and wild that few people ever got to experience them. The moist morning air was scented heavily with pine and cedar.

The quad was quite quiet, humming along the difficult trail, instead of growling.

As Brad guided the vehicle confidently over the steadily increasing steepness of the rugged trail, the grayness around them began to thin, as did the trees.

Faith realized what had seemed like cold fog was actually a cloud. And then they drove right through it, and came out on top of it, into dazzling sunshine and a bright blue sky.

They were just a few feet from the viewing point, which looked out over the steep valley that separated some of the most majestic peaks of the Fitzsimmons Range of the Coast Mountains.

Brad stopped the quad.

Even though it had not been very noisy, once the sound of the engine was gone, the silence of the mountains and the forest below them was immense. Faith slipped off her perch behind him, resting her precious cargo on the seat while she took off her helmet.

Then she picked it up her father's ashes, hugging that humble velvet bag to her. She walked to what seemed to be the edge of the earth.

She had forgotten how sacred these high places felt, the air beyond pure, the world swathed in clouds below them, the snowcapped, formidable mountain peaks marching off into infinity around them.

Brad came and stood beside her.

"Do you want to be by yourself?"

"No, actually, I think he'd like it that you were here. He liked you."

She took a deep breath. Her fingers, despite the gloves, were cold. They trembled on the drawstrings.

Without asking, Brad—just knowing what needed to be done—helped her with the strings, and then held the sides of the bag, peeling it back as Faith pulled out the plain white cardboard box that was inside.

She wondered if she should tell Brad this humble container was her father's wish, not hers.

But a glance at his face told her he was no more aware of the humbleness of the container than he had been of her suitcase.

In the hospice, Max had handed her an envelope thick with cash.

"This is to pay for it. A cremation. Don't put me in the ground," he'd insisted. "And don't let them talk you into any of their scammy stuff, funeral-home nonsense—fancy urns, and stupid cards with pictures on them. There's enough there to do it simple and to take me back to the high places."

"Dad! You don't have to pay for it yourself."

"Oh, Faith, what would I do with money where I'm going?"

She couldn't argue with that.

"It's the least I can do. You know, I never forgave myself for betting your college money."

"I know, Dad. We don't have to talk about it—"

"You let me say my piece. The worst of it was I played right into that wicked witch's hands."

"What wicked witch?" she'd asked, stunned.

He snorted. "I knew Deirdre Daniels couldn't stand it that her son loved you."

"I had no idea that you knew about Brad and me."

"I might not be great at playing the horses, but I was always good at reading people. I knew what was going on between you and the Daniels kid. I liked him. More evidence, as if I needed it, that rotten parents can have good kids."

His gaze had rested on her a little too long.

"You weren't a rotten parent!" she'd said.

"I gambled away your college money."

"Oh, Dad, everything worked out in the end. It's not as if Brad and I were going to go on and get married and have kids. Neither of us was ready for that. I was seventeen, for Pete's sake, he was eighteen. I've been happy with Felix. I wouldn't have changed a thing."

Again, his eyes had been on her face, so direct. He'd hesitated.

"You know there's something wrong with the old guy, eh?"

She hated it that he always called Felix that. "Wh-wh-what?" she had stammered.

"When was I here last?"

"Two years ago, at Christmas."

"Oh, yeah, that's right. The year I worked at Schweitzer. That's a good hill. You should go there sometime. Take Maggie and Michael. It's in Idaho."

He hadn't said it with recrimination, but she was pretty sure it bothered him that his grandchildren didn't ski, hadn't experienced the high places.

"You're not noticing," Max had said, his voice a tired whisper, "because it's probably happening slowly. But for me, not having seen the old guy for two years, the changes can't be denied. Can't miss them. I'm tired, pet. Maybe you can come back tomorrow."

But there had been no tomorrow.

And then she *had* seen the changes. Once she did start seeing them, she was not sure how she had missed them. Maybe because of a full life: graduations, a marriage and babies, her dad's illness, work.

But after Max had passed, it had been like there were alarm bells clanging in her head, accompanied by red and white flashing lights.

Felix's curious lack of affect about the death of her dad, and then about the birth of Maggie's baby, their first grandchild.

His increasingly insensitive and inappropriate remarks.

How could she have not noticed Felix, of all people, being inappropriate?

He started being mean. Last Christmas, after he complained childishly about the turkey being dry, he shook his head sadly at Maggie, and said, "I never thought I'd have a fat daughter."

Michael, who had traveled all that way to be with them, had set down his cutlery quietly, and said, "I've had about enough of you sniping at Mom and Maggie. You've been doing it since I got here."

In a blink, Felix had been out of his chair, towering over the seated Michael, his fists clenched. "What are you going to do about it then?"

Faith had had the shocking feeling that they were about to become *that* family, the one where the police arrived at their house on Christmas day.

The exact kind of family she had seen in Deirdre Daniels's judgment of her all those years ago, that she had spent her whole life trying to outrun.

"Are you okay?" Brad asked her now.

Was she okay? Her father had noticed the changes in her husband long before she had, but he had probably noticed the toll those changes were taking on Faith, too. Even before Felix's illness, Max had thought she was giving up parts of herself.

Was that why he had sent her on this mission back to Whistler?

To let him go?

But to find herself, too?

CHAPTER TWELVE

"I'M OKAY," Faith reassured Brad with a nod.

And then, she opened the box. She had not opened it before. Inside it was a thick, clear plastic bag, fastened with one of those impossible zip ties.

Without saying a word, Brad slipped a knife from one of those many pockets in his mountaineer pants. As cosmopolitan as he was, he had been born and raised traversing these backcountry trials. He would no more be caught in the wild places without a knife than he would be caught without water.

He slit the top of the bag open, and then he stepped back and behind her.

She was aware it was a physical gesture, but it felt symbolic, too. Brad had her back.

She lifted the bag up and away from herself. Slowly, she tilted it upside down. Some of the ash was light, like dust, and hung in the air, floated upward, suspended, almost glittering in the strong sunlight.

Some was picked up by the breeze and carried away.

And some fell into rocky crevasses and onto rugged outcrops. As she shook the last of her father's ashes from the bag, there was an incredible sense of relief, of rightness, of peace.

As if Max was finally home.

"Look," Brad said quietly.

And then from behind her, he put his arms around her waist, and she leaned back into him and tilted her head up to look at the intense blue of the sky.

Together, they watched as the bald eagle, possibly the largest one she had ever seen, danced and soared on the wind currents above them.

"In the end," she said softly, "this is what was left of a man."

"No," Brad said. "You're what's left of the man, Faith. You're his legacy. And you're a good one."

So it was not just her father who had come home.

With Brad's arms around her, and his voice stirring her hair, Faith felt she had come home, too.

She had expected she might cry when she let go of Max this final time. Instead, she felt a sense of closure, and having done right by her father.

He would have *loved* this.

Instead of feeling devastated by fresh grief, Faith felt an unexpected sense of euphoria and release as she silently wished Max well on his journey, and thanked him for all the gifts he had given her.

Among the best of them: to embrace the moment in all its unpredictability, to embrace the unexpected joys life gave you.

Brad contemplated how deliciously right it felt to be here on the mountaintop with Faith. It felt like such a grave honor to be trusted to help her with this most sacred of responsibilities.

"Do you feel the way I feel?" he asked her, finally releasing her. The eagle had vanished, riding a wind current up and up and up, until it was but a speck in the sky and then they couldn't see it at all.

She turned and looked at him. "Like a part of something bigger than us all?"

"Exactly," he breathed.

"Yes, I do. I feel at peace. And oddly happy."

"Exactly as Max would have wanted," Brad said. He felt oddly happy, too. To be with her, to be in the mountains, to feel such intense connection to all things.

He flattened the now-empty box and stowed it in the pannier of the quad. He saw her tuck the velvet bag inside her jacket, next to her heart.

"Do you feel ready for a hot drink? I brought a thermos with hot chocolate."

"You're spoiling me," she said again.

"I know," he said. "I like it."

Her eyes misted up. She was a woman who had not been spoiled nearly enough. At least not for a long time.

"Maybe not just yet."

Her eyes drifted to the trail, not the way they had been, but where it began to twist downward on the other side of the pass.

"Should we keep going then?" Brad asked. "We can see if we can get as far as the Mud Puddle, or if there's snow that will turn us back before we make it there."

The locals had created a tiny but beautiful rock pool around a hot springs that bubbled naturally out of the rocky earth around it. The water flowed in and out of that pool constantly, making it pristinely clean. Where it sloshed over the rock walls, it had created a decadently warmed mud bath, worthy of any spa.

It was probably the best-kept secret in all of Whistler. The locals did not tell. Anyone. Ever. It was code named the Mud Puddle, so that casual reference to it did not give away the fact there was an extraordinary secret up there in Feeney's Pass.

Some longing flashed through her eyes.

What was he doing, exactly? It felt like something more than just trying to draw that carefree part of Faith back to the surface.

"I can't," she said.

Thank goodness, Brad thought, that Faith was intent on being the reasonable one.

Still, he heard the reluctance in her voice.

"Why not?" he asked, pressing her.

She sighed heavily. "I have to start figuring out how I'm going to get on my flight on Friday if my purse isn't found.

I'm sure there's an overwhelming amount of phone calls that have to be made and paperwork that has to be done."

There. Get back on the quad, and fight all the things his arms wrapped so tightly around her were causing him to feel, and drop her off to do her tasks.

It would be the safest thing.

Safe. Not the choice that would honor her devil-may-care dad.

And yet, he could not miss the longing in her eyes as her gaze drifted again, not to the trail the way they had come, but the other way. To where it went.

He saw how she had carried the weight of the whole world on her shoulders for so long. "You can leave all the responsibilities behind. Just for today."

He had, after all. He'd sent Cassie a quick text this morning, from the new phone, telling her he would be out of cell range for the whole day.

"Nothing would please Max more than that," Faith said pensively, mirroring the thought Brad had just had.

It wasn't quite a yes. He nudged. "Do you want me to see if we get cell service here? I can call the resort and have someone start doing the legwork about getting on a commercial flight without documents."

"No, don't bother with the cell."

He was relieved by that because he was sure if he opened that new phone there would be a dozen messages from Cassie.

"Come to that, I'm sure Maggie is all over it, already."

"There's another option, too. I can get you home, Faith. I have a plane."

She looked at him, startled. "It's a long way in a small plane, especially at this time of year."

"Uh, it's not a small plane. It's, um, a jet." He needed her to know he was problem-solving, not boasting. "I mean I have access to a jet, I don't own one."

But then that felt dishonest, as if he was trying to downplay himself, and he was aware of wanting one-hundred-percent honesty between them.

"I probably would own one," he confessed, "except that my environmentally sensitive daughter would disown me for the hypocrisy of asking our guests not to have their sheets washed every day, while I'm indulging myself for the sake of convenience. She might say male ego."

To his relief, Faith laughed.

"Our daughters," she said, with a shake of her head. "Why are they so hard to please?"

"Because we raised them to not be afraid to have their own opinions," he said.

"True." And then she added, "And don't worry about the private jet! That hydrogen-fuel technology will probably be applicable to planes someday."

And the best possible thing happened.

They were laughing.

"What's one more day?" Faith said. "I'm sure I'll get home one way or another. Yes, let's see if we can get to the Mud Puddle."

He surreptitiously turned off the tracker that was clipped on to his jacket. Somehow, he did not want his daughter, unable to get him on his phone, looking at a GPS map, watching the little red dot that was him move closer and closer to the Mud Puddle.

It would just lead her to asking too many questions. Questions he was not in any way ready to answer.

He wasn't even sure if he had an answer, beyond following an impulse, and what kind of answer was that?

Faith got back on the quad behind him. The box that had provided some separation on the way up to the viewing point was gone.

Every bump and every rock brought her into closer contact with him. He could feel how snugly he fit between the V of her legs. He could feel her curves, even through the pillowy shape of the jacket she wore.

He could feel her heat.

And her heat seared him.

It filled him with something he had not felt for a very long time.

This was way more than an impulse. It was a *wanting*, raw and powerful, like a man who had crawled across the desert wanted water, or like a man who had not slept for weeks wanted to lay himself down, close his eyes and be taken by the abyss.

The snow, thankfully, blocked the trail before they reached the Mud Puddle, which would bring a lot more challenges to his impulses that he was not quite ready for.

They got off the quad.

The moment he was out of close contact with her, it felt—thankfully—as if the spell had been broken.

"End of the line," he declared.

Faith took off her helmet, ran her fingers through her messy hair. The spell threatened to curl around him again, like wisps of smoke coming up from a fire.

"It's not much farther, is it?"

"No, but it'll be slippery."

"Should we try it on foot?"

He cast an experienced glance at the trail. The snow was not deep enough to worry about avalanches, and yet, he felt that reluctance to give himself to the wild places that had so betrayed him.

"I didn't really come prepared for that. I didn't bring towels…or bathing suits."

His eyes met hers. She cocked her head and looked at him. She did not seem like the vulnerable woman who needed his protection. She seemed to know exactly where this could lead.

And what she wanted.

Of course, she had wanted to rescue that dog, too, which showed her decision-making skills might not be the best…

"Maybe it's not—"

"I can't believe you let me down like this, Brad. You've rescued me, you've fed me, you've given me a place to stay and money. You've offered to help me get home, but now this. You've forgotten the bathing suits."

She was teasing him. If felt wonderful. She smirked when he got it.

"Okay," he said, "turning in my Boy Scout hero badge. A bit of a relief, I must say."

"My dad used to say the Puddle was a healing place. That even the animals knew. That a sick animal would go lie down in the heated mud. I can't imagine being this close and not going there. What do you think?"

What he thought was alarming. He was not sure he could refuse Faith anything.

"Sure," Brad said. "We don't actually have to get in. Maybe just stick our feet in the mud."

"Does that make you a stick-in-the-mud, Brad?"

Was she suggesting she wanted to do more than stick her feet in the mud? His face felt suddenly hot.

"Am I remembering wrong?" Faith asked. "I don't remember anyone wearing bathing suits in the Mud Puddle, because the mud just wrecked them, anyway."

No, she was remembering that with one-hundred-percent accuracy. Was she actually trying to make him blush?

What else was she remembering? Because he was remembering youthful exuberance, laughter, both of them being kind of shy and kind of bold, the slipperiness of the mud, kisses hotter than that sulfur-scented water.

She rummaged around in the pannier and pulled out the thermos. He found a couple of bottles of water. With her free hand, she took his free hand, as if that was the most natural thing in the world. They began to make their way up the slippery trail.

They pushed and pulled and clawed through the snow, and over the icy patches, until they arrived at their destination, breathless.

Brad was pleasantly surprised by how this, his first venture into this kind of country in a long, long time, did not feel anxiety-provoking.

The opposite.

He felt his soul soothed by the pristine atmosphere of the high alpine, where the Mud Puddle was located, well above the tree line. Its smell—strong and sulfury—like rotten eggs, alerted them to how close they were before they actually saw it.

It was tucked behind a wall of rocks, well off Feeney's Pass, which was probably why the locals had succeeded in keeping it a secret so long. The slightly beaten path to it could have been mistaken for an animal trail, and indeed, there were some animal footprints in the snow, but no sign of human activity.

Brad watched Faith's face as they squeezed through the tiny little opening in the rocks and found themselves in an open area on the other side, a breathtaking view of the mountains around them.

"You know how some things aren't quite as you remembered them?" she breathed.

"Yes."

"This is better than I remembered it." She sat down on an outcropping and removed her light hikers and socks. She rolled up her pant legs and then sank her feet into the mud.

"Oh, my," she said and made a sound in her throat of deep and sensual pleasure. Then she opened her eyes and looked at him. "This isn't going to be good enough," she told him solemnly. "I can't come all the way here, and not get in. I would regret it forever."

CHAPTER THIRTEEN

BRAD QUESTIONED IF he had ever really thought they were going to get up here and just be satisfied to soak their feet and drink hot chocolate.

Twenty-four hours ago he certainly could not have predicted being at the Mud Puddle with Faith Cameron. Saint-John.

In fact, everything about his life with Cynthia had been ordered. Predictable. If you had asked him, he would have said he liked it that way.

But then the way she had died… Who could have predicted that? It was as if it was in total defiance of her own highly structured life.

He thought of that eagle soaring on the updraft, just letting life take it.

Live, something whispered to him. *Live.*

He took off his jacket and cast it aside. Now what?

She was looking at him to show the way. He could see it in her eyes, that she was wrestling with the insecurity of not being young anymore. Neither of them were young anymore. And they had both probably seen plenty of bodies in various circumstances.

"We can pretend we're Icelandic," she said, but her uncertainty was endearing. "That whole country is covered in hot springs. I don't think anyone worries about bathing suits."

"I've been there. On business. They're global leaders in geothermal technology. You're right about there being hot springs everywhere. Almost every town, even ones so tiny you wouldn't expect it, has a pool heated geothermally. But everywhere I went, people had on bathing suits."

"Oh," she said. "Did you go to the Blue Lagoon?"

"Yes. It's amazing. There are pockets of white mud in it, called silica, that you smear all over your bathing-suit-clad body."

She laughed. "It's on my bucket list. What's on yours?"

He'd lived an extraordinary life, he realized, where if he wanted to do anything, he had always been able to make it a reality.

He was surprised to hear himself reveal something. "I hope someday I'll be painting a nursery for Cassie."

He realized she was looking to him for leadership. He took a deep breath and stripped to his shorts.

The mountain air bit into his skin. He tried to keep his eyes to himself as beside him Faith peeled off item after item of clothing, until she was in her underwear, too.

"It's no different than being at the beach," she said bravely.

"Exactly."

"Except I haven't worn a two-piece since my first baby. So don't look!"

He tried hard not to look. Despite the fact they were barely dressed, Brad felt oddly comfortable with Faith, as if they had been married for a hundred years, as if being like this together was as natural as those springs bubbling out of the earth.

His hand found Faith's once again, and together they went to the edge of the pool.

It felt closer to the very edge of the earth than they had been at the Feeney's Pass viewing point.

"The silica in the Blue Lagoon can't have anything on this," Faith said, sliding down into the mud, until she was completely prone, letting its delicious warmth ooze over her body.

She was grateful that this morning, after just a moment's

hesitation, she had chosen the underwear he had given her yesterday, unable to resist how pretty it was in comparison to the utilitarian offerings in her own suitcase.

Funny, how what a woman had on, where no one could see it, could make her feel pretty.

Sexy.

Of course, now he could see it, but he was being a perfect gentleman and not looking at her at all.

She scooped up handfuls of mud. It was going to wreck the underwear beyond repair, but she could buy new things. Things more delicate and feminine. Maybe she'd even use that credit card he had given her and check out the Cobalt Lake Boutique before she went home.

She gave herself more completely to the mud, and covered herself thoroughly, partly shy and partly because the warmth of it was so compelling.

She contemplated the fact that with all her imperfections, here she was, nearly naked, in a very sensual setting, with the very gorgeous Brad Daniels.

What would her children think if they knew that after a less-than-twenty-four-hour reunion, she was frolicking in the mud, in her rather sexy undergarments, with her old high-school lover?

Faith decided, firmly, she would not go there. She had long been captive to what other people thought and she would not give away one second of this experience to the imagined re-criminations of others.

She had played it safe her entire life.

Where had that gotten her?

She was so tired of being the responsible one. Setting the example, being so damn *good* all the time.

Objectively, she and Brad were just two mature people giving themselves over to enjoying an unexpected experience.

She slid a glance over at Brad. He had stepped out in the mud, sinking in to his ankles. His broad back was to her. He had on boxer briefs, and was choosing not to lie down, but was standing, bending, cupping his hands in the mud and pouring it—it had the consistency of thick gravy—over himself.

It didn't really feel *racy* being in their underwear together. They were both now also clad, from the tips of their toes to the tops of their heads, with brownish-gray mud.

He looked like the clay form that they cast bronze around. And he was beautiful enough to be replicated into a statue.

Brad was a perfectly made man. Age had not diminished that. If anything, he seemed to have come even more into himself. Broader. More solid, with his long legs, wide shoulders, deep chest, taut belly. Even clothed as he was in mud, she could see the dimples above the band of his shorts, at the small of his back. The little indents were just above the lovely cut of lean buttocks that showed quite clearly through his mud-plastered shorts. Faith was surprised by how clearly she remembered that feature.

She had loved those dimples then. It had felt like a wonderful little secret she knew about him. Her sense of delight seemed undiminished by a very long hiatus!

Should she feel guilty? What was there to feel guilty about? It wasn't as if she had to submit a report to her children or to anyone else.

It struck her, in a way that it had not before, that she was free. To do and be whatever she wanted.

And at the moment, she was delighted to discover a sense of the mischievous in herself. When was the last time she had been playful, if her grandchildren had not been involved?

Even then, because of the stress of Felix, sometimes it had felt as if she was just going through the motions, playing the role of cheery granny, but not feeling it. At all. Her mind always elsewhere, her heart always numb.

She raised herself on her elbows, picked up a fistful of mud and tossed, aiming toward one of those dimples above his backside. It landed with a satisfying splat, square on one of his broad shoulders.

He turned and gave her a narrow look. At first, she thought he clearly expected more maturity, but then, she saw him gathering his own great fistful of mud.

"Prepare for a muck smush," he said, and stalked toward her, his expression theatrically menacing.

Laughing, she tried to get up, but the mud held her captive. She tried harder and then, with a great slurp, the mud released her and she moved to dash out of his reach. But it was impossible to build any speed with the mud sucking on her feet.

His hand found the middle of her back, and he gleefully ground mud into it. She bent to swiftly reload with a mud missile. When she turned around, he was already sloshing away, throwing taunts over his shoulder.

And just like that, she and Brad were playing like the children they had once been.

Sliding, shrieking, throwing mud balls. Soon, not an inch of skin was visible on either of them. Their hair was caked with mud. Her belly actually hurt from laughing.

He had just dodged her again, and with the mud dripping off him in twisted ropes, he looked like a mythical, hairy beast.

"You're the Sasquatch people claim to see in this area!"

"It's true," he confessed. "My mud-wrestling name in Sasquatch Sam."

"And here's me without my phone! That's a million-dollar photo right there."

"Absolutely not! I protect you from publicity, you protect me and my true identity."

It was pure silliness, and she welcomed it like parched earth welcomed rain.

She closed in on him again, arm raised to slam him with mud, but then when he pivoted to run, his feet skidded out from underneath him, and he was down, sliding through the mud on his butt.

Chortling, she lunged after him, and hovered over him. She was going to get him right in the face.

"Have mercy," he cried. "Man down."

"There is no mercy from the world-famous mud-wrestler, Greta the Barbarian. Prepare for annihilation."

He drew in a deep breath and closed his eyes, as if he was a warrior surrendering to his fate.

Faith chuckled and cried, "Victory!"

But before it was a complete victory, an unbelievably strong hand snaked around her ankle. When she tried to kick free of it, her balance tilted, then tottered, and then she was falling, their mud-slicked bodies coming together with a dull smack.

She was sprawled on top of the whole length of him. The mud-slicked underwear was a poor barrier, indeed. They might as well have both been naked. Slipping and sliding against each other, Faith thought it might have been the most sensual thing she had ever felt.

Only the whites of their eyes showed as they stared at each other, creatures from the deep, warm mud oozing out from between where their bodies were pressed together.

"Greta, I surrender," he whispered.

She freed an arm from between them, and with her thumb, cleared the mud off his lips. But before she could claim them, he slipped out from underneath her, stood and held his hand out to her.

Hand in hand, they walked to the small, rocked-off pool. He helped her slide in, then went and retrieved the thermos. She ducked under the water, and felt the mud melt off her hair and body.

He came, set down the thermos on the ledge and then slid into the pool beside her. He ducked under the water and came up restored to himself. The pool was tiny, with only one way to sit in it, side by side, and shoulder-to-shoulder.

After their dunk, the water turned the same color as the hot chocolate that he'd poured.

But, because it was constantly fed from the spring, it slowly cleared.

Utterly content, they sat on a ledge within the rock pool, water up to their chins, naked shoulders touching, stinky steam rising around them, sipping their hot chocolate.

"I needed that," he said, smiling at her, his dark eyes dancing with merriment. "To laugh like that. To let go."

"Me, too. I can't tell you how much."

"You don't have to. I get it."

And Faith suspected he was the one person on the planet who did get it, entirely. How sorrow was a cloud you walked under, thinking it would never break. That you would never see the sun again.

And yet, right now, both literally and figuratively, she could feel the sun again. She lifted her chin to it and closed her eyes.

CHAPTER FOURTEEN

"Can I ask you something?" Brad said to Faith, after a long comfortable silence.

"Or course."

"I've always wondered," he said, and she could hear the caution in his voice, so at odds with the carefreeness they had just experienced, "what happened all those years ago. One minute, we were like this—" he motioned at the pond and the mountains, a gesture that included them "—and the next you were gone."

What was the point, after all these years, of throwing anyone under the bus? Her father's terrible error in judgment, his mother's ability to pounce on an opportunity to control the unfolding of her son's life?

"The money for school just dried up," she said, her tone as careful as his.

"But why didn't you tell me that? I could have helped."

Over his mother's dead body.

But, of course, Mrs. Daniels was dead. There was no sense sullying her memory now.

"I was embarrassed," she said, "and scared." That was so true.

"But what happened? You just disappeared."

She hesitated. "A benefactor came along and tossed me a life rope. A full scholarship at U of T. It was a once-in-a-lifetime thing, and I had to make some hard decisions really fast."

"I still don't understand why you cut off contact so completely. Not a phone call, or a letter. Not even a Christmas card?"

Because Mrs. Daniels had made the terms abundantly clear.

"Brad, it's a long time ago."

She didn't realize her brow had furrowed until he pressed his thumb gently into it.

"Yes, it is," he agreed. But she could see the pain in his eyes.

"I'm sorry if I hurt you. I really am."

"That's part of what I couldn't understand," he said quietly. "It seemed so unlike you. To hurt anyone."

"I'm sorry," she said again.

He looked at her, deeply, as deeply as anyone had looked at her for a long, long time. It felt as if he could see the *truth* of her, even though most days—though not today—she felt she didn't know that about herself.

"I thought you loved me," he whispered. "As much as I loved you."

I did, she said silently.

Out loud, she said, "Brad, I was seventeen. You were eighteen. So young. I don't think we realize how young that is until we have our own children, and watch them hit those milestones. How would you have felt if it was your daughter, making decisions that could alter the course of her whole life based on that fierce, unflinching first love?"

"That's true," he said with a sigh. "I felt like she was a baby at seventeen. Sometimes, I still do. But you have a good point. Still, I feel as if there's something you're not telling me."

"Let's just leave it," she suggested quietly, though part of her wanted to trust him with all of it.

Brad sighed.

"You're right. Let's leave it. It's all a long time ago."

There was simply no point in saying to him *My dad gambled away my college money, and your mother was waiting like a vulture to pick over the bones of our lives.*

She had said to her father, on his deathbed, that it had all worked out. And yet, she was aware, in this moment, that didn't mean she didn't feel a residue of resentment around it.

But she didn't need to influence Brad's vision of the world, and his family, by sharing that with him.

For a while, the deep silence of the mountains was comfortable between them.

"Did you have other plans for your stay in Whistler?" he asked her.

She smiled. "I was going to go have dinner at the Mountain Hideaway where my dad would have never been welcomed. And tomorrow I was going to hit some of the shops and buy a few things he would have never been able to afford."

Because, she remembered sadly, Max was saving for her college, a noble gesture that he had spoiled with one impulsive decision. The worst of it was not his decision, but his guilt. He'd put walls around himself, imprisoning him in ways he had never allowed himself to be imprisoned before.

"I guess I was going to kind of thumb my nose at Whistler for Max Cameron. But now, I won't."

"If it's because of funds—"

She held up her hand. "It's not. It's not because of the lost purse. I'm pretty sure that credit card you gave me would cover even a breathtakingly expensive dinner at the Hideaway. But sitting here, where the world is so pure, and so wild, and so free, I don't want to do those things anymore.

"It feels almost as if it would dishonor him. If there was one thing my dad was not, it was into the *show*. To him—" Faith swept her arm over the views all around them, much like Brad had done earlier "—this was true wealth. Living fully. Experiencing creation deeply."

"Maybe it's just as well not to have dinner at the most well-known place in town given the interest of the media in locating the damsel in distress, the hero and the dog."

"Just tell them your hero badge had been revoked, remember?"

"If only it were that easy. They're hounds and the fox is their story. I don't think decency or sensitivity is part of their world."

"Thank you for being decent and sensitive in a world that isn't, Brad."

His hand found hers, and squeezed. She felt the length of his leg touch hers through the heat of the water. She felt a jolt of primal hunger go through her that was both alluring and alarming.

She stroked his leg. In response, he turned to her, gazed at her for a moment and then dropped his lips, nuzzling her neck before pulling away.

"I'm sorry. It just feels so much the way it always felt with you. As if you are steel and I am a magnet, helpless against your pull.

"Don't be sorry," she whispered, stunned—but delighted—that he still found her as attractive as he once had.

Brad's lips on her neck had awakened her awareness that there was a need inside her, not just to be seen as attractive, but to be a woman again. To feel a deep awareness of her own body, to feel that rush of desire, that exquisite moment of fulfilment.

To feel the tenderness of a man's lips, the rasp of his voice, the worship of his hands, the power of his need.

To experience physical intimacy.

All those things suggested hope for life.

Faith felt the enchantment of the world she found herself in—more, she felt healing blossoming inside of her.

Some barrier—some adherence to the rules she had followed her entire life—dissolved inside Faith with all the resistance of sugar meeting hot water.

"If it's too fast," he told her, "we can slow it down. We don't have to—"

But she put her hand behind Brad's head and drew his lips down to her own, and silenced him. His lips were so soft and so beautiful.

How was it possible to remember a sensation this accurately? And yet, she did—she remembered exactly what it had been like to be with him. And, at the very same time, as the kiss deepened, it felt brand-new and exquisitely exciting.

Her hands explored the water-slicked silk of his heated chest. His belly. She reveled in his hard lines. In letting her hands *know* him.

"Faith," he whispered huskily, "do you know where this is going?"

"Oh, yes."

"Are you sure?"

She laughed against the delicious column of his throat, nibbled it and then reached up and nipped his ear.

"Of course, I'm sure. It's not as if I can get pregnant."

"I was hoping," he growled against her ear, "it was because you found me completely irresistible."

"Ah, yes, and that."

And then they were laughing together, but the laughter was heated and breathless. He lifted her with astonishing and easy strength, setting her on a rock shelf as he stood before her.

Brad reached behind her, and his hands found the snap on the bra. It fell away, and his eyes drank her in.

Not seeing imperfections at all.

She found the band of those lacy panties, and both of them tugged them off. He stepped out of his shorts.

Faith did not feel self-conscious as his hands took ownership of her, as his eyes worshipped her, as his voice anointed her with blessings.

She wrapped her arms around his neck, and her legs around his hips, and he pulled himself into her.

You are so beautiful.

You are a miracle.

You are so good.

You are so strong.

After, they lay side by side, on a cold, smooth rock, the heated vapor coming off the pool and their own supercharged skin keeping them warm.

"So," she said, utterly content, "this is what it feels like to be a sinner."

She wondered, really, why she had waited so long. All through Felix's long illness, people had told her what a saint she was, until she had hated that label.

"If we're sinners," he said, "why do I feel I'm right at heaven's gate?"

The sinner and the saint, she thought, resided side by side in most people, probably in about equal measure, circumstances drawing out one or the other.

It was life in balance, really.

Like this rock they were lying on, hot and cold residing side by side in the perfect unison of healing.

A phrase ran through her head, and she was vaguely aware it was from the story of Adam and Eve.

They were naked and not ashamed.

Since the beginning of time, this was what a man and a woman had been meant to feel together.

The sacredness of connection.

It seemed as if the creation that was at the heart of that story was thrumming with life around them. The entire universe felt as if it was in harmony right now.

Joy and sorrow danced together, like the motes of her father's ashes caught in sunlight, until they melded together, until she could not tell one from the other, and they became neither joy nor sorrow, but that substance that made up life itself.

Hope.

There was such a sense of *rightness* to the way Faith's arms felt, wrapped around Brad, as he guided the quad back down the mountain.

Realistically, it was not that different than when they had headed up Feeney's Pass, but she was not trying to be proper anymore. She was giving herself fully to their connection, nestled comfortably into the back of him, her cheek resting on the back of his shoulder.

Brad was freezing. He had given Faith his shirt to towel off with as best she could, but now that wetness next to his skin was a terrible thing. His hair was also wet, under the helmet, which intensified the feeling of being cold. He hoped he was blocking the worst of the icy wind from her.

Protecting her.

It felt good to be protecting Faith.

Had he been so protective of her when he was young?

He thought, suddenly, of her words: *It's not as if I can get pregnant.*

He slammed to a halt so abruptly that her chin jabbed into his shoulder. He cut the engine, twisted to look at her.

Her hair was ice-tipped where it poked out from under the helmet.

"You weren't pregnant, were you?"

"What?"

"When you left?"

She shook her head, bemused. "No, Brad. I was taking precautions."

"Did we talk about it?"

"Brad! You're making me feel as if I'm on the witness stand for a cold case." She changed her voice, and it became deep, stern. "And what exactly was Mr. Daniels wearing on June sixteenth, thirty-some years ago?"

Not a condom, apparently.

"Sorry," he muttered. He turned back abruptly, facing forward, feeling guilty.

She was taking precautions.

Where had he been? Had they talked about it, or had his brain just been completely on hold, in that stupor of first love, or more bluntly, first sex, that pushed every single other thing out of the way?

Of course, the *first* aspect of it wouldn't explain why he'd gone on to repeat the very same pattern with Cynthia. She had told him she was protected and he'd happily left that responsibility to her.

He restarted the engine and piloted them down the hill. It was nearly dusk when they pulled up outside of Wolf's Song.

Faith slid off the quad. He could tell she was cold, despite him blocking the wind.

"You look like you need a hot shower," he said.

She pulled off the helmet and ran her fingers through her crushed hair. The curls sprang back, and she grinned at him in a way that made her seem unchanged from her seventeen-year-old self.

She tilted her head and grinned at him. "Are you joining me?"

CHAPTER FIFTEEN

THE TEMPTATION TO join Faith in the shower was nearly over-powering. But Brad made a decision that he was not going to be the same self-centered, instinct-driven jerk he had been when he was eighteen.

"No," he said, his firmness directed at himself more than at her. "Have your shower. I'll find us something for dinner."

Did she look faintly disappointed as she turned and went into Wolf's Song?

Here was the thing. She hadn't been pregnant, but she could have been. Funny, he had not once considered that possibility.

He recalled himself in those younger days. He'd said he loved Faith. And she had pointed out that, at that age, really, what did they know of love?

He had relished every moment with her, but when she had left, she had not trusted him with the truth that her family was in financial distress. He probably hadn't been worthy of it. Full of himself, enjoying the moment, reveling in the ex-quisite, all-encompassing sensation of his first really physi-cal relationship.

He remembered going to see Max, all those years ago, ask-ing where she was, pleading for information.

In retrospect, Brad was shocked Faith's father had not punched him in the nose. Because that's what he would have done if some young jock had gone after his baby, which he could now clearly see Cassie had been at seventeen.

But now, Brad thought, as he contemplated how he and Faith had slipped so naturally back into intimacy, he had the rarest of things.

A second chance.

An opportunity to get it so right this time.

Did he love her? Despite the self-centeredness of his eighteen-year-old self, he had been sure he loved her then.

Sure, almost from the first minute he'd seen her, the new girl in town, when she'd arrived at their school at the end of the eleventh grade.

He remembered saying to his mom, getting ready for senior prom, "I'm going to marry Faith Cameron someday."

Since then, though, love had taught him so many hard lessons about loss and powerlessness.

Maybe the new mature him didn't need to think of Faith in terms of love. Instead, he would see that he'd been given an opportunity to have a relationship with his equal, and an adult.

To treat her with respect.

And honor.

To spoil her rotten.

He didn't recall spoiling her rotten having anything to do with their twelfth-grade romance. He recalled almost everything in his young—and, admittedly, exceedingly horny—mind had been being about finding ways to be alone with her.

No wonder she had left without a backward glance.

And yet, he had felt as if he loved her madly, and beyond reason. Still, he was aware, again, he would want to kill anyone who had treated Cassie the way he had treated Faith.

After he had dropped off Faith, he parked the quad at his place. He raced in, and after changing into a dry shirt, and brushing his teeth, and running a comb through helmet-flattened hair, he took out his replacement phone and looked at it for the first time all day.

It occurred to him that it might have been years since he had not looked at his phone for this many hours.

It felt amazing. Freeing.

There were several messages. The first was from the police saying Faith's purse had been turned in.

He contemplated his sense of disappointment. No doubt that meant she would be able to go home Friday, as planned. Today was Tuesday. That would mean only two more full days together.

Somehow, he had hoped to stretch out that *spoiling time*. And maybe he still could. He could just ask her to stay longer, couldn't he?

The other message was from Cassie. Thankfully, she sounded annoyed rather than frightened by his sudden disappearance.

What should he tell her?

Nothing.

The loss of Cynthia had made him and Cassie unusually close, but maybe it was time to back off from that a little.

His daughter did not need to know all the details of his personal life, particularly given the fact she might place herself in charge of a romance project, and she also seemed to think his and Faith's experience out on the ice could be used to benefit the lodge.

He called her.

"What's going on with your phone, Dad?"

He told her about it blowing up over the rescue on the ice so badly he'd had to put it away and temporarily get a new number.

"I've seen pictures of that rescue now. That photographer posted some on social media, with the caption 'do you know these people?' It sure looks like you. The other person looks like a little kid, but I hear it was a woman. The whole town is talking about it."

Yay.

"Another media person posted an interview online with the lady whose dog it was. Its name was Felix. So adorable!"

"That dog was about the furthest thing from adorable that I can think of."

He didn't like it, one little bit, that something that was so highly personal to Faith—her husband's name—was out there in the public. Was it just local, so far? Or was it spreading?

It felt as if the jackals were circling, playing on the fact that everybody would think that was a heartwarming, poignant story. They would only like it *better* if they ever discovered that she had gone after that dog because it shared the same name as her now deceased husband.

But her pain being on display for the world would cause Faith so much suffering. She specifically did not want her daughter to know. He was going to have to look it up himself and see if the story was gaining steam or if it had stalled. He didn't want to ask Cassie because the less he expressed interest in it with her, the better.

"Dad, you should talk to them."

"Them?"

"The media. That photographer was in here again today."

"Did you let him know Gregor's gone?"

"No!"

He wished there was a way to tell Cassie that Faith needed the same kind of protection that his daughter went to such lengths to give their celebrity guests.

But how to make that request without letting on how deeply he was getting involved?

"Because they're going to run with it, anyway, and you probably have the best perspective of the whole thing."

Yes, he did, and knowing the secret of why Faith had gone out on that ice was something he planned to keep to himself.

He didn't like it that they were circling, closer and closer, to Faith's life.

"I'm not talking to them," he said firmly.

"I still think…"

He let her tell him what she thought, but didn't offer any comment. She sighed.

"You're so stubborn sometimes!"

"Now you know where you got it from."

She laughed, forgiving him.

"How was your day?" he asked her, and just as he had hoped, it threw her off the scent of the rescue-on-the-ice story. He listened to her talk about Christmas, how she was going to start on the cottages first—she was thinking of changing out the lights from white to colored around Cobalt Lake, she couldn't find some ornament or other, but she had found the perfect tree…

He was aware, a little ashamed, that he wasn't really listening to her. No, he was ticking off things he needed to get done in his head.

The first thing he did when he hung up was look for the rescue story online. It didn't pop up immediately, which was a good thing. When he found it, the video was pretty lousy. Maybe Gopher needed to improve his skills if he was looking for a break, instead of preying off the talent of others. It had about five thousand views, which in the online world was next to nothing. All it meant was that half the population of Whistler had had a look.

Relieved, he refocused on his mission of making up for the callow young man he had once been.

He snagged another bottle of wine from the very fine collection and then called the Hideaway and placed an order.

Brad hopped in his vehicle and headed into the village. First stop: the cop shop. Though technically the purse probably shouldn't have been surrendered to him, because he was the one who had reported the loss and had standing in the community, and was this week's hero, it was handed over to him without question.

His next stop was the floral shop on Main Street. They were getting ready to close, but again, he was able to use both his community standing and his local-hero status to coax an extraordinary bouquet out of them.

"Something special," he said.

"Any particular color?"

"Maybe just white."

"Budget?"

When was the last time he had purchased flowers? It had been too long, he thought. He wished he would have made small gestures that let his wife know how much he'd appreciated her more common. Marriages would be in a different place if everyone had the awareness he now had, that time was not a guarantee.

"Don't worry about budget," he said, "just the prettiest bouquet you can make."

He exited with a huge paper cone, stunning white blossoms peeking out of it. He wasn't sure what they were, but his whole vehicle filled up with the fragrance.

Then, finally, he stopped at the Hideaway and picked up the dinner he'd ordered for two. By the time he pulled up in front of Wolf's Song, Brad was feeling exceedingly pleased with himself.

Faith opened the door for him, before he even knocked. As if she had been waiting for him.

That did something to his heart.

She had showered and done something with her hair that made all the little curls stand up individually. She'd put on a hint of makeup, which made her eyes look huge and her lips look luscious. She was wearing a white turtleneck sweater, and slacks. It was casual and yet it made her look so feminine and womanly that it would be way too easy to forget his mission, and behave like a besotted teenage boy all over again.

But what he liked most was when he saw the light in her face when she took the bouquet from him and buried her nose in it.

"Did you buy the whole flower shop?" she teased him.

"I tried," he confessed.

"Gardenias!" she said. "They last about three seconds, so such a treat! Hydrangeas and roses. All my favorites!"

He would have liked to have been able to say to his daughter, *See, Cassie? Panic room? Are you kidding? The old man doesn't need any help from you in the romance department.*

"Do you want the good news or the bad news?" he said, stepping back from the door.

"Okay," she said, "I've fallen for this twice, so give me the bad news."

He laughed. "There isn't any."

Well, that wasn't exactly true. There was the video that had popped up online. He reminded himself to look again later and assess what was happening with the number of views. He didn't want her to worry if it was nothing, a local story that stayed that way.

He held up a finger to her, then went back to the truck, and came back up the walkway with the bag of food from the Hideaway. He had tucked the bottle of wine inside.

Faith took the bag, looked at the restaurant label on it and met his eyes with gratitude.

And then, he turned back once more to his vehicle, and came up the walk with her purse. Her mouth fell open. She nearly dropped the bag of food—with that very expensive wine in it!—but she caught herself, and instead, she set it down, took her purse from him and hugged it.

With those huge eyes so intense and soft on his face, she said, with the faint disbelief of someone who no longer believed good things could happen to her, "It really is all wonderful news."

Brad felt as if it had just become his life mission to keep it that way.

Faith could not believe she was holding her purse! It was such a relief and such a gift. She had just finished a conversation with Maggie, on the borrowed phone, before Brad had arrived.

She had been right about one thing. Maggie had spent much of the day figuring out how to get her home. It involved filing police reports, swearing affidavits, showing up at the airline customer-service hours before the flight. It had felt overwhelming, and like it would take up a great deal of the time she had left here.

And now, she had been granted a reprieve. She could just focus on *this*.

This really being *him*.

She had told Maggie, briefly, about the beautiful releasing of Max's ashes, but nothing else about the day.

Well, what was she going to say?

Oh, by the way, Maggie, you know that guy you thought was so gorgeous? He's actually my first love from high school and we did a very sexy version of mud-wrestling and I can't wait to see what the evening has in store.

Even a sanitized version would have probably given Maggie fits and led to stern advice-giving. It seemed like there was a growing list of things she was keeping from Maggie.

Well, she could let her know one thing that would reduce Maggie's worries. While Brad carried items to the kitchen, she pulled her phone out of the side pocket on her purse. Amazingly, it still had a tiny bit of battery life, and so Faith sent a quick text.

Purse found!

She added a few smiley faces.

"What can I do?" she asked, following Brad into the kitchen.

"You can sit right over there, look beautiful and try this wine."

Faith felt like the princess her father had once wanted her to be, as Brad completely pampered her. He poured wine and set the bottle on the table. It was even more exquisite than it had been the night before.

"Do you need to charge that phone?" He flipped open a panel behind her that completely concealed a charging station.

Was there anything they hadn't thought of at this resort?

She plugged in her nearly dead phone, and then decided to look up the wine. Maggie would be impressed if she served such an impressive vintage at Christmas dinner.

She stared at her phone, disbelieving. They certainly wouldn't be having it with Christmas dinner.

Now, she wasn't sure what to do. She didn't want to appear gauche, but surely he must have opened this bottle by mistake.

"Brad," she squeaked, "do you know what this wine is worth?"

"No," he said, unconcerned.

"It's worth eight thousand dollars a bottle."

He stopped what he was doing, obviously as startled as she had been. And then he started to laugh. "Oh, well, we can't put the cork back in, so we might as well enjoy it."

"But where did it come from?"

"We have a private cellar, separate from the resort. I'm afraid I have no idea what anything in there is worth. I told you, I'm not much of a wine guy."

She got it. Like the suitcases, the wine must have been his wife's thing.

"I don't think I can enjoy it, now," she said. She used her phone to do some quick calculations. "It's approximately fifty-three dollars and thirty-three cents a sip!"

"All the more reason to enjoy it," he said. He took a small taste out of his glass. "Ah. Fifty-three, thirty-three." And then he took another one. "One hundred and six, sixty-six. One fifty-nine, ninety-nine."

She started laughing. "Please stop."

But he didn't. "Am I impressing you with my math skills?"

"Brad," she said with a sigh of surrender, "you're impressing me in every possible way there is to be impressed."

He grinned at her, pleased, and she found herself relaxing, as he set the table, lit candles, plated the food.

There was an awareness of him, physically, that was startling. The squareness of his wrists, the shape of his fingers, the sensual curve of his lips, his economy of movement as he worked in the kitchen, his innate air of confidence.

He was really so out of her league in every single way! And yet, here she was, Brad Daniels's lover.

CHAPTER SIXTEEN

"BON APPÉTIT," Brad said, setting a plate in front of her with a flourish, and then sliding onto the deeply upholstered bench seat beside her, so close their shoulders were touching.

The scent of him mingled with the scent of food.

The afternoon's escapades—never mind drinking an eight-thousand-dollar bottle of wine—seemed to have left her senses heightened, acutely so. Even though she was wearing a sweater, she could still feel the fabric of his shirt against her shoulder, and beneath that the sinewy strength of him.

She sighed with pleasure, and took a bite of the food.

"This is delicious," Faith said. "I don't even want to know what it cost."

"In comparison to the wine? Peanuts."

"Thank goodness." She took another bite. "I think what we had last night was just as good."

"Take that, Hideaway. I'm going to tell Anita, our chef who prepared last night's meal. She'll be so pleased. Our restaurant is a little competitive."

Faith liked these small things about him so, so much. He was a man with an eight-thousand-dollar bottle of wine in his cellar and an innovation investor with a portfolio that was probably worth billions, and yet, Brad would take time out of what was no doubt a very busy schedule to make sure one of the staff felt valued.

Unlike his mother, she thought, but brushed the feeling

away. Tonight, particularly with her purse back, it felt like she needed to just relax. Enjoy what was being given to her.

He insisted on cleaning up after, and she let him, since really, it just involved scraping the plates and loading the dishwasher.

The fire had not been started, and Faith liked watching Brad's easy competence with it. Paper, kindling, small pieces of wood, match, then a slow feeding of larger pieces until a cheery fire crackled invitingly.

Then he settled on the couch beside her, and threw a companionable arm over her shoulder, kicked off his shoes and put up his feet.

She admired his socks: bright yellow tonight, with orange and black.

He squinted at them. "I think they're ducks," he said, wagging his feet at her. She looked more closely. Definitely ducks!

"You know what duck rhymes with?" he whispered evilly in her ear.

"Truck," she ventured, pretending innocence.

"Exactly!"

After a moment, he leaned over and said, his tone husky and suggestive, "Do what you're dying to do."

What she was dying to do was so X-rated it made her blush.

"I mean we're halfway down that road, anyway," he whispered. "With ducks and trucks."

She held her breath, thinking of the word she *never* said, that rhymed with both of those.

"Go ahead," Brad said softly, pulling away from her just enough to let his gaze slide to her lips.

She leaned toward him, her eyes half-closed.

"We both know what you're dying to do. That's a fast charger. Your phone is probably ready to go. So show me the pictures of your grandchildren."

Faith burst out laughing. She loved it that he was teasing her. She loved how easily the laughter came. She gave Brad a solid thump on his shoulder. "That's not what I thought you were going to say."

"Really?" He lifted a sexy eyebrow. "Dirty mind."

"Maybe we should give the phone a little longer to charge," she suggested.

Without another word, he lifted her against his chest, and she curled her arms around his neck, and snuggled into him. He carried her down the hall and into that bedroom as if she was light as a feather.

He put her down on the bed, and they undressed each other, with wonder and deliberation. This wasn't something that was *just happening*, as it had been at the Mud Puddle. This was a choice.

They used every inch of that bed, which just yesterday, she had thought was so ridiculously large.

This second time, there was an exquisitely slow tenderness to their lovemaking. They were two people who had been cast adrift, who had found each other. Who were rescuing each other, who were celebrating being pulled back from the abyss of a dark, roiling, endless, uncertain sea.

Much later, Brad, completely naked, completely confident in his nakedness, padded out of the room to retrieve her phone. Oh, those dimples!

Faith was pretty amazed by how she didn't feel self-conscious, either. Was there an opposite to self-consciousness?

If there was, he had drawn it out of her. With his hands and his lips and the look in his eyes.

It might be, she mused, with him out of the room, a good time to ask herself where all this was going. But the truth was, she didn't care.

She had cared all her life. She had made plans, lived by rules and behaved a certain way, and despite her best efforts, nothing had turned out the way she expected it to, anyway.

Now, for once, she would try to just breathe. To just enjoy, to the fullest, the pure sensual sensation of being in the moment.

He came back in, gave her her phone. Clothed only in sheets, she opened it and showed him some pictures.

"This is Maggie and Michael," she said. It was a picture taken of them in front of the Christmas tree, last year.

"They're extraordinarily beautiful," Brad said. "Maggie looks a lot like your dad. Your son has your hair. Look at that mop of curls. I bet he has to fight the girls off."

When she looked at this picture, though, she didn't see how gorgeous Michael was. She saw the tension around his mouth, the baffled anger. Would she ever be able to overcome the barriers he had erected around himself, as if family was so painful for him, he no longer wanted to be a part of one?

"Everything okay?" Brad asked, pushing a little strand of hair away from her forehead with his thumb.

He was so sensitive to her.

"Felix being so changed was really hard on the kids. I can see it in Michael's face in this picture."

"You are undoubtedly an extraordinary mom. I'm going to say you gave them what they needed to come back from it."

How had he happened on the most perfect thing to say?

"These are my grandchildren, Tanya and Chloe."

"There's those curls again," he said, as if those curls were the most amazing thing in the entire world!

The image was of them in the kitchen, the girls on chairs, in aprons she had made them for Christmas, wooden spoons raised to lips, a big green bowl between them.

"That's the cookie bowl," she said, and then glanced at him. In his glamorous world, did it all seem just a little domestic and dull?

But if the smile tickling across his lips was any indication, no.

"Your face," he said, handing her back the phone, and touching her cheek with a fingertip, "when you look at those girls."

"You'll know someday."

He sighed. "I hope."

"Show me your daughter."

"I'm still on the temp phone."

"Oh, no. Is your phone still blowing up?"

He shrugged. "I haven't looked at it all day. Such a sense of reprieve. I'll grab the temporary one, though, and see if I can pull up her social-media page."

So Faith and Brad sat in that huge bed—it could have been a twin for as much of it as they were using—backs propped up on luscious pillows, swathed in crisp white Egyptian cotton sheets, admiring each other's families.

When she yawned, he turned off the phone. "Sorry. I forgot the time difference. I'll head out."

"Please stay," she whispered.

He sighed. "I was hoping you'd ask."

And he settled back in the bed beside her, gathered her in her arms and took her all the way home.

Just before she slept, she thought of how just last night this bed had seemed too big and too lonely. In her journey through grief, this is what she had least expected.

How swift and bright was the light of hope. With those thoughts swirling around her, Faith thought she would have the best sleep ever.

Instead, she woke to pitch-blackness, trembling from the remnants of a terrible dream.

"Hey," Brad said softly, and Faith found his arms around her. "I think you had a bad dream. You were yelling."

He pulled her close to him, nuzzled her neck, buried his nose in her hair.

"I did have a bad dream," she said, shaken, so comforted by his arms and his warmth in the bed.

"Tell me," he invited huskily, and nudged her to turn over and face him. Her eyes were adjusting to the dark, and she took in the lines of his face, the sweep of his lashes, the curve of his lips.

She felt safe, the opposite of how the dream had made her feel.

"Tell me," he said again.

And so she did.

"I was out walking in a park in Toronto," she said, taking strength from the beautiful calm of his dark eyes. "It was a nice summer day, and there were lots of people in the park. Families picnicking, young couples strolling hand in hand, little kids laughing. And then this loose dog came toward me. He was quite lovely, a big dog with a thick brown fur coat, and soft eyes. It was really friendly, wagging its tail, its tongue hanging out, almost like it was grinning.

"I stood still and the dog came to me, and I was so delighted, like somehow it had picked me out of all the people in the park that day.

"But when I reached down to pet it—more like to welcome it—it turned into a bear. And it stood up on its hind legs and it grabbed me in this hold. It was so strong. It was crushing me. I couldn't get away. That's probably when you heard me yelling because then I woke up."

"That's powerful," he said. "I see a pretty clear meaning in it."

"I agree. I have variations of it, all the time. This is the first time with the dog, though. It's a dream where I think I'm safe and happy, and I'm amazed I'm the one having this experience.

"But then there's some danger lurking, or something familiar becomes extraordinarily terrifying without warning. Once I dreamt I was in my kitchen, making cookies, and a gunman burst in, and started shooting everything, my beautiful kitchen being ripped apart by machine-gun blasts."

His arms tightened around her. His silence encouraged her to continue.

"I guess my subconscious is trying to help me deal with my

life. Everything that I thought was safe, this feeling of being blessed by love, suddenly being wrecked, turning into something dangerous and unpredictable."

"Faith," he whispered. "I'm so sorry. Did your husband…? Was he dangerous and unpredictable?"

"That was the hardest part. That this kind and dignified and gentle man became a complete stranger to me. It happened slowly. At first, he'd say or do something strange, and I'd just brush it off. 'He's tired. He's stressed. He hasn't been eating right.' My dad hadn't seen him for two years when he came back to Toronto, sick. And he noticed right away that Felix had changed a great deal.

"And then I wasn't so quick to dismiss things. It was quite alarming, watching how reckless he had become, agitated, like a hyperactive child. Forward motion with no thought. So there were accidents, like catching a frying pan on fire, and incidents like getting caught shoplifting in a neighborhood store. He became so unbelievably nasty. He had no filters, whatever he was thinking he just said. He had no comprehension that he was hurting people. Last Christmas, he challenged our son-in-law to a fight. So, yes, I guess he did become dangerous and unpredictable.

"It was even worse because I felt as if I couldn't tell anyone what was going on, because I wanted to protect him. I didn't want people looking at him through the lens of something I had said about him."

"How lonely was that for you?"

"You have no idea."

But his hand squeezing hers made her think maybe he did have an idea.

"The only people I wanted to tell were doctors. I had this naive idea the medical system would step in and help you if things went sideways.

"But that's not how it works, at least not with brain disorders. A doctor, who would spend ten minutes with Felix, would think he knew way more about him than I did after thirty years together. My calls for help—increasingly desperate pleas—felt as if they fell into an abyss. It was so unbelievably hard to get a diagnosis. Because I couldn't get a diagnosis, the kids just thought Felix was becoming horrible with age, and that I was making excuses for him.

"But in the end, what difference did that diagnosis that I finally got make? There was not a single thing they could do to change it or stop it."

Faith couldn't believe she'd unloaded all of that. She was not sure she had ever told her story so completely.

"You have lived through the nightmare you just woke up from."

"You know what the worst of it was? All these nasty things he was saying and doing? What if the kids were right? What if that's who he always had really been—what if he'd always nursed these horrible thoughts about people—and the disappearance of his filters just allowed it all to come out?"

After a long time, his voice strong, sure, something a person could really hold on to in the dark of night, Brad said, "I don't believe that."

"Why not?"

"First of all, you would have never married a man like that. But second, you know how people are when they're drunk? You know how they say and do all kinds of things they would never normally say and do?"

She could not help but think of her father at her wedding.

"There's a saying—*in vino veritas*. It's Latin, it means 'in wine there is truth,' but I've never quite seen it that way, either. Cassie had a friend once, in her teen years, the sweetest girl you could ever meet. Kind, helpful, quiet. Cassie brought her home one night after they'd had too much to drink. She was so awful. Loud, rude, vulgar. The next day she didn't even remember. But how could anyone look at her and reach the conclusion that how she behaved, for those few hours out of her whole life, was who she was?

"It's an altered state. It's not who people really are," Brad concluded quietly. "And I'm sure that's what it was for Felix, too."

She felt an amazing wash of peace when he said that. A sense of understanding, not just for Felix, but for her father, too.

"Thank you," she whispered to him. "Those are just about the most comforting words anyone has ever said to me about this."

CHAPTER SEVENTEEN

FAITH FELL ASLEEP AGAIN, but Brad didn't. He marveled at the way he felt with her in his arms.

The truth was, he hadn't ever thought he would feel this way again.

Whole.

Complete.

So, so alive.

It was very much like that eighteen-year-old boy who had declared with such fierce certainty, *I'm going to marry Faith Cameron someday.*

He felt wildly and ridiculously in love, as if his every sense was humming, vibrating electrically within him.

He couldn't just come out and say that. A declaration of love at this early stage would scare Faith into next week. After all, he was even scaring himself.

But he could *show* her. Slowly, he could try and heal what the last few years had given her. He could do that by giving her these last two days and making them as carefree, as fun and as full of adventure as was possible.

Wednesday and Thursday. Friday she was supposed to go home.

But maybe, if the next two days went well, he could convince her to stay.

He could see if what he thought he was feeling could stand up to the kind of reality tests only time could give it.

He couldn't change what had happened to her, or the way his teenage self had behaved, but he could make her laugh.

Feel young again.

Have hope.

Embrace adventure.

Feel confident in her own beauty.

Maybe even have faith, as her name called her to do. That life would be good again. That the dogs would not turn into bears, that she could feel safe and secure even if she was doing things that weren't exactly safe and secure.

"What are we doing here?" she asked, the next morning, getting out of his car. Brad had been up since 5:00 a.m. laying the groundwork for this. "What is this place?"

"It's a zip line."

She digested that for about two seconds. "What a terrible idea."

But underneath the words, he heard the fear of a woman who had friendly dogs turn into killer bears in her dreams. And in her real life.

"It's not such a bad idea," he said softly. "An adventure like this is about facing your fears. It's about discovering your competence in dealing with them. Life throws us all kinds of stuff. We can't control that. The one thing we can control is ourselves."

This is part of what he had learned in search-and-rescue.

"The way I see it, life has thrown some unbelievable stuff at you. Stuff you probably thought would crush you. But it hasn't. Embrace that. This lesson is as much for me as it is for you. Do you know I haven't skied since Cynthia died?"

As he knew it would, as soon as he made it about a benefit to him—about helping him—she was right on board.

She took a deep breath, and regarded the course, and then they walked up to the entrance kiosk. It was such an act of trust.

She laughed when she saw the sign on the window, not even trying to hide her relief. "Look, it's closed for the day. A private event."

He laughed, too. "The private event is us."

"What?"

"It's not their busy time of year. I didn't want to have to worry about either of us being recognized."

She actually put her hands on her hips and glared at him. He thought he'd better not smile, even though she looked as adorable as an angry kitten.

"You booked the whole park?"

"I did."

"Don't you think that's unnecessarily extravagant?" she asked him sternly.

"Hey, it doesn't even hold a candle to that wine last night."

"I think your money would be better used for something else."

He was not entirely certain she wasn't just using this indignation as a shield to avoid zip-lining.

"Such as?" he challenged her.

"How about the food bank?" she ventured.

He gave her a long look, then pulled his phone—still the temporary one—out of his pocket. He couldn't remember the accountant's phone number, but he found the website and dialed it that way.

He got by reception with ease.

"Graham. How are you? Brad Daniels here… Cassandra's fine, she's getting the place ready for Christmas. How about Brenda?" After they got the pleasantries dealt with—Graham's daughter, who had gone to school with Cassie, was expecting grandchild number three—he said, "Speaking of Christmas, I'd like to make a donation to the hamper fund at the food bank… Oh. I already have? How much?… Okay. Double that."

He clicked off his phone and put it in his pocket.

"Now, you're just showing off," she said, but a smile was tickling her lips.

"Just trying to impress my lady. Did it work?"

"Oh, yeah," she said softly. She took a deep breath. Her grip tightened on his. "Okay," she said, "I'll do this."

"It's just the beginning," he said. "I have a few other things planned, too."

She regarded him thoughtfully for a minute. Then she said, "Okay, Brad, you can have the rest of today. But tomorrow, I'm going to make the plans."

He frowned at that. He had it all in place for tomorrow night. He looked at his watch. Maybe, he could move it up to tonight.

"If you'll excuse me just a sec, I have to make another phone call."

A few minutes later, he stood on the precipice, harnessed in and wearing a helmet. He helped Faith buckle hers in place.

"If this is so safe, why are we wearing helmets?" she demanded. "And what possible good will they do as we are falling to our deaths?"

"We won't die of a head injury?" he teased her. "You first, my lady."

"No, no, you first. I insist."

"Okay, but you have to promise you won't chicken out and leave me stranded on the next platform by myself."

"Okay," she said. "I promise."

Her promise felt as if it carried the weight of a cargo full of gold.

Brad was surprised his hands were a bit clammy. He couldn't let Faith see that. He'd never get her to go. He took a deep breath, and pushed off the first platform. The harness caught him, and suddenly he was whooshing through the air at breakneck speed.

He realized the sensation of a total loss of control was not one he particularly liked. He had to clamp his jaws shut to keep from yelling his dismay. He was very happy when his feet found the next platform.

He turned and gave Faith a thumbs-up, hoping she wouldn't be able to see the slight shaking in his hands. She squinted at him, took a deep breath and leaped.

What had he done? She was screaming in terror! But then he realized, it wasn't terror at all! She was screaming with laughter.

Her feet found the platform and she tumbled into his arms, gazing up at him with absolute delight.

"That was the best! The wind! The feeling of freedom! It was like flying." She suddenly stopped, and looked at him more closely.

"You didn't like it," she said, despite his best effort at a brave expression.

"Terrified," he admitted, pressing his forehead to hers. Just like that, she was the strong one. He saw exactly how she had gotten through Felix's illness. Because she had a core of pure steel.

She leaned into him, and whispered, "Brad, it's the closest sensation to sex I've ever had without actually having sex."

"That puts an entirely different spin on it," he said.

"I hoped it would."

And somehow, after that, he surrendered to it. To the speed, and the sense of not being in control, and of the bottom falling out of his belly and his world. He loved how she imparted her joy and her confidence into him.

He realized that discovering something brand-new, even if it was frightening, gave the world a shimmer it had not had before. Or maybe that shimmer was from sharing the brand-new experience with her, just as they had when they were younger.

A few hours later, Faith stood in front of him. He helped her unsnap her harness. The look on her face made the private booking of the zip line a bargain. It would have been a bargain at twice the price.

"I *loved* that," she said, unnecessarily, since her enjoyment was shining out of her eyes.

"Me, too," he agreed, and realized he really, really meant it.

"I think that's the most exhilarating thing I've ever done," she told him.

"Since you've already compared it to sex, my ego feels quite deflated," he said, for her ears only, with mock sullenness.

"Okay, the most exhilarating family-friendly thing I've ever done. I'm going to see if there's any zip lines close to us in Toronto. I mean, the girls are too young, but it would be a great thing for Maggie and Michael and Sean and I to do together. It's exactly as you promised, a chance to embrace the exhilarating side of fear."

He liked it *so* much that her first thought was how to share an experience like this with the people who meant the most to her.

"I have something even better planned for tonight," he told her.

"Better than that?" she said skeptically.

"I think so. It's formal, though."

"I didn't bring anything formal to wear."

"Go get something. You never had a chance to use that preloaded credit card I gave you." He sighed at the look on her face. "I'll make another donation to the food bank."

At this rate, the recipients of his generosity would be having steak and lobster for Christmas dinner rather than turkey.

"How formal?" she asked him a little later as he dropped her off in front of Wolf's Song.

"As formal as you can make it." He looked at his watch. "I'll pick you up at six."

Faith entered a Whistler boutique that she would have never ever been able to afford when she lived here. She remembered how stressed she had been going to prom.

She had taken the sea-to-sky shuttle into Vancouver and

used her chambermaid earnings to buy an exquisite dress at a secondhand store. She had traveled that distance so that none of her classmates would see her dress and recognize it as one they had discarded.

She had owned many gorgeous gowns since then, for faculty events, weddings, graduations, alumni reunions. And she had never owned another secondhand one. But she had never owned one like this shop was selling, either.

In fact, this was the kind of shop she avoided. The tasteful displays, soft lighting, good furniture, mirrors with gilt around the edges might as well have been neon signs blinking *expensive*. She had always harbored a secret sense that the sales staff in a place like this would know an impostor when they saw one!

But it must have been a new staff member today, because she didn't have the good sense to kick Faith out as not belonging.

In fact, she smiled at her, waved a hand and called, "Let me know if I can help you find something."

Which was probably the same as saying "I won't bother, because I can tell you can't afford it."

She went to a rack of evening dresses, and flipped over a price tag on a midnight-blue one. She tried not to gasp. On the other hand, the man had probably spent the equivalent of a new car on her today.

She could suck it up for once in her life.

The saleslady materialized at her side, as if she knew, somehow, a decision had been made. But she wasn't in the least snooty. In fact, she reminded Faith of one of Maggie's friends who went to the young-mothers group.

"I'm Bridgette," she introduced herself.

"A special-occasion dress?" she clarified once Faith had told her what she was looking for. "My favorite. I've got just the one. I thought of it the minute I saw you looking at this rack. Come with me."

And just like that, Faith found herself in a very posh changing room, looking at herself in the most gorgeous gown she had ever laid eyes on.

A little later, handing over her own credit card, not the one Brad had given her, she was not sure that how wonderful she felt buying that dress could be considered sucking it up.

That parcel tucked under her arm, Faith's next stop was the grocery store. She felt, acutely, the juxtaposition of the dress with her purchases there.

Perhaps she could change her plan for tomorrow. But really, there wasn't time. And in a way, it was a bit of a test.

Hours later, despite wearing a dress about equal to a month's salary when she'd been teaching, Faith felt as nervous waiting for Brad to come as she had felt all those years ago in her secondhand dress for prom.

She looked at herself in the mirror.

The dress was dazzling and elegant. Like Brad's hair, all the shades of gray in the silky fabric reminded her of storm clouds with the light behind them. The dress was beautifully cut, with a deep V at both the front and back, belted at the waist and then flaring out to midcalf. This was obviously why people paid so much for these dresses: the design of it *loved* how women were made. It hugged all the best parts of her and skimmed over others.

She looked beautiful.

And yet, when she looked at herself, she was aware the beauty did not come from the dress, or from her painstakingly tamed hair and her carefully applied makeup.

The beauty was from surviving the lake.

The beauty was from riding behind Brad on the quad.

The beauty was from honoring her father's last wish.

The beauty was from allowing herself to experience every single pleasure the Mud Puddle had offered her.

And the beauty was from having loved—and lost—and somehow finding within herself the courage to try it all again.

The doorbell rang, and, feeling really nervous for some reason, Faith opened the door.

Brad stood there looking very James Bondish, in a black jacket, a crisp pleated shirt, a bow tie, knife-pressed black slacks and mirror-polished black dress shoes. Gregor Watson did not have a single thing on him.

She was glad for every cent she had spent on that dress, but she wasn't sure even that was enough to bolster her confidence in light of how suavely perfect he was.

"Show me the socks," she whispered.

He lifted a pant leg, and he had on blue socks with purple polka dots. Just like that, he was *her* Brad again, fun-loving, devoted to his daughter, not taking himself too seriously. She didn't need to be the least self-conscious of him.

Tonight, he had a different vehicle, parked in front of Wolf's Song, sporty and low-slung, and nearly as hard to get into as his bigger SUV had been.

Of course, the shoes were unreasonable. But she'd had to have them. And her new best friend Bridgette had insisted.

They weren't in the car very long. In fact, he drove around the corner, to the bottom of the Timber Wolf run and the chairlift station.

She gave him a quizzical look, but he stopped the car, came around and opened her door. He guided her through the dark to the front of the station.

A voice greeted them. "Evening, Mr. Daniels. Ma'am."

Brad took her hand and settled her on the waiting chair. The lift attendant handed him a thick blanket and Brad put it over her shoulders and his, cocooning them together.

"Thanks, Mel," he said. "Remember—"

"Top secret," the young man said.

Faith shivered with delight. It really was all very secret agent. She loved it. The chairlift hummed to life, clanked once or twice, and then they were riding higher and higher, as the cables lifted them above the ground.

CHAPTER EIGHTEEN

FAITH SNUGGLED INTO Brad and took in the views. Soon, they could see all the way to Whistler. Cobalt Lake and Whistler both looked like miniature Christmas villages, their lights winking in the darkness.

By the time they reached the top station, they were in snow. The moon had risen and the world felt silver and white, as if it had all been designed to match her dress.

It was utterly magical. Adding to the magic, it somehow felt as if taking her to the top of a mountain on a chairlift was a subtle, but beautiful nod, to her father.

The chair halted, and Brad took the blanket from his shoulders and completely wrapped it around her. Even so, it was very cold up here. A path had been shoveled to a small café that Faith recalled served hot chocolate and coffee during the ski season.

Tonight, Brad held open the door for her, and a wall of welcoming warmth embraced her. There was a single, candlelit, white-linen-covered table, set for two, the chairs next to each other, rather than opposite each other, so that they could both face the view.

A formally attired waiter glided out, and filled their wine-glasses.

"Don't even ask," Brad warned her.

So she didn't. She didn't ask what the wine had cost, or allow herself to wonder what this exquisite dinner experience had cost him.

The waiter came out again, this time with a tray covered in a silver dome. He set it carefully in the center of the table, and with a flourish removed the cover.

Tears sparked in Faith's eyes. "Oh, Brad," she whispered, as she looked at the two Zippy burgers wrapped in their distinctive red-and-white paper.

"The funny thing is Zippy's is still there, and the place we were supposed to go that night has long since shut down."

It flooded back to her. Prom night. She had felt like Cinderella in the beautiful gown she had managed to pick up secondhand. But she felt like Cinderella in more ways than that. Because Brad had insisted he was picking her up at her place, the run-down trailer on the edge of town.

When she had come out of her room in the gown, Max had stared at her, flummoxed. And then he had bowed before her, and kissed her hand, and asked her for a dance.

Dancing with her dad, she had looked up at him to see the tears in his eyes.

"My little girl," he'd whispered, "all grown up and I'm not ready for it."

And it felt as if it was only then that she, too, had realized exactly what that night represented. A transition. The end of one chapter and the opening of another. High school would be over in a few days.

And then, Brad had arrived, standing nervously at the door with a corsage in his hand, and a limo idling behind him.

Max had put him at ease, chatting and teasing, and then he'd noticed the limo. "Wow," he said to Faith, "you're beating your old man to a first ride in a limousine."

And then Brad, with that amazing generosity of spirit that had made her love him, had said, "We're going for dinner first, Mr. Cameron, why don't you come with us?"

Faith supposed there were some girls who wouldn't have liked that. But somehow, to her, it felt perfect, saying goodbye to this part of her life with the two men she loved most.

And so the three of them had climbed into the limo, her and Max equally as wide-eyed and how luxurious it was. And then Max had said, "My treat tonight, kids." And he'd tapped on the glass and said, "Zippy's and step on it."

And so instead of the dinner at the fancy restaurant where Brad had reservations, the limo had pulled up in front of Zippy's and let them out. It shone in her memory. Maybe because it was so soon after that everything fell apart.

"Funny," she said, "how sometimes when things don't go according to plan, they turn out so perfectly."

"One of the best nights ever," Brad told her quietly, and raised his wineglass to her. "To remembering old memories and making new ones."

After the dinner things had been cleared away, the transformed café was filled with music and Brad held out his hand to her.

They danced together.

Again, she was drawn back to senior prom, to how it had felt to sway against him, how aware she had been of every detail of him: his scent, the thickness of his lashes, the full bottom lip, the way his hand had felt resting on her waist.

She gazed up at him now and felt that familiar intensity.

"You know what I love best about an older Faith?" he asked softly.

"What?"

"Everything," he responded with such sincerity her heart stopped.

"Oh, Brad," she said, "wrinkles and extra pounds—"

He put a finger to her lips. "Life," he said. "When I look at you, I see your life in your eyes. I see the layers of it. I see you holding sick kids in the middle of the night, and choosing a prom dress with your own daughter. I see you and Felix making sacrifices so that she can become a lawyer and Michael can go to Scotland. I see the depth facing sorrow has given you. And I see the courage in your undiminished capacity for joy."

Out the expanse of windows, the stars twinkled above them, and the lights of the village twinkled below.

Faith was so deliciously aware that somehow she had left her real life behind her and stepped directly into a fairy tale.

Only Brad was saying this was the *real* her.

Just as it was the real him. He had grown into his great promise of generosity, of humor, of sensitivity.

She melted further into him, felt the cradle of his arms close around her, and wished for this to never, ever end.

It was the wee hours of the morning before they were back at Wolf's Song. They fell into each other's arms.

Despite the exhaustion, a need was there, that had been building and building as they had danced together on the top of that mountain. It was as quiet as the hum of a bee, as immutable as the waves of the ocean, as powerful as a sudden summer storm.

They undressed each other with reverence, they worshipped at the altar of life. Faith had a sense of each of them bringing everything they had ever been, everything they now were and everything they would ever be.

They began as separate people, kissing, tasting, touching, giving and receiving pleasure, exploring sensuality from a lovely place of maturity. But as the intensity built between them, the sense of separateness was lost.

Not just between them. As they exploded, the barriers of the universe came down, and they collapsed. Into everything.

She lay in the circle of Brad's arms after, feeling the steady rise and fall of his naked chest beneath her cheek.

Beyond content.

Happy.

She was the one thing she had wondered if she could ever be again. She marveled at it. She was happy.

The smallest niggling of doubt pierced that happiness. She'd volunteered to make the plan for tomorrow.

What could she give the man who had everything?

Especially since his daughter had already beaten her to the sock idea?

She could give him the one thing he had missed.

But suddenly, in the light of everything he had given her, her humble, homey idea felt *not good enough.*

Tomorrow felt as if it was going to be a test. She fit into his world. Would he fit into hers? Somehow, she didn't feel ready for that test, or for the possible answer.

But it was too late to make a different plan.

In the morning, she was familiarizing herself with the kitchen when he came in. He was so darned cute first thing with his tousled hair, and sleepy, sexy eyes.

"I'm going to go to my place and grab a shower and a change of clothes. Any wardrobe suggestions for your plan?"

Insecurity clawed at her. No fancy dress required. No quad helmets. No adventure-sturdy mountain wear.

She was going to introduce Brad to ordinary life. After the magical worlds he had invited her into, it was sure to fall flat.

Faith debated canceling.

She debated telling him he could come up with the plan for the day, after all.

But no, it was time to see if their worlds had any overlap at all.

"No," she said, "just come dressed for comfort."

He came and kissed her, full on the lips, and it almost made her insecurities vanish. Almost.

"So what's the plan?" he said, when he arrived back.

Comfy for him was a pair of dark denim jeans, a crisp shirt paired with them. He looked way too sexy for what she had in mind.

She took a deep breath. "We're going to bake cookies this morning."

She watched him closely for signs: that it was too domestic for him, a little dull, boring.

Instead, he grinned at her with such real enthusiasm that she felt her heart melt. In fact, it felt as if any little piece of herself she had been holding back from him, suddenly and completely surrendered.

"Look what I found," she said, leading him over to the counter.

He looked at her find. "I don't have a clue what that is. A device dropped from the ship of an extraterrestrial?"

He was going to make the differences in their worlds seem fun, like exploring a new place.

"It's a stand mixer!"

He inspected it. "As opposed to a sitting mixer?"

"It's a chef-worthy piece of equipment. What kind of vacation cottage is equipped like this?"

"This cottage actually has a commercial kitchen, because it's the largest of the cottages. Sometimes people rent all of the cottages, particularly in the offseason, for weddings or conferences or family reunions. This one becomes the central meeting place, and it's set up for caterers."

Soon, they were measuring ingredients together. He had put on his playlist. The kitchen was filled with sunshine, laughter and music.

She handed him one of the beaters after they had creamed all the cookie ingredients together. She took the other one for herself. She licked the cookie dough off it.

"Oh, my," he said, watching her with narrowed eyes. "So that's how you learned to do all those remarkable things with your tongue."

He closed his eyes, and began to do very wickedly exaggerated things to the beater with his tongue and lips. Soon, he was adding sounds, until he had her howling with laughter.

In fact, she had never laughed so much while baking cookies in her entire life.

Now, the first batch of cookies was cooling on the counter, and the second was in the oven. He was sitting, casually, on the island. She had taken the beaters out of the beautiful stand mixer that was built into the cabinet system.

It occurred to Faith she had wanted to show Brad what ordinary looked and felt like. Instead, he had shown her the extraordinary hidden among the ordinary.

Suddenly, without anyone knocking or the bell ringing, the front door swung open. Brad slid off the counter and turned to it, quizzically.

Faith recognized his daughter. Cassie came in and pecked him on the cheek, took in the cookies, acknowledged Faith with a lifted hand.

Faith noticed Brad had set the beater down, almost as if he was hiding it. In fact, he had a bit of a deer-caught-in-the-headlights look.

"I thought I'd start Christmas decorations over here later this afternoon. I don't like to do the public areas until after Remembrance Day, but I thought I could get a head start on this."

"Sure," Brad said. Faith tilted her head at him. It was their last full day together, and her plan for the afternoon hadn't involved working around his daughter setting up Christmas decorations.

"Dad, you must be in charge of cookies for the next search-and-rescue meeting. I think hiring a caterer is cheating."

Faith waited for Brad to correct his daughter, and make an introduction.

Instead, Brad said nothing.

His daughter came over and offered her hand. "Hi, I'm Cassandra, Mr. Daniels's daughter."

"Hi, Cassie," Faith said warmly. "I'm Faith." She glanced at Brad. Nothing.

"It's Cassandra," she said. The correction was ever so casual, but it put up the faintest of barriers. The *staff* did not call her Cassie. She helped herself to a cookie, as if she owned the place, which come to think of, she did.

"These are delicious," she said. "Can you make sure Anita gets the recipe?"

"Of course," she said, and heard a bit of tightness in her own voice.

"What time do you think you'll be wrapping up? I won't come in until after you're gone."

Again, here was an opportunity for Brad to indicate Faith was not the caterer, that they were friends. And that the cottage was in use until tomorrow.

When he didn't say anything, Faith said, a little sharply, "Not to worry. I'm done."

Cassandra left with that same surge of busy energy she had come in with.

Faith took off her apron, folded it carefully and set it on the island. "I'm not sure I understand what just happened there, Brad. I thought I was staying here until tomorrow."

She'd also had some pretty hot plans for him this afternoon, that involved that huge, jetted tub in the en suite bathroom, and a container full of rose petals.

"We have lots of rooms," he said with a shrug.

"Why didn't you tell her I wasn't a caterer?" Faith asked softly.

"It just seemed less complicated not to mention it."

Suddenly, it occurred to Faith that the lift attendant last night had been sworn to secrecy, not because of the media chasing a story, but because Brad hadn't wanted his daughter to know about her.

"Really? It never occurred to you that your daughter mistaking me for staff might be hurtful to me, particularly since you didn't seem eager to correct her perception?"

He looked puzzled, the same as when she had mentioned her suitcase not being up-to-snuff.

"I was staff here, once. Do you remember that?"

"You were a chalet girl," he said, eying her uncomfortably, apparently sensing her rising temper and bracing for it.

"A chalet girl. Your mom's euphemism for a chambermaid. You know what I did, Brad? I stripped dirty sheets off beds, and cleaned toilets. I bet you've never done either, have you?"

"I'm not sure where this is going," he said uncomfortably.

"Your mom told me all those years ago that I wasn't good enough for you and I can see nothing has changed. You didn't even introduce me to your daughter!"

"My mom said that to you?" He looked genuinely shocked.

But she had started now, and she couldn't have stopped, even if she wanted to. It felt as if she had been keeping the secret to protect him. But now, she saw she'd been protecting herself, as well, as if the grown-up her might be able to slip into his world, her lack of social standing no longer applicable.

She was telling him *everything*.

"Brad, my dad lost all the money he'd saved for college gambling on a horse. A sure thing, he said. I'm not sure your mother set that up, though I wouldn't put it past her. But she sure didn't let an opportunity get by her to get rid of the *chalet* girl who had *designs* on her son."

"What are you talking about?" He looked angry now.

"You know who my mysterious benefactor was? You know who paid for my college, in the east, far away from her precious son? You know who made a stipulation that I wasn't to contact you *at all*? *Ever*?"

Brad looked utterly stunned.

She marched by him. He reached out to stop her, but she ducked easily out of his grasp and kept going.

She went down the hallway, and into the bedroom. She closed the door and locked it behind her. She ignored his soft knock on the door.

She pulled her shabby suitcase out of the cupboard, threw things in it, including that stupid bag full of rose petals she'd saved from the bouquet he'd bought her. She zipped it shut.

She ignored his rattle of the handle.

"Faith, we need to talk about this."

She pulled out her phone and called the hotel she'd originally had a reservation with. Thankfully, they had a room available for tonight.

The dress she had worn last night was still hanging in the closet. She realized she didn't want it. It was part of a world she could never belong to. One in which she had been an impostor.

She fished through her purse and put the unused credit card he had given her on the dresser.

Taking one last look around, feeling like Cinderella after the clock had struck twelve, Faith opened the double doors that went out to a deck off the bedroom.

She softly closed them and, tugging her suitcase behind her, took the boardwalk around Cobalt Lake toward Whistler.

When she got home, she'd send him a check for the jacket, and the toque and the clothes.

And then she'd burn them.

As she walked around the lake, she could almost see herself, out there, nearly drowning, thinking, laughably, that her father or Felix had somehow taken pity on all her suffering over the past years.

That her fate had been altered.

But she should be way more familiar with fate than that by now.

CHAPTER NINETEEN

IT WAS QUITE a while before Brad realized Faith had left.

He'd gone and sat in the living room, waiting for her to cool off. She would understand when he explained to her that he didn't want Cassie figuring out who she was because of the media thing.

And he certainly didn't want his daughter thinking Faith was a romantic interest.

She'd probably laugh when he told her Cassie would have them locked together in a panic room in no time.

Though if he was going to be locked in a panic room...

A horrible shrill noise startled him and he leaped off the couch. Smoke was roiling out the oven door and the fire alarm was shrieking its outrage.

He went and opened the oven door, and was nearly overcome with smoke inhalation. Brad slammed the door shut, held his breath and then opened it again. He pulled the second batch of now scorched cookies out with a tea towel. In his haste, he burned his hand.

Standing there, sucking on the burn, he waited for the bedroom door to fly open, for Faith to dash out, worried about him. She was the kind who would worry and fuss over any injury. She'd probably want to look at his hand, run it under cold water, insist on a first-aid kit—it might be just the thing to soften that unfamiliar anger he had seen flare up in her eyes.

But the door didn't open.

And then he knew.

She was gone.

The cookies suddenly felt like an illustration of his life: scorched.

He wandered back into the great room, nursing his hand, and sank back down on the couch. Eventually the smoke alarm stopped shrieking. Brad thought about what Faith had accused his mother of.

He wanted, desperately, for it not to be true. But in his heart, he knew it was. The pieces of the puzzle of Faith's sudden departure from his life just fit together a little too snugly.

His world felt strangely perilous, as he challenged what he had believed to be true his entire life. His mother had been part of that life—one of the biggest parts—for forty years. Of course, he'd known she had flaws. His mother had never been going to win a popularity contest. But he would have never imagined she was capable of something so controlling and so conniving.

How could he possibly have spent that kind of time around her and not know who she really was?

And couldn't the same be said of Cynthia? Twenty-eight years of marriage, and he was not sure he'd known her at all.

And Faith? He'd been wooing her for days. Protecting her. Contemplating a life with her, because he wanted to capture the feeling he had around her.

Of being engaged.

Connected.

Of being alive.

He'd felt he'd been as open and transparent with Faith as he had ever been with anyone. And she thought he was judging her? Not finding her good enough?

It was an insulting misread of him.

But it was certainly more evidence that when it came to the women in his life, he didn't know them at all.

It was good that she was gone, he told himself, because he'd been about to get himself into big trouble with her.

As head over heels—as blindly—in love as he had been when he was eighteen.

He got up from the couch and let himself out of Wolf's Song before his daughter came back.

Faith was exhausted as she walked out of the frosted doors that separated the airline passengers from those picking them up at Toronto Pearson International Airport. She paused for a moment, watching the reunions, people so excited to see one another. Passionate kisses, hugs, greetings.

She realized she was holding up traffic, people streaming around her.

She had to focus on something other than the feeling of her heart breaking. Again. She told herself she had done the right thing.

It wasn't just that she and Brad came from two different stratospheres, that he came from a world that she could barely imagine, and she came from the world that served them.

It was *this*.

This crushing feeling of loss. It was bound to happen sooner or later. Even when someone got a puppy, the sad ending was already looming, waiting…

"Mom!"

Startled, she saw Maggie coming toward her. Her beautiful daughter, her face wreathed in happiness to see her. And just like that, she was part of all of the happy reunions happening around them.

Maggie's arms closed around her. "It's so good to see you."

As if she'd been gone a year, instead of five short days.

"I had no idea you were coming," Faith said. She had fully intended to call a cab. "It's your busy time of day. Suppertime, and baths, and bedtime stories…"

"I just needed to be here," Maggie said quietly. "I've been

so worried about you." She smiled. "Not being able to reach you that first day, and finding out you hadn't checked into your hotel, sent me into worry mode."

Before Felix, Maggie hadn't had a worry mode. Now, they all did, like survivors of a terrible natural disaster, an earthquake or a tsunami.

They walked to the carousel and Maggie spotted Faith's suitcase right away, and took it, then ushered them through the busy airport to her waiting car.

See? Faith told herself. She had family. She didn't need a man to look after her, to give her this sense of belonging and home. Maggie was her home. Maggie was quite capable of spoiling her on occasion.

She watched how Maggie handled the traffic with such aplomb, chattering about the girls and how excited they were as the day care and the school were already gearing up for Christmas plays.

"Chloe's been chosen to be the donkey in the manger scene. She's over the moon. Of course, I have to listen to her practicing her braying every waking moment." She demonstrated the bray and Faith laughed.

It was a reminder that laughter waited, even after the heartbreak, like sunshine waited behind the rain.

Not that her heart was broken!

She barely knew the man.

Liar, her inner voice reprimanded her.

"I was hoping you could help with the costume," Maggie said. "I don't even know where to begin."

Faith felt a warmth growing in her. Because she knew where to begin. She could already imagine the costume taking shape, the comfort of feeding the nubby gray fabric through her sewing machine.

This was her life. Being with her children and her grandchildren, making cookies and sewing costumes, and being in the front row for the Christmas concerts.

Her life was not erotic experiences at secret hot springs, private zip lines, exquisite meals on mountaintops.

In his heart, Brad knew that. That she could not fit into his world. That was why he had gone to such lengths not to introduce her to his daughter.

They pulled up in front of Faith's house, and Maggie parked in a spot Faith wouldn't have even dared to try. Again, she marveled at her daughter's competence, at the lovely feeling, that despite it all, she and Felix had done so much right.

Maggie brought the suitcase to the front door, and Faith found her key. How would she have gotten in without her purse? She wouldn't have thought about it until just this minute, she'd be standing out here in the cold calling a locksmith.

It had been a miracle, really, that her purse had been turned in.

But where had the miracle been when she had most needed it? No, best not to believe in such things.

Or one could think their first love rescuing them from certain death was also a miracle.

She missed Brad. Crazy to miss him so acutely after just a few days of being with him. On the other hand, when she had seen him after all these years, she had recognized a part of her, a secret part of her, had missed him that whole time.

Maggie was looking at her oddly. "Mom, are you okay?"

Secrets felt as if they took too much energy.

"Have you got time to come in for a minute?" Faith asked her. "I have something I need to tell you."

"Of course, I have time for you, Mom!"

Such a simple statement, and yet it brought tears to her eyes.

"What's going on?" Maggie asked a little later as they sipped hot tea—not fine wine. "I knew I should have gone with you. You shouldn't have tried to look after Grandpa's ashes by yourself. And then losing your purse…"

They sat on the slightly worn love seats in the living room, facing each other. Faith felt her spirit flitting around her house. She could see the marks on the doorjamb of the upstairs bathroom where they had measured the kids every year. Over there was the spot where Maggie had drawn on the wall with a permanent marker when she was five, and no matter how often they painted over it, it eventually bled through again.

There was the place, on the carpet, where Felix had spilled his coffee, and the dent in the wall where he had fallen.

"I think it's time for me to move," she told Maggie, surprised to realize she had made that decision sometime in the last few days. "The house is at an age where it needs things I can't give it. I've leaned on Sean quite enough over the past few years. He has his own house to look after."

"Don't make that your reason, Mom. We don't mind."

Her memories of the children were imprinted on her heart, not on a growth chart on the bathroom doorjamb.

"It's not the reason," she said. "I'm just ready for a different life."

She and Maggie's phones pinged at identical times. That meant it was either Michael or Sean sending them both a message.

"That's great news," Maggie said, smiling down at her phone.

It was Michael.

I'm going to come home for Christmas. I'd like to see it one last time, in case it ends up being sold.

The timing of the text seemed serendipitous. Almost as if, even though the seas separated them, he had sensed the decision, sensed Faith looking around that space, getting ready to say goodbye…their energy joined in ways she would never fully understand, but was grateful for.

She was aware, as she looked at her phone, it was quite

possible she misinterpreted what had seemed like Michael's indifference. While she had been thinking her son was insensitive, was it possible he was the most sensitive of them all?

"Mom? Is that what you wanted to talk about? The house? I'm not sad. I was actually hoping you'd arrive at that decision."

Faith took a deep breath. "No, that wasn't what I wanted to talk about. I want you to know what happened the day I arrived in Whistler."

She wanted, suddenly, for her daughter to know all of it—and maybe all of her—good and bad. Because wasn't that really what home was, not four walls, but being accepted for who you were?

So she told her about her ill-advised attempt to rescue that dog.

As she told it, she was aware she felt it had been an exceedingly stupid thing to do. On the other hand, if she had not done it, she would not have met Brad.

And for all the heartache she was going to feel over the next while, would she trade those days of laughter and adventure and discovery for anything?

The hope they had given her that someday life was going to be okay again.

Maggie was staring at her, open-mouthed. "You broke through the ice and ended up in the lake rescuing a dog?"

Faith nodded. "Please don't say how dumb it was. I already know."

"Is that why you didn't tell me?" Maggie asked softly. "Because you thought I'd think you were dumb?"

Faith nodded. "Getting old. Incompetent. You needing to look after me, instead of the other way around. A repeat of what we went through with your dad."

"Oh, Mom," Maggie said softly.

Faith drew in a deep breath. "There's one more part. The dog's name was Felix."

Maggie was silent for a long time. When she finally spoke, her voice was fierce, and Faith was shocked to see she had started crying when she told her the dog's name.

"Mom, I need you to listen to me. I don't know what's made you feel I think of you like that. Maybe I'm tired sometimes, because of all the things that come from juggling two little kids and a career. Maybe it makes me seem impatient and judgmental.

"But you going out on the ice after that dog? That had Dad's name? That's the bravest thing I've ever heard. You are the bravest person I know. When everybody else, including me and Michael, had given up on him, you hung in there. You got up every single day and did what needed to be done. You went on living, when you must have wanted to just lie down and give up a thousand times.

"You have a warrior spirit. Even when the battles were so hard, even though you knew you could not win, there you were, strapping on your armor and taking up your sword.

"You know what you taught me, Mom? Love can take on anything. Love will get you through things so horrible you cannot even imagine them, let alone prepare for them."

Faith took a sip of tea, stunned by how badly she had misinterpreted how her daughter saw her.

"Speaking of love," she said softly. "There's more. The man who rescued me was Brad Daniels."

"Mr. Hottie," Maggie said, and then it fully registered what her mother had said. "Love?" she squeaked.

"He was my first love, in high school."

And then she told her daughter things she had never told her. About growing up with Max, and working as a maid at the Cobalt Lake Resort, and finally about Mrs. Daniels, letting her know she was not good enough.

And then she told her about Brad spoiling her.

And his daughter finding them in the cottage together, and how she had felt he was ashamed of her.

"Oh, Mom," Maggie said softly. "He wasn't spoiling you. He was romancing you."

CHAPTER TWENTY

FAITH COULD ALMOST allow herself to be persuaded. She had to remember, Maggie was a lawyer. She convinced people of things for a living.

"Until his daughter came along," she said firmly. "And then he couldn't put enough distance between us. I realized he knew I couldn't fit in his world. Ever."

"Out of the hundreds of possibilities," Maggie said gently, "that's what you came up with? Could there be another reason for the way he acted?"

There was that lawyer again!

"I doubt there's another reason for Brad not introducing me to his daughter," Faith said stiffly, almost flinching as she remembered being corrected, and asked to call her Cassandra.

But then she thought, if she was capable of misinterpreting her own son, and her own daughter, had she misinterpreted Brad as well?

"I'm going to tell you what I think," Maggie said, in that tone that let Faith know her daughter was going to tell her, whether she wanted to hear it or not.

"You are that warrior. You are the bravest person I know. But that battle with Dad has left you bloodied and exhausted. And you feel you can't ever do it again. Did you worry if you did hook up with Brad, that you might end up going through it all again someday?"

First of all, she wasn't going to be one-hundred-percent honest after all, because she wasn't going to confide in her daughter she had *hooked up* with Brad, if Maggie was using the term in the way young people seemed to use it.

But, second of all, she was a little surprised that, no, she had never thought of Brad, not even once, of needing her care someday.

Maybe that had been part of his appeal. That he was so healthy, and so vital, the least likely person to ever become dependent.

"You worry about Michael and I, don't you? Carrying the genetic makeup for it?"

As much as she had not thought of Brad in those terms, Maggie hit a nerve with that one.

"I do," Faith admitted, sorry she had not done a better job of hiding that particular concern.

"I did at first, too," Maggie said. "But then I realized all the worrying in the world wouldn't change what was going to happen in the future. All it would do was steal the joy away from today."

"How did you get so wise?"

"Look who I have for parents."

Parents.

"After you've spent your formative years trying to figure out how to keep squirrels out of the bird feeders, believe me, you got some smarts going on."

Faith was so grateful that Maggie had pulled that memory from all of them. She could remember the three of them— Maggie, Michael and Felix—in the backyard, building bird feeders with an impossible-to-penetrate squirrel obstacle course around them. She could remember the laughter, and the intensity with which their latest creation would be observed. In the later years, there had even been cameras set up.

"In my heart, I was always kind of rooting for the squirrel," Faith admitted.

"Me, too. I think we all were."

We.

The family they had been.

It was worthy of gratitude that the last years of struggle had not permanently stolen from Maggie all the incredible gifts her father had given her, when he was still able.

And Michael was going to come, too. He'd called it *home*. She hoped it was those kinds of memories drawing him here.

"See, Mom?" Maggie said quietly. "We'll start to remember the good things again. And that will make us less afraid."

"I suppose," Faith said, hoping for her son and daughter and grandchildren, but dubious for herself.

"You're afraid of loving Brad," Maggie continued, her voice the same soft voice Faith had always marveled at hearing when she explained something to her children. "You're afraid you can't have a happy ending. You're afraid you don't have the strength to battle the uncertainties that love can lay at your doorstep ever again. I think, as brave as you are, you were looking for an excuse to run away from what the universe has given you."

Faith went very still. Regardless of the fact she had never once looked at Brad in terms of health concerns, loving someone took unbelievable courage. She looked at her beautiful daughter, and saw that she was not only wise, but also intuitive beyond her years.

This, too, was what tragedy did—there were roses hidden among the thorns.

"I think you're right," Faith said. "I have no bravery left."

Maggie smiled softly at her. "Sometimes you have to let other people be strong, Mom. I bet Brad has enough bravery for both of you, to carry you until you're strong again."

"I think you're reading way too much into how he feels about me."

"I hope I'm not. That man was absolutely dreamy."

"Well," Cassie told Brad as she came into his office, set a coffee on his desk for him and settled in a chair across from him with her own, "that was an opportunity missed."

He stared at her, startled. Did she mean Faith? How did she know?

"Gregor has been spotted on the French Rivera, with a new girlfriend. They're all gone. Every media person who was here who was interested in that story about your rescue on the lake has disappeared."

He laughed at that. He was pretty sure it was the first time he had laughed in—

"I guess it was time-sensitive, anyway. No one cares about it ten days after it happened."

Ten days. Ten days since he had laughed, since Faith had left, each day longer than the one before it and not just in terms of the winter darkness that was descending on them.

"Ah, well, Cassie, you did a great job keeping them off Gregor's trail for all this time. They still thought he was here, and they had the possibility of that side story to keep them occupied while they waited for a glimpse of him."

"I know," she said with an impish grin, and lifted her coffee cup to him.

He saluted her back. "You're doing a great job getting everything ready for Christmas."

"It isn't a season," she said, "it's a feeling."

He looked out the window. Snow now blanketed his views. He could see skaters on the lake. The trees twinkled with bright lights and decorations.

One season shifted to another. Grief had already taught him that. Everything kept moving, regardless of how you felt about it. He didn't have the *feeling*. But he wasn't going to tell his daughter that, when she was working so hard.

"It's picture-perfect," he said, trying for enthusiasm and missing.

"Dad, is something wrong?"

"No," he said, and then, just barely refrained from adding, *Don't give too much energy to perfection, Cassie.*

"Christmas," she said, cocking her head at him. "It's such a hard time of year. I miss her, too."

"I know, sweetheart."

She looked at her watch, gasped and catapulted from her chair. "So much to do. Oh, by the way, did you get me that cookie recipe?"

"Uh…sorry, no."

She gave him a look of faux annoyance. "Another opportunity missed. Possibly the best cookies I've ever tasted."

And then she was gone. Brad waited until the door had closed behind her, and then, ever so slowly, opened his drawer and took out the letter. He suddenly had to find out if his wife was one more woman he had never really known.

Beloved

Brad was aware of a faint tremble in his hands as he opened the flap of the envelope, the glue long since dried.

A single sheet of folded paper, as yellow with age as the envelope slid into his hands. He closed his eyes, and unfolded the paper.

And then he took a deep breath and opened his eyes.

Beloved, my beautiful girl, you are now hours old and so utterly perfect.

Relief swelled in him, as well as a trace of self-loathing for his own doubts about his wife. The letter was to their newborn daughter.

I am terrified of the huge responsibility you represent. Is there any hope at all of keeping all this perfection intact as you grow toward womanhood? I feel your father and I did not have good role models for this adventure called family that we have entered.

My mom and dad, already gone, were so hardworking and down to earth. But hugs? "I love you"? As foreign to them as a trip to a far-off land. I grew up with "make yourself useful," not "I stand in wonder of your perfection"!

And your grandmother Daniels! I often wonder how did someone so harshly judgmental and so impossible to please, ever raise a man like your father? He is the finest man I've ever known.

My hope for you, darling girl, is this:

From your father, I hope you get qualities of decency, generosity, calm...and the world's best eyelashes.

From me, I hope you get qualities of order and adaptability, an ability to see what could be, instead of what is.

But my greatest hopes aren't about what you inherit from each of us, but what you discover within yourself. I hope you find courage, and independence, and creativity, and joy. I hope as parents, we give you the gift of being you in the world.

And most of all, beloved Cassandra, I hope when love knocks on your door, you say yes to it.

And now, you are stirring, and our new life as a family begins. I am putting this note away for you. I will take it out when you are thirty, and we will look at it together, and see how much of what I have wished for you has come true.

With all my love,

Mom (the happiest word I have ever written)

Brad held the letter for a long time, humbled by his wife's words about him, her words to their daughter.

He looked at the photo of her on his desk. In it, Cynthia was smiling, but he could see the faint tension around her mouth, the faint wall up in her eyes.

It seemed every question he'd had about his wife and their marriage had been answered by what Faith had said, and what this letter confirmed.

His mother had always been a difficult woman. She'd moved from Austria when she was a teenager, but never lost her accent. He suspected she had been made fun of. Once, in a rare moment of softness, Deirdre had told him something that had happened to her own mother during the war.

After that, he'd seen his mother—whom the staff called an old battle-ax behind her back, and the kids at school the dragon lady behind his—in a different light.

She was in some way a tormented soul, and so perhaps he had forgiven her things he shouldn't have. He'd told her once that he would not tolerate her being bad-tempered and judgmental with his wife.

He had never seen her behave that way toward Cynthia again, but after Faith's story, he wondered if he hadn't just forced his mother's aggression underground.

Looking back, he could see the daggers hidden in comments that had been seemingly innocent, that he had not given a thought to at the time. It occurred to him his mother might have subtly—and even not so subtly—tormented Cynthia when he was not in earshot.

And then Cynthia had felt a need to earn her way into the family. She probably had never once stood up for herself, thinking if she was good enough and perfect enough she could win her place in the Daniels family.

He thought of her relentless quest for perfection, the way she had put on airs, and pronounced things *marvelous* when they achieved her impossible standard.

Impossible, because no matter how hard she tried, she had probably never been able to get out from under the harsh judgment of his mother. She had set herself an impossible task if she'd been looking for Deirdre's approval.

It was even possible his mom had been even more ruthless when, after succeeding in getting rid of Faith, she had come up against the exact same challenge a few years later.

Had his mother made Cynthia pay the price for that accidental pregnancy again and again and again?

And he'd been blind to it all, engrossed in his work, thinking Cynthia was just as engrossed in her life, happily turning the resort into a world-class destination, collecting those incredible bottles of wine.

After Cynthia's death, he'd begun to question the strength of their marriage, but now he saw the flaw so clearly.

His mother had bullied his wife, and he had not seen it, beyond that first time. He should have been more vigilant. Instead, he had not protected Cynthia, not assured her she was absolutely enough exactly as she was.

No wonder, since the early days of their marriage, Cynthia had begun taking those bold midnight skiing excursions.

He'd thought they were out of character for her. She was so controlled, so *not* spontaneous.

But in actual fact, maybe that was the place—the only place—where she had felt free of the oppression of perfection, free to be herself, free to let her hair down, free to scream at the moon if she wanted.

Free to go out of bounds.

Free to shake her fist at all the rules and order that had been imposed on her, first by his mother, and then by herself.

He suspected by the time his mother had died, the patterns had been set. Cynthia had been so far behind the wall of her defenses—making her appearance and the resort and her wine collection so perfect—that she didn't even know that she was behind a wall anymore.

"I'm so sorry," he whispered to the picture. He slid the letter into the top drawer of his desk, added a reminder to his phone for way, way in the future.

He would give it to Cassie, as Cynthia had wanted, on her thirtieth birthday.

He'd known all along that Faith was about second chances to get things right. He just hadn't known how many levels it was on.

He picked up his phone and sent a quick text.

Cassie, are you still nearby? Do you want to walk around the lake with me? I'll tell you what happened that day.

He realized what he was really going to do was ask his daughter's blessing.

She answered back right away.

I'd love that.

Even with her busy schedule, she still loved being with Dad. For all the mistakes he was sure he and Cynthia had made, he could be assured in this.

His daughter was evidence of the triumph of love.

He picked up his jacket and headed out the door. For the first time since Faith had left, he felt optimistic, a stirring of hope chiseling away at the heaviness in his chest.

At the same time, he wondered if what he was about to confide in Cassie meant there was going to be a panic room in his future.

CHAPTER TWENTY-ONE

A PART OF Faith had really hoped that Maggie was right, that Brad had enough bravery for both of them.

But as she clicked off the days of November, it seemed if he was going to be the brave one, there was no sign of it. In fact, that time with him had a dreamlike quality to it, as if it had happened to someone else, unfolded on a movie screen or between the pages of a book.

Real life was enjoying the frenzied excitement of Chloe and Tanya after the first snow. Real life was beginning Christmas shopping, and watching decorations go up, bringing light and color to a dreary time of year.

Real life was helping Michael find a reasonably priced flight to come home.

Real life was starting that donkey costume for the Christmas play, and making paper snowflakes with her granddaughters that were now displayed in every window of her house.

Real life was realizing this would be her first year without Felix, though in truth, she knew she had lost him a long time ago.

Real life was taking action on her decisions about the house.

The house had actually been too big for her and Felix, once the kids were gone. But she had held on to it knowing that those kind of decisions were beyond his capabilities, and also that the familiar brought him some comfort.

Faith thought, with longing, of the woman she had been for a few short days in Whistler: carefree, bold, sure of herself.

She knew letting go of the house that had brought her such a sense of safety was part of embracing that woman.

That sense of safety had been an illusion. Just like in her dreams, the dangers had lurked, benign, in plain sight.

Yes, on that terrible last day with Brad, she had lost that certainty about herself—given in to old, old insecurities—but she knew now, her confidence was right there, waiting for her to invite it back into the forefront of her life.

A week later, she said goodbye to the real-estate agent, closing the door behind him against the snow that tried to swirl in.

So they would have one last Christmas here. One more time, with the kids and the grandkids gathered around the tree, the house smelling of turkey.

She thought she should feel sad, but she didn't.

As she looked around, she felt oddly free. Selling the house would leave her financially secure for life. That short time with Brad had filled her with longings.

All kinds of longings, she acknowledged with a blush, and yet the one that remained was to embrace adventure.

To travel. To explore. To discover.

The doorbell rang. She thought the real-estate agent must have forgotten something, and went back and opened it. But no, Brad Daniels stood on her doorstep.

He was stunning, just the way she would expect a man to look who had just stepped off his private jet.

But underneath that sophistication, she saw he looked exhausted. Gray stubble—that she had such a desperate need to touch, she had to stuff her hand behind her back—dotted his face. He looked faintly haggard. Thinner.

And then she remembered Maggie saying he would be brave enough for both of them.

His number, from that call Faith had made from the hospital would have been on Maggie's phone.

"Did Maggie call you?" she asked, mortified.

What would her daughter have said? *I think my mom's in love with you.*

And Brad, with his need to rescue…

He looked surprised. "Did Maggie call me? No, I called her. Her number was on my phone from when you called her from the hospital."

"She knew you were coming?"

"I wouldn't go that far. But she surrendered your address without much of a fight." He smiled that wonderful, delicious, crooked-grin smile at her.

She stepped back and let him in, aware of how humble her house was compared to the opulence of nearly every space at the Cobalt Lake Resort.

But he did not appear in any way aware of the humbleness of her house, just as he had not been aware of the differences in their worlds because of his watch, his car, her luggage, his ability to rent an entire park, or open up a ski hill for a private dining experience.

He had never been aware of those things, so Faith could suddenly see Maggie had been right.

It had been her who had seen the differences in their worlds, it had been her who had jumped to the conclusion that he had not introduced her to his daughter because she was not good enough.

With that realization, Faith felt the door of her heart squeak open one alarming inch.

Just enough that she said, "Come in, Brad. Sit down. Should I make us tea?"

So different than the expensive wines he had offered her. And yet, he tilted his head, and smiled. "Tea sounds wonderful."

And so, a while later, they sat across from each other, sipping tea from her bone-china thrift-store finds.

Then he set down his teacup, and drew in a deep breath.

"I want to clear the air with you."

"It's not necessary."

"I think it is. I had two reasons to keep you hidden from my daughter, neither of which had anything to do with your perception of not being good enough. First of all, she seemed to think the publicity from my rescuing you would be good for the resort. I knew you did not want Maggie to find out what had happened, so it seemed wise to keep you and my daughter in separate worlds for the time being."

He had been protecting her, Faith thought.

"Secondly, Cassie is very type A. Whatever she does, she does with incredible focus, smarts and zeal. And the very morning of the day I pulled you out of Cobalt Lake, she had indicated that if I was ready to move on, she would be there to *help* me. You cannot even imagine my terror at the prospect."

Faith found herself giggling.

"When I told her I wasn't interested in the awkwardness of dating, she suggested a panic room. A panic room!"

Now, she was laughing.

Oh, how he had a way of doing this to her.

"I was really, really angry when you told me you thought I hadn't introduced you because I felt you weren't good enough. And when you told me about my mother, my sense of shock and betrayal were off the charts. I had been struggling with a feeling of not really knowing Cynthia, and when you said that, I felt like I didn't know you, either. That I was the worst man ever at reading the truth about women.

"What was the truth about you? Twice, you had let me fall in love with you."

Faith felt her heart stop.

"And twice you had abandoned me. But as a week went by, I realized the truth. There's usually something else underlying anger. And for me, it was fear. Not the let's-jump-off-the-edge-of-the-world kind of fear of zip-lining. A deeper fear. A soul fear of the uncertainties of life. Of how you can think everything is going just fine, and then have your whole world collapse from under you.

"And then I had the thought, if I'm feeling this way, how much worse is it for you? I lost my partner to an accident. But you lost yours in the most cruel way I can imagine. What I realized, Faith, was that it's not about being perceived as not good enough for you. It's the terror of saying yes, once again, to the very thing that tore your world away from you."

Somehow, she was getting up and crossing to him. She found herself, not beside him, but on his lap, her arms around his neck, her tears wetting the crisp white linen of his shirt.

To be *seen* so completely.

"I'm scared, too, Faith. Both of us have learned things do not always go according to our little human plans. But we should have also both learned that life is short. Each breath is precious. We are offered gifts beyond what we can possibly believe we deserve. I want to see where this is taking us.

"I want to explore the physical world with you, but also the world of the heart. I feel we can show each other, and our children, the resilience of the human spirit. We can give them the gift of hope. Yes, bad things happen. Unimaginable things.

"But we pick ourselves up and go on. Not necessarily stronger, but deeper somehow. More compassionate. More in touch. More connected. Not less, not pulling back from the world, but going forward into it, saying a loud, impossible-to-miss *yes*.

"To all of it. The good and the bad."

There, in the circle of Brad's arms, Faith came home. To herself, to her heart, to a world that required the bravery, her daughter had seen, and she had doubted.

Until this very moment.

When he whispered, "Let's embrace our second chance. Let's jump into the abyss, hand in hand. I want you to marry me," she said the only word that was left in her.

"Yes."

EPILOGUE

CASSANDRA STOPPED IN the lobby and took a look around. So much to do, and so little time to do it in. Normally, she probably would have taken out her phone and made a few quick notes.

But the truth was, she was a little disoriented.

She had just met her father's girlfriend.

Soon to be more than his girlfriend, if the looks Brad and Faith had been exchanging had been any indication.

Dad had sent his company jet to get Faith specifically for them to meet. The meeting had been so touchingly important to him.

Cassandra had thought it might be awkward to meet Faith. The truth? She was just a tiny bit miffed that her dad had managed his own romance without a single bit of input from her.

From the anecdotes around the table tonight, it sounded as if her dad had not only done it without her, but had also absolutely dazzled his new love.

Well, not really his new love. His old love. His high-school sweetheart.

It had been apparent to Cassandra almost as soon as her dad had taken her for that walk around the lake and told her about Faith, that some sort of destiny was at play here. It was powerful that fate had brought them together on the lake, coupled with the odd fact that the dog she had rescued had born the same name as Faith's late husband.

But now, seeing them together, it was so much more than that. Her father and Faith *fit* in some remarkable way.

Even if Faith had not passed her the cookie recipe, she would have recognized her as the woman baking cookies in Wolf's Song. She didn't even want to think of what they had been doing together in there, besides baking cookies!

Still, she could not have conjured someone better for her dad.

Faith radiated a kind of wholesome goodness. She was the type who made cookies, and she had mentioned she was making a donkey costume for one of her granddaughter's Christmas plays. How adorable was that?

There was a sense of family and sturdy values around Faith, and Cassandra found herself loving the fact that Faith made it so apparent she was going to be welcomed into that thing, as an only child, she had always missed. A brother, a sister, nieces!

A sense of home.

But along with that wholesomeness, that sense of family, there was a kind of quiet strength about Faith. It was the strength of someone who had known suffering and loss as surely as Cassandra and her father had, and decided it was worth it to love again, even if it hurt.

This was the part Cassandra didn't really like: the looks that had flashed between Faith and her dad, the way their hands had intertwined, and their shoulders touched, had filled her with the strangest sensation.

Added to that was how alive her dad had looked. Cassandra wouldn't have even guessed something was missing from his life, until she saw how different he was now that it was there.

It. Love, of course, so evident, shimmering in the air between Faith and Brad like fresh snowflakes twinkling silver in moonlight.

And that strange sensation it had made her feel?

She didn't even want to admit what it was.

Not with Rayce Ryan, her own high-school crush, about to arrive here as their newest ski instructor.

It wasn't quite the same. She hadn't been his sweetheart. Ha. She hadn't even been on his radar. And yet, being near him, catching a glimpse of him in a hallway, had always made her heart race and her color deepen embarrassingly.

And then that one night, their final dance ever, as high-school students, it felt as if he had awakened to her.

Seen her.

And for one astonishing moment in time, she had felt as alive as her dad had looked tonight.

And then Rayce Ryan had wanted to kiss her.

And she had run away!

And, of course, in the years that followed, like everyone else in Whistler, she had followed his racing career with avid interest.

But had anyone else experienced that frightening sense of longing that she had nursed ever since she had run away from his kiss?

Had anyone else wanted to coax the tenderness from that devil-may-care man who had challenged the rules of the universe—and gravity—until he had lost?

Impatiently, Cassandra shook off the residue of yearning that seemed to be clinging to her in the face of her father and Faith providing evidence of happily-ever-afters.

Of course, other people had entertained those thoughts about Rayce! He was gorgeous, he was a celebrity, he was a world-class athlete. He'd probably had women, prone to romantic fantasy, throwing themselves at him for close to a decade. Certainly, he had been the heartthrob of at least half the girls in high school, and maybe more!

Cassandra might have secretly indulged the childish notion of endless love when she was young and naive. But she was not that anymore.

She had a million things to do.

A million.

So why was she going back to her place, to look again at all those clippings of Rayce Ryan's career?

Just one more time.

She was just doing her due diligence on the new employee, she told herself, nothing more. Before she put them away.

And before Rayce arrived. A man like that—with all that energy, who had no patience with rules or the laws of order, who was endlessly and effortlessly charming—could turn a world upside down in one blink.

If you let him.

And Cassandra Daniels was not going to let him, not any more than she had let him kiss her all those years ago!

* * * * *

Look out for the next story in the
A White Christmas in Whistler duet

Their Midnight Mistletoe Kiss
by Michele Renae.

And if you enjoyed this story,
check out these other great reads
from Cara Colter:

Accidentally Engaged to the Billionaire
Winning Over the Brooding Billionaire
Hawaiian Nights with the Best Man

All available now!

THEIR MIDNIGHT
MISTLETOE KISS

MICHELE RENAE

MILLS & BOON

To everyone who has tasted snowflakes and
engaged in snowball fights filled with laughter.
And if you haven't—what are you waiting for?

CHAPTER ONE

CASSANDRA DANIELS SNAPPED photographs of the massive floral display in the Cobalt Lake Resort lobby. It had been delivered an hour earlier and it had taken two delivery men to carry in the heavy vase overflowing with white and red poinsettia, deep red roses, sprays of glittered baby's breath, and sprigs of wispy greens. A plush red velvet ribbon wove in and around the bouquet.

"Marvelous." She studied the few shots and then color-adjusted her favorite to post on the resort's social media feed. "Mom would be pleased."

In fact, her mother, Cynthia Daniels, would only employ her approving "marvelous" when something was worthy of praise. Be it decorations around the resort, a chef's special dinner or even the sound of boots crunching fresh-fallen snow on a peaceful Christmas morning.

With a heavy sigh, Cassandra's shoulders dropped. It had been two years since her mother's death. An avalanche while she was out skiing had taken her from this world much too early. Grief still teased at Cassandra and seemed to attack at the most unexpected moments. Tears in front of the guests? Never. She could hold them back until she retreated to her apartment. Yet the invisible emotional tears in her heart seemed never-ending.

Christmas had been her mom's favorite season. As the

resort manager, Cynthia Daniels had taken seriously the task of decorating for Christmas. Each year she employed a crew of temporary workers for a week to make it all come together. From the guest rooms to the lobby, the spa, the exterior and all through the outer areas, including the cozy wooden walkway that curled around the lake. Not a patch of property remained untouched by the festive spirit.

Last year Cassandra hadn't been able to summon the spirit necessary to put up more than some interior garlands and ribbons. Her heart had felt the lack of her mother's presence in those missing decorations. This year she was determined to pull herself up from the grief, rediscover her own joy and create a Christmas that would make her mother declare, "Marvelous."

The outdoor decorating had been completed by a local crew. The trees were kept strung with lights throughout the year, as well as the lake walk. Inside the resort everything sparkled, glimmered and danced with sugarplums, tidy presents, tiny snowmen and snow-sprinkled figurines, poinsettias, holly and the requisite mistletoe. The spicy aroma of cinnamon and nutmeg greeted guests in the lobby. Each guest room was subtly touched with Christmas. And the last of the ornaments were currently being placed on the twenty-eight-foot blue spruce that greeted guests as they entered the lobby.

Cassandra heard someone call her name. One of the night maids had begged to help with decorations because *Christmas was her jam*, and she'd stayed on this morning to help.

"It's finished," Kay announced with a gleeful clap and a Vanna White–like splay of her hand toward the massive tree.

"It looks amazing," Cassandra enthused.

She strolled toward the tree, her eyes moving up, down and around to take it in. She'd given exact instructions on how the decorations should be hung. The ribbons strung evenly, yet artfully. Tinsel used sparely. No two similar ornaments close together. The red glass ornaments hung equal distances apart…

Yes, she was aware of her need for perfection. But Cassandra never asked for more than was possible. And if she did notice something out of place she'd never call out an employee for what wasn't a mistake but rather a misplacement. Her dad had once let her in on the backroom talk that the employees thought she could be demanding but they didn't mind because she countered it with kindness and respect.

Kindness was never difficult. It should be a person's normal mode; that's what her mom had taught her. And if you put out a warm welcoming vibe, it would return to you in greater amounts.

With a touch to a handblown glass sleigh that she remembered her dad giving her a few Christmases earlier, she then trailed her fingers over the shimmery silver tinsel. Astringent pine filled her nostrils. The ever-present scent of burning cedar emanated from the fireplace opposite the tree. Nearby a trio of peppermint candles sweetened the air. Cap that with the cinnamon sticks hung here and there within the pine boughs. The delicious perfume epitomized Christmas.

Cassandra stood back, hands on her hips. The tree looked Instagram-worthy. More photos were necessary! Could this mean she was almost finished with decorating? Save a few smaller tasks she had on her list—

"Wait." Her eyes darted over the tree hung with ornaments the Daniels family had collected over the twenty-eight years her parents had been married. She didn't see it. The one ornament she'd requested Kay take special care in hanging front and center. "Kay?"

"Yes, Miss Daniels?"

She loved Kay like an aunt who tended to smile at her and then sneak up close to tuck in a stray tag or remove a bit of lint from her sweater. Just as fussy about some things as Cassandra could be.

"Where is the ornament I told you about? It was my mom's favorite ornament. I made it for her when I was eight."

"I didn't see the ornament you described. A wood star?"

"Yes, a star made from twigs I collected in the forest. I glued them together. In the center was a photo of me and my mom. It gets front and center placement every year. It had to have been with the other ornaments. Did you check?"

"The bins are over there." Kay pointed to a rolling cart stacked neatly with clear plastic storage bins. All of them empty. "The boys brought in all the bins labeled for Christmas yesterday evening. Should I send them back to the storage room to check for more?"

"Of course. Or no, I'll do it." They'd done their part. Besides, she was the best person to recognize the missing item.

"This is not right. It's… It can't be Christmas," she said, her voice wavering. The courage she'd summoned to step away from the grief over the loss of her mother began to falter. Her stomach clenched. "Not without that ornament."

She noticed someone near the wall behind the tree bend down. "No!"

The employee who held the light switch box connected to the tree froze, half bent over. He flicked Cassandra a wondering look.

"No light! Not until it's perfect," she said, a bit too loudly. She sucked in her lower lip.

"But shouldn't we check to see that they work?" the startled man asked of her.

Cassandra shook her head adamantly. "Not until the ornament is in place. I'll look for it. You can clean up and return the bins to the storage room. But no one turns on the lights until you get the go-ahead from me. Understand?"

The half dozen employees standing around muttered their agreement.

Cassandra gave her sweater hem a commanding tug and nodded. Christmas simply would not happen until that ornament held the place of honor on the tree.

Someone seemed very agitated about a missing ornament.

Rayce Ryan observed the commotion in the resort lobby. No one had seen him enter, though that was by choice, given he purposely stood near a frothy display of pine, ribbons and sparkly snowflakes; Christmas camouflage. The entire three-story open lobby was decorated to the nines with red, green, sparkles, snowflakes, wreathes—it even smelled like Christmas.

It had been a long time since he'd celebrated Christmas with family. Memories of cozy flannel pajamas, hot chocolates by the fire and opening presents leaped to his mind and gave him a rare genuine smile. He'd had a great childhood. But when he hit his teen years, life had changed in so many ways. Most of it good. The worst of it? He'd lost the only family he'd ever known.

Might he dream to someday have family again? And along with that, a real home?

Some dreams were impossible. Besides, he'd once had the sweet life. A guy had no right to complain. Even as broken as he was. Rayce had begun to make a new life for himself. To perhaps capture a bit of that sweet life again. And it started here at Cobalt Lake Resort.

Rayce veered his attention back to the lobby. Something

wasn't right. And it seemed to circle around the petite blonde wearing a white sweater and slacks. Her hair was silver-white as well. Visions of sugar pixies danced in his head. Er, no, it was plums or snow princesses—he always got his song lyrics confused.

With a swelling of his heart, he suddenly recognized the pale beauty. It had been years since he'd last seen her, but he'd thought of her often in the interim. That she seemed upset by a missing ornament didn't surprise him. She'd always been—what did they call it—type A? Or more appropriately *driven*, as he'd once labeled her.

"Driven and unobtainable," he muttered.

Another grin stretched his travel-weary jaw. His flight from Florida had been delayed, turbulent, noisy—two crying babies—and alcohol-free. It was mid-afternoon and he was ready for a nap. Or a beer. Probably both. As an Alpine ski racer, he'd once thrived on six hours of sleep and eighteen hours of training, skiing and partying. Now? Life had decided to shove him on his face. Hard. And he was still recovering.

After the snow princess commanded to those standing around the Christmas tree that there was to be no light, she then grabbed a clipboard and turned to look right at him. The recognition on her face was a mix of surprise, curiosity and...disappointment?

A look with which Rayce had become all too familiar. Had *everyone* watched his colossal crash when he'd lost an edge at top speed on the giant slalom at last year's winter Olympics? Well, if they hadn't, they'd likely seen memes of it on social media. His most immense failure endlessly repeated and looped, and even set to farcical music. All because he'd been betrayed by a woman he loved.

Stupid heart.

No, he couldn't be reading the snow princess's expression right. She was involved in taking care of business. Ever busy. Always on the go. Always out of reach.

He waved. She had to know he was due to arrive today. He'd dealt with her dad, Brad Daniels, throughout the hiring process. The man had picked him up from the airport. They had chatted about their hopes for good ski conditions and that Rayce would have to establish his own teaching schedule. Brad had dropped him off with apologies because he'd had to return to town to pick up some parts for one of their snow machines.

Left to himself to figure things out? Not an issue. Rayce was a self-starter and could pick up anything on the fly. This should be an easy gig. Thanks to far too many years of training, he was disciplined as hell. But while his body was in the program no matter the challenges presented, it was his heart that usually ended up bringing him down.

Thus, his reason for standing here in the Cobalt Lake Resort. He'd been hired for the season as their guest ski instructor. Like it or not.

He hadn't decided if he did like it or not. The experience would reacclimate him to the slopes. And, with hope, allow him to start over. To figure out his next step. To…be a normal person for once in his life. Not some guy who had devoted over fifteen years of his life to training, competing, media appearances and giving 200 percent, including blood and sweat. And most of those years without family to keep him grounded and remind him that he was loved.

Rayce missed his grandparents. Was there anyone out there who could show him the immense love and kindness Roger and Elaine Ryan had? If there was, he desperately wanted to swerve in their direction.

With a nod toward Cassandra, he grabbed his suitcase

and rolled it toward her, even as she started walking away from him while gesturing that he follow. He remembered her well. They'd attended the same high school in Whistler. He'd been a jock; she'd been all brains and academic achievement. She had been The One He Could Never Have.

He knew because he'd tried. And failed.

But did that mean he had to give up on the dream? No, Rayce Ryan never gave up—until the task injured him so badly he had no choice but to bow out.

Cassandra looked as beautiful as ever. Probably even prettier because she'd done something with her hair; it was snow-white instead of the sunny blonde she'd once been. Her mouth was soft pink. And the sway of her hair with each of her strides, the way it dusted her elbows...

Rayce knew his heartbeats weren't skipping from exertion right now.

"Rayce Ryan!" She paused and turned to shake his hand. "Dad must have just dropped you off?"

"He did, with instructions to take the place in and get comfortable. I know the slopes. I did spend every winter here my entire childhood."

"Right. How many times did my dad have to send out security to rein you in after midnight?"

"Too many to count." He chuckled. "You can't keep a ski bum off the powder."

"No, you can't. But I think you should claim professional over bum."

"Eh. I'll always be a bum, living for the fresh pow and carving my line through the corduroy."

She smiled but caught her mirth quickly and adjusted her mouth to a tight line. "We've set up security cameras now. Just a warning if you have any midnight black runs planned. It's for the safety of our guests. Is that your only baggage?"

"I left my skis and equipment in the side entry where your dad let me off."

"Perfect. You can claim an employee locker later; that should fit most of your gear. If you'll walk with me." She strolled past the reception desk and down a long hallway. What a sensual sway to those slender hips. The woman was obviously a skier. She knew how to move. "I'm a bit busy right now," she called over her shoulder.

Her wavy hair bounced, enticing him to catch up and consider touching it. Admiration from a distance had been about all he'd managed with Cassandra Daniels. Yet seeing her again after nearly ten years did inspire him to wonder if he could broach that distance. Walk alongside those swaying hips that reminded him of a skier's schuss down the slopes.

"I'll get you to your cabin and leave you to take the place in on your own," she continued. "You're familiar with the layout of the resort. Not much has changed since our teen days, though we did add another lift and the outdoor amenities have doubled. Do you have a schedule prepared for next week?"

"Not yet. Your dad said I could take a few days to familiarize myself with the slopes and figure out my schedule for private lessons."

The look she cast over her shoulder judged him nine ways up and down. Rayce was used to that look. From everyone. Often it was accompanied by expectation. Everyone demanded so much from an Olympic athlete.

And he had let everyone down.

With an assessing nod, she finally said, "In a few days I'll touch base with you and get your schedule entered into the database."

Cassandra pushed open an outer door and barely broke stride as she took off down a heated sidewalk that curved around the backside of a high snow-frosted hedgerow. It was only ten degrees today, but she didn't flinch from the chill. Rayce, on the other hand, had grown accustomed to the Florida weather over the past year he'd spent in recovery. Jet Skiing and scuba diving warmed a man's soul in ways a frigid Canadian winter never could.

"This is the employee route," she said over a shoulder. "You're welcome to walk through the guest area, but it's quicker and more efficient this way."

"I suspect efficiency is your superpower."

Another judging glance. Or was it curiosity this time?

The woman had changed little since high school. Still pretty, still put together when it came to clothing and makeup. Still holding her head a level above all others. Because she was smart, or because she felt entitled? Had to be the smarts. The Daniels family had owned this resort since he could remember and held a trusted place in the Whistler community.

As Rayce followed her sure stride, he couldn't resist wondering if he might wiggle under her skin, nudge the snow princess off her throne to see if there was a warm, caring individual underneath the stoicism.

What the heck, man? His heart was interfering far too early. *Keep your eyes off her hips.*

"I mean," he corrected his comment about her superpower, "from what I remember about our high school days. You were driven."

"And you were a star." She marched up half a dozen wood steps to a small cabin capped with an A-frame roof and a frosting of pristine snow. She tapped a digital code into the box by the door. "Here's your new home away from home. The code is 5489. That's your code for all entries around the resort. It's written down in the welcome materials inside."

A home away from home? Rayce hadn't labeled a domicile *home* in—it had been since he'd left his grandparents' house to travel the racing circuit. Since then, hotels, airports and the occasional couch had served as shelter. This cabin was merely another place to sleep and eat while life tried its hand at him.

Cassandra pulled open the door and he walked up. Before crossing the threshold, he stopped and when he tried to meet her gaze, she suddenly seemed nervous, avoiding eye contact and pushing her hair over one ear.

"Are you…okay with me working here?" he asked.

Her pale blue eyes darted between his, speculating, perhaps even making decisions that only the female species made; things he could never comprehend. Her soft pink lips parted in wonder. "Whyever wouldn't I be?"

He shrugged. Because he recalled her walking away from him once. It had been ten years ago. They had been teenagers. Surrounded by friends and anyone who mattered in their lives. Oddly, that moment still hurt his heart. Rejection proved a more brutal wound than failure could ever inflict.

"The Cobalt Lake Resort is excited to feature Rayce Ryan as our exclusive ski professional this season," she said, or rather recited like some kind of marketing promotion.

"But what about you?" he tried. "Are you…excited?"

"I… I'm pleased you're here?"

"Are you asking me or telling yourself?"

"I don't understand the question." She checked her watch. "I really hate to leave you, but I need to get back to the task at hand."

"Something about an ornament?" That didn't sound so pressing, but what did he know?

"Exactly."

She offered her hand to shake, which he did. Despite the

frigid temperature, her skin was warm, and it allowed him a few more seconds to stand in her atmosphere. Take in her beauty. And wonder about the thoughts that were bouncing around inside her head. What did she think of him? Dumb jock? Handsome not-so-strange stranger? Just another employee? Failed Olympian?

Her phone rang and she checked the screen.

"That's my dad. I'll catch up with you later, Mr. Ryan. You have free run of the resort. But do alert security to get an employee badge before you head off to a slope. The GPS in the badge constantly pings the security office, so if there's ever an accident…"

"Will do."

And then she was off, as quickly and efficiently as was possible, the phone pressed to her ear as she chatted with her dad. The moment was so—

Déjà vu struck Rayce with stunning precision. She'd run away from him during the high school dance. After he'd bent to kiss her. In that one precious moment when the world had stopped and his heart had leaped for the stars.

And he had fallen.

Running his fingers through his hair, he watched until Cassandra disappeared beyond the hedges.

"She's going to disturb your heart again, dude."

Or maybe, she'd never stopped.

CHAPTER TWO

"I KNOW, but that ornament means so much to me," Cassandra said to her dad, who had called from the parts supplier in town to see if she needed him to pick up anything. She'd mentioned that the tree was almost ready to be lit. Almost.

"Cassie, the tree is the big welcome to the resort. We have to turn on the lights."

"Just let me find the ornament first. Please? It won't take long. Give me a few days to comb through the resort?"

His sigh reminded her that they'd been through a lot these past few years. He'd been there with an arm around her shoulder and a kiss to the top of her head whenever she'd felt her lower lip wobbling and the memory of her mother emerge. He had gone through the same grief but remarkably had recently been able to welcome his high school girlfriend, Faith, back into his life after thirty years apart. They'd just announced their engagement.

"I'll give you a week," he said. "But that's far too long to allow the tree to sit there dark."

"I promise I'll find it sooner." And now to change the subject… "Can you pick up some of those monster cinnamon rolls from the bakery for me? I know you're going to make a stop there."

"I do love those cinnamon rolls." Despite the Daniels family's love for health and fitness, they were a favorite treat. Who could resist that gooey, sweet cream cheese frosting? "Oh, did you run into Rayce Ryan?"

"Yes, I gave him a quick lay of the land and showed him to his cabin."

"Take care of him, Cassie. He's going to attract new business as our resident ski professional. And the guy's a looker, eh?"

"Oh, Dad, I think I hear a cinnamon roll calling for you. Talk to you later. Bye."

She clicked off and rolled her eyes. A looker? Why on earth would her dad imply she might find Rayce attractive? On the other hand, her dad did have a tendency to tease whenever she'd dated. He thought his jokes were much funnier than they really were.

Well. Rayce Ryan *was* all kinds of sexy.

She opened the back door used by employees and, starting toward the main areas, picked up her rounds that had been interrupted by the missing ornament debacle: ensuring all decorations were perfect.

It had been ten years since Cassandra had seen Rayce in person. Sure, she'd seen him on the news. The bar in the resort always had at least one of the TVs streaming the sports networks and especially focused on winter sports. Over the past decade, Rayce's face had been everywhere. The golden boy. The skiing wunderkind. The Olympic gold hopeful.

The man who fell.

On Rayce's first trip down the giant slalom at the Olympics last year, something had distracted him and he'd crashed. Hard. The viewing public had watched as he'd been carted off on a stretcher, only to surface a few days later to announce that his injuries had been devastating. He may ski again, but never professionally.

Cassandra recalled how her heart had dropped as she'd

watched that interview. Tears had even rolled down her cheeks. To have trained and worked so hard for something and then to have it torn away in literal seconds. It had to have destroyed Rayce in ways she couldn't even imagine.

When her dad had suggested they hire Rayce as their seasonal ski professional, she'd thought it an interesting idea, but hadn't believed it would come to fruition. Was he even ski-ready? Did he want to continue in the sport? Even if only as an instructor? And really, would taking a teaching job fulfill him in the manner that Alpine ski racing had? It could only be a step down for the man who'd once reigned as a local sports hero, and she didn't have to wonder how occupying that lower step might affect his ego. *Cocky, charming* and *confident* were the keywords the media often used to label him.

As well, she hadn't said anything to her dad about Rayce having been The Boy She Could Never Have. All through high school she'd been entranced by him. Every girl with eyes and a gushy swooning heart had been captivated by his charming manner. He'd been a jock, a confident cute guy who knew all the girls wanted him and who had used that to his advantage. Rayce must have dated half her senior class at Whistler Secondary.

But he'd never given Cassandra a glance.

Until the Last Dance the night before graduation. When Rayce had walked across the gymnasium floor and asked her to dance, her friend Beth had literally shoved Cassandra forward. She'd been too stunned, utterly at a loss for words. The Boy She Could Never Have wanted to dance with *her*? Following the momentum of that shove, she had moved across the dance floor under the dazzling disco ball as if under a spell. Dancing with the dreamy guy! Hand in hand! Face-to-face!

Yet when he'd bowed his head to kiss her, warning bells had clanged. And she had made a run for it.

Cassandra regretted not accepting that kiss. Because she had always wondered: *what if?*

And she still did. Could they have been a thing? Might the kiss have led to dating and something more? At the time, she hadn't been aware of his plans to move. Rayce had left Whistler right after graduation to devote his life to skiing and travel the Alpine ski racing circuit, so it could have never become serious. But if she were honest with herself, over the years she'd never chased away the fantasies of *what could have been.*

Are you excited I'm here?

Yes, she was. But she'd had the presence of mind not to feed his ego.

Shaking her head and smirking, she shook away her silly thoughts and redirected her attention to the decoration hung on the wall just outside the lobby. There were twelve identical arrangements of blue spruce wreath and red velvet ribbon nestled with green paper presents throughout the resort. This one needed a little nudge to the left…

"Hey!"

Cassandra startled at the deep male voice that, after her initial surprise, settled into her skin as if a welcome burst of sunshine warming the crest of an icy summit.

"Sorry, didn't mean to startle you." Rayce looked over the arrangement, his summer sky eyes bright with enthusiasm. He twisted one of the tiny presents to the left, then nodded. "Perfect."

Cassandra adjusted the present back to the correct position it had been in. "Did you find the cabin to your liking?"

"Yes. I appreciate that I can live on-site for this gig. It's cozy. And the tiny fridge will store my protein drinks and veggies." He tapped the present, tilting it off-center.

Cassandra moved the present again, and this time held her hand over it. "You have access to our chef and the cafeteria. All included in your salary. Feel free to use it anytime it's open." She swatted at his hand as he moved toward the present again. "Don't touch!"

He mocked affront and then chuckled. A laugh capable of making her lose her train of thought. "Did you find the ornament?"

Ornament? Uh… Don't think about his laugh!

"Not yet." And now she had a deadline thanks to her dad. "I'm headed to the supply room now to go over it with a fine-tooth comb."

He hooked his thumbs in his jeans' front pockets. "I'll go along with you."

"What?"

"I'm offering my services, fair lady. The wind has picked up so I'm putting off my survey of the slopes until tomorrow. And lame excuses aside, I'm whipped from today's travel. Two airports with long layovers and screaming babies. I'm good at finding stuff. I once found a snowboarder buried under four feet of snow in the middle of a blizzard."

Cassandra swallowed. The image of a body buried under snow arrested all thoughts about making things perfect, replacing it with a hard press against her heart.

The Whistler ski resorts had their occasional accidents. With the Pacific Ocean so close the weather was unpredictable. Blizzards and avalanches were a part of the deal. She'd grown up with a healthy understanding of safe skiing conditions and when to give Mother Nature a wide berth.

"Cassandra?" He bent to search her gaze.

She didn't want to explain how his casual mention of

finding the buried snowboarder affected her. And she had promised herself she'd move beyond the grief this holiday season. Which couldn't begin without that ornament.

"Sure." She nodded. An inhale drew in courage. "I'll accept your offer to help. Come along with me."

"Any day, all the time," he sang as she sailed down the hallway and turned to take a stairway to the lower level where the storage room was located. "So how's life been treating you since high school, Cassandra?"

Descending a few metal stairs, they landed in the basement, and she flicked on the lights. The main room was neatly ordered with storage labels placed high on the walls to designate different sections. Her mother's doing. Everything was neat as a pin.

"Life is fine, as always," she responded. Fine. But not marvelous. Yet.

With a regretful wince, she veered toward the interior decorations. All the plastic bins that had held the Christmas decorations were placed back on the shelves. Some had a few items sitting inside—probably broken ornaments—so she pulled one down and opened the cover. "You?"

"Well, you know, took a little spill recently. Turned my life upside down. Now I'm trying to get back into fighting form."

Nothing but a cracked red glass ornament inside this one. She replaced the plastic bin and pulled down another next to one Rayce tugged out. "Fighting form? Do you intend to train again? For more competition?"

He'd only signed on as the resort's guest instructor for the season. And her dad had thought that perfect. See how he worked out. Then they could decide whether to extend Rayce's contract. Cassandra had thought his injuries had been so serious he wasn't able to ski competitively again.

The media had reported he'd gone through numerous surgeries to repair broken bones, torn muscles, followed with intense rehabilitation. Though she noticed no outward signs of damage, no limp or painful movement.

"I'm always training," he said. "Docs tell me I'll never be able to achieve the level I was at, but when someone tells me no…"

She caught his wink. It lifted a gasp at the back of her throat. And something warm did a little spin in her core. The man wielded a useful charm with that wink. And he was very aware of it, she felt sure.

"This job is my introduction back to the slopes. A way for me to test my body, see if it's willing and able to fight back to competition form. I have to give it a go. Prove to myself that it's possible."

"It's good to know you have recovered."

"Recovery is a state of mind. Or so my physical therapist tells me." He rapped the cover of the container. "What am I looking for?"

Reining in the rise of desire his wink had summoned, Cassandra focused on the task. "Star-shaped ornament made from tree branches. It has a photo of me and my mom in it."

With a nod, he checked the bin, then placed it back on the shelf. There were dozens of the containers, which they methodically worked through.

"So you're the manager of the resort," he said as he worked. "I always knew you'd accomplish something great."

"You did?" Which meant…he'd thought about her achieving that greatness? Interesting. "You never gave me a glance in school. I find it hard to believe you had taken a moment to consider my future."

He turned his back to lean against the plastic containers and crossed his ankles. A soft gray sweater stretched across his noticeably hard pecs and abs. Once she'd stared at his blue eyes in a magazine spread and decided to call his iris color *caught* because any woman who peered into his summery blues long enough would surely be so.

Rein it in, Cassandra!

"I thought about you a lot, Cassandra. Watched you, too."

"Seriously? Sounds a little creepy to me."

But really? He'd watched her? No. Impossible. It had been her who had slid the sly glances his way as they'd passed in the hallways, or who had always taken the route from math class to science by the gymnasium so she could peer through the glass doors and catch a glimpse of him spiking a volleyball or netting a basketball. He'd played all sports when not training for the slopes.

"Not like stalker watching you," he said. "But every time you passed me in the hall? I gave myself whiplash."

She laughed, then caught herself. How to handle such a revelation? Of course, it meant nothing now. If only she had known ten years ago that they'd been secretly exchanging glances. Might her fantasies have come to fruition?

"You don't believe me?" He reached for the highest bin, which was filled with ornaments, and set it down for her. He bent beside it and watched as she sorted through the damaged and faded pieces.

With his proximity, she inhaled. He smelled subtly of cedar, but more so of pine and an icy winter day. Which was about the best scent ever.

"You're hard to not notice, Cassandra. You were smart. Pretty. Still are. But your hair has changed, and I like it. Very snow princess."

She paused in her sorting. After high school she'd decided to brighten her natural blonde hair, and now she regularly went to the salon to touch up the few places where some strands of gold fought to be seen. She liked the platinum look. It suited her. Snow princess? She'd never thought of it like that, but she did have some repressed need to *let it go*.

Or at the very least, get on with life and stop allowing memories of her mom to bring her down. This Christmas would be filled with joy and happiness. If it killed her.

"What'd I say?" He tilted his head wonderingly.

The man's blue irises were edged with black. Stunningly sexy. Add to that his stubble and messily cropped hair that looked as if Christmas elves had run wild through it, and he was everything and more. There was a reason why all the sports magazines had featured him on their covers. Why major sports products had paid him millions in sponsorships. And one of the largest cologne manufacturers had tagged him to hock their product. Women melted when Rayce Ryan looked at them.

Cassandra was not immune to such melting. Every part of her felt warm and loose. *Caught*. If he were to lean closer…

"I think I've lost you." He thunked her forehead with a finger. "You in there, Snow Princess?"

The rude touch prompted her to lean away. "Don't do that. I was just thinking."

"Yeah? I know, you're thinking about that night we danced, aren't you?" His voice lowered to a husky baritone, which teased at her inhibitions. "I still think about that dance once in a while, too."

So did she. And yet. She was an independent, capable woman, and certainly not prone to romantic delusions. "Why? That was ten years ago. We were in high school. We've grown up now, Rayce. We've moved on. We've…"

So why was she making a big issue about him asking now? Did she still have a thing for Rayce Ryan?

Of course you do, and don't deny it!

And they were not delusions. Romance was…something she hadn't taken time for in years. And she felt the ache of that lacking connection and emotion as strongly as she grieved for her mother. Though certainly she didn't have the time or heart space for a romantic liaison right now.

"I wish I'd had the courage to ask you out," he said. "But you occupied an echelon I could never manage to reach no matter how high I jumped." He shrugged. "Guess it served me right that you wouldn't kiss me."

A delicate glass ornament clinked against another and Cassandra shoved the container aside, standing. She'd analyzed that unclaimed kiss in the days following the dance.

"I couldn't kiss you," she explained. "Did you expect I'd put on a show for the whole class? We were standing in the middle of the dance floor. Everyone was watching. I…" She stepped away from the bin and wandered toward the door.

And really? He'd left town but days later. She would have been left with a kiss and dashed hopes for something more. She'd made the right decision. At the time. She did not live in the past and would not respond to the regret that rose with memory.

Before leaving, she said, "I wanted my first kiss to be special. I didn't think it meant anything to you at the time." She made a show of checking her watch. "I need to be somewhere. Meeting. I'll catch you later."

She fled. Just as she had fled the dance floor ten years ago. And it felt as silly and heart-wrenching now as it had then. She didn't want to run away from Rayce. She wanted to lean in closer. Inhale his subtle cologne. Savor his body heat. Feel his muscles meld against her body.

Kiss him.

Like she'd dreamed of doing for years.

* * *

Her reason for running away from his kiss had been because she'd wanted it to be special? To not be a performance before their entire class?

Standing atop a sunlit slope on his second day at the resort, Rayce's smile beamed brighter than the sun. If he'd understood Cassandra correctly, she *would* have kissed him if the conditions had been right. Which meant she hadn't fled his kiss because she hadn't liked him or because he'd somehow offended her. She had simply required the right moment.

Who would have thought? Since that night of the dance, Rayce had carried her rejection in the back of his heart, and it had often peeked out when at a party and he'd wanted to approach a woman. Would she like him? Would she want to kiss him? Or would she run away, leaving him standing there, the laughingstock of all those around?

Despite those anxieties, he had dated a handful of women over the years. But none of those entanglements had ever been so serious that his heart had relaxed enough to allow in contentment. Those women had been friends, lovers. A few weeks of excitement and fun between training camp and traveling from country to country. But dating seriously while he'd been on the racing circuit? Not easy. Except for that one time that had resulted in the ultimate betrayal.

Never date a team member, his coach had often advised. But had Rayce listened to that stern warning?

"Stupid heart," he muttered.

Now he was encouraged to learn that the rejection hadn't been because Cassandra hadn't liked him. Could he possibly find that moment with her once again? The perfect moment that would allow her to kiss him without an audience or the feeling of putting on a show.

He liked to make goals and exceed them. But this felt like more than a goal. It was...a quest! For a snow princess?

"Yes!" With a deciding nod, he pushed off down the slope.

His skis glided through the fresh powder. His plan this morning was to take things in, assess the runs he hadn't skied for years. There were hundreds spread across two mountains and various ski resorts. He'd take it slow and steady and focus on those closest to the Cobalt Lake Resort. He wasn't going to admit it to a soul, but a healthy fear made him cautious. One wrong move and the scarred muscles in his back would scream with pain. Not to mention his wonky leg.

The finest doctors had put him back together after his crash, but medical miracles weren't always possible. And while the surgery on his hip had been successful, the pain associated with the surgical scarring could quickly go from barely there to excruciating, shooting up and down his spine. It made him too cautious, fearful even, and that was never a good thing when racing down the slopes.

Rayce Ryan was broken. Yet admitting that to himself felt defeatist. Like giving up. Had the doctors been right? Would he never again achieve competition form? Was he really out of the game for good?

He knew those answers. But his heart was playing stubborn and didn't want to accept that his future may look exactly as it did right now. Playing the role of ski instructor at a swanky resort.

He'd not trained for more than half his life to teach others how to navigate the bunny hill, or even to give cocky young ski-racing wannabes tips on how to hold their balance and find the fall line. But here he was. Life had dropped the Cobalt Lake Resort in his lap.

Might he possibly put back together his broken pieces here? Teaching required he listen and give others suggestions and approval. Yet how to get that personal coaching for himself? Was there anyone left in this world to pat him on the back and offer him the reassurance and love he craved?

That he'd included love in his mad-making thoughts surprised him. Yet it was the truth. He'd been alone for the last year. Perhaps for much longer than that, when he considered that racing, while surrounded by millions of spectators, was an insular sport.

Rayce craved the emotional support he'd once received from his grandparents. And no, he'd never felt close enough to any of the women he'd dated to call it love. Rayce wanted a mixture of the approval and adulation racing had served him but with an even bigger portion of quiet acceptance. Maybe even respect.

And most certainly love.

Might he find that with Cassandra? She seemed to keep herself at a distance from him. There had even been a few moments when he thought she'd gotten lost in her thoughts—ah, shoot. He recalled his conversation with Brad on the way here. He had lost his wife, Cassandra's mom, two years ago in an avalanche. He'd mentioned Cassandra was still finding it hard to move forward, that grief was playing a real number on her.

And stupid Rayce had gone and said something about finding a person stuck in the snow after an avalanche.

"Idiot," he admonished himself.

Jabbing a ski pole into the snow, he shook his head. He might have already spoiled things with Cassandra, but that would never dissuade him from trying again and again.

CHAPTER THREE

THE NEXT DAY, while Cassandra waited for Kathy, the receptionist, to print up a copy of an invoice from a recent delivery, she adjusted the display of tiny resin snowmen featured at the check-in point. Five snowmen were seated around a fake fire warming their mittened stick hands. She couldn't remember if her mom had picked it up or it had been a gift from one of the guests. They were always receiving tokens and gifts from people who returned to Whistler year after year to spend their holidays here at the little boutique resort tucked between two larger establishments.

The Cobalt Lake Resort was a ski-in, ski-out that catered to an elite and moneyed clientele. They hosted many celebrity guests. Their security detail was top-notch, and Cassandra prided herself on the fact that not a single paparazzo had managed to invade their walls for a sneaky shot. They didn't close their doors to such individuals, but they did make it difficult to snag a room when certain high-profile celebrities were booked.

Rayce was considered a celebrity and she and her dad had discussed whether the hire would be wise. Certainly his presence would attract more guests, but for what reason? Merely to snap a shot with the famous skier? No, they'd decided Rayce would add another layer of polish to the resort's excellent reputation with his skills and easy charm. Fingers crossed, they would not be disappointed.

"What's up, Snow Princess?"

Cassandra jumped and one of the snowmen toppled. Was it the man's life purpose to sneak up on her?

"Must you do that?" she asked.

"I think I must. I like to shake things up. And you need to be shaken," he said with a huge helping of sly charm.

Shaken or caught in that beautiful blue gaze, she wondered. Feeling her jaw fall slack, Cassandra quickly noticed her swooning reaction and straightened.

Kathy, who stood over the printer, glanced over her shoulder at them. Cassandra did not miss the receptionist's bemused smile.

Rayce turned a snowman to face away from the fire. Cassandra turned it back to sit in line with his fellow snowmen.

"There's always one in the crowd that goes against the grain." He turned the snowman again. "Gotta have those sorts. They make life fun."

She curtly turned the snowman back. "Life requires a certain amount of order and..."

She almost said *control*. The need for order and perfection was naturally embedded in her DNA. Her mother had passed that gene on to her. And she would never *not* want to be like her mother.

"Talk to you later, Kathy," she said and resumed her morning route.

"I took a tour of the slopes." Rayce followed her through the lobby. The next stop was the spa to ensure they'd received the laundered towels and check that all the decorations were in perfect order. "Place looks great. You guys updated Lift Number Three. It's smooth. And a hot chocolate bar at the bottom of the Surf's Up run? Genius."

"We have three hot chocolate bars and a s'mores bar near the fireplace out on the patio. They are always busy."

"Your man, Eduardo, mixed me up a spicy cinnamon hot chocolate." He kissed his fingertips and followed with an, "Ahh…"

"You'll never get back to racing form if you indulge in those decadent treats."

"Eh. I'll work it off."

Out the corner of her eye she noticed him ease a palm down his thigh. The injured leg? She wanted to ask, but she also wanted to respect his privacy.

"I'm going to do a run-through of a private training session tomorrow," he said. "Work out my game plan before you unleash me on your guests."

"That sounds like a good idea."

"It does, right? But I need a guinea pig. Someone to role-play the guest. Can you spare anyone to fill the role of newbie for me?"

"I'm not sure. Tomorrow we're training some new serving staff. Most other positions will be running extended shifts as the holiday rushes in on us."

Rayce spun around in front of her and landed his palm against the spa door. His eyes slowly took her in from head to toe in a manner that touched every nerve ending she possessed. Tiny fires ignited at each point. For once Cassandra regretted that she always wore white. The warmth suffusing her skin—was she blushing?

"What about you?" he said with a waggle of his brow. A suggestive move. And not at all businesslike.

Must she draw a line about lusting after employees? The resort didn't have any fraternization rules. It seemed an unnecessary intrusion into a person's private life. But how to stop sexy thoughts of Rayce when his wink was engineered at a DNA level to make a woman blush?

"Me? Uh…" Surely there was an employee she could spare for a few hours?

"I know you're busy. You are always on the go," he added. "I was thinking of asking your dad. I probably should—"

"I'll do it." Her heart answered before her logical brain could stomp a foot down in protest. Because really? There was nothing whatsoever wrong with working with the man to ensure he had his game down right. The bonus would be that she'd have reassurance their instructor had been a worthy expense. "I can mark some free time into the afternoon."

"Awesome. Find me on the bunny hill tomorrow. You can play my newbie skier."

"I'll see you then."

"Not if I see you first." She caught his wink as he opened the spa door for her and gestured grandly that she enter. "On the slopes, Snow Princess. I can't wait."

The door closed behind her, and Cassandra stood there a moment in the steamy, humid atmosphere to register what had just happened. The man had seduced her into working with him. She wouldn't call it anything but. Trying to resist that sexy wink and his charming manner had been futile.

And yet. The practice session may be more than an employer assessing an employee. Especially if that wink were doing its job correctly. And yet…skiing. She hadn't been on skis since her mother's passing. And she wasn't sure she was ready for it yet. Would it seem rude if she canceled? No, she didn't want to cancel. And it wasn't as though it were a date. Just a friend helping a friend.

Oh, how she wanted to allow a man into her life. Thing was, she wasn't sure her heart was in the right place to handle romance when grief still managed to overwhelm her at the oddest of times.

Honestly? Cassandra Daniels was incapable of change.

On the other hand, spending more time with the exuberant and charming Rayce might inject a little joy into her life. And that was a necessity.

Cassandra lived in the family wing of the resort, whereas her dad lived in the family home in town. Occasionally she considered moving back into town, finding a nice cozy condo, but the job kept her busy and staying close to work was key.

Or that was the story she told herself. She was no busier than most resort managers really, and she could have managed time off and even a vacation if she'd wanted it. But without children of her own, or even a boyfriend, it had been easy enough to lose herself in the job. Owning a home equaled a settled heart to her. Only a dream.

Her top-floor apartment looked out over the tiny Cobalt Lake and consisted of a bedroom, a small kitchen, a living area with a balcony that she spent a lot of time on even in the winter months, thanks to the heater, and an office corner, where she now sat going over the day's to-do list. It was the morning of her practice lesson with Rayce. Concentrating on the list was difficult due to the nervous flutters in her stomach. Why had she agreed to a ski lesson? Of all things?

A quiet knock on the door was expected. And a welcome distraction from *other* distractions.

"Come in, Anita!"

The sous chef stopped in every morning at seven o'clock with a pot of thick creamy hot chocolate. Cassandra had never asked her to do so; it was simply a continuation of what Anita had done for her mother. After Cynthia's death, Anita had taken a few days off, then quietly returned to work. Cassandra still hadn't spoken to her about her mother's death. They knew they shared a mutual grief and that was enough.

"With a touch of peppermint today," Anita said as she set the tray beside Cassandra's elbow on her desk. They never chatted overmuch. In the mornings Anita was busy prepping the day's meals for hundreds of guests. She turned to leave, but at the door paused to say, "The surprise is not my fault."

With that, she quickly closed the door.

"Surprise?"

Cassandra twisted her mouth as she studied the tray. A white porcelain pot of hot chocolate and an upside-down cup. A serving of Chantilly cream always accompanied the drink, and a mint cake sat beside it on a small plate. That woman would fatten her up sooner rather than later with all her sugary offerings.

Turning the cup over Cassandra gave a start and almost dropped it but managed to catch the cool porcelain before it clinked against the plate. Sitting under the cup was a tiny resin snowman. The very snowman Rayce had wanted to turn against his fellow snowmen sitting around the fake fire.

"Seriously?"

Shaking her head, she plucked up the figurine. What did this mean? It had certainly come from Rayce. And the fact that he'd learned where, exactly, to place it, and who he needed to know to do so, must have taken some sleuthing.

Interesting. Did that mean he was pursuing her? Or just making fun?

Probably the latter. And yet he'd told her he'd noticed her in school. A lot.

Cassandra pressed the snowman against her heart. "I should have never run away from that kiss."

On the other hand she was a private person. Even as a

teenager she'd had the sense to be cautious. Had she kissed Rayce Ryan on the dance floor in front of their classmates, surely the gossip would have blazed. And in those situations it never ended well for the girl. And then with him leaving a few days later?

She'd made the right choice. At the time. But might the opportunity for a kiss again present itself?

"I wouldn't run away if it did."

With a nod, she set the snowman on the tray. Pouring the hot chocolate, she then topped it with a plop of Chantilly cream. It was a recipe from a famous Parisian restaurant that the resort paid to use exclusively. It was literally the reason some guests stayed; for the rich soul-hugging hot chocolate.

With a sip of the thick sweet concoction, she closed her eyes and remembered the first time her mom had told her about the Paris she dreamed about visiting, and how some-day they would visit together. They'd climb the stairs to the top of the Eiffel Tower, stroll through the city's many formal gardens and share a pot of hot chocolate, even if it was summer.

They'd never gotten a chance to go to Paris. Tickets had been purchased for a spring trip. The spring following that deadly winter two seasons ago.

With a sigh, Cassandra caught her chin in hand. She'd gifted those tickets to a friend and her new husband as a honeymoon trip because she hadn't been able to bear going alone or with anyone else. She was trying to honor her mother with the beautiful decorations this season, but every time she thought about Cynthia Daniels's bright smile and tendency to use the occasional French word because she thought it was chic her heart dropped.

"I miss you, Mom."

And no amount of decorations—no matter how perfect—would ever bring her back.

Her dad had fallen in love with Faith, his new fiancée, just a month ago. Brad Daniels was moving forward in life. And Faith had two children Cassandra's age. She was going to be a stepsister! And that felt exciting. Yet every so often, if she were honest with herself, she felt as though her dad were cheating on her mom.

Silly, really. Her mom and dad had been not so much a perfect couple as a perfect team. Yet Cassandra, being an astute twelve-year-old who learned a lot about relationships from social media—and who could add and figured out she had been conceived months *before* her parents' marriage—had asked her parents if they'd *had* to get married because of her. The explanation had been simple: on the same day as their engagement party they'd also found out they were pregnant. Best day ever! Since then Cassandra's life had been filled with love and happiness. Brad and Cynthia Daniels had shared twenty-eight years together. Happily.

Yet even knowing her mother for twenty-eight years, it had still been too short a time. How to move forward as her dad had? When Cassandra felt memories tugging at her, she tended to grow straighter, become more controlling. While her dad had tended to head out for a run to be by himself with his memories.

The stress of the past few years, of holding back her sadness, had begun to weigh on her. She'd exploded over a missing ornament. She should have never done that in front of the employees. And this silly little snowman didn't have to be facing a specific direction to look inviting and cute to the guests.

Always one that goes against the grain.

Like Rayce Ryan?

Yes, the man—an adrenaline junkie to the core—went against everything her heart agreed was safe. But why did she require safety? Why not enjoy a little fun with a guy who made her smile? It didn't have to become a relationship. She hadn't the room in her heart for that right now.

Cassandra sighed. "Not yet. But…"

Maybe sooner than she expected?

Rayce had joined Brad Daniels for an impromptu lunch. Meeting him as they'd turned to walk the same hallway, Daniels had invited him to try the new hot Cuban sandwich the chef had created. They currently stood in an alcove attached to the kitchen, which was stacked with cases of wine and a trolly loaded with fresh produce. The sandwich, spicy yet loaded with cool sweet slaw, had hit the spot.

"Ready to hit the slopes?" Brad asked.

"You bet. You've got some smooth runs. And the powder you're making on the Blackout run is nice and dry. Perfect conditions."

"How's it feel to get back out there?"

Rayce's back twinged but it wasn't from pain, rather expectation. He knew what Brad was implying. Are you capable? Am I paying for a wounded instructor who won't be able to give it 110 percent?

"I'm at ninety percent, Mr. Daniels. Honestly? I can't take the runs at top speed, and my balance sometimes goes out because…" The pain made him leery. No one was going to know that. And honestly? That 90 percent was closer to 80. "I've developed a workout routine. I'll be getting good use out of the weight room. I hope to live up to your expectations."

"Don't push too hard, Rayce. I don't have any expectations. Just give it what you've got and represent the resort with kindness and respect. The guests aren't expecting you to medal in their presence. Sharing your knowledge and demonstrating good skills is what they are looking for."

He fist-bumped Rayce, then nodded to the chef who had been lingering nearby for a few seconds.

"I have to give the chef my report on the sandwich. You good to go?"

"Thanks, I am. I've arranged a practice session later to work on my teaching skills."

"Sounds smart. I knew I hired the right man. Tell Cassandra I approve of the new menu item when you see her." He winked.

"I, uh, sure." How did he know Rayce was going to see her soon?

Before he could ask, Brad wandered into the kitchen and started chatting with the chef.

Rayce shrugged and made his way out the back of the kitchen and down a hallway that led him to an outer door. He stepped out into the crisp winter air. The sun was bright and after that conversation he felt weirdly bright himself.

The man didn't have expectations? Everyone had expectations of Rayce Ryan. He'd lived his entire life to achieve goals, meet expectations, then crush them all and soar beyond.

It felt unusual to hear someone say to just do what he could. Almost as if whatever effort he put in would be acceptable. And yet how to function without the approval of a job well done? A goal achieved? A time smashed by a tenth of a second?

This not-meeting-expectations was a new experience for Rayce. And navigating it was going to prove a challenge.

CHAPTER FOUR

IF A PICTURE were featured in the dictionary depicting *snow bunny*, then the vision walking toward Rayce would hold place on the page. Dressed in white snow pants and jacket, with a fuzzy pink hat topped by a big pink pom-pom, and spills of her snow-white hair falling out across her shoulders and back, Cassandra's pink lips drew his attention like a target. Each time he saw her, he felt like the high school jock who had zero chance with the smart girl all over again.

Of course Cassandra was hiding grief under that bright smile and carefree demeanor. During the interview, Brad had mentioned she hadn't hit the slopes since her mother had passed. That was crazy. But Rayce knew grief. It could level a person. He'd be cognizant of her feelings. But as well, he couldn't bear knowing she might never step into a pair of skis again. This could be good for both of them.

"I wasn't able to find an available employee," she said as she neared him, "so you're stuck with me."

She'd been trying to find a fill-in so she wouldn't have to work with him? Yikes.

"*Stuck* is the last word that comes to mind." He winced. Had he sounded too eager, too excited that he would get to spend time with her? Could she sense his growing warmth and the need to unzip his jacket—but he wouldn't do that, because what would he tell her? She was so beautiful. And she kept dashing her gaze from his like a gazelle dodging the hunter. Cute.

And yet she'd tried to find a replacement.

Chill, man. The woman isn't interested in you. Pay attention to your job.

"Feels like we're getting some snowfall soon," she commented. "Maybe it'll hold off until nightfall. I want the snow groomer to make a run over the slopes before then."

Rayce nodded in approval. "I do love a night storm. Especially when there's a full moon."

"Oh." Cassandra dropped her gaze and studied the snow. In fact he sensed from her body language she didn't want to be here right now. "Well, I don't think it'll be an all-out storm. Just some flakes."

Had he said something to upset her?

Keep it professional, idiot.

He did want to try out his instructing skills on a stand-in before the real thing happened, so he'd do his best to keep her smiling. "Should get enough to make guests happy campers come sunrise, eh?"

"Huh? Oh. Yes." She shook her head as if jogging something from her thoughts. "So. Here I am."

Oh, yes, she was. The one woman who seemed capable of throwing him off-balance with a mere look. Or a pause in her thoughts.

He had to focus.

"Okay, class!" He clapped his hands together, which lifted her chin, and earned him a small smile. Whew! "I understand you've never skied before, is that right?"

"Right," Cassandra answered astutely.

"Well then, we're going to spend a little time learning the basic maneuvers, ways to move and how to coordinate hands with feet before we even put on skis. It's all in the hips!"

He gave his hips a sway and that got a laugh from her, which made the pain that shot up his spine bearable. Just get through this, he coached inwardly. Don't let her see you fall.

"I knew you had a smile in there somewhere, Snow Princess. Show me your hip action. Let's go side to side and then in circles."

For the next twenty minutes he worked through basic motions that would allow someone new to the sport to get connected with their body and understand how certain movements would affect their placement on the snow. He kept it simple; if he sensed a skier was experienced, he would adjust his instructions accordingly.

Standing behind and near Cassandra was the best position to teach. And the occasional touch to her elbow to correct her arm position, or even to her shoulder to lower her line of balance thrilled him more than it probably should. It wasn't like he was touching her skin. But their intimacy teased at him. Her shiny hair beckoned for a nuzzle. And she smelled like flowers blooming under a crisp winter snow.

Keep it cool, he reminded. *Save the flirting for later, yeah? The quest for a kiss must be achieved.*

"Do you think that's helpful or a waste of time?" he asked when she laughed at another of his exaggerated hip swings.

"Very helpful. I see so many people stiffen up and try to prevent falls. If they were only taught the basics of body proprioception, they might not struggle so much. And we'd have less sprained wrist and ankle reports. Good call on the basics."

"That means a lot, coming from you."

"Oh, please, you're the Olympic athlete." She gave him a gentle punch to the bicep and he responded with mock outrage. "You know what you're doing."

"Sure, but I've never taught before. And was I kind? I

distinctly recall your dad using that word. Be kind to the guests."

"You are a mix of kind and sensual—er, I mean…" She twisted her mouth. "You're a natural, Rayce."

Sensual, eh? That had slipped out before she'd caught herself. *Interesting.* So maybe he was getting through to her in the manner he'd hoped for? Was it possible that her repeatedly asking him to readjust her stance with his hands to her hips had been not so much because she had no clue what to do, but rather because she'd wanted him to touch her?

"Good," he said around an inner grin of triumph. Wouldn't pay to get cocky while in practice mode.

Remain professional.

Was that even possible? "I hope my limp doesn't show too much. Wouldn't look good coming from someone who's supposed to be a master at the sport."

"I hadn't even noticed it!"

"Really?" Even if she had said that to be nice, it relieved a niggling self-conscious worry. "It only bugs me now and then."

"Will you tell me about the injuries you suffered? The press made it sound like you'd never walk again. Yet here you are, looking like you could do the giant slalom and the super G on the same day."

"On a good day? I might take that bet. On a not so good day, my entire left leg seizes up. I've got some pins and titanium rods here." He tapped his upper thigh. "And a plate that's still holding my femur together."

"Yikes. Can you feel all that hardware?"

"No, but I do get good Wi-Fi reception."

Her jaw dropped. Then she quirked a wondering brow.

"I'm teasing," he insisted. "But I had you fooled for a second there."

"Fair enough."

Man, she was gorgeous. And not like the ski bunnies he was used to hanging around and on him. There was something about Cassandra Daniels that set her apart from any woman he'd ever had eyes for. It went beyond her beauty. She was perceptive, listened and seemed genuinely interested in what he had to say. Yet she wouldn't agree with him for agreement's sake. The woman had a mind of her own and wasn't afraid to use it.

"Have you had physical therapy to help with the pain?" she asked. "What about medication?"

"Too much physical therapy. Spent a lot of time in a recovery unit. And then a rehabilitation house. I'm on my own now. Incorporating all that I've learned from physical therapy. I have some chronic pain from the hip surgery, which compromised my skeletal alignment. It's crazy. As for drugs, no way. I didn't want to take painkillers too long. So don't worry, I'll pass the resort's drug tests."

"We don't do that. And we wouldn't dream to do so. It's good to hear you're managing the injury. Just don't push it too hard. You've already shown the world what you are capable of."

"But did I?" Rayce stabbed the ski pole, which he'd been using to demonstrate balance, into the snow. "I crashed on my first jump out of the start house, Cassandra. That's hardly showing the world my stuff. It's a hell of a lot of failure if you ask me."

"Oh, come on, Rayce. Is that all you use to measure your success? How many World Cup Championships do you have?"

Two. And the World Cups were the sport's standard of excellence. Rayce had garnered the best and highest paying sponsorships from his World Cup wins. And by investing wisely, he had saved more than enough to live comfortably.

"The Olympics isn't the be-all and end-all," Cassandra said.

"Actually, it kind of is. If you can't medal in the big O, then you're nothing according to the media. Especially after your sponsors have invested so much in you. Millions, Cassandra. They certainly didn't get their money's worth from me."

"I guess I know that the energy drink dropped you."

"And the sportswear line. And the ski-gear line. And the protein drink that was going to be modeled after my own recipe."

"Yikes. I didn't know about those others. That's gotta be…"

"A mean slap in the face."

She sighed and nodded. "But you're not a failure, Rayce. Failing is not getting back up and moving forward. Failing is lying there and accepting it."

Her words sounded good. In theory. But. "Failure is not winning."

"Winning is everything?"

He blew out a breath. "Yes."

Winning used to be everything. But was it still? Of course it was.

And yet he knew that ultimate win was now out of his grasp. Much as he wanted to fool himself with training and therapy, the pain reminded him every morning that he could never go back to what he once had. No more World Cups. No more Olympics. He. Was. Broken.

"Whatever." He gestured dismissively. "I'll never come to terms with it. And I'll always pursue the next approving pat on the back. There's nothing anyone can say to change that. So!" He clapped his gloved hands together. "How about we strap on the skis and try the bunny hill?"

"Sure, but… Rayce, this probably doesn't mean much…" She lifted her eyes to meet his and he swallowed awkwardly. A certain truth glinted in her blue irises. It felt real, and familiar. *Comfortable*. "Whether or not you believe it, you have accomplished so much more than the average person. You don't need to prove anything to me, or my dad. We hired you—"

"Because everyone wants to train with Rayce Ryan. Don't deny it. And I get it. I am taking the paycheck."

"It's not all like that."

"But some of it is, right?"

She shrugged. His mood had soured since the conversation had switched to a focus on his weaknesses. And he didn't like to show that side to anyone, especially not a woman he was interested in.

And yet her father had said much the same. That Rayce didn't need to prove himself to him. He still didn't know how to process that declaration. But he'd have to learn if he wanted to glide toward the future instead of laying sprawled on the snow in the past.

"Skis," he said and handed her a pair.

He clicked into his own skis and waited as Cassandra set hers on the ground and took position with her boots placed on either side of them, ski poles in hand. She stared down at the skis for such a long time he wondered what she was thinking about. And then he knew. This was a test for her. Brad Daniels had said his daughter hadn't put on skis since her mother's death.

Due to an avalanche.

Was it too soon? Had his invitation been thoughtless?

"I can't do this." With a sudden jerk of the poles, she

stabbed them into the ground and stepped away from the skis. "I'm sorry. I…just can't."

She turned and walked off, her pace quickening to a jog.

Every bone in Rayce's body wanted to rush after her, but he'd felt something in her tone. A deep sadness. Tinged with fear. He knew that tone and that feeling. Man, did he know fear. He'd lost a part of himself during that Olympics' crash. He knew she had suffered a huge loss as well. It wasn't simply the lost ornament that was keeping her pinned to her grief; it was the memories of her mother, too.

He should go after her, make sure everything was okay. But the sadness in her voice reminded him so much of his own pain. A pain that had been with him far longer than since the accident. There were days he could barely deal with it himself. How could he help anyone else when he couldn't help himself?

Turning and stabbing his poles into the snow, he debated taking a run on the bunny hill. His leg didn't bother him today. Navigating the beginner hill would be like talking in his sleep: a no-brainer.

But.

Something compelled him to swing a look in the direction Cassandra had fled. Gathering the skis and poles, he put them away in the equipment shed, then went in search of Cassandra.

CHAPTER FIVE

THIRTY MINUTES AFTER she had fled the practice session with Rayce, Cassandra heard a quiet knock on her apartment door.

She swore softly and tugged the thick chenille blanket tighter about her shoulders. As soon as she'd gotten to her apartment, she'd kicked off her boots, shed her winter wear and plunged onto the couch. The tears that had been but a trickle had exploded and she'd engaged in a good sob session.

Now she sniffed softly and lifted her head to stare out at the sun falling behind the mountain. Her entire life had revolved around those mountains and the ski-bunny lifestyle. It had given her the greatest joy.

And it had devastated her family.

"Cassandra, I'm coming in," Rayce announced as he opened the unlocked door. He spied her sitting before the balcony doors. "No, don't get up. Is it all right that I'm here?"

Was it? She hadn't expected him to let himself in but asking him to leave felt rude. "Sure."

She nuzzled her chin into the blanket. No time to worry if she had red eyes or looked a mess. The man of her dreams carefully approached in the dimly lit room. Less than an hour and it would be completely dark outside. Still, the pale light seemed to outline his rugged jaw and even glint in one eye, softening him.

"I was worried about you," he said. He glanced around the room.

Everything was neat and in order. As it should be. All was well. Except her heart. Her grieving heart.

"Is it okay if I sit with you?"

Yes. No! She wasn't sure what she wanted right now. She'd never been one to share her emotions with others. And the only times she had, had been with her mom when they'd chatted over a hot chocolate. The Daniels family was not emotionally demonstrative.

But with Rayce's expression bordering on worried, she couldn't allow him to suffer.

She patted the couch beside her. "I'm sorry, I had a weird moment out there. Had to get away. I didn't want you to see me break down. And yet…" She shrugged and splayed her palms up in defeat. "Here you go. Cassandra Daniels. Undone."

"I'm sorry. I, uh… Your dad mentioned your mom's death during the interview. He also said you hadn't been on skis since then. So when I asked you to help me, well, I thought maybe if I could get you back on skis…" He sighed. "It was too soon. I shouldn't have pushed you."

She flashed a look at him. That he was so perceptive of her emotions startled her. It wasn't merely the light that had softened him; perhaps he did understand her. And it wasn't too soon, it was simply difficult. That he'd nudged her in an attempt to help meant a lot.

"I'm sorry, Cassandra. Losing a parent can be rough. Enough of a reason to need to get away when life zaps you with memory. Is that what it was out on the bunny hill?"

She sighed heavily and tugged up the blanket around

her neck like a protective piece of armor. "Mom and I were close. We shared clothes, spent weekends shopping and enjoying spa treatments. We were best friends. We were extremely type A and—fine, I admit it—controlling. But together we were a dream team. That's what dad always used to call us."

Rayce sat on the couch beside her, facing the balcony doors. Snow had begun to fall in thick goose down flakes. That she had allowed him in and shared something so personal with him startled her. She hoped he wouldn't overstep and delve too deeply into her pain. She didn't know how to open up completely.

Yet at the same time she was thankful he knew about her loss. His presence comforted her. She was glad he'd thought to check in on her.

"Your mom must have been beautiful," he said. "I mean, look at her daughter."

"She was gorgeous. Always dressed in gray and black. Very elegant, and looking like, well…if I'm the snow princess, she was the snow queen."

"I sit in the presence of royalty."

She chuffed. The man had lightened her mood by being himself. Letting down the blanket, she turned to face him, leaning her shoulder against the back of the couch.

"It was the skis," she confessed. "Standing there, looking down at them. The last time I skied was on a sunny afternoon with my mom."

He smoothed a hand over her knee. Patted it gently. But that he didn't try to offer condolences or empty sympathy meant so much. After the funeral many had come up to her and said *let me know if you need anything* or *call me if you need anything*. Really? Why couldn't they simply *do some-*

thing for her, without her having to put herself out there in her most vulnerable time and ask?

Rayce's silence shimmered as if gold. Like the best gift anyone could have offered regarding her loss. And she relaxed, settling into the couch.

"I'm not sure I'll ever be able to bring myself to put on skis again," she said quietly. "I... I see bad things when I even think about it."

"Bad things?" Now his gaze didn't so much catch her as offer her a soft place to fall.

She gave a deep exhaled breath laden with sadness. "My mom loved to ski at midnight. Under the full moon."

"Aw, Cassandra, I'm sorry. And I made that thoughtless comment about—I shouldn't have said anything."

He had said something about nighttime snowstorms. Which had been a catalyst to her mood swiftly changing. Yet she'd tried to remain light, not show him her angst, and paying attention to his teaching had helped some. There had even been a few moments of subtle flirtation she hadn't ignored.

"One night Mom went out alone." She spoke the words before her brain could hold her back from the confession. "She triggered an avalanche. It was hours before Dad realized she was missing. This was before we started using the GPS badges. Rescue crews worked through the night. We couldn't find her until the following morning." She buried her face in the blanket.

Her heart seized and her throat felt too narrow to breathe as her sobs renewed. She had cried often in those weeks following her mom's death. And every week after. Though the tears had lessened, the loss still felt the same in her heart. There was a hole now. In the shape of Cynthia Daniels. And nothing could fill that empty shape. Not even a silly ornament. That was still missing. The clock was ticking toward the turning on of the tree lights. She'd searched all the storage bins again, and the linen storage room. Would she ever find it?

Rayce gently squeezed her shoulder. Dare she ask him to wrap his arms around her? To hold her? It's all she had ever desired during those long winter nights following the funeral—to be held. Of course she and her dad had hugged, but he had been mired in his own grief. And initially neither of them had known how to interact with the other.

"Thank you for telling me that," he said quietly.

She wiped the tears from her cheek and braced her palm against the side of her head. "I hadn't expected such a visceral reaction to standing over the skis and looking down at them. Guess I know now that skiing is not in my future."

"It makes me sad to hear you say that," he said. "Skiing is such a joy, a passion, a way of life."

"I know." The sport affected a person not only physically, but also mentally. It provided health. Activity. Utter joy. To completely abandon it seemed unthinkable. Even Rayce, who had been damaged irreparably by the sport, had not given it up. "But I don't know how to be comfortable with it again."

"You don't have to put on the skis," he said. "Not yet."

She tilted her head, one eye revealed above the blanket. He brushed the hair from her lashes. That touch went a long way in broaching the soul-encompassing hug she desired. They were friends, but not yet close enough to ask so much from him. Just having him sit beside her calmed her worries.

"Someday you'll have to put them on," he said. "You can't run from it forever. Trust me. I know grief, Cassandra. It's a deep pain. But it softens over time. And I promise, when you're ready, I'll be there to hold your hand when you glide down the slope. I'm sure your mom would wish the same for you."

She'd never thought of it that way. Cynthia Daniels would never want to see her daughter in such emotional distress. So why had she done something so stupid as to go out on her own at midnight when she'd known the dangers and risks? Her selfishness had changed Cassandra's life forever.

"Is there anything I can get for you now?" he asked. "Some tea? A box of tissues?"

She smiled at his genuine concern. "I'm going to be okay."

"Good, because it hurts my heart to see you sad."

"I wouldn't want to be the cause of a man's wounded heart."

"I heal fast." He rubbed his thigh. "Some parts of me do, anyway. Hey, I was thinking about taking a walk around the lake once it's dark. Check out the lights. Do you want to join me?"

"I'm…"

"Not sure. I get it. I shouldn't intrude any longer. I know grief can be so personal." He stood and then picked up the blanket that had fallen to the floor with his movement. He tucked it on her lap. "I wanted to make sure you were okay."

Cassandra inhaled his delicious winter scent. It distracted her from her sadness. The man was handsome, talented *and* compassionate? There had to be something wrong with him—but what?

"I'll, uh…be at the path to the lake in an hour. If you want to join me, I'll see you then."

When he stood at the door she called, "The snowman under my teacup was evil!"

Rayce smiled a wicked yet sexy grin. "Yes, yes, it was. I did tell you I was here to shake things up."

"Mission accomplished."

"Don't give me any high scores yet. I'm just getting started. See you later, Snow Princess."

She was thankful for his quick exit. And while she should have asked for that hug, she felt the little she'd given him had been an opening into her soul. And that opening beamed out some light.

Spending time with Rayce made her less sad. And all he had done was listen to her. But he had said he knew about grief. Perhaps they were kindred spirits who could help one another?

She dared to think that could be possible.

CHAPTER SIX

AN HOUR LATER Cassandra bundled up for a walk in the chilly weather and headed outside. A sudden *meow* distracted her, and she caught a glimpse of that darn cat. The stray that had been scampering around the Cobalt Lake Resort grounds since summer. Snow-white, it was difficult to see against the snowy landscape and tended to surprise her. It was becoming a nuisance, stalking the birds who conglomerated at the various feeders and leaving tracks across the guests' snow angels. And she was pretty sure she'd found cat hairs on the cushions around the outdoor fireplace. But she had a resort to run so there was no time to consider pet patrol.

Wandering across the patio where the fireplace blazed and a few guests sipped hot chocolates before the amber flames, she felt drawn toward the interesting safety Rayce offered. When she arrived at the head of the wood-paved pathway that circled the small lake and sighted the handsome athlete, she could only smirk. He was doing it again!

"Seriously?" she announced as she approached Rayce.

The man adjusted the big red weatherproof bow attached to the wood railing. Dozens of the bows were posted along the pathway. Christmas lights were strung between them. The glow from the lights reflected off the glass ice pond in fairytale glimmers. Cassandra would never tire of the photos guests posted on social media along with comments that the lake walk was *magical* and *enchanting*. One couple had even gotten engaged on the covered dock at the halfway point around the lake.

"Now it's right," he said with a pat to the now-crooked bow.

Cassandra tilted the bow to the right. Perfect. Then, feeling the best way to win the argument was by distracting him, she started walking. "You like to disturb the norm!" she called back.

He joined her, their winter jackets brushing softly as their arms touched. "I like to push boundaries."

"I'm aware of that."

"Why is it you are so satisfied with normal?"

An interesting question. She did like to be challenged. Yet there was a certain safety in familiarity. "What's wrong with normal? You make it sound dirty. Taboo."

"Nope, you've got that wrong. All the taboo things I can think of are far from normal. And some involve whipped cream."

Cassandra's jaw dropped open as she met his grinning face. With a waggle of his eyebrows, she realized he'd done it again. He was tossing out zingers to see if he could get a rise out of her. Disturbing her norm. Inciting a tremor of desire.

"I love whipped cream," she volleyed, taking a bit of pride in the quick reply.

"Then you and I are going to get along just fine."

They reduced their walking pace to a stroll as the path curved and overhead the tree branches danced with colorful lights. Pinks, blues, greens and reds reflected in the snow, dusting the branches and shimmering across the glassy lake surface.

"This is incredible," he said. "It feels like a fancy light show yet cozy at the same time. And Christmas music?" A melody softly echoed through the speakers placed along the trail. "Love it!"

She pointed toward the center of the lake. "As soon as we get safe ice thickness, we'll open it for ice skating and pond hockey."

"Nice. I love an aggressive game of pond hockey."

"Yeah? We'll see how talented you are with the stick when we meet on the ice."

Rayce nodded in surprised approval. "I think you just challenged me, Miss Not So Normal."

"I suppose I did."

"So I take it you're not a puck bunny?"

"Please." Puck bunnies were over-styled fashion victims who fawned over professional hockey players and flirted their way into their beds and sometimes earned an expensive and sparkly gift. "I'd never be caught swooning over the players from the sidelines. I like to get into the action."

"I never would have guessed that of Miss Astute and Perfect."

"Don't call me that. And I'm not Miss Not So Normal, either."

"Sorry. But can I use Snow Princess? Pretty please?"

She made a show of thinking it over, then nodded. "If you must."

"Yes!" Rayce glanced over his shoulder. "But that ribbon…"

"Fine!" She skipped ahead and turned to face him as they walked. "I admit that I have perfectionist tendencies."

His swagger drew attention to his hips. Relaxed, easy. So sure of himself. "You like to control the world."

She performed an evil laugh and then pressed her pinkie finger to her lips. "Or perhaps just a small portion of British Columbia."

He laughed and jogged up to her, clasping her hand. "I love an evil plan. Now here's mine. Race you to the dock?"

"Doesn't sound very evil, but…" Dropping his hand, Cassandra took off. "I'm in!"

After a burst of energetic running, she arrived at the covered dock that had been built to showcase its Nordic design; it was made of clean pine, with traditional rosemaling along the rafters. Another couple leaving hand in hand nodded to her and she called to them to have a good night. That left the dock to Cassandra and Rayce.

Stepping up onto the cozy retreat beneath the glowing lights always lifted her mood. Spending time with Rayce seemed to do the same. Was it his teasing at her boundaries that felt so exhilarating? How odd. And yet she did enjoy inching closer to his idea of shaking things up. And she hadn't given a moment's thought to—no, she'd cried enough earlier. Time to take a vacation from work and her grief, if only for the evening.

With a leap over the two steps, Rayce landed on the dock floor with arms splayed triumphantly. "He makes it in a single bound!"

"I'm very impressed. I noticed your limp earlier and I thought you were in pain. Everything all right now?"

"Eh, there's some muscle twinges, but I'm still standing. And performing that stupid leap may seem silly but considering I couldn't even walk a year ago? I'm taking it as a win."

"You can have it."

"Thanks. That'll go a long way when I know I'll be suffering in the morning."

"Oh, Rayce, then why do you do such things?"

"How can I not? I'm stuck with an injured leg and tweaky back while all I want to do is push my body to the limits. If I keep pushing maybe my leg will take the hint and get over this stupid pain."

"Either that, or you'll cause more damage. Sorry. I shouldn't be a naysayer. What do your doctors say?"

"That I need to take it easy."

"Even the sports doctors? The ones who work with the Olympic team?"

He shrugged. "I lost access to them a month after being in the hospital."

"Really? That hardly seems fair."

"I don't want to talk about the politics of it all. I've survived and that's what matters."

"Fair enough." She tapped one of the hanging icicle lights. "So what do you think?"

"This place is cool." He looked out over the pond. Red and green lights dazzled the circumference, and a fancy laser light painted a show of Santa's sleigh being pulled by reindeer across the iced surface. "Promise you'll include *The Little Drummer Boy* on the playlist for me?"

"Oh?" She assessed him. His eyes sparkled in the glow of the white icicle lights. And that hair…always tousled and so tempting. She'd like to run her fingers through it. Tug him closer and— "Is that your favorite Christmas song?"

"It is. I like the story of the little boy playing his simple drum for the newborn Christ. It…" He shrugged. "Gets me right here every time." He thumped his chest. "But don't tell anyone Rayce Ryan has a soft spot."

She crossed a finger over her heart. "Promise."

"I suspect you are an excellent secret keeper."

"The best. But if that's the only secret you've got…?"

"Eh, I have plenty. The press exposed most, though.

Crazy how the paparazzi became so interested in a regular guy from a small town, isn't it? And yet I make one monumental mistake, and they've ghosted me."

Cassandra hadn't realized it but, yes, about a month after the Olympics snafu, all news of Rayce Ryan had fallen off the radar. What fickle allies the press could be. And the public, for that matter.

"Does that bother you? Not getting the attention anymore?"

He leaned against the railing, cocking his head to the side. Their breaths condensed before them in tiny puffs. "I am a guy who likes to put himself out there, be seen, make connections, talk to anyone willing to talk to me. The media fed that need. It's the part where my coach ghosted me that really cuts."

"Your coach? Seriously? You mean you haven't talked to him since...?"

"Not since about a week after the accident. He stopped into the hospital. Tossed a wilted bunch of flowers at the end of my bed and proceeded to tell me how disappointed in me he was."

"Oh, Rayce, I'm so sorry."

"Eh." He shrugged. "I deserved it. The man invested a lot of time and money in my training. And look what he got."

"He got a double World Cup champion is what he got. Not to mention you were rated number seven overall in Alpine racers. That's an accomplishment."

He sighed and scruffed his fingers through the hair she wanted to feel against her skin. "I know, but that didn't seem to matter much in that moment when he stood in the doorway to my hospital room. Coach had been there for me since I was a teen. He wasn't exactly a replacement for my grandfather, but he was protective and stood up for me and had my back. Until I crashed. He blamed me for making a stupid mistake. And he was right on the mark."

"Rayce! How could he have possibly blamed you for that? It was an accident."

His heavy sigh spoke volumes. "My mind wasn't in the game. I forgot that my goal was to please others. And now? Who will approve? Cheer me on?"

"You need the cheers but without the flashes," she stated.

"Maybe? But I'm not here to talk about my screwups," he said. "I thought we were talking about our social skills?" He slapped his chest. "Super extroverted. Complete opposite of you."

Cassandra conceded to his sudden need to change the subject. Though she wanted to know more, to delve deep into his soul and—really? She wanted to go soul-deep with the man? What had happened to just friends?

That charming smile and easy demeanor is what happened. Rayce defined irresistible. And that made her want to learn as much about him as she could. And might that abandoned kiss be claimed?

"I'm not an utter introvert," she said. "I can turn on the smile for our guests and clients."

"But I suspect you're happier when you get some downtime. You go all day, make the world perfect, and then…?"

That he pinned her so easily made her wonder if it was as obvious to everyone else. Of course she'd observed as much about her mom. When Cynthia Daniels turned in for the evening, she shut down. Soak in a hot tub, sip some tea and forward all work emails to the *save* file. That had also been her time to spend with family. And while her mother had worked sixty-hour weeks, she had still found time for Cassandra, and made that time special.

But Cassandra had no one to give her attention to so

pushing her workweek to seventy hours had been a natural progression. A social life? What even was that?

"After the world has been perfected," she said to Rayce's question, "I shelter in my room and have a cup of tea or hot cocoa and relax."

"Ah, so you are capable of relaxing."

"Oh, come on! I'm relaxed right now." She waggled her shoulders, letting her hands flop. The tension that usually strafed the back of her neck was, surprisingly, absent. "See?"

"Well, and there are no people watching right now." He made a show of casting his glance around them in a one-eighty.

Cassandra glanced around the pathway that circled the pond. The night glistened like a fairyland. The atmosphere around them encouraged her to be present, completely. To accept what life wanted to give her. "No, there aren't. But what—?"

"I did bring this." From his jacket pocket Rayce tugged out a plastic piece of greenery with white berries—mistletoe.

"Where did you get that?" She made a grab for it, but he easily dodged her. "You broke it off from some display—"

She swallowed back her protest as he held it high. Above and between the two of them. The unspoken question was so loud: *do you dare?*

"Don't run away this time." His voice was laced with a quiet request to meet his heart halfway. A heart that had been battered, beaten and put through the ringer.

In his eyes shimmered a softness. Gone was the cocky, confident skier who had once held the world's attention and who had thrilled the crowds with his swift and agile performances. The part of him that called out to her now felt almost innocent. Lost.

Similar to how she felt when grief overwhelmed her.

Stepping up to him, she eyed the piece of green plastic that dangled a few white berries. Suddenly they stood in the center of the high school gymnasium, disco lights flashing across their faces. Hands sweating. Heartbeats thundering.

But this time, they stood alone. No audience to dissuade her hopeful fantasy.

Cassandra tilted onto her tiptoes and—a snarling *meow* parted them both. Rayce spat out something about "a critter" and dodged to the left.

Cassandra now saw the white cat had gotten tangled in the Christmas lights strung along the pathway. It struggled manically. Crouching, Rayce approached the creature carefully.

From down the path some kids shouted to, "Catch the snow monster!"

With a quick move, Rayce succeeded in untangling the cat and it leaped from his hands, landing on the glassy lake surface. The cat struggled to find its footing on the slippery ice.

Two teenagers jumped onto the dock and raced to the railing to watch as the cat scrambled away.

"You guys weren't chasing that cat, were you?" Rayce asked in a surprisingly parental tone that impressed Cassandra with the added innuendo of admonishment. "Leave it alone."

"We won't hurt it, mister," one of the kids responded. "We just want to see if it makes it across the lake. It slipped! Did you see that?" He poked his friend in the arm.

The look Rayce gave her said exactly what Cassandra was thinking: once again their kiss had been foiled. And it was obvious their window to try for another kiss would not return out here.

He held out his hand and she took it. They started toward the resort at a slow stroll. Little was spoken. The tension was palpable. The desire heating her neck had not lessened. She had been so close to finally kissing the one man who could knock her out of her self-imposed boundaries.

That darn cat!

When they neared the patio with the blazing fire, Rayce tugged her to a stop and she turned to look up at him. His skin and eyes glowed from the reflected Christmas lights.

"I'm not sure I'll be able to walk within your vicinity without wanting to kiss you," he said.

Same. And yet logical Cassandra leaped out to take control over mushy romantic Cassandra. "That wouldn't be wise in front of the employees."

His smile dropped. "You worried about some kind of fraternization thing? Because if you are, I'll quit the job right now."

"You haven't even begun!"

"I know, but that's the choice I'd make. Just so you know."

"It's not that. We're not so fussy about telling our employees who they can date. I'm a private person. I like to keep things like…" *their almost kiss!* "…that…sacred."

He stroked her cheek. "I get it. You're not into cameras flashing while I sweep you off your feet and into a kiss?"

The thought horrified her. To see her mug splashed on some front page, or worse, go viral online? No, no and most definitely, no. She shook her head.

"Well, the paparazzi are no longer interested, so no worries there." He twirled the plastic mistletoe. "But I may attempt the sweeping part again when you least expect it."

She snatched the mistletoe from him. "I would expect nothing less from the man sent to shake up my life. Now, from where did you steal this?"

He grabbed it back and stuck it in the back pocket of his jeans. "Not telling."

"But if there's a hole in a display somewhere…"

"That'll keep you on your toes!" He took off walking on the path.

"Rayce!"

"Merry Christmas, ya filthy animal!" he called back, then sped up, his chuckles echoing in the chill night air.

Cassandra shook her head. But then she smiled. Quoting one of her favorite childhood Christmas movies? The man was certainly all kinds of crazy mixed with charm and a dose of dashing.

And he had almost kissed her.

Let the shaking up of her life begin.

CHAPTER SEVEN

ANITA SET THE serving tray on Cassandra's desk and left with a few kind words to have a great day. Finishing off a letter to the local scout troop who had requested a field day at the resort, Cassandra then turned over the cup and gave a little chirp to see a little drummer boy figurine smiling up at her.

She chuckled. "Oh, he's good."

She tapped the drummer boy's head. "You are almost as cute as he is. But he is handsome. And sexy. And…"

She sighed. Oh, that almost kiss. Closing her eyes returned her to the dock, standing so close to Rayce. His outdoorsy scent had filled her senses. The soft melody of Christmas music played in the background. One more inch and their breaths would have mingled, their lips would have touched.

Her heartbeats thudded now. She sighed and caught her cheek against a palm, eyes still closed.

What was happening between them? Were they flirting toward something greater? The thought did not put her off. And it encouraged another smile. What a perfect way to spend the holiday season. With a man who intrigued, excited and surprised her. Cozy snuggles while sharing a blanket before the fire? Yes, please!

Of course she wouldn't expect anything more than a fun

time. He had, after all, only signed on for the season. And certainly she wasn't prepared to begin a relationship, what with—well. She hadn't the time for that.

And yet, why *not* indulge while he was here? She'd seen the happiness return to her dad's eyes after he'd fallen in love again. It was a special spark that only lighted when a person's heart sang. And there was no reason she shouldn't seek a relationship. Her workload wasn't so immense she couldn't devote time to another person.

What was stopping her?

She glanced to her daily list. The top item was *find ornament*. How many days had she left on her dad's ultimatum to find it? Half a week had already passed.

Was searching for the ornament a means to fill the hole in her heart? Could she fill that hole and make room for another living, breathing person? Why couldn't she be satisfied with memories of her mom, and just forget about the wood star? There were many more ornaments on the tree that her family had gathered over the years. Each with a different memory. Why not stroll out to the lobby right now and flick on the Christmas tree lights? Begin the holiday proper?

Something held Cassandra back. Pushed her toward the quest. And it was a different place in her heart that needed filling than that which was currently being entertained by Rayce Ryan.

It was the feeling.

Christmas isn't a season; it's a feeling.

Cynthia Daniels would often quote her favorite movie as Cassandra would follow her about the resort, helping to tidy.

That ornament had brought joy to Cynthia Daniels's heart. And by placing it on the tree this year, Cassandra would honor her mother's memory and move forward.

Only then could she exhale and allow another person into her heart space. *And feel*. For now she would steer clear of anything serious with Rayce Ryan.

They were eighty years old, the pair of them, and had been married for sixty years. Neither had skied a day in their lives. But it was on their bucket list, along with sky diving. That adventure was going to happen next week after they hopped on a flight south to Arizona.

Rayce got a kick out of watching Mr. and Mrs. Thorson glide down the bunny hill. Hands clasped to support one another, their elated hoots echoed in the crisp morning air as their extremely slow journey seemed to stir up more joy than any person should contain.

He shouted an encouraging, "Whoo!" and kept a careful eye on the twosome. They'd be fine. They wore enough winter clothing that should either topple, they'd probably roll in the thick snow like giant marshmallows.

With their general lack of ability and hearing, Rayce had taken his time with them, making sure they understood the movements and correct balance before allowing them to step onto their skis. He'd felt a flush of pride when they'd taken their first sweep down the hill. And not fake or false pride like an approving word that must be earned through hard work, pain and repetitive motions.

Now that he thought about it, Rayce wasn't sure he'd ever taken pride in his accomplishments. All his life he had known nothing but skiing. He'd read about it, talked about it, eaten on the slopes and dreamed about the powder through the night. His grandparents had pushed him down a hill when he was four and since that auspicious first descent, he hadn't stopped seeking the next thrill. What else existed beyond skiing? It wasn't as though he were qualified for a desk job or retail work. He didn't know how to exist away from the slopes.

The thought was crazy. And he knew it. But that didn't loosen the fear in his bones. Who was Rayce Ryan without the skis?

"Heck if I know," he muttered.

He winced as a step to the side tweaked the muscles in his back. That was the real fear that had become embedded in his bones. The pain made him tentative on the snow, even disconnected from his body at times. It challenged his balance. And ski racing was all about balance.

Was he a has-been? A loser? He didn't want to wear those labels. But the only way beyond them was by rising and taking back the win. Through immense and uncompromising pain. A win that he wouldn't know how to appreciate. So would it even be worth it?

A triumphant shout from the bottom of the hill redirected his thoughts.

Pushing off and taking the hill in a quarter of the time it had taken the Thorsons, Rayce arrived beside them as they both settled on a bench to rest after their strenuous but successful journey.

"You two rock," he announced. Mr. Thorson met him with a fist bump. Rayce hoped to remain as young at heart when he reached their age. "See you tomorrow same time?"

"For sure!"

"Glad you had a good time. Go have some hot chocolate!"

Helping them out of their skis, he then sent them off in the direction of the hot chocolate and s'mores bar. He collected their skis and poles and skied over to the rack to leave them for the groundskeeper who made a sweep every so often to return equipment to the warming room.

Thinking about hot chocolate reminded him of the clever

message he'd sent Cassandra this morning. Hey, it was the little things, right? Deviously, he knew she'd spend time trying to figure out exactly where that figurine had come from.

At the sight of Rayce's cocky smile, Cassandra straightened from inspecting the massive wreath hung on a wall in the lobby. It was filled with tiny festive figurines. Yet nothing seemed to be out of place.

"Not from that one," he said as he joined her side. He beamed. So proud of his intrigue. "But I've got some mistletoe in my pocket if you want to learn where that came from."

"You think you're so clever?"

He shrugged. "I do have certain talents."

Cassandra exhaled. Yes, he did. And the idea of utilizing said mistletoe flourished in her brain to a full-on make-out fantasy. No stray cats struggling in a tangle of lights to stop it, either. But with a glance to the reception desk, she quickly swept away that titillating thought.

Kathy set down her headset and with a wave got Cassandra's attention.

"What is it, Kathy?"

"I got a call from Lift Four. The Torgerson twins are at it again. I tried to contact your dad but he's in a meeting right now."

"The Torgerson twins?" Rayce tilted a questioning glance toward her.

"They are young, rich, spoiled and tend to hit the slopes drunk. Anyone hurt?" she asked Kathy.

"No, but the attendant at the bottom of the lift said they've planted themselves on a snowbank and are loudly booing the skiers' landings."

"They need to be redirected," Cassandra said. "I'll round up one of the grounds men to help me coax the twins toward the nightclub. It's a bit early for dancing, but I'm sure they'll appreciate the atmosphere in there."

"I'll help you."

She gaped at Rayce, but then realized he may be just the person to help her out. The twins were celebrity chasers, and she was quite sure they lived only to see and be seen with everyone who was anyone.

"You may be the bait we need to lure them away from the lift," she said. "Come on."

Half an hour later Cassandra and Rayce said goodbye to the twins and headed outside to walk the path toward the lake. A guest had reported seeing animal tracks on the path. Possibly a bear? Cassandra doubted that, but she'd give it a look.

As soon as the twins had seen Rayce, they'd asked for autographs. Rayce had signed the sleeve of the one's ski jacket. After some polite conversation, and Rayce hinting that all the ski bunnies were in the bar warming up by the fireplace, they'd convinced them to take their hijinks inside.

Cassandra exhaled for a job well done. With a lot of help from their resident celebrity. But watching Rayce chat about his World Cup wins and his secret maneuvers hadn't felt like witnessing an ego show. In fact, the ego that had always puffed up his chest and set back his shoulders during after-race interviews hadn't been evident. And she wasn't sure if that saddened her or if it was just Rayce taking a new turn. Had the accident crushed his ego?

Before thinking, she blurted out, "What did it do to you?"

Rayce slashed a gloved hand across a pine tree, releasing a storm of snow across his face. He turned and tilted his head. "What are you asking? About the twins? They're all right guys. Just needed some attention."

"I mean the crash." She shrugged. "You were so kind to

the twins. I would have expected grandstanding and boasting from Rayce Ryan, especially with two devoted fans of the sport."

"Boasting? You think I'm cocky?"

"Rayce. The whole world knows that."

He bowed his head but couldn't hide his smile. "Fair enough."

"Yes, but since you've been here at the resort I've noticed, well…you seem calmer. Maybe not so quick to grab the spotlight?"

He clapped his hands together and studied the wood pathway. No animal tracks yet. She'd made him uncomfortable. But it was too late to take the question back. And she genuinely felt he was a different person than the one who'd skied competitively a year ago.

"I told you about my mom," she said. "It changed me and the way I interacted with others."

"Really? Because you seem like the same go-getter I once used to notice in high school. Still on the fast track, everything perfect, woe to all those who don't meet your standards."

That was a shocking statement. But before Cassandra could reply that he was being hurtful, he put up a hand. "Sorry. That was, well, it was the truth. But that doesn't mean I haven't noticed your kindness toward the employees and your general goodness. You are a snow princess, like it or not."

"Does it come with a crown?"

He caught her teasing tone and winked. "Made of snowflakes. But you're right about me not grabbing the spotlight. Well. There are no spotlights to be found here at the resort."

"We keep a tight rein on the media."

"Appreciated. By all your guests." He scruffed his fingers

through his hair, an action that always made Cassandra's fingers itch to do the same to him. Then he said, "You're right. This past year has changed me. Is it for the better? Not sure. What do you think?"

"I think you're..." sexy, alluring, and oh, did she want to kiss him "...doing well with the guests. And the staff. You've won them all over. Especially Anita. You and Anita have a weird thing going on."

"We do have a secret alliance. Does it bother you?"

She thought about the surprises that appeared under her morning cup. "I'm not going to tell you who you can befriend and who you can form secret alliances with. Anita was good friends with my mom."

"I picked up on that from the chats I've had with her. She's very proud of you. Following in your mom's footsteps. You know, that's the only thing I've ever wanted to feel about myself."

"What? Pride? You don't feel pride in your accomplishments? Rayce!"

"If I don't have a coach yelling at me to do better, change an angle, do it again and again and again, I just..." He shrugged and his shoulders dropped. "Maybe I won't ever get back to racing form again. And maybe I don't want to."

That was a stunning confession. What else was there for an Alpine ski racer like Rayce Ryan? Guest ski professional at a local resort didn't seem to land even close to what he was accustomed to.

"Really? What do you want?"

"I can't tell you. It's..."

At that moment, a rustle came from beneath the pine tree, which spat out a snarling white cat. It leaped out and dashed between them on the path and scampered off.

"That darn cat. Again!" Cassandra declared as she studied the ground. "Those are the smallest bear tracks I've ever seen." And what terrible timing the critter had. Would she ever find a moment alone with Rayce to fulfill her fantasy of kissing him?

"You should catch it."

"Oh, no. The last thing I need is a pet cat. It's feral, I'm sure."

"Yeah, but what if it wanders onto one of the slopes? When there are skiers out there? I'm sure you have accident insurance, but I'm also sure you want to avoid any lawsuits."

"I hadn't thought about that. But what would I do with the cat if I did catch it?"

He shrugged. "Take it to the pound. They can rehome it. It could be someone's pet. Maybe they are looking for it."

He had a point. "I'll get one of the employees on the task. Uh…" He had been about to tell her why he didn't think he wanted to race again. She wanted to hear that. But she was starting to feel the chill. If a body didn't move in the winter air, it felt the cold much faster. "Are you hungry?"

"Always."

"Would you like to join me for dinner as thanks for the suggestion about the cat?"

"I'd like to join you because you want to spend time with me."

"Oh. I do want to spend time with you," she said breathily. "Meet me at my room in half an hour. I'll have a meal brought up."

"It's a date." He wandered off toward the employee cabins.

Cassandra muttered what he'd said. "It's a date. Is it? Maybe. I suppose. Yes." She settled into the idea of it with a swoony smile. "Yes, it is."

CHAPTER EIGHT

THE YARD LIGHT positioned above the big outdoor fireplace highlighted the thick fluffy flakes in their magical freef-all. They'd eaten a fantastic meal and shared a large slice of Triple Threat chocolate cake, dense and layered with cream cheese frosting and crumbles of chocolate bits and cherries. Cassandra only ate a few bites. When she'd pushed the plate across the table, Rayce had eagerly finished it off.

Now what better way to enjoy the snowfall than with a bottle of wine, while wrapped in a cozy blanket. The chilled fruity red hit her just right and she smiled as she relaxed deeper into the pillows propped behind her back and shoulders. This couch was deep and comfy, and placed before the windows for the perfect view of the mountains.

Rayce had commandeered a red-plaid blanket and sat close enough that she could breathe in his crisp winter scent and wonder how long it might be before they kissed. They were safe from any feline interruptions here.

"Favorite Christmas movie?" Rayce asked.

They'd been sharing their favorites while watching the snow flutter in the golden beam of light. Favorite sports, adventure spot, music, food, color, all the standards. It was a nice way to get to know him better. And that he had a favorite dance—the tango—had surprised her.

"'Christmas isn't a season, it's a feeling'", she quoted

from her and her mom's favorite movie. "Of course *It's a Wonderful Life*," she added. "It's such a feel-good movie. What about you?"

"*Home Alone*. 'Keep the change, ya filthy animal!'" Rayce laughed at himself. "So I'm juvenile. Sue me. I can relate to the little boy being left home alone."

"You can?" She turned to face him. Relaxed and wrapped in the red-plaid blanket, he seemed like an old friend. It was so easy to sit and talk with him. But his relating to the movie bothered her. An abandoned little boy? And the little drummer boy from his favorite song had been all on his own, too. "Have you been left alone, Rayce?"

"Not like in the movie. My grandparents were always there for me." Behind the couch was a long high table and with a finger he teased the little drummer boy figurine she'd set there. "Gramps and Grams died when I was in tenth grade. I was…nearly sixteen? I was left alone for weeks after that while the family tried to sort out who would assume guardianship of me. There was only the one aunt in Hawaii and a distant cousin in Europe. Neither were interested in taking in a teenage boy. It was a rough time."

"I can't believe I never knew that in high school. It must have been terribly difficult for your studies."

He shrugged. "I was a jock. Got by on my sports skills and good looks."

"And your devastating charisma, surely. I can't imagine any teacher flunking you after the Rayce Ryan–charm treatment. So who in your family finally decided to take you in?"

"None of them." He chuckled nervously. "When they started talking about child protective services, my coach stepped in. He gave me a room in his basement. I found an apartment after I graduated. By then I was already racing the Master's circuit and had nabbed a few local sponsorships, so I actually had an income to cover basic living expenses. But once I was out of school I moved into full-time competition and the World Cup series. Didn't need much of a place to stay. Just a bed to collapse on after a hard day of training. It's not so bad as it sounds. Don't give me those puppy dog eyes, Cassandra."

"I know training and competition is a full-time job. And you were incredibly lucky to have a coach to take you in. But I suspect living with the coach was more of a business arrangement than getting a replacement family?"

"Yeah, I would have never called Coach Chuck family. At least not when it came to an emotional connection. I don't think it was necessary for the life I was born to live, what with competing and all that."

"Sure, but Rayce, did you have *anyone* to love you?"

He tilted his head. The light that shone through the balcony doors glanced across his eyes, flooding them with a clear sadness. "That's a weird question. What do you mean?"

"Family is there to put their arms around you when you need it. To give you hugs, as you said. To love you."

"My grandparents loved me." He shifted on the couch and propped an elbow to rest his head against his hand. "They were the only parents I've ever known. They raised me because my parents weren't interested in the job after about four months of trying."

"What? Rayce…" Her heart thundering, Cassandra couldn't imagine something so awful. And he explained it with an utter lack of emotion. She immediately thought of what it would be like to never know her parents. Her mom…

"Don't worry, Snow Princess, I had a great childhood. I assumed you knew the story. News media likes to blast all that tragic stuff. It makes for a good lede. But from what my grandparents told me, my parents were hippies who wanted to travel the world in a van and live off the land. They weren't into kids. Something like that. And Grandma always said they showed me the most love by allowing them to raise me."

"So you never knew your parents? Do you see them?"

"Haven't heard from them. Ever. Nor did my grandparents, though I suspect Grandma tried to find them a few times. And after I started hitting the newsstands and had my ugly mug plastered on product displays, I wondered if they'd try to contact me. But no." He shrugged. "Grams and Gramps were the best. When they died, my world was shattered."

"I can't imagine losing them both. At the same time?"

He nodded. "The carbon monoxide detector needed a new battery. They didn't suffer. Passed away in their sleep. I had been away in Denver for a weekend training course."

"Oh, Rayce." She gave his arm a squeeze. "Your heart must have crumbled."

"That's exactly how I felt. And I'm not sure it's ever been put back together in the right way." He took her hand and kissed the back of it. "When I told you I know grief, I meant it."

"So how did you manage such tremendous grief and at such a young age? If you'll share that with me."

"You thinking about your mom?"

She nodded. Tears felt imminent but she fought them back. Now she felt the need to be strong for him, and to listen, to witness the emotional pain he suffered and may have never had opportunity to share with anyone else.

He stroked her hair and the soft touch threatened to make those tears spill. Was he aware of his easy kindness, his genuine concern? If so, that should have filled him with pride.

"I think of them every day," he said. "It used to crush me. But my constant and relentless training schedule forced me to find a place in my heart for them that wouldn't completely send me over the edge. So I put them here." He patted his chest. "I think about them when I need support and guidance. And when I do, I can only smile."

A tear spilled down Cassandra's cheek. "That's lovely. And very strong, especially for a kid who was forced to take care of himself at such a young age. I like that. Finding a place for them in your heart."

She pressed a palm over her own heart. Her mom had always been there. Yet now she felt the hole where she had once been. Could she do the same as Rayce had done? Keep her mom in a compartment that would allow her to move through life without always needing to cry or yell at others because silly things were not right, not "marvelous"?

He touched her cheek to wipe away a tear. "You'll find that ornament," he said. "But if you don't? She's always with you. I promise."

The promise felt real, and it settled into her heart like a warm hug. If Rayce could manage his life and get beyond his grief at such a young age, then surely she was capable of moving forward, too. With or without a silly ornament.

"We got into some deep stuff." He picked up the figurine and gestured with it as he asked, "You okay?"

She nodded. Whew! Even when she had been trying to be strong for him, her heart had stolen that moment to break down.

"Time to change things up. You want to watch a movie?" he asked. "You know I am calling this a date, so a movie generally follows dinner."

His wink seemed to disguise the inner struggle that he'd just revealed to her. Cassandra could feel his yearning desire to change the atmosphere in the room that had gotten heavier with his confession.

Wiping away another tear, she said, "I'm actually exhausted. It's been a long day of business and wrangling of drunk twins. Is it okay if I take a rain check on the movie?"

"Not a problem. I should probably head out. Keep my eyes open for that darn cat while I'm at it, eh?"

"Please do."

"It's been a long time since I've spent such an exceptional evening with a woman."

"Really? I agree it was nice, but it was also…emotional."

"Yeah, sorry about that." He tucked her hair behind her ear. Watching him study her hair and take her in filled her with a heady rush of desire. But acting on that feeling didn't feel right. "Are you going to be okay?"

Always in his presence. "Of course. What about you?"

"Eh… I tend to land on my feet. Usually." He winked. "We're survivors. Even if it doesn't feel that way to you now, you'll rise when the time is right."

The man was charming and outgoing and…always brought out the best in people. But to the detriment of his wounded heart? Was that his means of hiding his pain? His loss? By charming everyone into liking him? Perhaps cockiness was his armor? No, every move he made was genuine.

Standing, she grabbed his hand and walked him to the door. When he pressed his back against it, she felt compelled to make a connection with him. But a kiss didn't feel right. It was too sensual for the mood that lingered over them and with the ghost of her mother haunting her thoughts. And surely he needed some emotional space as well. But the moment demanded touch so…she hugged him. She made it quick, not allowing her body to respond to his warmth, the utter hardness of his muscles, the—

Cassandra stepped out of the hug. "Thanks for a lovely evening."

He marveled at her. "That was nice. We should do it again soon. I mean the date. But also the hug."

"I'm…" always busy and yet, not so busy as she liked to believe she was. Busyness had been her armor. Rayce had loosened it "…free most evenings."

"So am I. And we do live close to one another. Would be a shame if either of us sat alone in our places eating or doing whatever when it could be done with someone we enjoy spending time with."

"A very astute observation. Dinner tomorrow?"

"I'll bring the mistletoe."

CHAPTER NINE

THE SNOWSTORM DISSIPATED in the early morning hours. Snowplows were dispatched and snowcats from all the area's resorts set out on the slopes to groom the runs. Walking paths had to be cleared by hand. Thankfully Cobalt Lake Resort employed a crew of talented interns, whom Cassandra quickly dispatched, shovels in hand.

Fresh snowfall always worked like a beacon as skiers headed out early to enjoy the slopes.

From her balcony overlooking the back patio, Cassandra spied Rayce with his clients. He was an easy spot thanks to his neon-green gear. He'd started wearing the color after contracting with the energy drink. Their logo had been a riot of green splashes. They had also been the first to drop him after his accident. It must have been rough for him. And his coach dropping him while he'd still been in the hospital? That was nothing less than vicious.

Yet there he stood, out on the slopes, trying again. In a different format, but he was doing what he could in the profession he loved. He was not a quitter. His grandparents had raised him right.

That he'd opened up to her last night meant a lot. The information about his teen years, and the loss of the only family he'd known, helped her to understand him better. Despite the obstacles he remained determined.

She glanced to the table behind the couch. The drummer boy figurine was gone. He must have slipped it into a pocket on the way out. It was his totem, she decided, even if he didn't realize it. A boy alone in the world, determined to make his way and give what he had to others.

That day she had fled from him in fear of putting on skis returned to her. Later, when he'd come to her room, he had said something so wise. She would have to step into a pair of skis sooner or later.

Rationally she knew he was right. It wasn't because as the manager of a ski resort she needed to be seen participating in the sport. Rather it was because it had been a part of her life until her mother's death. Skiing felt like breathing. And she did miss it.

But later felt much safer, and more doable, than sooner. Because, when looking down at those skis as Rayce had waited, fear had jittered in her throat like the lump that had settled there that morning she'd learned her mom had been crushed by the avalanche. They'd closed the resort for a week, then finally her dad had made the tough decision that they couldn't risk further lost income, or disappointing guests, and had reopened. The show of support from the Whistler community had been incredible, as well as that from people all over the world. They'd been booked solid through spring, and most guests had sent notes with memories about Cynthia Daniels. It had been heartwarming, but also too much.

Following her mom's death Cassandra had wanted to take some time off. Like a month. But she'd also been aware of her father's pain. He'd lost someone he had loved for twenty-eight years. It would have been selfish of her not to stand by his side and keep the resort running. And her mom would have insisted they do as much. Admittedly last Christmas had been dull and lackluster to the guests. No fabulous Christmas Eve party, or even half the usual decorations.

By clinging to her grief, Cassandra was depriving others of something special. Of their own Christmas memories. Which was the very reason they came to the resort in the first place!

Could she fill the mom-shaped hole in her heart and make it like that place where Rayce kept memories of his grandparents? Always there, but not a heavy weight that overwhelmed her and insisted on keeping her down.

"I can do that," she whispered. "I have to do that."

But how? She already held her mom in her heart. It was the need to cling desperately to her memory that had put her in this funk. She needed to open her fingers, relax her grasp and know that the memories would never flutter away.

And it must start with the daily operations around the resort. She wouldn't allow her grief to interfere with the guests' enjoyment of their vacations. Cassandra decided that with every decoration she hung she would be saying "I love you" to her mom. Even making such a decision seemed to lift the heavy weight from her heart. But a small weight remained.

The missing ornament. How many days had she remaining to find it? A day or two, according to her dad's ultimatum. The email she'd sent to all employees last night to keep an eye out for the ornament had not resulted in a discovery. And every nook and cranny she'd checked only produced another letdown. She needed to resign herself to the idea that it wasn't going to be found. And while it was important to her, what really mattered in the long run was that she remembered making that ornament for her mom and the expression of joy on her face every time she had hung it on the tree.

With a nod and an inhale, she decided today would be a good day. A new day. One that would hold her mom's memory in a special place while also making room for everything else. She would not be a doom-and-gloomer, like Mr. Potter from her favorite Christmas movie.

A knock on the door prompted her to invite Anita inside.

"I brought you a new brew that we're thinking about adding to the menu. It's a creamy chai with lush vanilla bean and a kiss of orange. Really lovely."

"Ooh, sounds intriguing. I love chai." Cassandra inhaled the spices and immediately detected the vanilla.

The sous chef set the tray on Cassandra's desk. On it sat an upside-down cup and a porcelain pot. As usual.

Anita wandered back to the door but paused with her hand holding the door open. "The email said you were looking for an ornament?" she asked. "Did anyone find it?"

"Not yet."

"I will check the kitchen storage," Anita said. "You never know. Odd things end up in there on occasion."

"Thanks, Anita."

After the chef left, Cassandra inhaled the spicy aroma. It made her think of foreign places and exotic fabrics and designs. Someday she'd love to travel to Morocco to see the sights and marvel over the culture. She could manage a week's vacation, especially in the summertime when her dad, ever busy with his many business ventures, enjoyed a break from that busyness and liked to take more control of the daily management of the resort.

Catching sight of a spray of glittery snow from the corner of her eye, she wandered to the patio doors, which were edged with snow. It looked like a frame around a Christmas postcard. Must have been a hunk of snow dropping from the roof.

A flash of neon green caught her attention. Rayce skied slowly beside the Thorson couple. He met with them daily, and each time Cassandra happened to walk near the elderly couple, they regaled her with the ski instructor's kindness and fun manner.

Her dad's idea to hire Rayce had been spot-on. But for as much as she felt her heart loosening to allow him into her life, she had to remind herself that he'd only been hired for the season. Come spring he'd be gone. And she did not want to step into any sort of attachment that would eventually be broken. She'd lost too much lately.

Turning to the desk, she followed the spicy scent of chai. Turning over the cup, she gasped, and then laughed. Sitting on the plate was a figurine of a blond kid wearing a Christmas sweater. Upon closer inspection, she realized it was the boy from Rayce's favorite movie.

"Where did he get that? First the little drummer boy and now this guy? I know we don't have this decoration in the resort." Unless it was something one of the employees had brought in? Very possible.

Wherever he'd found it, it made her smile, and laugh when the movie mom's declaration of "Kevin!" struck her thoughts. She tucked the figurine into a pocket then poured the creamy chai. The first sip was amazing. This was definitely going on the menu!

A *ping* on her laptop alerted her. Twelve messages had been forwarded from reception. Good thing she had a pot of chai to get her through the afternoon.

Rayce could see her watching him. From this distance he couldn't quite make out her expression, but a figure dressed in white stood before the patio doors looking in his direction. Heh. She liked him.

More than a few times, as he'd traveled the world by planes, trains and buses, he'd allowed his thoughts to drift back to the good old days of high school, and that beautiful girl he'd always admired. Heck, he'd crushed on her hard. And then she'd run from him.

She wasn't running anymore. Now to get that kiss.

Where *was* he headed with Cassandra? Because it felt like a dating kind of situation. Last night had involved some intense conversation, and stories that he'd never shared with anyone. That stuff had been personal. But he'd felt comfortable opening up to Cassandra. She hadn't made him feel as though he were less than, or wrong for having grown up with a different family structure. And when he'd told her about his grief, it had been real and from the heart.

Yet the last time he'd tossed his heart into the ring, disaster had struck. In the worst way possible. It had robbed him of an Olympic medal. Because the woman he'd thought he loved had kissed another man.

"Stupid heart," he muttered as he glided over the fresh powder toward the Thorsons.

That couple had been married for sixty years! They were respectful and caring toward one another. Man, he'd love to have something like they had. Maybe he should ask for some pointers?

Having clicked out of her skis, Mrs. Thorson lifted a boot for him to loosen the bindings. Rayce knelt before her and made some adjustments.

"You're a good fellow," she said. "You always take your time with us, when you could be out there teaching the youngsters and zipping down the slopes."

"There's no place I'd rather be right now." He set down her boot and stood, only to have Mr. Thorson shake his hand.

"Good stuff, for sure," the old man said.

Rayce lifted his chin. The praise swelled in his chest. It felt like nothing he'd ever experienced on the racing circuit. These two were genuine and honest. They didn't care that he could take the giant slalom in a mere two minutes.

"Tell me your secret," he said to Mr. Thorson. "How have the two of you stayed in love and for so long?" He cast Mrs. Thorson a wink.

Mr. Thorson sat on the bench beside his wife and tilted his bright purple-capped head onto her shoulder. "She's always right. And if you have to go to bed angry, just be sure you're both happy by the morning."

Mrs. Thorson laughed at that seemingly personal comment, while her loving husband hugged her.

Rayce put up his hands in mock dismay. "All right, you two. Let's keep it safe for the kids. I hear they've got a new hot chocolate flavor with honey and caramel in it over at the nearby stand."

"Ooh." Mrs. Thorson immediately made a beeline for the stand that Rayce had pointed at.

Mr. Thorson slapped him on the shoulder and said, "Just be honest and kind. That's all they want from us." With another wink he went off after his wife.

Honest and kind. Rayce liked that. Simple rules for an amazing marriage.

When he was with Cassandra, their connection felt promising. Her smile. Her laughter. That lush snow-white hair that swept softly across his face when he sat close to her. And the genuine care he recognized in her eyes and her voice. It did things to his stupid heart.

A guy should be more careful. Heck, he was only here for a season. Getting involved would not prove wise. But Rayce Ryan never got anywhere by playing it safe.

Was it love he wanted? Cassandra had seemed worried

that he hadn't gotten love in his life. He had. From his grand-parents. Familial love. But what might it feel like to fall in love with a woman and to completely abandon his heart to that romantic feeling? Could he do that again? Without fear of injury, rejection or losing the ability to compete?

"Honest and kind," he muttered with a glance toward Cassandra's balcony. She no longer stood there. Was being with Cassandra worth losing his focus?

What *was* worthwhile to him now? If this broken body of his couldn't bring home a gold medal, he'd have to find something to replace his need for adrenaline and competi-tion. The cheers and adoration. The acceptance.

Her absence made his heartbeat stutter.

"Damn it," he whispered. "You're going to go for it, aren't you, stupid heart?"

CHAPTER TEN

A FIRE BLAZED in the outdoor fireplace and the s'mores stand was open for guests. The hot chocolate bar currently offered a dozen different flavors. Cassandra loved the white chocolate cherry version. And who could say no to the dark chocolate and orange spice?

During her rounds she frequently stopped to chat with the guests. But her focus would never be dissuaded. Was the hot chocolate bar clean and inviting? Was the outdoor music set at the right volume? Was all the soot cleared away with not a hint of it on the stone patio? All seemed in order, and the right amount of snow had been heaped behind the cozy chairs. A blanket closet was also heated to provide guests with a comforting wrap of cozy warmth.

"Marvelous," she whispered, hearing the word in her mother's voice.

Yes, Mom, it is marvelous. And...with or without an ornament, I can keep you close. I can do this. I can move beyond the grief. I am capable of changing...

"What's that?"

Spinning around and landing in Rayce's arms, Cassandra felt a brief effusion of joy that was quickly replaced by decorum. "Rayce, I didn't see you behind me."

"Keeping you on your toes. That's my job. So, what's marvelous?"

"Oh, nothing really. And everything. Well, not everything. It's what I strive for," she explained as she began to walk the path and he accompanied her.

A trip completely around the lake wasn't necessary but she did like to walk up to the first observation point to do a scan and make sure all the lights were working.

"You strive for marvelous," he recited. "Sounds unattainable."

"It's something my mom used to say. She was very fussy. Everything has a place and position. She would spend hours daily going through the resort, making it look perfect. The guests expected it."

"So that's where you got your need for perfection."

"There's nothing wrong with wanting the best and creating a memorable experience for others."

"Fair enough. So marvelous is the ultimate goal?"

"Absolutely. And… I think I've come close this year with the decorations. I just want to make my mom proud." She clasped her hands before her mouth briefly. "But that ornament."

"I can help you look some more?"

Once at the observation point, he stopped alongside her and leaned his elbows onto the banister where guests could walk out and gaze over the lake in the summer. The bench seating had been recently swept and weatherproof seat cushions were neatly placed in a cubicle for guests to use. While there wasn't an attendant posted, there was an abundance of treats in a small cabinet to satisfy any snack attacks.

"After our chat last night, I had a talk with myself about letting it go," she confessed.

"How's that going?"

A heavy sigh felt like a mutiny of her determination. "Letting it go is… It's become this *thing* that I need to clutch or accomplish or even defeat. I don't know how else to put it."

"You mean, letting go of the thing that connects you to your mom? And you'll never reach that particular marvelous if you don't find the ornament?"

She hadn't thought of it quite that way, but he was spot-on. She nodded and bowed her head. That he understood her always surprised her. He wasn't the unattainable golden boy she'd once put on a pedestal. Rayce seemed so normal, not like the celebrity persona he'd embraced with open arms. Had the accident brought him down or was it that he was new here and hadn't found his footing yet? Maybe the real Rayce Ryan would rise soon enough.

"So, what are we doing out here?" he asked. "Beyond listening to Elvis croon about Christmas?"

"Making the evening rounds before I turn in. One final check for—"

"Marvelous?"

"You got it. Let's walk back but take the path around the fireplace so I can check on the shoveling situation to the employee cabins."

"I can tell you right now it's all good, but I suspect you need to see it to believe it. I don't mind." He stretched out an arm, his hand open in invitation. "You can walk me home."

He winked at her and clasped her hand. She was wearing thin gloves and he wasn't. Never had she wanted to rip them off more than now to feel his warmth, the sureness of his skin against hers. When had she last walked with a man and held his hand? Such a silly thought, yet it was something that went beyond mere friendship. So…why not?

Tugging from his grasp, she bit the finger of her glove and pulled it off, tucking them both in her pocket. When she clasped his hand again, she said, "Much better."

He gave her hand a squeeze. "You always have been the smart one."

Smart, or rather hungry for his warmth and the feel of his skin against hers?

"How's the coaching going?" she asked.

"Better than expected. I really want to take Mr. and Mrs. Thorson home with me when this gig is over."

"They are a sweet couple. Oh. Do they remind you of your grandparents?"

"Maybe? They're just good, fun people. Honest and kind."

"Those are the best sorts of people."

"They make me think. A lot."

"About what?"

He jumped ahead onto the first wide log step that led upward to the employee cabins. It was well-swept and edged with bright strip lighting to prevent accidents in the dark.

"I don't know," he said. "Just life and love and things like that." He dashed up a few more of the massive log steps and she followed. When he pulled her to him, her heart leaped. "You're easy to be around, and that is a new experience for me. I like you, Cassandra."

It felt as though he were declaring his love for her, but she wasn't so foolish as to believe that. It was a delicious feeling, though, to hear that from him.

"You make me feel less broken. Come inside," he said with a gesture toward his cabin. "For a few minutes?"

Unable and unwilling to conjure a quick excuse, Cassandra nodded and followed him down a shoveled pathway to the small single-room cabin.

That word he'd spoken swiftly and softly—*broken*—disturbed her. Is that what he thought of himself? She supposed it was inevitable after what he'd been through. But it put an ache in her very soul to hear his confession.

Before following him inside, she heard a *meow* and turned to spy the white cat scampering across the path they'd taken.

"Is it that darned cat?" Rayce asked.

"Yes, but he darted away. I told the grounds crew to keep an eye out and catch it," she said, closing the door behind her. "Surely, someone would like to adopt the thing. It's so fluffy."

Rayce shrugged off his jacket and tossed it to the couch, but it missed and landed on the floor. "I haven't gotten groceries yet, but I do have snacks and beer. Want a bottle?"

Cassandra picked up his coat and carefully laid it over the back of the couch. "Sure."

He handed her an icy bottle of craft beer from a local brewery. "Have a seat."

She sat on the couch, finding it surprisingly comfy. When she was little, she'd followed her mom from cabin to cabin, helping her to straighten things out, take inventory and order new pillows and linens when necessary. All she could recall was bouncing on this couch, never actually sitting in it like a normal person.

"I know, right?" he said as he settled onto the couch beside her and put his feet up on the coffee table fashioned by a local artist who used fallen lumber rescued from the forest. "It conforms nicely and embraces you like a hug without being under-stuffed and uncomfortable."

"Wow. I just learned who the resident couch connoisseur is."

"When you spend your late teen years couch surfing, you develop a talent." He tilted his bottle against hers. "To big comfy couches and good conversation."

"What did you want to talk about?"

"Anything and everything, as long as it's with you. We've done the favorite things." Head tilted against the back of the couch, he turned his gaze to her. His summer sky eyes caught her instantly. Could a woman ever tire of staring into them? "Tell me something I don't know that no one would guess about you."

Cassandra considered that one as she sipped. "I'm not so fussy as I appear."

"Doubt it," he countered. "You couldn't let my coat stay on the floor."

"That's aesthetics. I'm a terrible mess in the bathroom. I leave towels on the floor, beauty supplies sitting everywhere."

"You're an absolute heathen." He chuckled. "Come on, give me something good."

"Like what? We've both shared our grief. Hmm, what about a true confession that doesn't involve a family member? Just about you. Personally."

"Fair enough."

He shifted to face her and she danced her gaze over his face. He had mastered the sexy stubble and finger-combed hair. No wonder he'd been on every magazine cover; the man gave good face.

"I'm not good at recognizing emotion," he finally said. "I mean, stuff like love and anger and indifference."

"Really? I would think anger an easy one."

"You'd think, but I've walked into more fights than you can imagine. People tell me I'm too easygoing. I like to joke and prod at people. It's a means of pushing them out of their comfort zones. I think I picked it up from Coach. He was always pushing me to see what I was capable of. Guess it makes me kind of one way or the other."

"I don't understand."

He shrugged. "Things are always either too far to the left or right. Too good or too bad. It's rare that I'm balancing in the middle. It's what I know. I'd like to be in the middle more often. To be more balanced."

"But I thought you enjoyed competing? The challenge. That must weigh heavily to the good."

"Actually it weighs on both sides. Competition is rough stuff."

"That's probably what trained your brain for those two extremes. I wouldn't think the middle ground would satisfy you."

"Right? But, well…" He let out a heavy sigh. "It's something I need to explore. After spending half my life in the extremes, I wonder what I've missed. Can I be a normal guy?"

"I don't think you'll ever qualify as normal, and I wouldn't want you to be so. You're too interesting, Rayce."

He leaned in closer and fluttered his lashes at her. "I think you like me, Snow Princess."

"Of course I like you."

"Do you like me enough to kiss me?"

Her mouth dropped open. Cassandra quickly closed it. And the first words out of her mouth were, "Where's that mistletoe?"

He dug in his back pocket and produced the plastic frond, which was growing crumbled and bent.

"Do you carry that everywhere?"

"If there's one thing I've learned over the years, it's to always be prepared."

"Scouts?"

"No, it's the 'not being willing to get the seat next to the bathroom if I'm late for the bus, train, or plane' kind of preparedness training."

Her laughter escaped in a burst and when she came down from it, Rayce met her with a kiss. Their skin still slightly chilled from the outside air, their initial connection caused a deliciously cool spark. It ignited and shivered through her system, quickly racing through her body to awaken all nerve endings. The crowd cheering in her head was really the thrill of her soul dancing to this moment.

Finally, it shouted. *That kiss you regret walking away from is finally yours.*

As they deepened the kiss, Rayce slid a hand along her

cheek and cupped the back of her head. It wasn't tentative or shy. They had connected. And the intensity of the moment surprised her. He knew how to move and met her with an initial softness that then became a little firmer, even daring. Yes, he dared to go deeper, to draw her in closer, to defy her to push him away. Of course she should expect nothing less from the man who was determined to shake up her world.

There wasn't an excuse in existence that would tempt her to push him away.

Reaching up, she glided her fingers through his hair. It was just as soft as she'd imagined it would be. The move pressed them even closer and she laughed a little as they tilted their heads to reconnect differently. The sudden rush of heated passion brewed the moment into a delicious and electric embrace.

As quickly as she had fallen into the joyous surrender, he pulled back and smiled at her.

"No audience," he whispered, with a dart of his eyes to illustrate their quiet surroundings. "It was a long wait, but I'm glad it finally happened."

"I am, too." Giddy swirls spun through her system. Her shallow breaths came as fast as her heartbeats. "I think… one more."

Gripping him by the sweater, she pulled him to her. This kiss was the one she'd craved for years. The one she'd regretted never accepting. The one she'd always wondered about when kissing anyone else. The one she would never refuse. This kiss melded them in a clasp of desire that she wasn't about to destroy by running from it.

But as well, this kiss answered her deep need for connection. For that hug she'd been missing. For an intimacy that fed her soul in a surprising manner, that went beyond mere attraction.

Rayce bowed his forehead to hers. "Something has started here."

Really? Because she was wont to believe that it had started a long time ago. At least in her heart.

"Another?" he asked.

She nodded.

They'd learned one another's mouths and moved quickly to kisses that were deep and long and, oh, so satisfying. And when the hand he had pressed against her back moved around to caress her breast, Cassandra arched forward against his body, wanting...

So much. And yet how dare she take such pleasure when she should be focusing on other things like honoring her mother by making the tree marvelous through the addition of the ornament? She had intended to get that settled before losing herself in a relationship.

Relationship? Why was she even *thinking* that word?

Breaking the kiss, she stood and tugged down her sweater. "I gotta go. Sorry. I'm... This...can't go any further tonight."

"Okay. Yeah. Sorry. That was moving a little fast."

"Just a little." She grabbed her coat on the way to the door.

When she gripped the doorknob, she bowed her head. She was attracted to Rayce. Her entire body screamed for more, more and more! And she wasn't so precious that she wouldn't allow herself to get involved with the man simply because he was an employee. It was her life; she could do as she pleased. And she did crave intimate contact with his naked body, the ultimate deepening of their connection.

"It's not what you want," he called from behind her. "I'm sorry. I was going to be smarter about romance. I think my stupid heart has overstepped."

Smarter about romance? His stupid heart? No, it wasn't stupid. It was being cautious. He'd been through so much in his lifetime. And they understood one another on the grief front. But this side of their relationship was—not so much a challenge as a step in a new direction for her. She wasn't sure what she wanted from Rayce. Or rather she did want something from him—body contact, his hand on her thigh, his mouth on hers—and she didn't know how to take it. Would it be fair to only take that from him without committing to something more?

Oh, she didn't want to talk now. She needed to be alone to sort out her feelings about him.

"It's not you, Rayce. See you tomorrow," she called, then closed the door.

At the bottom of the log staircase, she paused and turned back to the cabin. Soft downy snowflakes fluttered before her. She'd fled from him once again. And this time, she felt even more confused by her conflicting emotions. What did grief over her mother have to do with allowing Rayce into her heart? Surely she had room for both of them there? And since he'd arrived at Cobalt Lake Resort, she'd relaxed her staunch work habits and begun to enjoy herself.

So why the escape from what could have turned into a heavy-duty make-out session? The man could kiss! And she had waited ten years for him. Not that she'd stood around waiting. No, she thought she'd never see Rayce again after high school. But the fact that he was back in her life, in a surprisingly intimate way, made her flush warmer than a sip of hot chocolate.

Rayce had been right about one thing. She did reach uncomfortable quickly. She shouldn't have fled.

Was it too late to turn and go back inside?

"It is," she whispered.

Returning to Rayce's embrace would stir up a new conversation that would involve going deeper into her heart than she could manage right now.

CHAPTER ELEVEN

BRAD DANIELS CHATTED with the electrician who had stopped in to go over the resort's electricals with him. The twosome shook hands and he directed the man to take off on his own—he knew the building—then turned to face Cassandra.

"Dad, how's the wiring and all that important electrical jazz?"

"Just jazzy," he replied with a killer smile that always seemed to turn the heads of the female guests. But the addition of jazz hands went a bit too far.

Cassandra clasped her hands over his to make it stop. "Fair enough."

"So now we can flick on the Christmas tree lights."

"Uh…" She had been coaching herself to move beyond her grief and accept she may never find the ornament, but her heart still hadn't quite gotten the memo. Last night's desperate escape from the arms of a sexy man who had only wanted to get closer to her was proof of that.

Her dad's gaze switched from the massive, beautifully decorated tree, back to her. "The electrician said there's nothing wrong with the remote or any of the connections. It's the big welcome to the resort."

"Yes, but I still haven't found Mom's ornament. And I do have a day or two left on your ultimatum."

"Right. I forgot about that." He shrugged. "Maybe it's already on the tree. Got stuffed deep inside on a pine bow somewhere?"

Did he have no idea which one it was? Or how much it meant to her?

"No, I looked."

He rubbed his salt-and-pepper stubbled jaw. "It's just an ornament, Cassie. Don't you want the guests to *ooh* and *aah* over the fabulous lights? Your mother would appreciate that more than some silly little ornament."

"It's not silly!"

Startled at her outburst, her dad initially cringed, then he pulled her to him for a hug. As much as she didn't want anyone to witness such a moment, Cassandra's body leaned into the much-needed hug and she tilted her head onto his shoulder. The sudden rise of endorphins coursing through her body switched from manic anger to a soothing stream of comfort. Her dad was her rock, the man who had held her hand at the funeral and promised her she would survive, that they both would.

"I know you miss her, Cassie," he said with a kiss to the top of her head. "I think of her every day."

That was the same thing Rayce had said, that he'd thought of his grandparents every day. Was it easier for men to move on? No, that sounded ridiculous. Obviously her dad finding new love had helped immensely on the *moving on* front.

"But you've started a new life with Faith."

"I thought you were happy about Faith?"

The two had gotten engaged after a whirlwind romance. They had known one another from high school and reconnected after years apart. And Cassandra did approve of Faith. She was kind, smart and independent enough to not take any of her dad's nonsense. Not that he had an ounce of it in his bones, but he did have his trying moments.

A bit like Rayce and his needing to push her. Hmm… Was she attracted to a man who reminded her of her dad? Nothing wrong with that, especially since Brad Daniels was one of the best.

"I am happy that you're happy, Dad. I just… I'm moving slower than expected on this whole 'letting Mom go' thing, I guess."

"You don't ever have to let her go, sweetie. She's still right here." He patted his heart. "Got a nice little nest where she resides."

Cassandra spread her fingers over his chest, feeling his heartbeat, and imagining her mom so close. She felt much the same when things were just right—*marvelous*, as her mother would grandly announce. And Rayce had placed his grandparents in the same manner, right there, in his heart. It was beautiful. She could do the same…

"Give me another day to find the ornament," she asked more than told him. "It's…" She sighed. A weird, ineffable thing she honestly couldn't put into words.

"I get it. But think of our guests. And, you know your mother would not be happy to see the tree lights dark."

He was right: Cynthia Daniels *would* be upset about the dark tree. "One more day." Cassandra held up a fist and he met her in agreement with a fist bump.

"All right, I have to find Faith. She's convinced we need to start wedding planning sooner rather than later. Fancy invitations to order. Silly colors to pick out."

"Have fun with it, Dad."

"Speaking of fun, how's Rayce working out?"

"With the job?"

"Uh, yes? Is there anything else I'd be wondering about?

Like maybe the fact that I saw you two walking the path last night? Hand in hand."

Oh, bother, and here she'd thought they'd been all alone and unwatched. But they hadn't kissed outside. Nothing to give her dad reason to suspect they were anything but friends. Except the hand-holding.

"I like him, Dad. Both as a professional ski instructor who has been getting rave reviews from our guests and…"

He put an arm around her shoulder. "Anything that makes your face light up and your eyes sparkle is okay in my book. Maybe we'll have a double wedding, eh?"

"Oh, please, Dad, we're just…"

What *were* they? What did she want them to be? During their make-out session last night, she'd abruptly fled Rayce's cabin. By the time she'd returned to her apartment, she decided it had been nerves.

But she couldn't get what Rayce had said out from her thoughts: *I was going to be smarter about romance.* And he was always calling his heart stupid. What did that mean? It couldn't reflect well on her if his heart had chosen her in a moment of stupidity.

"I have to run, actually." She tapped her watch that blinked with a reminder. "I've got an appointment for… something or other. Talk later, Dad!"

She left swiftly, with her dad's chuckles trailing in her wake. He knew exactly what she hadn't been able to put into words. That she and Rayce were more than simply friends.

And when she considered it, she did want more from Rayce. But she wouldn't label them boyfriend and girlfriend. And certainly not lovers. Taking things slowly was all right by her. But it was not knowing how Rayce felt about the two of them that would drive her mad with wonder.

She owed him an explanation for her quick retreat last

night. And with hope, he'd let her a little further into his psyche so she could understand what sort of challenge Rayce Ryan's stupid heart presented to her wanting soul.

Standing at the top of one of the medium challenge runs, Rayce's thoughts were on the snow princess whom he'd kissed last night. Three kisses actually. He had been counting. But then he'd gotten cocky and made a move that was too fast for her. He'd scared her off.

"Not cool." He needed to be more respectful of her needs and…desires.

Never before had he been so cognizant of his actions, of how one wrong move might destroy something he wanted with increasing desire. He must follow Cassandra's lead. It felt like the right way to proceed with her. She required patience, honesty and kindness. Just like he needed the proverbial pat on the back.

He'd grown up knowing that unless he performed a skill perfectly, the pat would not be forthcoming. And…he didn't get them anymore. Not in the form of a coach nodding their approval, the cheer of an audience as they watched him speed by or even the flash of paparazzi cameras as he smiled for the fans.

Life had been so focused, and yes, rushed. If he hadn't been training, skiing or traveling with his coach, he was listening to performance audio tapes and practicing various martial arts to maintain a level of flexibility and skill that was unparalleled by his opponents. Always his eyes had been on the prize. Take a photo with the ribbon, medal or fake gold cup. On to the next event. Not a moment to savor his accomplishments. Not when he had to best himself the next race by a tenth of a second.

Now any chance of earning such pride had been stripped

away, leaving him but a man who had lost a dream and who wasn't certain how to move forward.

Life had changed the moment he'd crashed out of the Olympics. And in what had seemed like a split second, all the fans turned to look at the other guy, the newest Alpine racing sensation. The cameras had ceased their blinding flashes in his direction. And even the media, after the routine interviews in the hospital about the pitiful damaged skier, had tucked away their interest and moved on. Along with Coach Chuck. Rayce had never considered Coach a replacement grandparent, or any kind of family member, but he had been his mentor and guide and influenced his every move for so long.

While the cameras and attention had seemed to fill him up at the time, now he realized he did not miss the frenzy, the surface adoration and the false worship that had come along with it. None of it had been real. It was all a show. And he'd been the star of that show for a short time.

But if he didn't feel the innate pull to put on another show, what came next? Race, crash, recover, repeat had been his mantra throughout his competition years. He didn't feel compelled to *repeat* now. And that wasn't as alien a feeling as it should be.

Because lately, when he was with Cassandra, he experienced a different but similar feeling to the racing euphoria. Acceptance. Importance. Not being judged, but rather feeling he could fill the space and simply exist alongside her and she would make him feel like he had done something right.

Cassandra made him feel like he was a little less broken.

It was a feeling he wanted to chase, to inhale and absorb like oxygen into his muscles. But he didn't want to make a mistake and risk crashing out of what they had started. This could be something, and he had to recognize that and honor it without being thrown for a loop by the woman. And sacrificing his stupid heart.

"It is stupid," he muttered. "It's not smart enough to know what's real and what is just a game."

Cassandra didn't play games. Yet her abrupt departure last night after those amazing kisses had tugged at his softening heart, pulling it to a stretch until it snapped back with a sting. She hadn't wanted to remain in his cabin one moment longer. Had he done something wrong? He'd thought she'd wanted that kiss as much as he had.

Stabbing a ski pole into the snow, he flipped down his goggles. Here behind a line of trees, no one at Cobalt Lake Resort who happened to be standing out on their balcony could see him. Rayce didn't need Cassandra to see him; this was about proving to himself that he could do this.

With an inhale, he stretched his back. The twinge of pain didn't bite too sharply. And his leg wasn't bothering him at all. Excellent. He wasn't going to slow this one down. He needed to push himself, to test his limits.

Pushing off, Rayce tucked his poles back and his body bent and lowered to minimize resistance. The slap of the brisk winter air on his cheeks was the best thing in the world. Icy and biting yet burning a heat flash in its wake. A shift of his weight took the gentle curve and then he headed into a swift schuss toward the bottom.

Yes! This felt like his old normal. Free and always racing downward and striving for a goal. The goal right now? Make it to the bottom in one piece.

Laughing at his thoughts, he neared the base of the slope and…his thigh muscle twinged. Fear gripped his senses and his body tilted. His ski angled at the same time as a volt of pain strafed up his spine. A fall was imminent.

Knowing how to take a fall, Rayce readied himself. He

landed against the snowbank at the edge of the run in a graceless collapse and roll that spat up sprays of snow. His body settled lying on his back, face up, skis splayed and feet turned outward.

No one around to see that beautiful disaster, thankfully.

"Idiot," he muttered and pounded the snow with both fists. His hip burned. Pain scattered up and down his spine with sharp prickles that made him grit his teeth. "You think you can compete again?"

Who was he kidding? He'd never again be as effortlessly fearless on skis as he once was. He gritted his teeth and eased his fingers over the cramping thigh muscles. A reminder of what he had done to himself. Through emotional stupidity. One moment of self-absorption had cost him so much.

Rayce swore and slapped the packed snow. In truth? It wasn't that he *couldn't* do this; he simply *didn't want* to do this. He'd had a good run. Time to move on.

Because his life had changed.

Staring up at the icy blue sky, his breaths condensing before him, he recalled what Cassandra had said about her mother. Cynthia Daniels had triggered an avalanche. These mountains were dangerous. And with the ocean so near, the weather could change faster than a snap of fingers. Even the most experienced skiers risked death by a sudden avalanche. It would be an awful way to go. Buried alive. If it ever happened to him, he prayed his lungs would be crushed by the incredible weight of the snow, instantly taking his life.

Cassandra must have been inconsolable in the days following her mother's death, just as he had been when he'd learned about his grandparents' demise. Grandpa had been meaning to buy a carbon monoxide detector for over a year. Following that dreadful news, he'd wanted to skip training.

Coach Chuck had given him a week, then convinced him training was the best thing for his mental health. And his grandparents would be proud to know he hadn't given up.

Coach had known all the right things to say. And yet… Would Rayce have been better off if he'd taken a little longer to mourn and grieve the loss of the two most important people in his life? There were days he wished he would have, but honestly he could never know if it would have changed his future in any way. Coach had been insistent he return to training. But when things had come down to the wire, Coach had revealed his true colors in the hospital after Rayce's crash.

"You screwed up," Coach Chuck had said. The man's severe, unemotional tone was as clear as a bell in Rayce's memory. It was the foul language—something Coach had never used—that had shocked Rayce. "All that work. And for what?"

Coach hadn't stopped by again after that admonishment. And when Rayce finally called him, the man said he needed to step back. Give Rayce some room.

Rayce hadn't realized it at the time, but it had been Coach Chuck's way of dodging a bad situation. And of accepting a younger skier under his tutelage that he'd been talking to for a year and hadn't mentioned to Rayce. He'd learned about that from the media.

And now who was left in this world to care for Rayce Ryan?

He sat up and stabbed a pole into the snow. He hadn't twisted his ankle. He'd fallen correctly. He'd just feel a little sore for a while. Feeling sorry for himself was more stupid than throwing a race because he'd seen his girlfriend kissing another man.

Cassandra would never use his heart in such a cruel manner. She was true and kind, if a little perfectionist. But he liked that about her. And she gave him the emotional connection he'd lost following the accident. Or possibly it was a connection he hadn't felt since his grandparents were alive.

Who do you have to love you?

That was the real question, wasn't it? He'd succeeded in kissing The Girl He Could Never Have. Now, to trust his heart and follow it to the end? Or would he let her down as he seemed to let down everyone who had ever walked into his life?

CHAPTER TWELVE

NIGHT HAD FALLEN and the view from Cassandra's balcony boasted a fairyland of sparkles and colored lighting. The fireplace below had coaxed out dozens of guests despite the falling snow. It was that big fluffy, soft stuff that looked like goose down and she would swear to anyone that it tasted like candy.

It had been a while since she'd caught a snowflake on her tongue. Wrapping the chenille blanket tighter around her shoulders, she remained on the balcony watching the guests. And when a snowflake fluttered closer, within reach—a knock at her door startled her from catching it.

With a frown she padded inside to answer the door. Her thick knitted calf-high slippers with rubber grips on the soles made squidgy noises on the gleaming hardwood floor. She never expected anyone after ten in the evening so it could only be...

"Rayce."

He tossed and caught the plastic mistletoe a few times. The man was a master of the easy yet cocky smile. But that smile dropped when he noticed her expression. "Really? Is that disappointment? Way to make a man feel welcome, Snow Princess."

"No, it's not. Come in!"

"Are you sure? Because your face—" he gestured before her face with the mistletoe "—is saying something different."

She tugged him across the threshold, then led him through the living room to the open balcony door. "I was standing outside, trying to catch snowflakes on my tongue when you interrupted me."

"Oh." Seeming reassured he hadn't been the problem, he stood on the threshold. "And here I thought you were over me after last night."

"No, I—" They'd have the conversation about her fleeing him, but first things first. "Grab a blanket from the couch and join me!"

A moment later he stood shoulder to shoulder with her, blankets cozily wrapped about them. He leaned over the railing, tongue thrust out.

"It's not as easy as it looks," he said.

Cassandra tilted back her head and opened her mouth. Snowflakes *plished* on her forehead. A cool one melted on her nose. And… "Yes!" It melted on her tongue with a sweet kiss of winter. "I love that flavor."

"What flavor is that?" Rayce pulled her close and she hugged against him.

"The flavor of childhood," she decided. "I haven't tasted a snowflake in that long. It's a good memory."

"I'll remember that next time I do a face-plant in the powder."

She laughed. "I suppose you eat snow all the time, like it or not."

"I've consumed more than a man should, and never voluntarily. Maybe even recently—"

"Did you fall?"

"Eh… Took a stumble. Sometimes the ole leg…" He sighed. "We're not feeling sorry for ourselves tonight. So, can I see if the flavor of a snowflake still lingers on your tongue?"

Their gazes dropped to mouths and with a nod, she leaned in to meet his lips with hers. The winter kiss started with the sweet nip of chill, which quickly warmed. The change in temperature at their mouths was framed by the cool air, the hush of snowflakes dusting their faces and hair. *Magical* was an easy word to describe the moment. Maybe even... No, it couldn't possibly be... *Marvelous?*

"Kissing you is better than tasting snowflakes," he said against her mouth.

"I agree." She pulled him in for another kiss that could melt snowflakes in an instant. Was it possible to achieve the ultimate approval in a kiss?

Rayce's kiss lured her closer and she snuggled against his chest. He opened his blanket and she spread her hands around his back, as he did at her waist. His touch burned in the best way, warming her faster than the fire below. There was a certain perfection to their embrace that defied logic. He was the opposite of her, wild and cocky and a seeker of attention; she preferred the background and order and yet wasn't afraid to share herself when the moment was right. Like now. Rayce brought out things in her she had always known were there, but hadn't seen much of recently. Like passion and curiosity.

With a nuzzle of his nose along her cheek, he slid away the hair from her neck and glided a kiss to her earlobe. Erotic shivers tickled from her neck, over her scalp and down to her toes. Yet they stood outside on the balcony. Anyone below who looked up...

Rayce's hair was capped with white. She brushed off the snowflakes. "It's starting to pick up. Let's go inside."

Both shook out their blankets before going inside. "I want

to check out that massive fireplace one of these days," Rayce said. "There's always a lot of people huddled around it."

"Making s'mores and singing Christmas carols. So did you just stop by to kiss me?" Cassandra asked as she wandered to the kitchen to see what she had for wine or beer. A half bottle of red? It would serve. She grabbed two goblets and joined him on the couch. "Sorry. Leftovers."

"That's fine. Maybe I did come over just for a kiss," he said. "Or two. Or three?"

She clinked her goblet against his. "I'm in for three. I saw you this morning standing out on the Harmony run."

"Yeah? You can't keep your eyes off me, can you?"

"It was the glare from your ski visor that caught my attention. But… I admit you're not so terrible to look at."

"You say that as if a forced confession. Who's holding a knife to your throat, Snow Princess?"

"Sorry." Over a sip of wine she met his gaze. Using her best sultry tone she said, "You're very handsome. How's that?"

"And?"

"And? A great kisser. And very…"

He lifted a brow, awaiting her summation.

"Annoying, actually." She moved aside and poked him in the thigh. "What is that sharp thing? Seriously? You carry that mistletoe with you everywhere."

"It's my good luck mistletoe. Hey, my mistletoe maneuver got me another kiss."

"Have you ever used it on anyone else?"

"Never." He made a show of crossing his heart with a finger. "Promise. There's not a woman in this world who could lure this mistletoe above her head, except you."

He tugged the pitiful thing from his pocket and adjusted the wired branches but there was no saving the crumbled tangle of green plastic leaves and fake white berries. "I bet the real stuff would get me—"

Cassandra choked on a sip of wine. "Would get you what?"

They stared at one another as the silence caressed them with an intimate tension. She suspected he would have said *in bed*. And guilt did shade his expression. Though she suspected there wasn't a lewd comment in this world that would make Rayce Ryan blush.

Nothing wrong with expecting they move to the next level of intimacy. That kiss on the balcony had certainly stoked something inside her. Sleeping together was not off the table. Especially on a night like this. Cold outside but cozy inside. Goose down flakes falling softly from the sky. And moonlight enhancing it all.

"I didn't mean..." he started.

"I know what you meant. And you don't need real mistletoe to get that, either."

His brow quirked. On the other hand he wasn't going to be here forever. And she'd flinched the other night when his hand strayed, seeking a more intimate connection. And yet on the other, borrowed, hand she was a big girl. She could do what she wanted.

"Rayce, why are you tiptoeing around me? We can have sex like two adults if we want to."

"I... Right. Of course we can. I just..." He spread his arms across the back of the couch and put up his feet on the coffee table. "Well, you kind of ran away from me last night."

"Because you implied you were doing the dating thing wrong."

"I didn't—oh. Right. Don't take it personally, Cassandra. It's my stupid heart."

"I don't understand why you keep calling your heart stupid. It doesn't reflect well if it was stupid enough to kiss me."

"Kissing you is not stupid, Cassandra. That's the best thing in the world. I'm sorry." He shrugged. "I say that because my heart tends to get me in trouble. Big trouble. And I want to be careful with it. Not follow it too closely into danger."

"All this interaction between us, the dinners and romance, and the utilization of mistletoe, involves some risk. Danger, as you put it."

"I know." He took her hand and kissed the back of it. Summer sky eyes met hers over the top of her hand. How could he possibly believe danger was involved in their interactions? "This is different, Cassandra. I want to do everything right."

"Does my need for perfection prompt that?"

"Nope. I find that part of you adorable. It's… I really like you. And I don't want to send you running."

"Have you had many women run from you?"

"My stupid heart will never tell. Listen, Cassandra, some truths here? I'm not a big dater."

"Seriously? Because every time I've opened a magazine or scrolled online these past few years, I usually saw you with your arm around a woman."

"The rags! Half the time those dates were set up. Makes for good press."

"But what about the Grammys? I distinctly recall seeing you with Aliana Garnet."

"Ah, the infamous 'leaning in' pic that surfaced online and the whole world thought I was kissing her. In reality, we'd been set up for the evening. We didn't click. At all. She smelled like fancy perfume and the scent made me dizzy. And I was too short for her, even though I was inches taller. Those crazy high heels she was wearing! Anyway, that photo was taken when I was whispering something to her about needing to find a bathroom."

Cassandra laughed. "Really?"

"Hey, when a guy's gotta go… Aliana was not at all impressed with me. I didn't even score a kiss. Not that I wanted one. That *date*—" he crimped his fingers in air quotes "— was all for show. She should have thanked me, though. Her TikTok numbers soared. And I'm pretty sure I scored the *Rolling Stone* interview because of it."

"So it was a…business date?"

"Exactly. Super boring. Both of us were working the angles, making sure it served our own bottom lines. Admittedly I have had a few real girlfriends that I thought cared about me, and in turn I cared about them. But nothing that ever lasted. You may have noticed I have a big ego. If I'm not the star, then no one else can be. At least that's what one of them shouted while she was throwing shoes at me and telling me to leave her place. I caught one and took it with me. She texted me to return it, but… I can be a jerk sometimes."

Sounds like the woman may have deserved the theft if she had been throwing things at him. On the other hand there was always two sides to every story.

"Then why the job here at the resort?" she asked. "Seems insignificant for a man of your ego. The media are not allowed, and you're never going to get your photo on social media for being seen coaching an octogenarian couple on the bunny hill."

"Isn't that the truth! Honestly? This job was all that was offered to me. After the accident I lost my endorsements and the whole world forgot I existed. My manager tried to find me some action but other than a few movie roles—"

"Movie roles? Why didn't you take those?"

"I am not an actor. And I don't need the money. I've saved a good portion from my endorsement deals. And one thing I can do is invest wisely. I'm set for life."

"That's good to know. I'd hate to think you were destitute. What about the fame and attention? I know you miss that."

Letting out a hefty exhale, Rayce toyed with the blanket that he'd tossed across his lap. "I do like the attention. Crave it. But…"

"But?"

"I don't know." He scruffed his fingers through his hair. "I've only been at the resort a little while and have worked with some interesting guests. I was thinking about it as I lay at the bottom of Harmony."

"You were *lying* on the slope?"

"Had a minor misstep. My leg is intent on reminding me I'll never get back to racing form."

"Rayce, you have to be careful."

"Don't worry about me. Besides, I wear that GPS tracker badge when I'm out there. Resort rules, don't you know."

"Those trackers give me and my dad peace of mind. We've had to utilize them more than a few times."

"They are smart. But as for me and Cobalt Lake Resort, I like the smallness of it. The slower pace and personal attention and taking my time to show someone how to do something right. Don't get me wrong. If I sensed a camera within smiling distance, I'd slap on a grin and pose. That's nutty, isn't it? What's wrong with me, Cassandra? I don't want to be that guy who needs validation from others to exist."

"Seems like you're taking a step in a direction that may not require such validation. If you're enjoying the coaching?"

"Watching Mr. and Mrs. Thorson take their first run

down the hill was a hoot. They even clasped hands. It was cute. And, I don't know, it made me…feel."

"Feel like what?"

"Just feel."

"Oh."

It was half sad and half good to hear him say that. Had the man never experienced the joy of helping others? Of being validated simply for existing and not because he'd accomplished a task or won an event?

"You think I'm a nutjob. I can see it in your eyes."

She touched his jaw. The thick stubble enhanced the sensory appeal. Rugged on the outside yet a bit softer on the inside. Rayce Ryan did not cease to surprise her. And that he shared those complicated parts of himself with her meant so much. And yet…

"I'm a little sad that you haven't had moments of validation outside of your sport," she said.

"I have. My grandparents were loving and kind and always there to cheer me on. Even if it was walking in the Sunday school parade dressed like an Easter lamb. Life changed a lot after they passed. I don't know if I can ever get back to that place of comfort and love." He exhaled. "Will I ever have a family? Someone to care about me? Can I ever have a real home?"

"Rayce, you are worthy of all that and more. And you'll find your family, people who care about you. You've had a rough time of it this past…well, probably all during your competition years."

"I wouldn't call challenging myself rough. The physical part of it was awesome. It's that emotional stuff that baffles me. Like right now with you."

She tilted her head against his arm, which rested on the

back of the couch. "It's safe to talk to me. I'm glad you've been so open with me."

He inhaled and closed his eyes, nodding. "That's a validation I can embrace. Thanks, Cassandra. For listening."

"Anytime." She snuggled up closer to him and spread her arm across his chest, hugging him. "This is nice. I could do this every night."

"Same. But. I need to know something. Maybe a few things."

"Like what?"

"Do you have a boyfriend?"

She squeezed him. "Do you think I'd be hugging you like this if I did?"

"Right. Also, *would* you like a boyfriend? I mean, a guy you could hang around with, date, spend time with—"

She kissed him to stop him in his struggle to find the right words. And because she wasn't sure how to answer that question. *Did* she want to be his girlfriend? Well, yes, part of her jumped for joy over the label. But another part tugged her back and waggled its finger.

You don't have time for this! Where is that ornament? Why aren't you thinking about your mom right now? And really, he's only here for the season!

Outside the patio doors a flash of brilliant sparks caught their attention and they broke the kiss.

"Sparklers," Cassandra said with growing excitement. "Dad must have brought out the party fireworks. And is that..." They both listened and the sound of a guitar and people singing rose.

"It's our guest musician! Let's go listen." She tossed him the blanket and he grabbed it.

"We could do that or...we could make out some more." He glanced toward her bedroom.

Cassandra bit her lower lip. Yes, that did feel like the next step. The most handsome boy in the school had asked her to be his girlfriend. And there hadn't been a crowd to whisper and gossip and make it wrong. She should take that win. But something wouldn't allow her to rush into What Came Next. While her body craved Rayce, her mind pulled on the brakes.

Rayce nodded. "Music and fireworks, it is." He tossed the blanket over his shoulder and offered his hand. "My stupid heart is thankful for your common sense."

"Who's to say my heart isn't as stupid? I may regret not snuggling with you in a big cozy bed tonight."

"You won't." He opened the door and gestured she lead the way out.

"How do you know?"

"I don't. But I do know that the offer will come again. You can't get rid of me that easily, Snow Princess."

"I wouldn't want to."

They clasped hands, and this time sharing a blanket, they watched the impromptu concert dazzled with sparklers.

CHAPTER THIRTEEN

THE NEXT AFTERNOON the white cat mewled, dodged Rayce's grasp and scampered across the snow-frosted patio stones. He raced after it but turned right into Brad Daniels. The man held an armload of cut wood. Despite his salt-and-pepper hair, and the fact he was at least twenty years older than Rayce, he looked fit and strong. And Rayce had learned he jogged most mornings and was on the Whistler Search and Rescue team.

"Mr. Daniels, you need some help with that?"

"I got it. Looks like you're on critter patrol."

"I want to catch that cat before it does some damage on one of the slopes."

"Good call. Did Cassandra ask you to do that?"

Rayce shrugged. "No, but I like to help out. Do things that make her happy."

Even weighed down by the wood, Brad's smile beamed. "I can see that you do. Let's talk about Cassandra."

Uh-oh, what had he stepped into? Would the man be upset he'd kissed his daughter? Well, he didn't have to confess to that. Unless Cassandra had told him. Why would she do that?

Why was he panicking?

"Cassandra," Rayce said slowly. "Yes. Your daughter. The resort manager. My, uh…boss."

"Chill, Rayce, I know you two like each other."

"You do?" Rayce winced. "Sorry?"

"What for? I haven't seen Cassie smile so much in years."

Whew! He'd won the father's approval? One major hurdle in the quest accomplished. Come to think of it, he'd achieved the quest of kissing Cassandra and altered the goal to something only his heart could describe.

"But I'm worried about her."

"Why is that, Mr. Daniels?"

Brad shifted the weight of the wood in his arms. "The lobby tree lights are still dark. She's holding on to the grief."

"Yes, we've talked about her feelings about her mom. I think Cassandra is coming around. Well, I mean, everyone grieves differently. I'd never ask her to stop..."

"Sure, and I didn't mean it like that. I just..." Brad sighed heavily. "I wonder if I moved too quickly with Faith? Does my upcoming wedding bother Cassie more than I'd expected it would? It's not like I'm replacing her mother."

"I don't think she views your engagement like that, Mr. Daniels. She did say she was happy for you two. It's just that ornament holds a special meaning to Cassandra."

"You'll help her find it, yes? I did give her a deadline, which I believe is today. That tree needs to be lit. It's the focus. If you can help her find it, and in the process, if the two of you fall in love..." He let that sentence hang. Rayce wasn't sure he was supposed to reply so he didn't. And then Brad gave him a stern look that appeared more forced than anything. "Don't break her heart."

"Oh, I won't. Promise."

"Uh-huh." The man's assessing gaze did not preach trust.

As any father had the right, Rayce decided. And even if he were just playing with him, the implied warning had been received.

"I should get back out on the slopes. Got an appointment soon. Don't tell Cassandra about our conversation, please?"

Brad shrugged. "She's a big girl. She knows when a guy is genuine."

With that, the man strode off, arms easily supporting the heavy load, leaving Rayce behind in the cool shadows of the shed.

Did Cassandra know that he was genuine? *Was* he? What did that even mean? *Honest and kind.* The keys to a happy relationship.

His confession to her last night about having difficulty adjusting to a life lacking in fame and attention had been from the heart. Honest. She had seemed to support him. But she hadn't wanted to sleep with him. As well, she'd dodged the question about if she'd like to be his girlfriend. That had stung.

What was wrong with him? Sure, she could be taking things slow with him. Nothing wrong with that. In fact it was smart. He should follow her lead and do the same. Ignore the prodding thoughts that insisted he would never earn the nod of approval from her. Could he ever get beyond that need for validation and start to trust his own heart?

Because he'd never win the girl if he didn't get right with himself first.

The Grammy-winning musician staying at the resort had returned to the fireplace for another impromptu concert. He'd been doing so every day at random times. Two dozen guests, including Mr. and Mrs. Thorson, had gathered, hot chocolates and mixed drinks in hand, roasting marshmallows, tossing snowballs in the background.

Lured by the singer's raspy baritone, Cassandra had donned a cap and mittens and a plush comfy sweater that hung to mid-thigh to head out and enjoy the music. Thanks to their elite guest list, pleasant surprises like this happened on occasion.

The crowd was respectful, and surprisingly she only saw a few phones recording. She nodded to the security guard posted by the door and he got the hint. The resort respected everyone's wishes for privacy; they should do the same for others. When all phones were tucked away, her shoulders relaxed. Joining in on the chorus of a famous song that everyone knew, the makeshift audience raised their arms and swayed amidst the magical glow of snow-covered pine trees.

The next song, a romantic tune, lured some to dance with their partners before the massive stone fireplace.

"Would you like to dance?"

Cassandra spun to find Rayce standing behind her. His smile grasped her by the heart and squeezed. And his beautiful blue eyes made her sigh. *Caught.* And so happy for it. She nodded and as she hugged against his reassuring warmth they began to sway.

"I love this song," she said.

"Yeah, it's sappy, but the girls like it."

"Yes—" she tilted her head onto his shoulder "—we do."

With a slow twirl, they caught the Thorsons' attention. Mr. Thorson put out his fist and Rayce met him with a fist bump. The elderly couple smiled warmly and focused back on their dancing.

"Love that couple," Rayce muttered as he slid both palms across Cassandra's back and his body heat melted through her sweater. She swayed in the arms of a sure warrior. Every part of him was hard and strong, yet lean and agile. His sinuous strength made her feel protected, yet small inside his secure embrace. Like a bird protected from the wind. Closing her eyes, she succumbed to the moment.

In Rayce's arms nothing else mattered. Not the every-day troubles and astute commitment to detail required of her job. Not even that evasive ornament. And thinking that made her cling to him tightly. She didn't want this to end. He was kind, funny, and whatever was happening between them...mustn't stop. *Did* she want to be his girlfriend? At any other time she would have answered with an eager *yes*.

Why was it so difficult to step beyond her self-imposed boundaries? Were they even legitimate boundaries, or were they just silly fences erected to keep the grief inside?

Whoa. Now that was an interesting way to think about it. Was she keeping the grief in for a reason? What was it she didn't want to face?

"Song's over," he whispered as they continued to sway.

Beside them Mr. and Mrs. Thorson also still swayed to a slower tune.

The crowd sang along to a catchier tune now. Cassandra slid her hand into Rayce's. "Want to slip around the hedge?"

"Sure. Lights check?"

"No." *Move beyond that fence and kick down a few slats, Cassandra.* "Just a romantic nook."

"I am in."

Around the end of the snow-frosted hedgerow, they found a cove with a bench but they didn't sit on the padded cush-ion. Instead, they stood, hand in hand, in another slow danc-ing sway. The singer's melody echoed up and over the hedge. Christmas lights from the distant lake walk blinked in a col-orful background. If Cassandra saw fairy dust fluttering in the air right now, it would feel perfectly normal.

Rayce spun her under his arm and danced her a few steps. "I like dancing with you," he said. "I don't think I've danced since high school." He got a funny look on his face, realizing something. "With you. That was my last dance."

"Really? And I ran away from you like a—"

"Like a princess who needed to beat the clock. I get it now that you've explained. But we're all alone again. And I kind of get the feeling you like my kisses?"

"Where's your mistletoe?"

He patted his coat pocket and then the back pockets of his jeans. "Darn it."

"Don't worry." She slid a hand up along his stubbled cheek. "I'll issue you a rain check on the mistletoe."

A kiss in the middle of fairyland. A dance in the arms of a man she was beginning to realize held a certain soul bond to her own. They shared so much emotionally.

"Cassandra, getting to know you has been amazing. And I think about you all the time. It feels weird to say, because it sounds so juvenile, but I like you. A lot."

"Like a lot?" She laughed. "Same."

"Really?" He bobbled the yarn pompom on the top of her white cap. "Well, what do you know. The snow princess likes me."

With a pump of his fists and a shout to the sky, he gave a hoot like the one he always shouted at the end of a winning race.

Cassandra glanced nervously toward the hedge. A crowd of guests stood just on the other side.

"Don't do that." He turned her head to face him.

"Do what?"

"Worry what others think. You're allowed to kiss a man around other people. It's not salacious. It's kind of sweet. We're not high schoolers anymore. The mean girls aren't going to whisper about you and the jock isn't going to tell all his friends he made out with you."

"I…wasn't worried about that in high school, but now I

wonder if I should have been. Seriously? You would have kissed and told?"

"No, Cassandra, I mean, we're grown-ups now. We can do what we want when we want. Or is it that you don't want anyone to know you like me? Oh, that's it."

"No, it's not."

"It's an employee thing, then, right?"

"No, Rayce, I already explained—" She decided kissing him was the easiest way to end what had no strength as a viable argument. "It's just uptight me. I need to loosen up."

"I've noticed that," he said calmly, not accusingly. His eyes danced with hers. So easy to fall under his spell. Save for the one thing tugging her off course.

"Yes, well, everything surrounding me this time of year makes it hard to relax and…accept."

He took her hand, tugged off the mitten and kissed her rapidly cooling skin. "You want things perfect for your mom. I get that. But can you manage a few moments here and there for the guy who thinks you're the greatest thing since the giant slalom?"

That race had been his masterpiece. He'd never gotten the opportunity to show that to the world in the Olympics.

"I want to."

"But…?"

"But nothing." She released her breath with a nod. "Right. I'm a big girl. I've got this. And I need to stay in the moment. Right now I am standing before the sexiest, kindest, goofiest man I know, and I don't want him to think I'm not interested."

Another kiss ended what might have become an endless pep talk.

Rayce whispered aside her ear, "Let me walk you back to your room."

She hooked her arm with his. "Gladly."

* * *

Once inside Cassandra's dark apartment, they swayed before the balcony doors. The outdoor lights beamed a romantic glow across the living room.

Rayce nuzzled his nose into her hair that smelled like snowflakes, tasted sweet, with a tinge of memories. Everything about her was soft. Even her heart. Because he knew if they detoured toward the topic of that ornament, the mood would flip and he'd be spending the night in his cabin.

That wasn't going to happen. It couldn't. The moment felt right. And when she looked up into his eyes and smiled, then began unbuttoning his shirt, he leaned in to kiss her behind the ear and down her neck. Her soft sigh turned into a wanting moan.

"Stay," she whispered. "Please?"

Rayce nodded. "Wasn't planning on leaving."

CHAPTER FOURTEEN

STARTLED AWAKE, Rayce tapped the off button on his watch alarm, and turned on the bed. Cassandra slept still, tucked between the cozy white flannel sheets. Beautiful, peaceful, gorgeous, sexy Cassandra.

Wow. That had been some sex. He really should snuggle up and—nope. He had a 7:00 a.m. appointment with a guest out on the slopes. Which was twenty minutes from now.

Swearing under his breath, he carefully slid from the bed and gathered his clothes, dressing as he made his way across the room. The curtains were pulled but subdued morning light permeated a crack between them and glowed across the bed. It dashed a line across Cassandra's pale hair.

Did he really have to leave her looking like a sleeping beauty? He'd love to wake her with a kiss and glide right back into making love. He'd be a fool to do anything but.

And yet she was so peaceful. For as hard as she worked, and all the stress she'd been dealing with regarding her mom, she probably needed the sleep. As well, if he wanted to keep this job, he'd best make his way directly to the slope. He'd detour through the dining room on the way out. Anita would have waffles or pancakes and some form of protein to fuel his day.

Pulling on his shirt and buttoning his jeans, he stepped

into his shoes at the door and wondered if he should leave her a note. Sneaking out felt a little…sneaky.

Then…he had a better idea.

Waking in the bed by herself was normal for Cassandra. But it shouldn't have been so this morning. Rayce had snuck out without even saying goodbye. Before allowing anxiety to even stir, she had the common sense to glance outside and spotted his neon green winter gear on a slope. He must have had a guest appointment this morning.

After a long hot shower she wrapped a robe about her body and wandered to the desk to check her schedule for the day. Usual rounds and then some thank-you notes, along with gifts to their best guests. This time of year her mom had always sent out gift baskets to a list of dozens. Champagne, chocolates and pastries made by local artisans, and a set of Cobalt Lake Resort branded cozy slippers and a winter scarf along with a handwritten note.

Assembling everything and writing the notes would keep her busy all day.

A knock at the door was followed by Anita slipping in. "Good morning!"

"Thanks, Anita. How's your day so far?"

"Busy. No time to chat."

"Do you have the chocolates boxed for the thank-you gifts?"

"I do. I'll have Zac bring them up right away."

"Thanks!"

The door closed and Cassandra put her feet up on a padded stool and leaned back in her chair. A relaxed coziness had encompassed her since she'd slid out of bed. Like she hadn't a care in the world. There was no rush to get things done. No one required her approval or answers to resort-related questions. She could simply exist.

Then she realized this feeling was that of having been well-pleasured last night. Had it been that long since she'd had an utterly soul-shuddering orgasm? The lingering dopamine was truly the best kind of anxiety medication. Seriously, she needed to take care of her physical needs more often. With Rayce.

She wondered if he felt the same? Had it been difficult for him to leave her this morning? Or had he snuck out, relieved to have escaped the awkward "morning after" chat?

She hoped it was the former. But there was something about Rayce that he kept closed off. Not that she expected him to reveal all and be super open—everyone had their secrets—but…she was putting too much measure on their having slept together. Maybe?

Most definitely. Let it be fun and exciting, she told herself. Just like the Christmas season should be.

With a sigh she tugged up the thick robe and closed her eyes to imagine Rayce's hands gliding over her body. His kisses tasting her. Their heat melding in a hot and heavy lovemaking session. She wanted more than lighthearted fun and excitement.

But what did that mean? Did she desire a relationship with the man she hadn't known very long but whom she had dreamed about on occasion over the last decade? A man who was only here until spring?

She had no grand designs on her future regarding relationships, but it was a "back of the mind" goal to someday have a husband, some kids and a house at the base of a mountain. Never far from the resort. This place was truly her life.

But was it her home?

That odd question startled Cassandra. Of course, the resort was her home. Well. It was her workplace. The apartment was—no, it wasn't a home, exactly. It was where she landed after work, and continued to work, and…

"I don't really have a home," she whispered. Much like Rayce. The realization sunk heavily in her chest. "I want one." But that would involve…

Moving forward. Leaving behind the things she'd become accustomed to calling a home. Opening her heart to more than work. Letting go of some of the control. Sharing herself with another person in every way.

The thought that her mother would never be able to watch her walk down the aisle saddened her. And that switch to memory reminded she did still have a mission.

"Guest thank-you boxes to assemble," she said, "then one last ornament search before Dad realizes I've stretched the deadline by a day."

Turning over the cup on the tray, this time she sighed and caught her chin in hand at the sight of the little drummer boy. A second appearance? He could show up in her life all he wanted.

Rayce noticed Cassandra walking from the direction of the storage room. That ornament haunted her like—a precious lost mom. He'd allow her that need to hold a piece of memory in her hand. He hadn't anything but photos on his cell phone to remember his grandparents by, and he cherished them.

He wasn't sure if he dared talk to her now when she had clearly been looking for the ornament. She might be in a fragile state of mind. And him walking up to her and asking if she'd enjoyed last night would not exactly go over in the resort lobby and—who was she talking to now?

Cassandra greeted a man at the reception desk. Then he leaned in to *kiss her on the cheek*.

"What the heck?" Rayce murmured. That had been more than a friendly European greeting. And they were not in Europe.

Anita strolled toward Rayce with a tray of what looked like stacked egg cartons. She nodded acknowledgment. When she drew parallel, he asked, "Who's Cassandra talking to?"

The sous chef paused and glanced over a shoulder, her eyes taking in the pair at reception. Then she chuckled. "Oh, him! He comes every December to see her."

"What? Why? Who is he? He looks about our age. And he's…" He didn't want to admit it, but the guy was handsome. In "a crisp white shirt and slicked back hair" kind of businessman way.

"She used to date him. For a season? I don't recall how long."

Used to was good. But. Rayce's neck muscles tightened. A flash of seeing Rochelle kissing the American skier made him wince. The catalyst to his crash.

"Do they…still have a thing?"

"A thing?"

He shrugged. "You know."

How to explain, or simply ask the woman if Cassandra was getting it on with the tall handsome man she had just hugged?

"Not sure," Anita said. "Like you mean sex?" She winked.

He managed to nudge up his shoulders in an "I could care less" manner. "Not that it matters."

"Oh, it matters to you." She smiled as she walked away and called back cattily, "It matters!"

Yeah, it mattered. Because he didn't sleep with women just because he could. Despite the way the press had portrayed him as a rogue of the slopes, Rayce was a gentleman and he never slept with a woman unless he thought there was something between them. Like he had with him and Rochelle. And he'd thought that something existed between him and Cassandra. Really, they had established a connection that felt genuine.

He watched from behind a frosted white wreath smelling of spiced oranges as she led the man toward the back patio door. Really? She was going somewhere with him? Should he walk out there? Introduce himself? Or play it cool and observe them from afar?

Since when did spying fall on the *cool* side of the scale? Rayce shook his head. They looked cozy. And if they'd once dated…

Shoving his hands in his pockets, he turned the opposite way. Just when he'd thought he'd gotten on a good run, found someone special, he'd crashed. That had been a fast fall.

With a sigh and a lift of his shoulders, he shook his head. "No," he muttered. "I will not fall this time."

It was late by the time Rayce completed his guest appointments and gathered the necessary accoutrements to visit Cassandra's room. The fresh flower arrangement in the café was now minus a long-stemmed red rose, but he'd been sneaky and squished two flowers together to hide the spot. He'd combed his hair instead of sliding his fingers through it a few times. And he'd shaved carefully so there were no nicks. He smelled like a cedar cabin—subtle, one spray of cologne—and he wore an ironed shirt.

Now he knocked on Cassandra's door, holding the flower behind him as he waited.

After seeing her talking to that man in the lobby, he'd initially grown angry. And defeated. The horrible memory

of watching Rochelle kiss another skier had made it difficult to breathe. But then something inside him had sat up.
That stupid heart of his? Yeah, it had grown smarter over
the past days. And it suggested to Rayce the man he'd seen
talking to Cassandra had probably been a friend, or a guest
she'd known for some time. Nothing for him to lose his cool
over. Not worth his anger.

But something niggled at him still. The twosome had
walked outside together. And Cassandra had not tried to find
him this evening. She knew his schedule. Which made him
wonder if she was avoiding him. For what reason?

The door opened and Cassandra, standing in a fluffy
white robe, smiled at him. "Rayce. I was hoping I'd see
you again."

"Again? I do live here at the resort. Why would you think
you wouldn't see me again?"

Her smile dropped. "What's up with you?"

*Don't let your heart grow stupid again and ruin this. Be
honest. Be kind.*

"Sorry. Nothing's wrong. Well. Can I come in?" He
whipped around the rose and offered it to her.

"Oh, that's beautiful." She stepped aside to allow him
entry as she sniffed the flower. "Wait a minute. Where did
you—"

He turned and winced just as she realized the answer to
her inquiry.

Putting up a palm, she shook her head. "Doesn't matter.
It's the thought that counts, right?"

"It is." Whew! He'd narrowly avoided that little tiff. "So
it looks like I caught you getting ready for bed." He looked
around. Low lighting in the living room. The humid scent
of a recent shower lingered. "You have a busy day?"

"It was a long one. A bunch of reservation switcheroos

and we've a high-profile celebrity staying in a week. I've already received a call from the local newspaper wanting the scoop. One of the most difficult parts of my job is detouring the media. How was your day?"

She wandered into the kitchen and found a vase for the rose. Rayce rubbed his jaw. How to ask about the man? Was it really necessary? He should ignore it—but his heart couldn't. He just needed to do it, get it out of his brain, and then he'd know it was nothing and that he could trust her.

"My day was great," he offered. "The Thorsons have graduated from the bunny hill to Harmony. They're going to be world-class skiers in no time. I love that couple. They've taught me a lot."

"Really? Like what?" She sat on the arm of the sofa, pulling a blanket over her legs. Undone and fresh from a shower, she looked so simple and perfect. He wanted to pull the robe from her shoulders and kiss her skin. Inhale her "flowers under snow" scent.

Concentrate, man!

"Uh…right. The Thorsons have shown me that I can be proud of some things. I taught them how to ski. That is an accomplishment."

"Of course it is. You have many things to be proud of, Rayce."

"I like that you're on Team Ryan, but…" He exhaled. He probably didn't have to bring it up.

Just move on. It was nothing.

"But?"

He scrubbed the back of his head, then blurted out, "I saw you talking to a guy at reception earlier. He…gave you a kiss."

"A guy? Kissed me? Oh! You mean Clint?"

Clint? Ugh.

"It wasn't a *kiss*-kiss," she said lightly, unaware of his inner emotional torment. "Clint is just a friend. Oh, wait. Did you and your stupid heart think otherwise?"

He winced.

"Oh, Rayce."

"Hey, you can do whatever you want."

"Really?"

He shrugged. "Not like we're dating."

"We're not?"

What was she getting at? He *wanted* them to be dating. They'd made love, for heaven's sake! But... Clint?

"Rayce, I don't sleep with any man who crosses my threshold."

"Well, I just—"

"Is that what you think of me?"

Her outrage stung, and he checked his cocky attitude. "Of course not. Cassandra, I thought..."

But his heart held a rein on his tongue, not allowing him to state what he really wanted. Because this felt like a race he'd forever fail.

She stepped up to him. Her soft blue eyes melted him like a snowman puddled before a bonfire. Rayce recalled the slip of her silken hair over his skin last night. Too luxurious. A treat he hadn't deserved. And yet the woman made him feel less broken.

"You thought?" Testingly she repeated his last words. "You thought what? That we *are* dating?"

He nodded subtly.

"So did I!" she declared with a gesture of her hands. "I never sleep with a guy unless there's something there. Something I want and like and well—no. I'm not going to beg for your forgiveness, Rayce. Especially since there's nothing to forgive. Clint and I did date. Years ago. But Clint stays at Cobalt Lake Resort every December. I ran into him at reception and he told me about his engagement. From there I walked with him for a while as we caught up on the past year. So if you need to do the he-man affronted act after learning that, then I guess you're not the man I thought you—"

Hearing that information snapped his self-imposed reins. Rayce slid his hands through her lush hair and pulled her in for a kiss. An urgent kiss that he'd been holding back since he'd opened the door to see her standing there like a lost snow princess desperately in need of a warming hug. She shivered in his embrace. That wasn't from the cold. Because the same shiver shuddered through his system and warmed him from the inside out. Kissing Cassandra never felt wrong. Had he been angry with her? Thought she'd gone behind his back with another man?

"I'm sorry," he said and bowed his forehead against hers. "It's my stupid heart."

"Stop calling it stupid, Rayce. I can understand how you might have taken seeing Clint give me a kiss on the cheek. But you're the only man I'm interested in. We shared an amazing night last night. I wanted to find you all day but was so busy and I know you worked late."

He kissed her again. "My he-man gene reared its ugly head. I'm a guy, Cassandra. I don't like seeing my girl with another man."

"Your girl?"

He shrugged. "I'd like that, but…"

"But?"

"It's this." He took her hand and placed it over his heart. "My luck with women tends toward the life-destroying."

"Rayce, what are you talking about?"

Could he be completely honest with her? It would allow her to know exactly where she stood with him. And why he'd reacted so strongly to seeing her with Clint. If he didn't confess now, he may lose her. And this wasn't a race he was willing to forfeit.

"Sit with me."

She snuggled up beside him on the couch. The moment was too intimate to destroy with his truth, but it was now or never. He'd come here to make sure he did not stew in anger over something he'd been mistaken about. He owed her his truth.

"The reason I keep calling my heart stupid?"

He peered into her beautiful gaze and his anxiety lessened.

Safe here with her.

Never had he felt so sure of that.

"It's because it doesn't know how to judge a good thing from the bad. The last girl I dated resulted in my crashing at the Olympics."

She twisted in his embrace to stare up at him and did not assault him with numerous questions, and that made a difference. He needed to exhale and summon downright bravery for the next part. Would the truth change the way she thought of him? Would it send him crashing again, only this time metaphorically, but in an even more painful manner? The idea of another rejection after he'd experienced so much letdown following the accident tensed his muscles.

When her fingers threaded with his, Rayce closed his eyes and focused on the warmth of her skin. Cassandra helped him to think forward instead of wallowing in the past. She would never do anything to hurt a person or manipulate them in any manner.

"I was secretly dating a girl on the Canadian team," he started. "Rochelle. Thing is, Coach had a rule about us dating while on tour. He said dating a team member was bad news. He even encouraged us not to date at all because we're always training and competing. Intimacy before a big race? It doesn't work for some people. It's never affected me. Until I let my stupid heart into the act."

The squeeze of her fingers silently reassured him in a way he couldn't believe he deserved. When had a woman ever sat quietly with him and listened to him spill open his heart? Never.

Because he'd not trusted someone until now.

"It had only been a few weeks of us sneaking around behind everyone's backs, meeting in dark freezing start houses, slipping into a bathroom at restaurants. I really liked her, thought it was more than sneaky stolen moments behind Coach's back. My heart thought she loved me. And I thought I loved her. Maybe I did."

Tilting his head against the couch, he then shook it, utterly amazed that he'd allowed himself to soften like that. Race, crash, recover, repeat could be construed as date, crash, recover, repeat. He'd been given a hard lesson, that was sure.

"On the night before the giant slalom at the Olympics, she broke it off with me."

"Seriously? How awful!"

"Yeah, well. In hindsight we were both in it for the sex."

"But what about your stupid heart?"

"My stupid heart thought something was real when it wasn't."

"Love is love, Rayce. It comes in all forms. You probably were in love with her."

"Maybe." Yes, at the time he had thought he was in love. Yet dismissing that feeling was the only way to set it aside and turn his back on it. "But that wasn't the most devastating part. The next day, as I made my way to the start house for the big race, I saw her standing on the sidelines. I winked at her, because even though it was over…" He sighed. "Stupid heart."

Cassandra slid her hand across his chest and hugged him closer. She was so sensitive to his need for a listening ear!

"Anyway," he continued, "when she saw me, she turned and kissed the guy standing next to her. He was on the American team and my biggest rival. And it wasn't a short peck. It was—" He swore quietly. "It ripped at me. It shouldn't have, but it did. I didn't want to believe she did it on purpose to mess with my race. I mean, we were on the same team. My loss was her loss! But it happened."

"So when you went down the slope…?"

"I thought my head was in the game, but seeing that kiss messed with my focus. I couldn't maintain my balance when my right ski hit an ice ridge on the seventh gate. I can't even recall how I went from upright on two skis, to lying on my back, sprawled, staring up at the sky. And as I lay there in a mangled mess, in pain, all I could think was, you did it to yourself, buddy. You shouldn't have been fooling around. Coach Chuck warned you. Your stupid heart."

"Oh, Rayce, I'm so sorry. I can't believe… Have you talked to her since?"

"She stopped into the hospital—" he swiped a hand over his face "—with the American skier. She acted like that sideline kiss never happened and we had always been just friends. It was another sound blow to my heart. I know I should have been stronger, but I'd never had anyone toy with my heart like that before."

"I can't imagine how that must have felt."

"Worse than the pain of the accident."

"Sorry, Rayce." She rested her head against his shoulder. "Thank you for telling me that."

They clasped hands over his heart. That she wasn't admonishing him for his stupidity and loss of focus over something so ridiculous as seeing a woman kiss a man meant the world. No judgment. Just a quiet acceptance.

"Yeah, well, it wounded me. Beyond the scars and surgeries and all the physical therapy. It hit me here." He tapped his heart. "The pain from the scarring puts an unwanted fear in my bones every time I hit the slopes, but I think that betrayal twisted its way into my soul. I don't want to crash again because some woman touched my heart and then crushed it. So when I saw you talking with Clint..."

"I understand. But I hope you realize it's not the same thing. Clint is engaged. The two of us are old news. I would never do anything to make you crash, Rayce. Promise."

"That sounds...like something my heart needs to hear."

"But you don't believe me?"

Yes, he did. Most of him did, anyway. One thumping section of his heart still held back. "Maybe I need to put on the brakes and take it a little slower. Make sure my heart..."

"Your heart isn't stupid. It's real and wanting, and—I can imagine how you must crave love and attention after all you've been through in your life."

She rested her chin on his shoulder and placed a palm over his chest. Right over his thundering heart. He'd never told anyone about seeing Rochelle kiss the American skier. Never wanted anyone to know it had been his stupid romantic heart that had caused him to crash and literally alter his life forever.

Did she really understand that he had to be careful with his heart now? It had been him who had pursued her. Another quest, like a race, he'd had to complete. Chasing after something that might have given him the love he desired? Was that it? *Did* he crave love and attention? That sounded so needy. And yet he felt good when with Cassandra. Less broken. He didn't know if she loved him. But he did know it felt great to be with her. To receive her attention.

How could that be a bad thing?

"I care about you, Rayce," she said quietly. "And I never would have slept with you last night if you didn't matter to me. So you know, I consider us a pair."

"Yeah?"

"And if you don't, then we're going to have a different discussion."

"I like being a pair with you. But…" There was another elephant in the room that he couldn't be sure wouldn't trample them both. "Is *your* heart really in this?"

"What do you mean?"

"I know what it's like to lose someone, Cassandra. Two someones. Can your heart be in this pair with the distraction of grief?"

"You don't think I can care about you while also grieving my mother?"

"I'm sure you can. It's just, I don't want to step into a situation where you're trying to work something out, and then make it more difficult by introducing romance and love and all that jazz."

"All that jazz sounds kind of nice. But you're right. I am having a hard time of it." Twisting to settle her side against his, the back of her head nestled against his shoulder. "I know it's not about the ornament. But my heart is convinced it is. I've thought about making a special and private place in my heart for my mom, but it feels like shoving her away and reducing that heart space for her. It doesn't feel right. What am I doing wrong?"

"You're not doing a single wrong thing." He kissed the top of her head. "Everyone grieves differently, Cassandra.

I can't tell you how to do it. But I can say that for myself, it was a process. I mourned. I screamed. I kicked things. I had the distraction of training to not let me get mired in falling apart after losing the two most important people in my life. But I also believe they would have been upset to watch me fall apart. The way Gramps and Grams died was an accident. But me holding a candle for them without seeing the world around me wasn't right.

"I thought about it one night. What if my mourning for them was somehow keeping them tied to the earthly realm? What if every thought I had about them anchored them to me and kept them from moving onward, going to Heaven or a new life? The best thing I could do was release them. Not from my heart. But from the part of me that needed to hold tight."

"That sounds—" she swallowed "—difficult."

"It's an adjustment. I still thought about them before every race. Gave them a nod. Gramps, who was an armchair astronomer, believed we are all stardust. I like to think the two of them are out there...stars in the sky."

"So you think I need to release my mom's memory to move onward?"

"No, you should always hold on to the memories. Don't be afraid to live your life. Don't you think that's what your mom would want for you?"

"Yes. She'd be angry to see me moping about some silly ornament."

"It isn't silly. It's something very personal to you. But you remember it, don't you?"

She curled up against his side. "I remember getting the glue all over my fingers and being so worried it wouldn't be perfect. But it was. Mom hugged me for the longest time after I gave it to her."

"That's an awesome memory. One you'll always have, even without the ornament. Just give it a think, Cassandra. I'll be here for you. But I don't want to get in the way of you finding what works for you and the memory of your mom."

"That's the kindest thing anyone has ever said to me," she said with a sniffle. "At the funeral everyone was like, *let me know what you need*. Well. I'm not going to reach out to anyone and say help me or hold me. That feels too scary, and needy. I wanted them to just do it for me without being asked. It's so weird when someone dies."

"Same happened to me. I wanted someone to hug me and make me dinner and clean my house."

"What?"

He shrugged. "My place was a mess after the funeral. I'd been out of town for months beforehand. And I wasn't in the headspace to do any cleaning. It's the little things that matter."

"That's so right. I laid in bed for days following the funeral. Then Anita knocked on the door and set a tray with hot chocolate on it by the bed, kissed my forehead and said she'd see me tomorrow morning to start the rounds my mom usually did. And you know? I did see her the next morning."

"Anita's a good one."

"She and Mom were close. I—gosh, I should talk to her about Mom someday. She's never said much. And I haven't known how to talk to anyone about it other than my dad."

"It might be a meaningful conversation for both of you. Anita knows things. She's a keeper."

"You have a weird relationship with her."

Rayce chuckled. "I think I've charmed her."

"That's one of your talents." She hugged him. "Will you stay with me tonight? No making love, just…us?"

"Definitely."

CHAPTER FIFTEEN

SLIPPING OUT OF BED, Cassandra tiptoed into the kitchen and pulled out a pitcher of orange juice. They'd slept in their clothes, snuggling until they'd fallen asleep. That quiet embrace had seemed even more intimate than sex now that she thought about it. Trust had grown between them.

With no breakfast food in the fridge, she decided that making an order with the chef would be best. Peeking into the bedroom, she saw Rayce was awake. "You hungry?"

"Always." He rolled onto his back, stretched out his legs and wiggled his feet covered with thick wooly socks. "What are you making?"

"Oh, dear one, you need to know I've become very reliant on the chef since I made the resort my permanent home. I can call Anita and put in an order for us."

"Sounds like a plan…" He glanced at his watch and winced. "Shoot. It's quarter to nine."

Had they really slept that late? She'd been so utterly comfortable lying beside him, like being with him was the only place she belonged. "Lesson?"

"In fifteen minutes. I'm sorry, I don't have time for food." Swearing, he tumbled out of bed. A few swipes of his fingers through his hair worked his coiffure into place.

Were they destined to forever see him fleeing the scene

following any night of shared intimacy? It was funny to consider.

"I can't have the boss knowing I was late because I was sleeping with his daughter. Even if it was just sleeping."

"You most certainly cannot. I'll…"

"What's so funny? You've got a laugh just waiting to escape."

She took in his unruly hair and noticed the crinkled skin on his cheek from sleeping on that side. So cute. Utterly cuddly. And about the sweetest guy she'd ever known. "You're adorable. I'll have breakfast sent out to the slopes. Something you can eat on the go."

"Thanks." Rayce grabbed his jacket and threaded in an arm. He stalked over to her with one boot on and bent to kiss her. "I gotta go! The Thorsons need me!"

As he rushed to the door, Cassandra called out, "Your grandparents would be proud of you, Rayce!"

He paused with the door open, still shoving one foot into his boot. "That's the nicest thing anyone has ever said to me."

"I wasn't trying to be nice. I just know they would be. You've got something, Rayce. People are comfortable around you. They trust you. And you're a world-class skier. Put them all together and you make a great teacher."

"Never would have thought I'd want to do what I'm doing now. But I do enjoy it. I only signed on for the season, though. Your dad just wanted to try me out."

"Would you stay longer if he asked?" And if her heart insisted?

"There is a lot here at Cobalt Lake Resort to want to stay for." If he used that wink one more time, she may have to drag him between the sheets and strip him bare. "Meet me later for some real food?"

"Sure. When do you have a break?"

"Not until four."

"Meet me back here then."

"It's a date!"

The delivery truck had picked up the thank-you gifts, all boxed up and addressed to guests. Cassandra had made up extra boxes, one for each of the resort employees. She'd handed Kathy at reception a box and the woman had eagerly dug into it, swooning over the chocolate truffles and thanking her with a high five.

After a long day, Cassandra recalled her conversation with Rayce as he'd scrambled out the door this morning. They had a dinner date this evening. She called in an order to the kitchen and was on her way to pick it up when she overheard a conversation in the lobby between what looked like an eight-year-old girl and her mother.

"Mommy, can I turn on the lights and make the tree pretty?"

"No, dear, they probably only turn them on at night."

"But it's already dark outside!"

"I know." The mother cast a glance around the lobby. It was obvious she wanted to make her daughter happy and that child's frown was something Cynthia Daniels would have never allowed to slip past her quality control.

A heavy lump rose in Cassandra's throat. She was denying a little girl a simple Christmas joy because of her adamant refusal to do one thing. That ornament may never be found. It could have gotten crushed or broken. Perhaps last year, when the decorations were packed away by staff, someone had decided it was too damaged and tossed it.

Or it was simply missing. And she needed to come to

terms with that. She'd already pushed her father's deadline beyond the past due date.

You can do this, she coached herself inwardly.

Rayce kept a place in his heart for his grandparents. Time to arrange that place in her heart specifically for her mom. A place that would allow her room for others—like a sexy ski instructor—and to move forward.

With a heavy inhale, Cassandra drew up all her bravery and walked over to the pair. "Did I hear you wonder about the lights?"

"Why don't you turn them on?"

"Uh…"

Never lie to a child.

Slipping over to the present at the back of the tree where the controls were kept safely out of the hands of curious guests, Cassandra plucked out the remote. Her mom had always let her do the honors after the tree was decorated. And she'd pronounce "Marvelous!" as Cassandra would step back and display the glowing tree with a sweep of her hands.

"I was just going to turn it on."

I love you, Mom. This is for you.

She handed the girl the remote. "You can do the honors if you'd like to. Maybe your mom will take a picture of you doing it?"

The girl nodded eagerly and cast a glimmering gaze toward her mom, who was already lining up the shot with her phone. Cassandra slipped to the side and crossed her fingers behind her back. An immense welling of emotion flooded her system. The picture that she'd pasted into the ornament had been of her laughing in her mom's arms. A precious moment forever preserved. They'd shared so many of those moments. And she remembered them all.

Out of the corner of her eye, she noticed her dad standing

near the reception desk. His nod and thumbs-up to her spoke volumes. It sent her courage and approval at the same time.

With that reassurance…she relaxed. This little girl would have many memories of her mother as well. Together they may even preserve one of them in a special way, as Cassandra had.

As the Christmas lights blinked on to the cheers of the girl, Cassandra's heart opened a little wider and she embraced the moment with an accepting nod. That special place in her heart beamed.

"Thank you," she whispered, though the girl couldn't hear her through her elated cheers.

Feeling as though she'd received an approving hug from her mom, Cassandra accepted the remote back and clutched it to her chest, watching as the mother and girl took a few more shots before the beautifully lit tree. Behind, at the reception desk, her dad gave a hoot and the few guests loitering in the lobby paused to take it in.

It wasn't perfect. The ornament was still missing. But it was close enough. And maybe this time, Cassandra decided, close enough would do. Because the memory of her mom flushed her system and made her stand tall and smile. All was well.

Mostly. Maybe?

No, she had to accept this. She *could* accept this.

Meeting her dad halfway across the lobby, they collided in a long and generous hug. He kissed the top of her head and then brushed the hair from her face. "I'm proud of you, Cassie."

She nodded, the burgeoning tears making it difficult to speak.

"She lives in our hearts."

Yes, she did.

At that moment, Rayce strolled into the lobby, spied the lit tree and his eyes met hers. She shrugged. He smiled and tilted his head in a gesture that suggested she join him.

Giving her dad's hand a squeeze, she thanked him in a whisper as she kissed his cheek. "Thanks for always being there for me." They bumped fists and he wandered over to talk to the mother and her daughter while Cassandra met Rayce beside the hot chocolate dispenser.

"You just turned those on?" he asked as she joined him. "Did you find the ornament?"

"No."

He kissed the back of her hand, then held it against his cheek for a moment. "It's a good thing, Snow Princess. The tree is beautiful. Are you going to be all right?"

He understood the struggle of emotion she currently battled and knowing that settled her rising anxiety.

"Yes, I think I am. I made a place here." She tapped her chest over her heart. "For her. And I couldn't deprive the guests of such an iconic Christmas sight any longer. But that doesn't mean I'll give up my search."

"Is that where you're headed right now? On the search?"

"Actually, we had a date, didn't we? I was going to pick up our dinner and head to your cabin."

"Sounds perfect. How about after we've eaten, we drive into town and catch a movie? Like a real date?"

The hopeful tone in his voice made her smile. They hadn't gone on an official date outside of the resort.

"Sounds like the perfect way to spend an evening," she said.

His smile beamed so brightly that it extinguished any remaining anxiety she'd had about lighting the Christmas tree. With a wave to her dad, she left the lobby holding Rayce's hand.

* * *

After the movie the twosome strolled a sidewalk in Whistler Village. Christmas decorations adorned the streetlights, storefronts and even the trash receptacles, and enhanced the festive atmosphere. Rayce had spied a cozy café on the way in and wanted to stop for something sweet following the buttery theater popcorn. He'd let Cassandra pick the movie and it had been, as she'd called it, a rom-com.

"That was a cute movie," she said, clasping his hand.

"It was…too easy," he decided. "I don't think life is like that. It's more messy. Hearts and emotions can change on a dime."

"Are you talking about the movie right now? Because it sounds to me like you've switched to real life and you're not entirely convinced that what we're doing here is going to work."

"Sorry, I guess I zoned out after the hero offered to make cookies to help her win the competition." He sighed and lifted her hand to kiss it, even though she wore a glove. "Yeah, real life, eh? I want it to be like in the movies. Believe me, I've thought ahead. Like years ahead."

"And what do those future thoughts involve?"

"I think about how I'd like to have a family and what that might look like. Having a home, for sure. I'm not going to tell you much more. Don't want to jinx it."

"A home…" Her tone went wistful for a moment, but she snapped out of it in astute Cassandra fashion. "I never think much further ahead than the day or the week's schedule."

"You're kidding me? You must have princess dreams of wearing a white dress and walking down the aisle like the chick in the movie?"

She wobbled her head. "Eh."

"But white's your color!" he said more as a prod than in disbelief.

"Okay, fine, but I've always thought a simple summer ceremony would suit me. Wearing a floral dress. Barefoot. Flowers in my hair."

Now she was just being romantic. Rayce swallowed as the image of Cassandra Daniels adorned in flowers and twirling down a grassy aisle toward him gave him some kind of hopeful quiver right…there. He caught a hand over his heart.

"What's wrong?" she asked while simultaneously pointing across the street toward the café. "All that buttered popcorn acting up?"

"Yep." And he was sticking with that story. Wouldn't feel right to confess he'd had a romantic thought about his future. A future that included his snow princess.

"Let's pick up some fancy treats to take back with us." He tugged her ahead to a chocolate shop that displayed bonbons in the window.

"You do know the way to my heart."

Honestly? He *was* navigating some sort of passageway toward her heart. And it felt like a fresh run down a new slope: adventurous, a little risky and filled with the unknown around every slight curve. But that was exactly the kind of risk Rayce Ryan liked to take.

CHAPTER SIXTEEN

THE FOLLOWING MORNING, Rayce had lingered in Cassandra's bed. They'd kissed. Made slow and intense love. Dozed off in one another's arms. Then repeated. The man did like to practice a thing until he got it right.

He most certainly did get her right.

Bright sunlight finally coaxed them to rise and get dressed. Rayce had offered to pick up something in the café and bring it up to her, but she declined. She had morning rounds to make and he did have a client. It wasn't a rush out the door to make the appointment, though. They'd kissed all the way to the door, and when he'd gotten ten feet down the hallway, he'd spun and rushed back to give her one more long lush kiss.

Getting it right.

Now she stood before the vanity mirror after having blown out her hair and put on some makeup. She'd never felt so utterly relaxed and at the same time *desirable* in her life. It was a heady feeling. Better than Christmas morning.

The best present she had received so far this holiday season was rediscovering Rayce. Being able to share things with him. Talking about both the good and bad times. He seemed to understand her, and she understood him. They had bonded through grief. But she wanted it to go beyond that. And it did. They shared amazing chemistry between the sheets. And even when dressed and walking hand in hand or eating or enjoying life, they seemed to fit in one another's atmosphere with ease.

Finding love couldn't be so easy, could it? Because, when she thought about it, she cared about Rayce and adored every little thing about him. From his cocky grin to feeling he needed to wield the plastic mistletoe to get a kiss from her. And her heart was all in. Which meant...

Was she falling in love? So quickly?

Her dad had done as much with Faith. But he and Faith had known each other since high school.

She and Rayce had gone to school together, too, but hadn't really known one another. That hadn't stopped her from crushing on him. And, apparently, he'd had a thing for her, too. Was it only now that life had decided they should become a couple?

Why fight it? Or better, why not take it day by day and enjoy the moments? Yet the deadline for his departure lingered. If she ransomed her heart to him this winter, would she have to take it back when he left in the spring?

"Don't think like that," she admonished herself.

When he'd mentioned his plans last night, the word *home* had seemed to cling to her. More and more she really did wish for a home away from work. An escape from the place where it felt necessary to exercise control. Yet since she'd begun to loosen the reins on that control, the longing for a place to genuinely relax was real.

Dare she dream of a future with Rayce in a home they'd created together?

"Nothing wrong with dreaming," she whispered.

But the thought wasn't as convincing as it should have been. They were in a new relationship. Anything could happen. It was far too early to start picking out patterned China and silverware.

"But I can allow the fantasy," she whispered with an approving nod to her change toward a more relaxed and open future.

Dressing quickly, she combed her hair and pinned it up in a neat chignon, then headed out for her usual morning rounds.

Afterward, bundled up against the cold, she wandered over the boot-tracked trail that curled around behind the main patio and fireplace. When a *thunk* of cold snow splatted her back, she at first thought it was snow falling from the pine trees. But a distant whoop of triumph revealed to her she had been attacked. And she recognized that cocky whoop.

"Really?" Cassandra surveyed the snowy ground, spying the best patch for ammunition. When another snowball hit the back of her boot, she swung into action. Bending, she scooped up a handful of moist yet moldable snow and began to pack it. "Are you aware that I am the snowball-throwing champion of the Girl Guides of Canada?"

Rayce splayed his arms out in mock challenge. Then he tapped his chest and lifted his chin defiantly. "Take your best shot!"

He was close enough for the direct hit that she lobbed toward him. Snow dispersing at his shoulder, he took it like a man. But he quickly bent to reload. As did Cassandra.

She threw another, and another, each time landing a hit on her opponent. He missed her a few times because, now that she could see them coming, she dodged like the professional she was. They moved closer and closer, and her snowball craftsmanship grew messier until finally she held two handfuls of loose snow as Rayce ran toward her. She flung them at him, getting him in the face. His chuckles matched hers as he grabbed her about the waist and took her down in the fluffy snow.

Their kiss was cold and silly as they rolled in the snow and took turns flinging loose snow at one another. Kiss. Attack. Kiss. Pleads for mercy as snow began to sink under her scarf and icy water seeped through her sweater.

"Mercy?" Rayce defied as he hovered above her, a snowball in hand.

"Please!" she shouted.

"Then I guess we know who the new snowball champion is, eh?"

"I'll alert the Girl Guides immediately." She flapped her arms out across the snow as she lay on her back, looking upward.

Rayce flopped down next to her, and he started reshaping the snowball he had in hand.

The sky glistened with a beautiful pink tinge that floated at the tops of the snow-dusted pine trees. It had been a long time since Cassandra had lain in the snow and took things in. Lived in the moment. As well, she'd missed the utter abandon of a good snowball fight.

"Turning on the tree lights wasn't as heart-wrenching as I thought it would be," she confessed.

"I'm glad." He worked diligently at his snowball. "I bet it made your mom happy."

At the thought of her mom, smiling and laughing with happiness, a tear came to Cassandra's eye. But she wasn't going to freak about her sadness. Instead she opened that place she'd reserved in her heart and sat with it a while.

"Here." Rayce handed her the snowball.

"What's this for?"

"You."

She took the snowball; it was no longer rounded. He'd formed it into a heart.

"It's my heart," he said lightly. "I trust you'll treat it well."

She carefully held the snow heart with both gloved hands. "I'll treat it as kindly and respectfully as you've treated mine."

He rolled over to kiss her until they were laughing and wrapped in one another's arms, legs and scarves. He smelled like winter cedar and sensual heat. And he tasted like snowflakes and adventure. Amidst their make-out session, she managed to set the heart down.

Rayce looked aside to spy the snow heart. "Let's leave it there so it doesn't melt."

"Deal. Race you back to the resort?"

"If I claim an injured leg, will you give me a head start?"

"Ha!" She pulled herself up and then before dashing off, she bent over the snow heart and drew a bigger heart around it with her finger. "There. Now it's official."

"What's official?"

"Our hearts belong to one another."

"That's freakin' romantic."

"Yeah? Well, this isn't." She blasted him with a kick of snow, then took off toward the resort.

He followed, his laughter the best balm to the few slivers of grief that the thoughts of her mom had produced. But with Rayce she realized she could hold all those emotions, and still rise to embrace the good times.

He didn't want to wake the sleeping beauty, so Rayce finished a note for Cassandra and set it on her desk. Yes, he'd developed a habit of slipping out of her bed while she slept, but not every time. Invigorated by a night of making love and a newfound intimacy that included trust and honesty, he wanted to challenge himself this morning. And his back wasn't bothering him, so it was now or never.

The sun wouldn't rise for another hour, but he was eager to catch the fresh powder. He grabbed his ski jacket and headed out.

An hour later he landed at the bottom of the run. Exhilarating! The powder was deep and dry. Perfect conditions for a speedy descent. And despite a few painful twinges along his spine, his leg hadn't given him trouble.

But now that the sun had risen, the slope was crowded with skiers. Had he really left a warm, gorgeous Cassandra alone in bed just to catch some powder?

"Fool," he muttered.

However he'd had to prove something to himself. And now that he thought about it, the invigorating feeling that encompassed him may be pride.

"Nice." He could push his body. But as well, he'd learned that he'd hit the limit in those runs. Any faster and he would have been in agony. There were no gold medals in Rayce Ryan's future. No more cheering fans. No more endorsements or sponsorship deals. Retirement was a real thing.

Strangely he was okay with that. Because he'd found something more fulfilling.

With an accepting nod he skied over to the hot chocolate vendor. When he went to flash his employee badge for a free drink, he patted his jacket. Where was the tag?

"Sir?" the elder gentleman manning the bar prompted as Rayce patted down his clothes in search of the badge.

It must have fallen off somewhere. Probably when he'd been flying downhill. Ah, well, he had some cash in his pocket. He handed over a bill and received a steaming cup. It was far from the thick fancy stuff the resort served their guests, but the sugar worked the same, rushing through his system with a scream.

When he tossed the cup in a garbage bin and turned around, his path was blocked by three women wearing various shades of pink and purple. Snow bunnies, each with diamonds glinting at their ears and around their necks. Their sort never zipped up their jackets against the chill. How else would anyone notice their bling? They were not here for the skiing; they were here to be seen and to party.

One of them called him by name and asked him for an autograph. She offered the pink sleeve of her jacket and a black Sharpie. The others joined with their sleeves as he whisked his John Hancock down each arm. Despite the crazy good feeling of pride he was still riding, his ego would never tire of the attention. This retired Alpine racer had to take advantage of it when he could.

"We saw you fly down that slope. You're so talented, Rayce. You make it look so effortless."

The last sleeve was signed and she tipped the capped marker under his chin. Her bright pink lips curled into a seductive twist. "You want to join us in our room for something stronger than cocoa?"

"We have so many questions. If you answer them, we'll make it worth your while," she sing-songed coyly.

Rayce's eyebrows rose. The pheromones coming off them in waves were dusted with perfume and lust. He could feel it permeate his skin.

"Sorry, ladies, I don't think my girlfriend wants me answering questions."

"Girlfriend? The media reports say you haven't dated since the accident. That you were incapable of ever..." She shrugged. "You know."

Now that one stung. And it was a cruel cut at his manhood. The media had never reported any such thing!

As the trio laughed wickedly, Rayce pushed away and slid toward the track leading to the resort. They'd started out amiable enough, but when he'd refused their advances, they'd grown just plain mean.

His mood dove from the high of the early morning fresh powder run to the dredges of a bruised ego.

Cassandra found the note after Rayce had slipped from her bed without so much as a kiss goodbye. It sat next to the little drummer boy figurine and read:

Heading out to catch the fresh powder. See you later.

Seriously? He must have snuck out extremely early because the sun was only just now rising. Which meant he'd hit the slopes before they were open to the public. There was a reason the runs weren't open until the sun came up. They were dangerous; what kind of idiot went out on his own to ski in the dark?

She bit her lip and shook her head. Her mom had gone out at midnight all the time, much to her dad's protests. Such reckless abandon had cost her her life. And while Cassandra knew Rayce was a professional—it didn't matter. Mother Nature cared little about a skier's skill.

Stepping on something with her bare foot, she winced, then bent to pick it up. It was Rayce's employee badge. She turned it over. A fragment of neon green fabric stuck in the rivet clip. It had torn from his jacket.

She glanced out the patio doors. The slopes were busy; it was always a rush to get to the fresh powder in the mornings. She couldn't see the green jacket out there. Had he gone down a slope before the sun had risen and…had trouble?

A terrible darkness clenched Cassandra's throat. She didn't want to think the worst. But as she clasped the badge and the plastic edge dug into her palm, she could only think of avalanches and skiers missing their mark and careening off the slope to crash into rocks or tree trunks.

Or worse.

She swore. Just when she had been so close to accepting the loss of her mother and moving forward, now this had to happen. *If* anything had happened.

No. He was fine. Right? If an avalanche had occurred, the entire mountain would be cleared and emergency protocol would be instituted. Her dad, a member of the search and rescue team, would have alerted her. Rayce was perfectly fine. He knew what he was doing—but why would he torment her like this? He knew about her fears.

With a swallow she closed her eyes and pressed a hand against her thumping heart. Praying nothing had happened. Her heart may never recover!

Wrapping a scarf around her neck, she stepped into her boots and opened her door to find Rayce standing there with his fist up in preparation to knock.

"Rayce!" She grabbed him by the front of his jacket. "Get in here!"

"Glad to see you, too." He wandered inside and turned to give her a wink. "Is this urgent welcome because you missed me and need to strip me bare right now?"

"What?" Oh. He was talking about the fabulous sex they'd had last night. But she could not get beyond her fear and anger to soften to that pleasure. "No! You are so reckless!"

His jaw dropped open. "Reckless? Me?"

"Yes, you. Going out before the slopes opened? Were there even any patrols out there? It had to have still been dark. Did anyone see you?"

"Cassandra, are you seriously upset because I—a professional skier—wanted to take a few runs on my own? You know I know what I'm doing, right?"

"The slopes don't care if you're a professional or a newbie. You could have been hurt and no one would have known where you were."

"I left you a note. And I—" He patted his jacket and winced.

"And you left without this!" She held up the badge. "Didn't you notice it missing?"

"Not until after I'd finished my run, and then I got distracted because I was shut down by a bunch of snow bunnies with flashy bling and bad attitudes."

"Snow bunnies?" Her shoulders dropped as she exhaled. So that was what he'd been doing? "You were out there flirting while I was in here worrying about you?"

His smile grew. "You were worried about me? Does that mean you care about me?"

"Of course I care about you. But I don't like that you believe you're so expendable. I would think that the accident curbed your reckless need to endanger your life."

"I am not a reckless skier. And that accident was not due to anything but a broken heart. I told you that!" He swore. "Please don't tell anyone about that. It's humiliating. And now you're chastising me as if I'm a child!"

"Only because I would be devastated if you were injured or…or worse! I can't believe you don't understand that. After my mom—I thought we had something."

"We do. Cassandra, I wasn't thinking about your mother. I realize now that finding that badge must have freaked you out.

You thought I was out there with no means to be found if… if anything had happened to me. I'm sorry. I should have—"

"Yeah? Well, my mom is never coming back because she was reckless. I'll never get to hug her again."

Something inside Cassandra closed. All the emotional work she'd put in since Rayce had arrived sluiced away. Her heart went still as the armor fitted back around it.

She lifted her chin and shook her head. The adrenaline junkie standing before gave her a bewildered look. "I can't do this. You're not the man for me, Rayce. I can't handle any more grief right now."

"Cassandra, I'm fine."

When he made a move to embrace her, she put up her hands in protest. "I need someone stable, Rayce. Someone who is willing to stick around Cobalt Lake for me. Someone who will be there for me and who won't take risks."

He sighed heavily. "Skiing is all about the risk," he muttered. "You know that."

She bowed her head and nodded. "Would you please leave?"

"Really? We have to talk about this, Cassandra. I don't want this thing we've started to end. And I'm not a loser like those ladies on the slopes implied. I can't be. But if I lose you…"

She winced. So much was unspoken in that pause. He'd lost a lot. She should be more sensitive to that. But right now, with her fractured heart, she couldn't handle another heartbreak.

She opened the door, holding it for him. "I'm sorry. I can't do this."

With a heavy sigh Rayce walked to the door but paused alongside her. She couldn't look at him. Or she'd fall into his summer sky eyes and melt.

Without a word he took a mangled piece of plastic from his jacket pocket and handed it to her. Then he left, closing the door behind him.

Cassandra clasped the mistletoe to her chest. Tears spilled down her cheeks. She didn't want him to go. But she didn't know how to ask him to return.

What was she so reluctant about? It couldn't be because of his reckless behavior. She was bigger than that. The man knew what he was doing. And no matter how safe she attempted to keep her world and those in it, she could never monitor everyone all the time. Accidents were just that—accidents.

She had been so close to allowing love into her life.

Leaning against the door, she crushed the mistletoe against her chest and closed her eyes. "I wish you were here, Mom. I need you."

CHAPTER SEVENTEEN

AFTER AN AFTERNOON class with four kids all under ten years old, Rayce helped an intern return the skis and poles to the storage shed. It had been gently snowing for an hour. Thick flakes quieted the atmosphere in a way those who weren't familiar with a snowy season could never understand. Though the slopes were still packed with skiers, it was as though sounds and conversations were muted. Nature insisted on being noticed.

With an eye to a lift on Blackcomb peak, he shook his head. His back, which had been tight and painful all day, warned him to stay grounded. A deep tissue massage and maybe even a soak in the hot tub felt necessary.

Take care of yourself, buddy. It's the right thing to do. Besides, you're retired, remember?

As well, after the argument with Cassandra this morning, he didn't need a streak of pain in his spine to warn him against taking a risky run. If he'd been feeling low after his encounter with the snow bunnies, Cassandra had shoved him even lower with her announcement that she didn't want him in her life.

As he walked slowly toward the employee cabins, he veered off behind a line of pine trees where the snow blanketed a short length of open field. He'd heard some kids out here the other night making snow angels. And despite the falling snow, he could still see impressions of an angel or two as he walked by.

The pale sky fluttered with flakes. He sighed. His two angels were up there. Somewhere.

"Are you out there?" he asked the sky. "In the stars? Do you miss me as much as I miss you?"

Talking to his grandparents helped him to forget the rough parts of life that tended to sneak up on him. Like an injured leg keeping him grounded. Or an upset woman who had told him she didn't want someone as reckless as him in her life.

The fact that Cassandra had talked about needing someone to stick around long term had been buoying. But at the time his heart sunk. Because in the same breath she'd erased *him* from that possibility.

Cassandra had made a choice. And it hadn't been him. She insisted on swimming in her grief and not allowing anyone to dive in to float alongside her. He could have done that. He thought he *had* been doing that. Talking with her. Sharing his grief with her. Being there for her.

If that badge hadn't fallen from his jacket, he'd be in Cassandra's room right now, holding her in his arms, nuzzling his nose into her hair. Being the man she wanted him to be because that was the kind of man *he* wanted to be.

Eyeing an undisturbed patch of thick snow, he turned and fell backward, arms out. He landed with an *oof* and a chuckle because he'd made an old man noise. At the very least, his leg hadn't done anything weird like twitched him headfirst into a snowbank.

Spreading out his legs and arms, he fashioned a snow angel and closed his eyes to the falling flakes. The taste of them melting on his lips reminded him of his snow princess.

Well, she wasn't his anymore, was she? She'd declared he wasn't the guy for her. That he hadn't cared enough about her to not go skiing on his own. At the time he couldn't have known the angst he was causing Cassandra. It hurt his heart to think that something he had done had upset her.

"She's very special," he said to the sky. "I thought we had something. I...don't want to be alone. I'd give it all up if I could have someone in my life. Someone to love."

He'd already lost it all, so he had nothing left to sacrifice. Was that it? He had nothing to offer someone like Cassandra Daniels. No comfy home. Not even a strong proud warrior of a man who could protect her. An injured leg did not make for a hero.

"I could fall in love with her," he confessed to the sky. "I know what love feels like. You guys made me feel safe, happy and loved. Did I ever tell you how much I appreciated what you did for me? Allowing me to go on those ski trips and funding my training. Buying all my gear. I know you weren't rich. But, Gramps, you never said no. And, Grams, you always had a hot meal and a hug for me whenever I returned home from camp or a ski event. I miss you guys!"

The wind shushed through the pines and redirected a glittering sweep of snow across his face. If that hadn't been a message from Gramps, he didn't know what was. The old man had always been funning with him, trying to get him to laugh.

He sat up and brushed the snow from his ski pants. His cap had fallen off and he twisted to pick it up. He traced a finger over the embroidered Cobalt Lake Resort logo. Could this place ever be a home to him?

"I could settle here and be happy," he said to anyone who would listen.

They were listening. They always were.

"The skiing is first class. And... Cassandra."

His snow princess.

He most certainly was not the best guy she could have

in her life, he thought to himself. Not smart enough, that was for sure. And too cocky, certainly. Complete opposite of her careful and neat ways. And…reckless.

But she made him believe his heart was not so stupid. Heck, the darn thing had to be smart. It had led him to Cassandra.

Should he beg her to give him another chance? That's how it worked in the movies. Grand gestures seemed to be a thing in a successful romance. Rayce shoved a hand in his pocket. He'd handed Cassandra the mistletoe in a moment of surrender, of forlorn sadness at having been given the boot. There was no easy passage back into her heart now.

But if a passage still existed, he hoped the gate wasn't locked.

"Do I dare fall in love?"

The pale sky was serene and quiet. A few snowflakes brushed his face. Kisses from his grandparents. He knew what their answer was.

Now did he have the courage to live up to their expectations? To show them that he could accept love and give love in return?

The next morning Anita dropped off a tray of hot chocolate as Cassandra was stepping out of the shower. "Have a great day!" she called.

"Wait, Anita!"

"Yes?"

Cassandra pulled on a fluffy robe and hustled out to the living room. She knew the sous chef's time was valuable, but now more than ever she was determined to honor the connection with her mom in any way possible.

"I appreciate you bringing me hot chocolate in the morning. I know you always did the same for my mom."

"Your mother and I…" Anita pressed a palm over her chest.

"You two were close," Cassandra confirmed. "She mentioned you often."

Anita nodded, not looking up. Cassandra could sense her nervousness and heard the catch in her breathing. "I cared about your mother. She was very good to me. To all of us. We chatted in the mornings. Sometimes I would take tea with her if I wasn't too busy."

"That's so nice to hear." Cassandra hadn't known that. Perhaps they'd been more than respectful coworkers, friends even. "I have wanted to speak to you about her since, well, since she passed. I want you to know that you were special to her."

"Thank you, Cassandra. She was special to me. I miss her." Now she tilted her head back and sniffed at a tear. "I know it's hard for you now. And seeing your dad with his new fiancée…"

"It took a while for me to accept Faith, but she's good for my dad. And I look forward to meeting my new step siblings. Are you okay, Anita? I mean…have you ever talked to anyone about…?" About Cynthia.

Anita shrugged and shook her head, and that action compelled Cassandra to hug her. Initially Anita resisted, but then she pulled her into a hug that drew tears from Cassandra's eyes as well.

"She is missed," Anita whispered. "But always remembered."

Cassandra stepped back from the hug and swiped a tear from her cheek. "Yes, remembered. Every day."

"But you mustn't let sadness stick to your bones," Anita said with a deep inhale as she settled her shoulders. "That's not good for anyone."

She'd never heard it put in such a manner, but yes, the grief had stuck to her very bones. And it wasn't good for her.

Anita clasped her hand and squeezed. "Thank you. I needed that hug."

"So did I."

"You are so much like Cynthia," she said. "I know she is proud of you. And you know? I think she would like that handsome Rayce Ryan a lot."

Cassandra chuckled. "I think she would, too. And if she didn't, he'd charm his way under her skin one way or another."

"He is a charmer. So, uh…"

"What is it, Anita?"

"I just think he's falling in love with you."

"You do?" Cassandra wasn't at all surprised at such a declaration. Her heart felt much the same about Rayce. But to hear it declared so simply forced her to own that feeling. "I… Well. Rayce is kind. Funny. We have fun together."

So why had she let him leave? Kicked him out, even? She'd told him she couldn't do this. That hadn't been her talking. Not rationally, anyway.

In that moment Cassandra had allowed fear to rise and overwhelm her. She hadn't been acting in accordance with her true feelings. Rayce calmed her and embraced her every quirk, mystery and even her perfectionist tendencies. Her mom would certainly approve.

Was she looking at Rayce as an option for her future? The other options being…no boyfriend, constant work, no social life, all her free time consumed with work-related tasks?

"Anita, do you think I've lost myself in this job?"

"Honestly? You do spend an awful lot of time here. Your mother had her home in Whistler Village to go to after work. Where do you go?"

"Here." Cassandra's shoulders dropped.

The words Anita didn't speak were clear: *where is your life?*

"I do dream about having a home away from work. And about having a relationship with Rayce."

"Your mother would be happy to hear that." Anita took Cassandra's hand and gave it a squeeze. "Take a chance on him. He's a great guy."

Well. Rayce did have his reckless moments. And that would never change. Also he didn't trust his own heart. She hated that he called it stupid. A person should never use that word to describe any part of themselves. The body listened to those words. And if he couldn't get beyond not trusting his heart, that could present a problem should she decide to offer up her own.

But did *she* trust her heart?

"I do want to give him a chance," she said. "Or rather, I did. We had an argument. Oh, I wish my mom were here to talk to. But…" She inhaled and let it all out through her nose. *Let it go.* "I can't thank you enough for letting me talk to you like this. It means a lot."

"Anytime, Cassandra. And don't worry. People argue. It's what we do to learn about one another, yes? And then we realize it's not worth the anger. If you care about him, tell him."

Cassandra nodded as Anita left and closed the door behind her. She did care about Rayce. And she had come down from her anger enough to realize their argument had been hasty and not at all what her heart desired.

So much had happened since Rayce Ryan had set foot in the resort. Her heart had altered in many ways. She had conceded and turned on the tree lights without finding the ornament. Because it had made others happy. And in the process, it had brought a smile to her face. It had lightened her grief to know her mother would have approved.

This was supposed to be the happiest time of the year. A wonderful life! Yet one moment her heart swelled with joy, the next it sank into sadness.

Closing her eyes, she pictured her mom. Pale blond hair and tall lithe figure. Always elegantly dressed and, though Cassandra knew Cynthia Daniels's brain always spun one hundred kilometers an hour and never slowed down, she wore a smile for others and her kindness was always genuine.

"What do you think, Mom? About Rayce? He's special. He makes me laugh. I have fun with him. I forget about work and striving for perfection when I'm with him. I think I could love him."

Silent, she waited in quiet wonder for a vocal reply she knew would never come.

Did she need a sign? She liked hearing how Rayce thought of his grandparents as stars in the sky, always there, watching over him. Maybe her mom was up there, too. And if so…

"I have to follow my heart, with you as my guide."

With a nod she confirmed the conversation with Anita had been worthwhile. Her mom, who never took time to slow down and chat with anyone, had spent time in the mornings over tea with Anita. Another wonderful memory to store in that place in her heart designated for Cynthia Daniels.

Eyeing the tray, with the pot and upside-down teacup, her heart skipped. Would she find a surprise under the cup this morning?

Her heart sank. Probably not. She and Rayce had come to some sort of ending. Much as she regretted it. Was it too late to change things? It couldn't be. The man was good for her heart.

If she wanted Rayce, she had to fight for him.

With another determined nod, Cassandra got dressed. Sitting before the desk to check her emails before she started her rounds, she again eyed the upside-down cup. The suspense was killing her, and yet…

She shook her head and tapped at the keyboard to go through a short list of emails. The RSVPs for the employee Christmas party were pouring in. They always held the gathering a few days before Christmas Day itself, and brought in a celebrity chef and entertainment from Whistler. Secret Santa gifts were exchanged while photos were taken. No one ever missed it.

An email from Faith reminded her she had promised to go wedding dress shopping with her and her daughter after the New Year and gave her a few dates as options. The idea of gaining not one but three new family members had initially shocked her. Then she'd decided it was good for her dad. He needed the companionship, love and attention. And why not? Love did things for a person's heart.

And she was beginning to recognize that change in her own heart.

Typing a reply to Faith to say that any of the dates would work, Cassandra then absently reached for the teacup and turned it over, completely expecting the saucer beneath to be bare—

Cassandra let out a surprised chirp. Sitting on the plate was a small silver star that she knew had come from one of the wreathes in the lobby. Made of resin, it glittered when she tilted it. She recalled again how Rayce thought of his grandparents as stars in the sky.

With a tearful smile she tapped the star. "I haven't given up on you, either, Rayce."

CHAPTER EIGHTEEN

RAYCE SPIED THE white cat scampering over a snowbank
and toward the equipment sheds. He took chase. Angling
toward the employee cabins, he swung around a tall birch
tree only to collide with Cassandra. He caught her by the
forearms and steadied her from taking a fall.

"Are you okay?"

"Yes. Thanks for catching me. But what are you doing
out here?"

He had not planned to literally run into her after their
breakup. They'd both said terrible things. Had put their
hearts out there. And it hadn't ended well. He owed her an
apology. More than that, he wanted to talk until they moved
beyond the argument and back into the trust and empathy
they'd created.

Look at him, feeling all, well…the feelings!

"I'm on the trail of a wayward cat," he said. "You?"

"Same. I think it went that way." She pointed toward one
of the vehicle sheds.

He bent to study the snow. "You are correct. Tracks!"
He grabbed her hand and led her quickly across the snow.
To talk now or wait until the moment was right? The moment might never be right. But what if he made the wrong
move? Again!

A *crash* from inside the shed averted his attention. "Let's get that cat! I'm sure it went into the shed."

"I don't know how it could get inside. The building should be locked and…"

As they neared the shed, both were shocked to see one of the windowpanes was broken. Nearby on the ground lay a broken pine branch. Evidence that it hadn't been a purposeful break-in.

"That's a very crafty cat." Rayce inspected the tracks that leaped from the ground and landed on the windowsill to disappear inside. He peered through the broken window. "Here, kitty, kitty!"

"Let's check inside." Cassandra led him around the corner to the front door where she entered the digital code.

Inside the open-beam structure sat a fleet of the resort's vehicles. A Jeep and a four-wheeler were parked on one side, as well as some of the facility equipment. There was no need to flick on a light switch because daylight beamed through the half-dozen glass ceiling panels.

Rayce scanned around the room filled with assorted vehicles and his gaze landed on the scatter of broken glass. "You got a broom in here?"

"Don't worry about it." Cassandra inspected the glass that had fallen inside. "I'll send the groundskeeper out to clean it up and repair the window. We'll use the fallen branch in the fireplace tonight."

"You've always got everything under control. I adore that about you."

"Hmm, well, I do fall apart on occasion."

He opened his arms and gestured with his fingers. "Come here. Fall into me."

In her moment of reluctance, he watched as caution played over Cassandra's face, only to quickly wriggle into something familiar and much more welcome: trust. Cassandra plunged into his embrace and the two kissed in the dim quiet. Broken in different ways, they had learned to understand themselves through one another.

"You make the world kinder," she said to him.

"I don't know about that. We need to talk, Cassandra. I'm sorry."

"I am, too."

"Yeah? Well, hear me out." He exhaled a cloud of breath. "I'm willing to risk rejection for the prize. The crowd can boo all they like. If I feel what I'm doing is good, that's all that matters."

"What does that mean?"

"I like it here at the resort, Cassandra. I'm going to talk to your dad about staying on through the summer."

"Rayce, that's wonderful. We'd love to have you for as long as you're willing. I know my dad would agree. But what prompted your change of heart? I thought you had intended to train…?"

"That was boasting, Cassandra. It'll never happen. And you know? I don't want that anymore. The competition and relentless training? That was the first part of my life. Retirement feels right."

"It does?"

"It does. So now? Here? It feels like a new beginning. One I want to follow to the end."

"I'm proud of you."

He studied her face, beaming at him beneath her pink pompom cap. In Cassandra's eyes he never felt like he had to prove himself. Yet hearing her say she was proud of him felt like a million sparklers had just been lit in his body. He absolutely hummed with a jittery excitement. "Really?"

"Yes. You're following your heart. A very smart heart

that may make mistakes sometimes, and then other times makes some very good decisions. It's not stupid. It's real. We all get hurt, Rayce. I'm sad that you were so devastated by what you thought was your heart, but you know, maybe that was the way life intended your path to go."

"Those are profound thoughts. I'm not much for destiny and all that fate jazz. I just…" He had to go for the gold if he wanted this to work. The anticipation of the moment felt as bright as his inner sparklers. Could she see his nervous excitement? NASA space satellites must be able to see it. "There's another reason I want to stay here. It's because of you."

"Oh, Rayce, I…"

"I know what you said about me being reckless. I promise to do a badge check every hour. To never be off your radar."

"Thank you, for that reassurance. I shouldn't have gotten so upset. I know you are a professional. You can take care of yourself. It's just…"

Just what? Some of the sparklers extinguished. She couldn't reject him. Please?

"Mother Nature doesn't care how skilled or smart we are," he said. "I get it, Cassandra. And I want to stay safe. Because you matter to me. And I'd hate to know something I did caused you any worry or pain."

He kissed her. First on her cheek, then on her lips. Her lashes fluttered against his nose as he tilted up to kiss her on the forehead. Marking her indelibly. Making a claim that could only be interpreted by his heart. He took her gloved hand and placed it on his chest. She probably couldn't feel his heartbeat through his jacket, but who knew? Every piece of him felt turned up to eleven. And he had to make her understand that feeling.

"This place feels like it could be a home to me," he confessed. "That's part of what I really want."

"It can be your home."

"I don't mean a little cabin behind the resort. I mean like moving back to Whistler, becoming a member of the community. Doing…life stuff."

"Life stuff?"

"Like owning a home and car and having a family. Making a career of teaching others how to ski."

"You have big plans."

"They are small compared to what I have with you right now. The other part of what I want is… It's you, Snow Princess. Do you think we can continue this relationship? I promise I won't break your heart."

"You don't need to make any such promise. I shouldn't have yelled at you like I did." Now she pressed both her palms to his chest and considered her words before finally saying, "I've been leery, too. Trying to relax my tight control on everything, including letting go of my grief. But I had a talk with my mom today."

"You did? I talked to my grandparents earlier."

"I know you were thinking about them."

She…knew? He gave her a wondering gape.

"I got the star under my teacup." She kissed him. "You were talking to your two stars up above, weren't you?"

"I was," he said in awe of her understanding. She got him. And knowing that made him feel even better than knowing she was proud of him.

"Mom would want me to enjoy life," she said. "To put my heart out there. For someone to catch."

He kissed her hard. Deeply. And in the process transferred those shimmering sparkles he experienced to her. Clutching her to him, Rayce whispered, "Caught you."

"Don't ever let me go."

"Promise I won't."

A sudden cloud of dust fluttered down from the rafters. "That's weird."

"Kitty!" Rayce called repeatedly.

She followed his sightline as he scanned overhead along the rafters.

"I think the critter is up there—watch out!" He grabbed her about the shoulders and tugged her aside.

A falling cat snarled through the air. A box crashed three feet from where they stood, tearing cardboard and scattering the contents in a tangle of Christmas tree lights, tinsel and plastic lighting clips.

Secure in Rayce's arms, Cassandra hugged him tightly. Her rescuing hero. Who simply wanted a home. A place for his heart to be happy.

The cat *meow*ed and wandered to the scatter of old Christmas supplies. Sniffed at it. Then looked up to Cassandra and Rayce. Its next *meow* sounded insistent.

"I think it's okay," Cassandra said. "Seems to be walking on all fours without trouble."

Rayce let out a heavy exhale and his embrace loosened. "Whew! I didn't want you to get hurt."

"I'm okay, Rayce." She kissed him. "You made sure of that. I always feel safe in your arms."

She laughed a little because speaking her emotions surprised her and at the same time felt better than right—it felt…marvelous.

Rayce took a deep breath, and said, "Cassandra. Would you be my girlfriend?"

"Yes." She smiled.

"Yes?"

She nodded. "You need more than that?"

Meow!

He looked over her shoulder. "That darn cat is getting into the fallen—Cassandra, look!"

He took her hand and plunged to the floor over the tangle of lights. Cassandra plucked up the star made from twigs. A twist of silver tinsel had been twined around the sticks and glued here and there. And in the center was the photo of her and her mom.

"I can't believe it." She pressed the ornament to her heart. Tears spilled down her cheeks. "It's almost as if the cat led us here."

The cat, seemingly proud of its accomplishment, *meow*ed happily.

Cassandra had just been given a hug from Heaven by her mother.

The next morning after Rayce left for an appointment with a guest, Cassandra ordered a few things from a local craft shop. Later in the afternoon, using the delivered supplies, she put the finishing paint touches to an ornament. It had been years since she'd felt the crafty urge, but this had been necessity.

"A little odd looking, but it's the thought that counts. Right?" she said to herself.

Tucking the ornament in a box, she then picked up the star made of twigs and studied the photo of her and her mom. "Thanks for leading me to this, Mom. You've made this a perfect Christmas. And I think I can do the same for someone whose one wish is to have a home."

That evening the staff met in the lobby for Christmas carols and a festive Christmas cookie exchange with the guests. Heading toward the party, Cassandra could already hear the carols jingling down the hallway. The scent of cinnamon and pine enticed her further, and the jingle of bells brightened her smile.

She saw Rayce leaning against the reception desk, wearing a sweater emblazoned with the face of the kid who had been left home alone, palms to his cheeks as he realized his situation. She gestured and got his attention. He beamed at the sight of her. As did her heart.

He strolled over and she tugged him around the corner away from the crowd.

"What's up, Snow Princess? I figured you'd get into all the singing and merrymaking."

"I do. Does that comment mean you don't?"

He shrugged. "It looks like fun, but I don't have any cookies for the exchange. Feels wrong to participate."

"Oh, please, Anita brings enough for everyone. Besides, you're the little drummer boy. You bring your charm and kindness to the event. It's your talent."

"Really?" He shrugged sheepishly. "I can work with that."

"I love the sweater. You never did tell me where you found that figurine."

"Eh. It's sort of a good luck charm I've carried with me through the years. Along with the drummer boy."

"I know you claimed the drummer boy after you gave it to me. You can have Kevin back, too, if you want him."

"How about we share them?"

"I like that. I seem to recall Kevin got a happily-ever-after ending?"

"He did. His family returned and he was once again safe in his home." Rayce sighed. "Corny, but it gets me every time."

"You'll find your home one of these days," she encouraged.

"I know I will. Did you bring the ornament to hang on the tree?"

"Of course." She showed him the star. "But first." She handed him the small box. "I have an ornament for you. You can hang it on the tree or keep it for your own tree."

"I've never had a tree…" He accepted the box.

"Someday you will."

He kissed her. "I love you, Snow Princess."

The announcement landed in her heart like the warmest winter kiss. True words, spoken clearly and with meaning. They echoed her own heartfelt beliefs. Cassandra nodded eagerly. "I love you, too."

For a moment the two held each other's gazes, their smiles growing. Love zinged back and forth between their eyes, their smiling mouths, their beating hearts. A kiss was necessary. Slow, soft and sweet. Didn't matter if the crowd witnessed this wondrous sign of affection. This was their marvelous kiss. No mistletoe required.

After a sigh and a bow of his forehead to hers, Rayce jiggled the box she'd given him. "So what do we have here?" He pulled out the tiny resin model of the Cobalt Lake Resort that they sold in the gift shop.

Before his smile dropped, Cassandra rushed to point out the detail she'd added. "It's our resort, but look there. The little man standing in the front?"

He studied it curiously. "Oh, yeah. He's wearing a green jacket."

"That's you! I painted the figure. Rayce, the resort is your home now."

He looked to her, his eyes going watery.

"You are always welcome here, in Whistler and…in my heart."

"I don't know what to say." He clutched the ornament against his chest. "It feels like a home. Especially when

I'm with you. Thank you. This is the nicest gift I've ever been given."

She kissed him and then tapped his lips. "Oh, I've got a better one for you later. When we're in bed."

A single eyebrow zipped upward.

With dramatic flair, Cassandra pulled something out of her pants pocket and brandished it between them.

"Are you kidding me?" He studied the crumbled plastic mistletoe. "That thing has certainly gotten a lot of good use."

"Are you going to kiss me again or marvel over a silly piece of plastic?"

He didn't need any more motivation than her flutter of lashes.

"You've changed my life," he said after the kiss. "I love you."

"I'm so glad you came to Cobalt Lake Resort. You helped me to find a place in my heart for my mom's memory. And I have another place right here." She patted her chest.

"What's that for?"

"For you of course. You can stay there as long as you like."

"In that case me and my figurines are moving in."

"You'll all fit. My heart is your home." She tapped the ornament she'd made for him. "Shall we hang these on the tree?"

"Definitely."

They snuck in behind the guests who were singing in harmony to a Christmas song that Kathy played on her portable keyboard. Cookies were munched and hot chocolate sipped. Her dad, clad in an outrageous Christmas sweater decorated with tinsel and real flashing lights, stood across the room with an arm around Faith, who wore a matching sweater. He winked at her and nodded.

Lured by the twinkling lights on the Christmas tree, Cassandra led Rayce around to the front of it. He studied the pine boughs filled with tinsel and ornaments, and then hung his ornament in the front. "How's that?"

"I'll notice that little green jacket every time I walk by."

"You did get my charming good looks right." He tapped the tiny man. "Your turn," he said.

With a squeeze of his hand and a reassuring nod from him, Cassandra placed the star ornament front and center. Then she stepped back and into Rayce's arms. The place she felt most comfortable. And loved.

The memories she held of her mother were now safe in her heart. And this new memory of love and acceptance was exactly where it belonged. Now everything was…

"Marvelous," she announced.

EPILOGUE

ON BOXING DAY Cassandra glided slowly down the slope with Rayce by her side. She'd chosen a gentle run for her first time on skis in almost two years. But after a pep talk and a kiss from her boyfriend, confidence had flooded her system. And she felt sure her mom was watching her from above. Another star in the sky twinkling next to Rayce's grandparents.

Rayce skied closer and reached for her hand. "You're doing it, Snow Princess!"

"I am! I missed this so much!"

"Let's ski together every day," he said.

"Works for me!"

They neared the bottom of the slope and with a twist of her hips Cassandra came to a stop, followed by Rayce. He tugged off his gloves and leaned over to kiss her. His wink sparkled brighter than her heart. Oh, she'd been captured by his eyes. And his incredibly smart heart.

"I have a crazy idea," he said.

"Does it involve more cat-wrangling?"

"Hey, Caspar adopted me after the incident in the shed. He won't leave my cabin. I know it's because of my handsome good looks."

"Naturally. It couldn't be anything but." How she adored

his self-effacing slips into ego. It was who he was, and she wouldn't wish him to change.

"But taking in a stray cat is not the crazy idea."

"Do tell?"

He took her hand and bowed his forehead to hers. Standing there for a moment, they shared the quiet stillness of the crisp winter day. And when Cassandra started to ask about his idea, he suddenly kissed her forehead and asked, "Do you want to look for a house together in Whistler?"

The question didn't even startle her. In fact it felt like the perfect next step in her dream that had come true.

"You mean a *home*?" she asked.

His smile beamed. "Most definitely. A home."

* * * * *

*If you missed the previous story in the
A White Christmas in Whistler duet
then check out*

The Billionaire's Festive Reunion
by Cara Colter

*And if you enjoyed this story,
check out these other great reads from
Michele Renae*

Two-Week Temptation in Paradise
Consequence of Their Parisian Night
Cinderella's Billion-Dollar Invitation

All available now!

COMING SOON!

We really hope you enjoyed reading this book.
If you're looking for more romance
be sure to head to the shops when
new books are available on

Thursday 21st November

To see which titles are coming soon, please visit
millsandboon.co.uk/nextmonth

MILLS & BOON

MILLS & BOON®

Coming next month

CHRISTMAS BRIDE'S STAND-IN GROOM
Sophie Pembroke

'Okay, so what are you suggesting?'

Giles's head was spinning with all the contradictions. She didn't love Charlie, but she loved the idea of marrying him. She *desired* Giles, it seemed, but not the life *he* wanted. So what *did* she want, really?

'A pre-wedding fling,' she said bluntly. 'No expectations, no *feelings*, even. Just…scratching an itch.'

'No, really, stop…you're embarrassing me with your flattery,' he replied in a monotone.

Millie rolled her eyes. 'You know what I mean. You don't love me. You don't *want* to love me. And nothing that happens between us is going to change your feelings about marriage, is it?'

'No.'

That much, at least, he was sure about. Everything else seemed to be shifting sands.

'And I want my future with Charlie too much to risk it by engaging in anything more than a fling with you,' she said simply. 'But…I can't ignore this feeling between us, either. I've tried—trust me, I've tried.'

'So have I,' he admitted.

'I know that passion…chemistry…doesn't equal love or for ever. It's just sex. It's far safer than love. So I figure the best thing to do is to get it out of our systems before the wedding,'

Millie explained. 'I mean, it would only be worse if we kept on feeling this way *after* I was married, wouldn't it?'

'That's true.'

He was certain there was a flaw in her logic somewhere, but he was struggling to see it right now. Was that because she was right or just because he was just hypnotised by her eyes.

'I haven't… Since I broke up with my last boyfriend—and that was a while ago—I haven't been with anyone. I might even have forgotten how, it's been so long. And it would be… useful to have a reminder before I get married.'

'So this is purely practical?'

He raised an eyebrow at her and she blushed, shaking her head a little.

'No. It's not. I just… I want this. I want to settle down and have the life I've planned with Charlie. But I also want *you*. I want to enjoy these last weeks before the wedding, and I want to see where this connection leads. Don't you?'

Her eyes shone with determination as she met his gaze, and he could see the fire behind them. The passion.

And, God, he wanted to taste it. Taste her.

Giles didn't have it in him to deny it any longer.

So, instead of answering, he leant forward and captured her lips with his own.

Continue reading
CHRISTMAS BRIDE'S STAND-IN GROOM
Sophie Pembroke

Available next month
millsandboon.co.uk

Copyright © 2024 Sophie Pembroke

FOUR BRAND NEW BOOKS FROM
MILLS & BOON MODERN

The same great stories you love, a stylish new look!

OUT NOW

Eight Modern stories published every month, find them all at:

millsandboon.co.uk

LET'S TALK

Romance

For exclusive extracts, competitions and special offers, find us online:

f MillsandBoon

X @MillsandBoon

⊙ @MillsandBoonUK

♪ @MillsandBoonUK

Get in touch on 01413 063 232

For all the latest titles coming soon, visit
millsandboon.co.uk/nextmonth